lies
and
letters

A Sam and Bump Misadventure, Book 2

cader idris
press

Also by N. Gemini Sasson:

lies
and
letters

A Sam and Bump Misadventure,
Book 2

N. GEMINI SASSON

LIES AND LETTERS
(A SAM AND BUMP MISADVENTURE, BOOK 2)

Copyright © 2015 N. Gemini Sasson

ISBN 978-1-939344-11-3 (paperback)

Library of Congress Control No. 2015920455

For more details about N. Gemini Sasson and her books, go to:
www.ngeminisasson.com

Or become a 'fan' at:
www.facebook.com/NGeminiSasson

You can also sign up to learn about new releases via e-mail at:
http://eepurl.com/vSA6z

Cover art by Cheri Lasota at Author's Assembler
Editing by Clio Editing

This book is dedicated to *all* dogs.

Big or small, black or white, long-haired or
short-haired, purebred or mutt —
None of those differences matter.
Dogs remind us that true love
is unconditional and infinite.

LIES AND LETTERS

A Sam and Bump Misadventure, Book 2

There's a drug lord corrupting the youth of sleepy Wilton, Indiana —
and he'll get rid of anyone who stands in his way, including an
innocent witness. Even a drug-sniffing dog.

When Sam McNamee decided to chuck her dreams of living in
the Florida Keys and instead settled in rural Indiana to raise her
daughter and look after her aging father, she didn't expect to be
caught up in the middle of a drug ring investigation. But someone has
it out for her. Or to be more precise, her dog, Bump. And they'll stop
at nothing to run her out of town — including framing her daughter.

All Sam wants is to give her relationship with veterinarian Clint
Chastain a chance. But matters get complicated when Clint's ex —
sexy humanitarian Dr. Danielle Townsley — invades Sam's territory.
Clint keeps reassuring Sam that she's the one he wants, but his actions
leave room for doubt. Meanwhile, firefighter Archer Malone is the one
constant in Sam's roller coaster life. And he's looking better all the
time.

Then, Bump disappears — and the one person who could help
her find him is the same one she's trying to avoid.

chapter 1

PAIN SPEARED MY EYEBALL. I reeled backward, both hands pressed protectively over my eye socket, the point of impact pulsing white hot like someone with deadly accuracy had jabbed me with an acupuncture needle. Or something larger — like a javelin. In reality, I'd poked myself in the eye with a mascara wand.

Flailing a hand at waist level, I knocked several items from the bathroom counter onto the floor. As I leaned forward to flip up the faucet lever and grope for a washcloth, my balance shifted and I careened sideways. A tube of lip gloss rolled under my heel, cracking under my weight.

As if a gun had gone off, I ducked my head and swung my torso around. At just the right angle to whack my forehead on Ida's knickknack shelf. A porcelain chicken toppled to the floor, shattering into a dozen knife-sized shards and a hundred tinier ones.

I gripped the counter ledge to steady myself, careful not to move my feet. With my one good eye, I scoped out the washcloth, crumpled it up, and ran it under cold water. It was hard enough operating with one hand; now I could only see out of one eye.

Sighing, I glanced down at the brace on my wrist. The doctor had told me I'd been lucky it had only been dislocated, but I hadn't realized until I didn't have use of my left hand how difficult it was to do some things with only one hand. I'd been avoiding buttons since I came home from the hospital earlier that summer. Sometimes, though, you had to ditch the sweats in favor of real pants, and today was one of those days.

Paws plodded down the hallway, accompanied by human feet. Dainty knuckles tapped on the other side of the closed bathroom door. "Mom, are you okay?"

I sucked in a breath and held it, trying to collect my wits, which had been a pretty futile endeavor all day, starting with when I'd sprayed Lysol on my hair after I'd shampooed and dried it. I didn't know who'd swapped its location under the sink for the hairspray can, but at least I didn't have to worry about spreading flu germs if anyone rubbed up against my head.

"Yeah, Tara, I'm fine." A one-eyed wreck, but I'd live. Hopefully. If I didn't die from embarrassment.

My dog Bump — a stray I'd accidentally acquired when I ran into him with my Subaru Forester during a thunderstorm — snuffled along the door's bottom.

"Okay, just checking. We were all waiting for you in the dining room and we heard a great big crash." There was a pause as Tara waited for me to reply, but I was too busy alternately dabbing the black streaks from my face and pulling my lower eyelid down to check my cornea. She cleared her throat. "Did something break?"

Obviously. That was my snarky fourteen-year-old daughter's subtle way of chiding me for my clumsiness.

I looked down at the floor to assess the damages, but everything was blurry. So I shut my bad eye and squinted. Jagged pieces of shiny chicken were scattered from just beyond my toes all the way to the linen closet. A ceramic landmine. Kind of like those metal spiky things that medieval knights used to litter a battlefield with to thwart approaching armies.

"Uhhh, sort of," I confessed. "Say, can you bring me the little broom and the dustpan? I think they're behind the door to the pantry. And tell Ida I owe her a chicken. I kind of obliterated her red-and-green one. I hope it wasn't an heirloom."

"Sure." She started off down the hallway, Bump scrabbling after her, then they both came padding back. "Oh, hey, I almost forgot. He's here."

"He?"

I knew who she meant, but somehow I'd thought maybe he wouldn't show up. Even though I'd been preparing for his visit since I came home from the hospital over a month ago and Ida had announced she'd invited him to dinner. The date had been moved back repeatedly, on account of his busy schedule and me being too doped up on painkillers to engage in a lucid conversation.

"That hot firefighter guy. You know, the one who saved you — Mr. Malone."

Archer Malone. How could I forget? The man who'd not only rescued my dog from a blazing house fire, but hunted down the arsonist who'd kidnapped me.

Wait, Tara was only fourteen. She wasn't supposed to notice that Archer was 'hot'. Actually, she'd be blind if she didn't. How sweet. My little girl was growing up. Tears pricked the backs of my eyelids.

"I'll be right down," I told her as I sniffed back a wave of melancholy, "as soon as I clean this up." *And find my dignity.*

Their footsteps receded. The cool washcloth pressed to my eyeball, I flipped the toilet lid down and took a seat. After about fifteen seconds of holding my throbbing eye socket, I leaned over to look in the mirror. One bloodshot eye stared back at me, wiped clean of makeup. The other was framed with thick, curly lashes and pearly green eye shadow. Great, I could probably pull this look off if I just donned a pirate eye patch.

What did it matter? Archer was *just* a friend ... Wasn't he?

Butterflies swarmed in my stomach. I wanted to puke them up and set them free. My heart was fluttering at ninety miles a minute, too. I needed to calm down. Flinging open the medicine cabinet, I grabbed my oxycodone bottle and popped the top open.

Crap! Empty.

There went my plan for remaining calm and cool. I'd just have to be myself. Which so far today wasn't going so swell.

After wiping my good eye clean, I collected the compact from the floor and carefully reapplied the eye shadow to both eyes, sans mascara. The look was a little stark, but presentable — if you didn't look too closely at the eye I'd jabbed, with its lacework of red veins surrounding my green iris. Maybe if I just kept Archer on the side of my good eye, it would be back to normal by the time dinner was over. I leaned closer to the mirror.

Oh, shoot. Was that a goose egg forming on my forehead?

I scoffed. What was one more battle wound? I still had bruises from my ordeal with Jake Taylor, and here I was primping and putting on make-up. Like it would make a difference. Like Archer Malone would care what I looked like. He'd seen me bloodied and bruised, pummeled to within an inch of my life.

Three knocks. Louder than Tara's.

"Sam, can I come in? I thought you might need some help."

It was Ida Oldingsells, the retired neighbor from next door who'd taken us in after my childhood home burned almost to the ground. She was like the aunt I'd never had. Or the mother I wished I'd had. It was only in the past few weeks that I'd gotten to know her well enough to think of her that way.

"Sure," I said. "It's not locked."

Slowly, she twisted the knob, like she was afraid of what she might find on the other side of the door. With good reason. I probably looked pretty scary right now. The door drifted open.

Her eyes lowered to the floor. "Oh my."

"Sorry. I poked myself in the eyeball with my mascara and couldn't see. Then I hit my head on the shelf and … I'm really sorry. That chicken probably belonged to your great aunt. What was it — seventy years old, ninety, a hundred?"

"It could be from the Ming Dynasty, for all I know." Ida plucked up a few ginormous shards and plunked them into the wastebasket. "But not likely. I got it at a garage sale over in Oil City last summer for three dollars. I should've offered the gal a buck, but her place looked like she could use the money."

Tara appeared at her shoulder, holding out the broom and dustpan. Her brows flicked upward, but Ida shooed her away before Tara could comment on my debacle.

I went to grab the broom from Ida, but she waved me off. "You go down to the freezer and stick a package of frozen peas on that eye and forehead."

"Oh, come on. It's not *that* bad."

"If I can see it from the hallway, yes, it is. Besides, how are you going to sweep and hold the dustpan with just one hand?" Whisking the broom from side to side, she cleared a path to the toilet. "Now go. The guest of honor is waiting to see you, and he's fidgeting like a nervous groom."

I reserved comment. If Archer was nervous, it was because he had a hormonal teenager drooling over him, a high-octane hostess flitting around like a hummingbird on Red Bull, and a cranky septuagenarian staring him down. It was up to me to put him at ease and convince him this was just a relaxed dinner among friends. A little thank-you for his heroic efforts.

Girding my loins, I marched out into the hallway and down the stairs. From the shelf above the stair bottom, a row of naked Kewpie dolls, with their crazed eyes and cowlicks, ogled me. I quickened my steps.

At the bottom, I grabbed the handrail and swung around the

landing out toward the foyer — and plowed right into Archer's chest. His solid, muscular chest.

He gripped my arms. "Whoa, there."

His breath tickled my nose, we were that close. Leaning back, I plastered on the biggest smile I could muster without splitting my face open and patted him on the cheek, the same way your grandmother did when you were two and did something cute. "Whoa, yourself."

Whoa yourself? Was that the best I could come up with?

His hand slid down my left arm, stopping just above my brace, and then drifted away. He looked me over. Not like he was checking me out for date material, but like he would if he'd just come across the loser of a stalled car/oncoming train standoff. "You look … better."

Looking 'better' wasn't much of a compliment, considering that not too long ago I'd looked like roadkill.

I tugged a coppery curl over the lump on my forehead and turned my face toward the front door, so he could get a better view of my good eye.

"Thanks, but I'm sure I look better than I feel." Which was the truth. I didn't elaborate. Even now, my insides felt like I'd been steamrolled. My ribs were still so sore it hurt to breathe deeply, I could only turn my neck in one direction, and my face was still puffy and mottled with fading green and purple bruises. Even now, I couldn't remember the thrashing Jake Taylor had given me beyond the first couple of fist blows. And I didn't *want* to remember. Ever. Anyway, it was all over now. And the reason I was here, today, was standing right before me.

Archer squeezed my good arm lightly before letting go. "I'm sorry I didn't visit you in the hospital. Something came up."

Something more important than checking on the person whose life you saved? I waited for an explanation, but he just shrugged like he'd forgotten to pick up milk at the store. Was that all he was going to say? No 'My mother had a stroke and I had to fly to Phoenix to see her' or 'I was down with pneumonia and didn't want to infect you'?

The truth was that while I hadn't expected him to visit me in the hospital, I'd hoped he would. Saving Bump from the fire had been part of his duties as a firefighter. Hunting Jake Taylor down to find me had gone far beyond doing his job. He'd put his own life in danger to save mine. That connected us in a way nothing else could. That *had* to mean something, didn't it?

"Something came up, you say?" I prompted, slipping my hands into the back pockets of my stretchy, contour-revealing jeans.

"Yeah, sorry 'bout that." Archer glanced toward the dining room, where Tara sat staring at him with her chin propped on her fists. At the end of the table, my dad, Walter Schimmoller, had a newspaper spread across his plate, his finger tracing the words of an article, his lips moving. Archer looked back at me, but his body was aimed toward the dining table — a clear signal that he was more interested in supper than a one-on-one conversation with me. "You were probably wondering where I was."

Ah, so maybe he was going to tell me after all? There had to be a reasonable explanation. But if I plied him for information, that would seem like I was irritated with him for not showing up at my bedside. Even if I was a bit miffed, I didn't want him to know. So I, stupidly, said, "Oh, not really. I was so doped up on painkillers I didn't know what day it was. I now understand why people hold up pharmacies for that stuff."

A cloud drew over his face that said: 'Addiction isn't a joking matter.'

Somehow I'd teased a nerve. Probably a relative in and out of rehab.

I brushed past him, stopping at the empty chair next to Ida's, which was right across from Tara. Tara, who was mesmerized by Archer's very presence. I cleared my throat to break her trance. She blinked a few times, then looked down at her lap, as if suddenly realizing how obvious she'd been.

I pulled the chair out for Archer. "What would you like to drink? Water, milk, iced tea?"

"What, no beer?" he said very seriously. Sitting down, he spread the paisley napkin that Ida had set beside his plate in his lap.

"Oh, I ... I'd have to check. I'm not sure if Ida —"

"I was kidding." He winked at me. "Water's fine."

Now I was *really* confused. Drug addiction was off limits, but casual drinking was not? Apparently, men could be moody, too.

I shuffled off to the kitchen, planning to linger there while Dad entangled him in political talk. It took all of fifteen seconds. Meanwhile, I couldn't find the peas, so I plastered a lumpy package of frozen broccoli to my forehead for a few minutes, stalling.

Turning around, I almost tripped over Bump. He had his rump planted near the dishwasher and was sitting there stock-still, like one of those cement lions at the end of a long driveway. I followed his line of sight to discover that both of Ida's cats were perched on top of the cupboards, Mr. Jeeves hissing at him and Tiger Lily pressing herself into the smallest ball she could, probably hoping the big dufus down below would disappear in a puff of smoke.

I poured the drinks one-handed and lined them up on a tray, taking my sweet time as I waited for Ida to come back downstairs. If anybody could brighten the evening, it was her.

My prayers were answered when she walked through the kitchen carrying a small clanking garbage bag and dropped it into the trash can next to the fridge.

"Sorry again." Frowning apologetically, I stuck the broccoli back in the freezer.

"Never mind that. You did me a favor. Now I have an excuse to go garage-saling and find something nicer. If you want to come with me, there's a neighborhood sale in Bluebird Estates this weekend."

"Hmmm, not really my thing. Besides, I kind of don't have a

place to put anything right now."

"Sadly, that's true." She fluttered in close and, standing on tiptoe, peered into one of my eyes, then the other. At just under five feet tall, she would have had to climb up a small stepladder to meet me on eye level. "That had to hurt."

"It did, but I'm pretty tough."

She gave me a quick hug. "Also true. Now, let's get those heathens fed before they riot, shall we?"

Together, we carried out the food. Bump stayed in the kitchen, keeping watch over the fluffy gargoyles. Dad carved up the pork tenderloin while we passed the green beans and boiled potatoes around.

Ida reached for the gravy bowl at the same time that Dad lifted it toward her. A blob of a brown jelly-like substance spilled onto the table cloth. As they muttered simultaneous apologies, Ida popped up from her seat. Dad waved her back into her chair.

"I'll take care of that, Ida, dear." He shuffled off to the kitchen and grabbed a damp dish towel from beside the sink. "You've done more than enough today."

"Thank you, Walter." She smiled sweetly, looking pleased that he'd do such a simple thing for her. "But I really haven't done anything out of the ordinary. Just threw some food together and —"

"Oh, poppycock." Sitting back down, he proceeded to blot the stain away. "Any more of this and you'll spoil us all rotten. You're like Wonder Woman and Martha Stewart all rolled up in one."

I froze in shock with my fork halfway to my mouth. That almost sounded like a compliment. Maybe I still had too many painkillers in my system. And what was with the 'dear'? If I didn't know any better, I'd say they were acting like an old married couple.

Dad stabbed his knife into his pork and left it handle up. "What are you staring at, Samantha Ann McNamee?"

"Nothing." I shoved the green beans into my mouth and said

between chews, "Just wondering what was in the paper today."

In reality, I'd rather be tied to a stake at the Salem witch trials than have him recount the local headlines to me. Dad could go on for hours about minutiae in the news. Like he had a personal stake in every world event from here to Uzbekistan.

He'd barely started on the topic of how Oil City was getting another strip mall, when Ida, thankfully, interrupted.

"Say, Walt, did you notice anyone cutting across the pasture a couple of days ago?"

"You sure it was a person and not a dog or a cow?"

"Two people, actually. And why would I mention a cow cutting across the pasture?"

"Just wondering if you got a good look."

"Good enough to tell they were walking upright on two legs."

He shook his head. "Can't say I've seen anything. When was this?"

"Two days ago."

He shrugged. "Probably just kids sneaking a smoke. Or screwing around on a blanket in the…" — I faked a cough, and he instantly caught my drift and glanced at Tara — "Never mind. I'm sure it's no big deal."

Ida buttered her roll, then handed the basket to Archer. "I just thought it was strange, that's all. I don't mean to be paranoid, but living out in the country, you get suspicious when folks trespass."

"If it helps," I told Ida, "we'll all keep an eye out for you. If it's just kids, we can probably scare them off with a warning."

"Forget the warning." Dad stabbed some more pork. He brought a forkful to his mouth and stuffed it in, while asking, "Do you have a shotgun, Ida?"

I gawked at him. "Dad, you can't be serious. Wouldn't it be better to just call the sheriff?"

"Pffft." He waved his fork at the window. "What if they're not kids, but serious criminals? By the time the sheriff gets here, we could all be —"

"Dad! We have a guest."

"And? This is important, Sam. Stuff you should think about before something bad happens again. If you'd had a gun with you when Jake Taylor tracked you down, hell, even some pepper spray, then maybe —"

"Stop!" I inhaled a deep breath, then slowly, *slowly* let it out. "I ... I don't want to talk about this right now."

Silence filled the room. Poured into every crack and hole. A heavy, painful silence that said more than words ever could. I wanted so badly to unload on my dad. But Archer was there and, until now, things had been going relatively well.

I had to get out of there.

Without saying anything, I retreated to the front porch. The screen door banged behind me. I plopped down on the porch swing and kicked my feet, letting it glide back and forth, soothed by the rhythmic movement. The fading rays of an August sunset glowed a fiery orange against the clapboard siding of the house. I leaned back against the floral cushions, relishing in the momentary peace, and closed my eyes.

Inside, I could barely make out Ida's hushed voice, chastising my dad. His mumbled reply. More back and forth. I tuned it out. Focused on the hum of insects, singing away the final days of summer. And closer by, a pair of sparrows having a lovers' argument in a nearby viburnum.

A minute later, the screen door creaked, then shut softly. Feet trod toward me across the loose planks. Still, I didn't open my eyes.

"Can I join you?"

I opened my eyes to Archer. He held out a saucer with a slice of pie.

Taking the plate from him, I scooted to the side to give him room. The swing stalled as he settled beside me. Closer than I expected. Close enough for our thighs to touch. I didn't have room to scoot further away, so I just let myself get used to the feeling of his leg against mine. Which gave rise to all sorts of confusing thoughts.

But most of all, it just felt … right.

And then, pushing an arm against the back of the swing, he swiveled his body sideways so he could look at me straight on, breaking the physical connection between us.

It was me who looked away.

"He just wants to protect you," Archer said.

I shoveled the pie into my mouth so I wouldn't have to talk.

Then he added, "Too bad he has such a shitty way of showing it."

A little snort of laughter leaked out of me. A chunk of peach went down my windpipe and I coughed. When I finally recovered, I said, "I'm glad you get it."

He smiled. A devilish sort of smile. He totally got it.

We sat in comfortable silence for a while, Archer rocking the swing, me gobbling down Ida's heavenly peach pie.

"Have you been back there yet?" he asked finally.

"There?" I gulped my last bite down. Did he mean the park where Jake had abducted me?

A cold sliver of fear wedged itself between my vertebrae. What was I scared of? Jake was in jail. He wouldn't be out for decades. Unless local law enforcement had forgotten to read him his Miranda rights, or the judge overturned his conviction on a technicality, or he became Humboldt County's first jailbreak ever. Geesh, I had to stop watching those cop and lawyer shows Dad had on the TV every night.

"Your dad's house," Archer said. "Have you been back there? The fire marshal came over from Fullbright and looked it all over. Not much to investigate, since we know who did it and why. But then, you've barely been out of the hospital. You probably haven't felt like tromping up that hill to sift through soot. Has your dad gone over?"

I shrugged. "I don't know. We haven't talked about it. There's a lot we don't talk about."

His mouth tilted in a lopsided smile. "Yeah, I got that drift. I know how it is, believe me."

He braced his feet on the floor to stop the swing in mid-glide. Bending forward, he peered through the big picture window. At the table, visible on the other side of the archway at the far side of the living room, there was a cribbage game underway. Tara slapped her cards down and did a double-handed fist pump. Walt and Ida groaned simultaneously as they relinquished their cards in defeat. Dad thumped Tara on the shoulder, then popped the tab open on his root beer.

When I'd showed up on my dad's doorstep earlier that summer, intent on getting his house sold so I could speed off to Florida with Tara, I never imagined, not even for a nanosecond, that choosing to stay in Wilton could turn out so ... well, not perfect, but okay. 'Okay' in its own weird, dysfunctional way. It wasn't all roses, but there were moments when we all got along. Maybe Ida was the glue that bonded us all together. Maybe it was the passion for retro that Dad and Tara shared. Maybe it was Bump. Whatever it was, it was working. For now. Most of the time, anyway.

Except for when Dad was being a thoughtless ass.

I set the saucer on the porch railing. Inside, an overhead light flicked on. Dad shuffled the cards and cleared the pegs from the cribbage board as he grumbled about beginner's luck.

"Seems like this would be a good time to slip away." Archer nodded toward the hill beyond Ida's property. His close-cropped hair caught the evening light in burnished strands of platinum and gold. "Want to go before it gets dark?"

Standing, he offered me his hand.

I studied it, noticing all the calluses on his fingertips and how his knuckles were still bruised from where he'd tussled with Jake. I laid my palm in his, felt its warmth and strength. With an easy smile, he pulled me to my feet, so that we stood toe to toe. I raised my face to meet his eyes.

It was a moment. And an eternity.

Everything. And nothing.

Like we were both waiting for the other person to say or do something.

Which didn't happen.

Because far down the long driveway, tires crunched over gravel.

Turning toward the sound, Archer scrunched his brows in a questioning look. "Expecting anyone?"

I checked my watch: 7:35 p.m. "No, and I don't know who it could be."

Side by side, we went down the steps, pausing at the bottom beside the rose bushes, which were clinging to the last of their blooms. It was still warm during the day, but the nights were growing longer. On Monday, Tara would start at Wilton Memorial, my alma mater. It would be her first day of high school. At least she had four classes with her friend, Shannon Mullins. Wait … Tara had asked if her friend Shannon could spend the night this weekend. Maybe that was Tom and Judy bringing Shannon. But I thought it was supposed to be tomorrow night. Somehow I'd gotten confused.

Or not.

As I peered at where Ida's driveway emerged from around a bend, I saw not Shannon's parents' car, but Dr. Clint Chastain's sparkly white SUV rolling toward us.

What was *he* doing here?

chapter 2

NOT UNTIL ARCHER WINCED did I realize my fingernails were piercing his arm.

"Sorry." I uncurled my fingers and let my hands drop to my sides. "I just wasn't expecting … him." My lip contorted into a snarl. Either that or it was just my heart twisting around on itself.

As Clint's Lincoln Navigator pulled to a stop, Archer's gaze swept from my balled-up fists to Clint's car, then back to me. "I must have missed an important development. I thought you and he were —"

"No!" I squeaked. Then lower, "It was never anything serious."

He squinted at me. "Funny, I had a different impression."

Of course he didn't know. No wonder he'd been such a gentleman tonight and kept his distance during my recuperation. He still thought Clint and I were an item. Which we had been until Clint's ex, Dr. Danielle Townsley, had shown up at the veterinary clinic and rubbed up against him like a cat in heat. Apparently, *she* hadn't known about us, either.

Although there was no 'us' now, as far as I was concerned. I had moved on. Or intended to, at least. Soon.

Clint's car door swung open and he stepped out. All six feet and four inches of him. Dressed in a dry-fit top and his short running shorts. Those legs. Long and lean. Powerful. Graceful. Tan. Shaven. Wait, what guy shaves his legs except a competitive swimmer, to reduce drag? Totally narcissistic, and yet … he looked good that way. Damn good. Not that I cared.

"Sam?" Clint smiled. A big, melt-your-insides kind of smile. As if Archer wasn't even there, he walked straight up to me, took my hands, and kissed my forehead, right beside my new goose egg. He let go of my hands and stepped back. "God, you look great. Almost brand new."

Oh, he was slick. I'd throw myself at him if I wasn't so mad. Because for weeks I'd thought his wife was dead, but turned out she was just out of town, and *technically* they weren't even divorced when he and I had shagged on her wine-stained alpaca rug.

I had the sudden urge to knee Clint in the cojones. Archer must have sensed the tension boiling inside me, because he put an arm around my shoulder and pulled me close.

"Hey, Clint." Archer thrust his free hand out to shake Clint's. "Good to see you, buddy. Just come from a run?"

Clint gripped Archer's hand and released it as quick as if Archer had zapped him with a joy buzzer. "On my way, actually." He turned his face to me. "Your dad said I could swing by and pick the dog up for a run this evening. If that's okay? I mean, you look surprised. Or reluctant. I don't know which."

I hesitated. "It's just that … he forgot to tell me you were coming."

"You were asleep when I called. He asked if I wanted him to wake you up, but I told him no. I hope you're following doctor's orders, Sam. Trauma victims need a lot of rest for their bodies to repair." His fingers grazed the ridge of a slight scar along my jawline. As he lowered his hand to rest on my shoulder, his mouth quirked in a smile. "So anyway, I just told him I'd be by this evening sometime. I hope it isn't a problem. I figured Bump could use the exercise.

Besides, I miss the goofball."

To think, not too long ago I would've handed Bump over to him permanently, seeing how well they got along. But now, even though he was just taking my dog for a quick jog, it felt like the start of a custody battle. Tara would have been more than happy to take over Bump's exercise needs until I was a hundred percent. Still, I didn't have the heart to turn Clint down right now. He really did love that dog.

"Sure, I guess." I hooked a thumb toward the door. "He's inside with the *Let's Make a Deal* crowd. Just, nothing too long, okay? He needs to build up his stamina. His lungs haven't completely recovered from the fire yet. He still wheezes if he plays ball too long."

"No problem. I'll make it short." He finally looked back at Archer, his gaze hardening. "You two headed off somewhere?"

"Up the hill to check out the house." Archer's hand slid down and around my waist. "Sam hasn't been back yet."

Clint tipped his head back, a possessive glint flickering in his pupils. "Just have her back before she turns into a pumpkin."

"Last I checked, Sam was a grown-up. I think she can stay out as late as she wants."

Clucking his tongue, Clint fisted Archer on the bicep. "It was a joke, pal. Lighten up."

I wasn't sure whether to step between them and play Gandhi, or get a ringside seat. I picked neither and yanked Archer away.

"Thanks, Clint," I said over my shoulder, as we wedged past the rusty gate in the farm fence and headed up the hill through the meadow.

Clint was already at the front door, knocking. But even when Ida came and let him in, he was still watching us.

"Are you part owl?" Archer asked.

"Huh? Oh." I turned my face forward, but then I had to walk slightly sideways because my neck was so stiff. Why did it seem like I was marching through quicksand? We'd barely gone a hundred yards

17

and I was already gasping for air. My ordeal had set me back further than I realized. I sucked in a deep breath and shoved the words out before I could go into oxygen debt. "Just thinking I should've told him where the leash was."

He snorted ever so softly. "For someone you're not involved with, there was an awful lot of tension back there. I hope you didn't mind me putting my arm around you. I figured maybe if you wanted him to back off, he'd take the hint if I stepped in."

What? So he was just being gallant?

"Gee, thanks," I said, more snidely than I'd intended. Life with a teenager was rubbing off on me. I stomped to the left to avoid a patch of wild blackberry thorns. "Not like I couldn't handle him myself, you know."

"Hey, I didn't mean ... I just thought ..." Air whooshed out of him. "You're right. But if you ever want to tell me what happened with him, I'm here."

I swung around in front of him, planting my hands on my hips. The moment I stopped moving forward, I could feel the lactic acid burning in my leg muscles. We weren't even halfway there. Ever since I'd come home — or rather back to Ida's — from the hospital, even doing easy things made me incredibly tired. I felt like a rag doll, like I could just flop over sideways at any moment and crumple into a spineless heap. "Why would I do that?"

"Because I could give you the guys' perspective, that's all. Help you make sense of whatever he did to upset you." Tucking his fingers into his front pockets, he searched my eyes. He looked so dang ... sincere.

"More like what he didn't do."

Back at Ida's, Clint's engine started up. We both looked that way and waited for him to back up and start down the driveway before continuing. Like he could hear us that far away.

"Okay, I'm game," Archer said. "What *didn't* he do?"

I was still looking at the bend in the driveway around which Clint's car had disappeared. "Tell me he was still married."

"What?"

One glance at Archer told me even he didn't know.

His face twisted into a scowl of disgust. "I thought ... Everyone just assumed ... I mean, we all knew he'd been married to that doctor chick that he met in college, but everyone thought when he moved back here and wasn't wearing a wedding ring and didn't talk about her that it was long over." He touched my shoulder briefly, as if to make it clear it was a gesture of sympathy and not one of affection. "Hey, I'm sorry. That was scummy of him. What exactly was his excuse for not telling you?"

"He claims it was a technicality." I turned back toward the tree line at the top of the hill, behind which sat my dad's burned-down house, and started walking. I'd hoped the rest would have rejuvenated me temporarily, but it was just that much harder to get started again. Every bruised muscle protested. For a moment, I thought about turning back and doing this some other day. But somehow, with Archer here, it just seemed like the right time to come to grips with it. "Said that papers were misfiled by the local attorney."

"You mean that gal, Natasha Plappert-Knapp?"

"Sounds right."

"Most folk around here know she's fine for routine stuff, but if you need her to actually *do* something, well, good luck with that." He grabbed my elbow and guided me around a groundhog hole. "So, he's still married to what's-her-name?"

"Danielle Townsley. He swears it's final now. That all the legal ends have been tied up. That's why she was here in town recently. To sign papers."

"No kidding? And you found out when she just turned up?"

"More or less." I left out the part about how she was coming on to Clint right in front of me. But more than that, it was the fact that

Clint hadn't shoved her away and introduced me as his — what *had* I been to him? His girlfriend? His booty call? We hadn't formally declared ourselves a couple, but we'd been headed down that path. Maybe a little too quickly. Anyway, call me old-fashioned, but I kind of thought when you started talking about your 'feelings' for someone and got to know each other intimately that it implied a certain exclusivity.

I wasn't about to tell Archer that Clint and I had had sex. Because right now, that's all it was: sex. A normal, human activity. I didn't need to feel ashamed about it or like it had bonded us for life. If I was saving myself, I'd missed that chance. I sure hadn't preserved my virginity for my wedding night with Kyle, my high school sweetheart and husband until an accident claimed his life a decade ago. Besides, Clint hadn't forced me to do anything. Nor had he tricked me into dropping my pants by any measure. It had been a mutual grasp at pleasure. A few precious hours of two bodies enjoying the sensations created between them. A night of ecstasy. Of living completely and totally in the moment. And I had been *long* overdue for that.

So why did I feel so conflicted about telling Archer the whole truth?

Was it because of the betrayal I felt at Danielle's sudden appearance? Or something else entirely? Was I afraid of sharing too much personal information with him?

"Sam?"

Archer waved a hand in my face. He was standing in front of me. Close enough to kiss me. Not that I expected him to. Why was I even thinking that? And when had I stopped moving?

I blinked at him until I regained my bearings. Slowly, I leaned to the side to look past him.

There it was. A half-burnt hull. The remains of my childhood home.

Most of it, amazingly, was still standing.

Oddly, it wasn't the fire that almost took my dad's life that I remembered. It was growing up there. Before Mom left us. Zipped off to Europe with her boyfriend, Étienne. For a while, we'd been so … happy. And ordinary. At least in one little girl's eyes. Mine.

What had gone wrong? Likely, I'd never know. And I wasn't about to ask my dad about it. That book was closed. Still, there were the letters from her that I'd discovered … He'd said I could read them. Even encouraged me to.

No, the past was the past. Just like it was with Clint.

"Come on." Archer started toward the house. "Let's get a closer look."

My feet remained rooted. He took about five steps before turning back around.

"Sam, are you okay? We don't have to, if you don't —"

"No, I'm fine. Really." I started walking again. Slowly, baby steps. "I was just taking it all in from a distance. I really thought it'd look worse."

"It will up close." He took my hand in encouragement as I came abreast of him. His touch was comforting in the way that a warm soak with bath salts was, or a fuzzy blanket on a chilly fall evening. "The exterior may still be standing, but there was a lot of smoke damage inside, not to mention water damage from the fire hoses."

Dad's truck was still out in front of the house, untouched except for some blotches of soot that had fallen on it. His single set of car keys had been lost in the burned debris, and with Ida at hand to chauffeur him around he hadn't yet bothered to have another set of keys made. The house may have been uninhabitable, but at least he still had his truck. The direction of the wind that night had spared it from the sparks.

As for the house … the closer we got, the clearer it was. Archer was right. The façade was merely that: a façade. The windows were all busted out, the tops of their frames outlined in black smudges that

21

extended up to the roofline.

And as we swung around to the garage side of the house, toward the back, I was lost for words.

There were huge gaps in the roof, and the kitchen — or what was left of it — was open to the elements, no ceiling and two walls charred to cinders and crumbled down. All the boxes and stuffed shelves and cabinets were nothing but a collection of whitish-gray ash. I could just make out the melted upright box that had once been the refrigerator. Close by, under a heap of fallen drywall and blackened two-by-fours, sat the warped remains of the stove. I'd almost started a fire in that stove myself when Dad forgot to tell me the temperature gauge was broken.

Archer stepped through what used to be the back door and poked at a pile of ash with his foot. He hit something solid, kicked at it. A can rolled out, its label gone. "Pretty bad, huh?"

I joined him, turned around once, then looked up at the sky. "Just … wow. Doesn't look like there's anything salvageable here."

"Hard to say. You'd be surprised what gets preserved sometimes. But yeah, what the fire didn't get, the hoses did." Hands deep in his back pockets, he surveyed the ruins. "You know, your dad was lucky. Especially since his smoke alarms didn't work."

A pang of guilt jabbed me in the gut. More than once, I'd told myself to replace the batteries, but I'd always been too busy. Now I knew that nothing was more important than being safe. Which made me think a little about what Dad had said earlier. Given what had happened to me with Jake, maybe learning how to handle firearms was something I ought to give some thought to. But I had so many reservations … the least of which was that guns scared the bejeebers out of me.

A wave of dizziness struck me and I grabbed the burnt stud of the outside door frame for support.

"What is it?" Archer slipped an arm around me before I

could fall.

I clung to him, let myself steady in his hold. He helped me outside to sit beneath the boxelder tree. As I leaned back and gazed up at the paling sky, I noticed the leaves on the house side of the tree were all curled and wilted from the heat of the fire. Some of them had even turned prematurely brown. But the tree was still standing, and next year all the leaves would come back in full, as if there'd never been a fire at all. I let myself sink down, if only to be closer to the ground.

He squatted in front of me. "I'm sorry. I didn't mean to upset you by bringing you here. Obviously, it was too soon. I guess I didn't realize the fire had —"

"It's not the fire."

"Then what?"

There it was — that cottony feeling in my mouth. I worked my tongue around, trying to gather enough saliva to speak. "It's Jake."

"He's in the county jail, Sam. He won't —"

"I know, I know. But what if it happens again, Archer, and you aren't there to save me? Or what if it's not me who's targeted next time, but Tara or Dad or Ida?" I tucked both hands beneath my armpits, hugging myself tight. Life had been one contrast after another since I'd returned to Wilton. Here, I'd never felt more hopeful, more like I belonged. And yet ... I also felt less safe than I had taking public transportation after dark in downtown Chicago. Not to mention the roller coaster of emotions I'd experienced in such a short time.

My shattered love life, however, was not going to kill me. People like Dylan Hawkins and Jake Taylor were another matter altogether.

Archer didn't say anything. He just waited for me to put my thoughts together. If only I knew how. I didn't have any proof that anything else might happen to any of us. Jake Taylor, as far as anyone could figure, was working entirely on his own. A messed-up guy who'd lost his girlfriend and had been about to lose his job because of a drug habit. Still, why did I have this inkling of dread sitting in the pit of my stomach, waiting to work its way back up like I'd just downed a plate of greasy onion rings and a pitcher of beer?

The problem was I didn't know what the problem was.

It was just me being hyper vigilant. Which made it impossible to appreciate the fact that I'd come through everything all right. Because in truth, I wasn't.

I was scared. To death. Of what *could* happen.

Clutching my fists to my chest, I let it all gush out. "You agreed with Dad that we should have a plan — and I get that. I do. It's just … I know that you should have smoke detectors and a fire extinguisher for fires, but how do you make a plan to protect yourself from some moron who could attack you at anytime, anywhere? I mean, somebody could hide in the bushes outside the lodge and bean you with a crowbar. Or shoot bullets into your car as you're sitting at the ATM. Or slip drugs in your punch cup at a baby shower."

"Drugged punch, huh? You have a vivid imagination. You should be a writer."

"Thanks, I'll give that some thought." If only he knew I had a secret identity. "Anyway, you get my drift, right? What happened with Jake … it's gotten to me. I should feel safe knowing that's all settled, but I'm not. I don't want it — or anything even remotely like it — to happen again. Just … I have no idea what to do to prevent it. And that's making me sick with worry."

He plied my fingers loose from my fists. Holding them lightly, he turned his gaze toward the house, focusing on nothing in particular. He exhaled, long and slow. "You can let the past control you — or you can take control of your future." Then, just like that, he shook it off with a shrug.

"So what do I do?"

"I don't know what to tell you, Sam, except … do *something*. Have Ida install an alarm system, for starters."

"I thought that's what Bump was for. I've read that dogs are better deterrents to crime than alarm systems. Remember how he went off on you and Jake at the park that day?"

He met my gaze then, the reddish-orange light of sunset softening the contours of his stubbled jawline and a good-natured grin on his lips. "Yeah, I remember. Bump can sound pretty scary when he wants to. Still, he's not the bravest dog I've ever seen. I'm not sure how far he'd go to protect you. And he's easily won over. A couple of biscuits or a bit of hamburger, and he'd switch loyalties like that." He snapped his fingers. "You need something more. Not only do they have alarm systems you can control remotely through your phone now, but there are security cameras that will let you see what's going on in your house no matter where you're at."

"Ida shuns technology. It would creep Tara out. And Dad would be paranoid that Big Brother was watching him. He'd probably blind all the cameras with duct tape. That or cut the electrical cords."

"You could take a self-defense class after you're all healed up."

"Not out of the question, but I'm about as graceful as an elephant on stilts. Chances are I'd end up with another broken bone or a concussion before I got my money's worth out of the class. I'll think about it, though. Maybe I could talk Selma into taking a class with me." I thought briefly about asking Tara or Ida, but Tara had the quick reflexes and confidence of a teenager. Next to her, I'd look like a mom who was trying to be hip and failing miserably. Ida would make me look even worse. Even in her sixties, she was spry and dauntless. At least with Selma, I had a chance of appearing to be the coordinated and capable one.

"Okay, just think about it. As long as you do something. Let me know what you decide." Archer inclined his head toward Ida's house. "You ready to go back now?"

I pushed myself to my feet. Together, we strode around to the front of the house and started down the hill. I was grateful we were going down and not up again. I don't think I could have done that hill twice in one day in my current state.

Halfway to Ida's house, I got the sense that something wasn't quite right. I scanned the surrounding pastures. No cows, no skulking figures.

I shrugged it off and continued on, my attention momentarily diverted by Archer, who was quietly singing a Blake Shelton song. I only knew that because I'd seen the singer on a music awards show a couple of nights ago as I was channel surfing. Normally, country songs shredded my nerves, but Archer's voice had a soothing quality to it. The guy could carry a tune. Just as I glanced at him, something beyond him caught my eye. Something not quite as it should be.

There, along the fence line where the neighboring farmer's property was, a pair of tire tracks disappeared into the cornfield, leaving a gap in the neatly cultivated rows. When had that happened? I was sure it hadn't been there last week when I'd walked Bump out here to potty him.

Archer was five steps ahead of me before he looked back. "What are you looking at, anyway?"

"Remember Ida talking about seeing someone go into the field recently?"

He nodded.

I pointed to the opening in the corn rows, plowed wide by a decent-sized vehicle. "Looks like they've been there before."

A gunshot cracked in the distance. Archer and I locked eyes.

"A hunter?" I whispered.

"If it is, they're doing it illegally. Hunting season doesn't start for two more months."

Just then, a bullet whizzed through the air and buried itself in the earth close enough to startle us both. I latched onto Archer's arm. He pulled me behind a mulberry bush, took a quick look around, then motioned toward the house.

"Are you crazy?" I said.

"It's coming from the woods back there. I'm guessing whoever it is just wants us to stay the heck away and isn't going to come running after us."

"Well, I'm glad you're confident about that, but I think I'm going to stay right —"

Archer latched onto my good wrist and yanked me down the hillside, dodging brush and leaping over cow patties. The ground jarred beneath me with every footfall. The world blurred past. My legs wheeled uncontrollably. My lungs screamed for air. I stumbled, heaving for breath, and finally Archer slowed to a fast walk. We were almost out of the pasture.

When I buckled over the second time, he let go of my wrist. Hands on knees, I gulped in precious air, but as soon as I realized Archer was still forging onward, I hurried to catch up with him. We walked side by side, our panic subsiding but fear still thick in the air.

I glanced behind us. It was silent now. He was right. There was no one there.

Archer's shoulder bumped mine. I whipped my head forward — just in time to see the groundhog hole before me. My foot slammed down abruptly, jarring my jaw so hard I bit my tongue. I sank up to my knee, my upper torso twisting in the opposite direction from the one my feet had been going in.

"Sam!" Archer crouched beside me. He held his arms wide, as if to scoop me up, but just as quickly reverted to his medical training: don't move a victim if there's any chance of spinal injury. "Are you okay?"

"I … I don't know." My left leg was jammed in the hole past my shin. Somehow I'd had the presence of mind to put my right hand, my good one, out to break my fall. But it hadn't been pretty. I could taste the blood swirling around in my mouth. Leaning onto my right hip, I very gingerly pulled my foot out of the hole. Afraid to look, I screwed my eyes shut and rolled onto my back. "Is the bone sticking out?"

Archer scooted close and ran a hand lightly over my pants leg. "Doesn't appear to be. Can you bend your knee?"

I flexed my knee slowly.

"That hurt?"

"A little stiff, but I think I can walk on it." Truth was my whole body ached, so it was hard to tell if I'd done any new damage. But I was trying to save face, so I was going to finish walking to the house if it killed me. I started to sit up, but he gently pushed me back down.

"Not so fast there. I haven't finished checking you out. I'm going to remove your shoes."

Don't stop there, I wanted to tell him. But he'd no sooner lifted my ankle to take my left ballet flat off than I shrieked.

"Sorry, sorry. Bear with me."

Glaring at him, I dug my fingers into the long grass and twisted the blades murderously as he slid the shoe all the way off. He paused until the grimace faded from my face, then pushed my pants leg up carefully, the backs of his fingers sliding against my freshly shaven legs. If I wasn't in so much pain, I'd be turned on.

"Can you move your ankle for me?"

Nodding, I turned my foot in a tiny circle. Mobile, but I was starting to sense a dagger of pain to the outside of my foot. That was when he touched my little toe.

"Don't!" I yanked my foot out of his grasp. "Touch me again and I'll hit you," I growled.

He laughed.

"It's not funny! It hurts like hell."

"I'm sure it does. I was just thinking ... no kickboxing for you for a while."

"Why?"

"Because you've broken a toe."

"Ahhh, nooo." I slapped the ground beside me. I couldn't catch a break. "So what do they do for that? Cast? Put a screw in it? Don't tell

28

me it's going to require surgery."

"Not even crutches. An air cast, *maybe*. But usually just a lot of rest and patience. Luckily it's your left foot, so you can still drive."

Small consolation that was. I was going to be housebound more than I cared to be, and with Tara starting school in three days, I'd be reliant on Clint to exercise Bump and run some steam out of him. Wonderful.

"You were there beside me — and then all of a sudden you weren't." He took off my other shoe and handed them both to me. "Let's get you back to the house."

Like a groom stepping over the threshold with his bride, he scooped me up into his arms and carried me away.

chapter 3

"YOU CAN LET GO now." A pleading grin flitted across Archer's mouth.

I'd been clinging so tightly to his neck as he'd lugged me the rest of the way down the hill and into Ida's living room that my arms had locked. Besides, I felt safe cradled in the hammock of his bulky forearms. I really didn't want to let go, but I had to. I peeled my arms away and let myself fall back against the floral cushions of the couch.

"Mom, what happened?" Tara stood in the doorway to the dining room, her sleeves rolled up and a lilac-colored card dealer's visor on her head. Actually, it was one of Ida's many sun visors, but the effect was obvious. They were turning my daughter into a cribbage-swindling card shark.

"She stepped in a groundhog hole," Archer said. "They're all over the place, and with the sun behind the trees it was getting hard to see."

That was the polite version. The truth was there was only one groundhog hole in the entire field and I hadn't been watching where I was going. But no need to tell her that.

"Would you mind fetching her a cooler full of ice water, Tara?" Archer suggested.

She scurried into the kitchen.

Archer swung my legs onto the couch, then, sitting on the edge next to me, he propped my left foot up on a stack of pillows. "I'll call you in the morning."

How I wished he'd said those words in some other context.

"I'd suggest you have someone drive you to the doctor then. I'd take you, but I'm on duty all day. Not that you couldn't take yourself, but just to help you out. I don't see any reason for you to rush to the emergency room tonight."

"Good, because my insurance deductible is about the cost of a new car. Economy car, maybe, but still ..."

His fingers traced lightly over my good foot, then my left one. When I didn't jerk at his touch, he squeezed lightly. "Any better yet?"

"Well, I didn't feel like punching you that time, if that's what you're asking."

"That's a good sign. Might just be a sprain. The town doctor won't be in tomorrow, but there's an urgent care clinic on Highway 5 near Fullbright. They accept walk-ins. They might take some X-rays, they might not. Either way, they'll tell you to stay off of it, elevate it as much as possible, immerse it in ice water, and take anti-inflammatories. Standard stuff. Whatever you do, don't overdo it. You'll only make it worse. Got it?"

I nodded and a sigh leaked out of me.

"What is it?" he said.

"Just ... thanks. Again."

He patted my cheek, his fingers lingering beside my ear before he pulled them away. "No problem. I'm on shift in a couple of hours, so I need to head out. Let me know what they say after you get that looked at." Archer stood, but hovered over me, his face a mixture of fatherly concern and friendly tenderness. His sandy brows narrowed. "I mean it, Sam — make sure you see a doctor. And I *will* call. You still owe me details about Clint. In the meantime, call the sheriff and let him know about the gunshots. Until then, don't let anyone go into that pasture or near those woods. Got it?"

I nodded, trying to figure out how I was going to keep my dad away from there. Because if I told him not to go, he probably would.

At the door, Archer paused to repeat the instructions for my care to Tara, who had returned with a cooler sloshing with water and ice cubes. Then he said goodbye and left.

Capturing a breath, I squeezed Tara's hand and plunged my foot into the icy water. A blast of cold shot up from my little toe through my spine and straight out the top of my skull, like Mr. Freeze had zapped me with his freeze gun. I snatched my foot out, air whistling between my teeth.

"Mom!" Tara scolded. "Mr. Malone said you have to ice your foot to keep the swelling down."

"Archer did not say for you to cryogenically preserve me. What was that — absolute zero?"

She rolled her eyes at me. "Mom, you know that's impossible. Absolute zero is the temperature at which —"

"Spare me the science lesson, Einstein. The fact is I'm going to need this foot later. Take the cooler back into the kitchen and add a little warm water ... *please*."

Upstairs, the toilet flushed, followed shortly by the shuffle of Dad's slippered feet as he came down the stairs. He was already in his plaid bathrobe and pajama bottoms. It couldn't have been much past eight o'clock.

"What happened to you?" He paused at the far side of the living room, squinting because he didn't have his glasses on.

"Ninja groundhog ambushed me," I said. "Where's Ida?"

"Ran over to her friend's to pick something up. Planning some sort of fundraiser."

"Oh. Fundraiser for what?"

"No idea."

"Which friend?"

"Don't know that either."

"She didn't tell you?"

He wandered to the front door, looked out the little window at the top, then turned the lock. "She did, but I was only pretending to listen. 'Uh-huh' and 'Really?' go a long way in a conversation with any female."

I didn't argue with him. Whatever he and Ida had going was working so far, and I wasn't going to mess with it. She'd been kind enough to take us in after the fire, and if there was one place I had to hang out until our situation changed, this was it. Eventually, though, we'd either have to find someplace else to live or wait until the insurance company came through with a big fat check so Dad could rebuild. And that would take way too long. I voted for option A. For now, I wasn't too keen on living this far out of town, but you couldn't beat the view and peaceful surroundings. Perfect for writing. If I ever got back to it.

Dad muttered goodnight and shuffled back upstairs. Soon, a Beach Boys tune drifted down the stairs from the radio Ida had loaned him. Somewhere in that heap of ashes on top of the hill was Dad's entire record collection. Given what I'd seen tonight, we weren't going to find anything to salvage up there.

A couple of minutes later, Tara returned with the cooler. I dipped a finger in to test it. "This is barely colder than room temperature."

She huffed a sigh. "Who are you, Goldilocks?" Leaving the cooler behind, she stomped into the kitchen, came back with two trays of ice cubes, and shoved them at me. "All yours. I'm going upstairs to Skype with Shannon. We're making our weekend plans. You know, the last hurrah before summer comes to a screeching halt."

"Sounds good, but you know we can't Skype here."

Her face froze in shock. She clutched her hands to her heart. "What? But Ida gave me the password for the Internet."

"Satellite Internet. Not only is the connection crappy, but data's limited. One two-hour chat session and the whole system will freeze up. For days."

Throwing her hands in the air, she huffed some more. "How am I supposed to *talk to people*? What is this — an outpost in Antarctica?"

"Sorry, honey. Just text or e-mail her. Or ... call her. This is life in the country. It has its plusses and minuses."

She started to trudge up the stairs, her shoulders rolled forward. "When you come up with a list of the plusses, let me know. Fresh country air is not one of them. That hog farm on the corner is noxious."

Okay, I had to agree with her on that one. But it wasn't any worse than the stench of human urine on park statues. Or food rotting in a dumpster. Or raw sewage. Chicago had all kinds of interesting smells.

I no sooner had my foot dunked in the chilled water than I heard the smooth rumble of an engine. Clint. I'd almost forgotten about Bump. Since I'd been convalescing lately, everyone else had taken over doggie care duties. And because I'd gone most of my life without a dog, it was too easy to lapse into non-dog mode.

The car door slammed. Paws scrabbled over cement, clicked on the wooden planks of the steps, then skidded to a halt in front of the door, followed closely by human feet. Clint knocked twice.

Hugging a pillow to my chest, I stirred the ice cubes with my now numb foot. He'd see me alone and want to talk. I wasn't ready for this.

Tap, tap, tap.

Three times. He was getting more insistent.

"Come in!" I yelled.

He jiggled the handle. "It seems to be locked."

Of course it was. I'd sat here and watched Dad do it. I could holler for someone upstairs to open the door, but likely Tara had her headphones on and I didn't want Dad engaging Clint in any manner. So I pushed myself up from the couch and stood. Or tried to. Even with a half-frozen foot, I could feel that toe starting to throb.

For a few moments, I stood on one foot, looking like a wobbly flamingo.

"Uh ... Sam? Are you going to let us in?"

"Just a sec." I could crawl to the door. But then I'd have to pull myself to a stand once I got there, and there was nothing close by to grab onto. I couldn't walk. Or fly, last I checked. In lieu of a motorized wheelchair, that left hopping. I scooted on one foot, my balance remarkably good. Before I opened the door, I crossed my bad foot behind my good one and leaned against the wall.

"Hey." I let him in. Bump waggled in after him, his tongue hanging long to the side and a stream of saliva dripping onto the floor to pool in a small lake. He looked thoroughly exhausted. And delirious. But then, Bump never looked sad or even sober. He was a perpetual puppy, and as annoying as that could be at times, it also made him that much more endearing. Sitting in front of me, he cocked his head one way, then the other, those mismatched eyes twinkling with limitless mirth. I scratched the top of his head. "Thanks for walking him for me. Could you do me a favor and put him in the laundry room?"

Clint looked at me suspiciously. "Why? Are you busy holding up the wall? Not that I mind putting him away, but ..."

"Ummm ..." I made little swirly motions with my hands, then flapped them toward the kitchen as I waited for something plausible to spring to mind. Nope. I had nothing. I couldn't even think of a good lie.

His eyes drifted downward. "Why is your foot blue?"

I checked. It was. Time to wave the white flag. "Okay, so I stepped in a hole. The grass is tall out there. Practically waist-high. Anyway, I was looking toward the cornfield next to Ida's when I fell. Appears someone's been doing donuts over there in their truck. Annnd ... someone shot at us when we got near it."

"Shot directly *at* you?"

"Well, close, anyway."

"Sure it wasn't a hunter?"

"That was my first thought. But Archer says it's not hunting season yet and we should call the sheriff. He thinks whoever it was didn't want us near there."

"Huh. Maybe I'll check it out. How's your ... ankle, foot ...?"

"Little toe, actually. Just trying to stay off of it until I see the doctor tomorrow."

"Want me to take a look?"

"Thanks, but Archer already did."

"Oh." His face fell. He looked around the room, like he expected him to leap out from behind a piece of furniture and challenge him to a martial arts duel. "Well, then, I'll just get Bump a drink of water. Meanwhile, you stay put."

"Not a problem." Except that I might fall over.

He hurried past. Bump veered toward the kitchen, eager to stalk felines, but Clint gave him a sharp tug on his leash in the other direction. A few seconds later, the laundry room door shut and Clint returned to slide a steady shoulder under my arm. Once I was situated on the couch, he arranged the pillows behind me and under my foot, spread a throw over my legs, and handed me the remote control. I could get used to having attractive men wait on me hand and foot.

"Can I get you something to drink?" he asked.

"I'd ask for a glass of wine, but remember what happened the last time you handed me one?"

His lips curled into a sexy grin. "Yeah, bit of a mess, but I like how it ended."

"Oh. Right. Forget I said that." I couldn't, though. Judging by the grin still plastered on his face, he couldn't either. My body tingled just thinking about it.

Silence yawned between us.

The refrigerator kicked on with a low hum. Tiny paws plopped onto the kitchen floor, then scampered across it. We both looked in the direction of the noise. Mr. Jeeves poked his pink nose around the doorway to scan the premises. When he decided it was clear of any annoying canines, he slunk across the living room uneasily, then sprinted up the stairs to safety. Once the cat was out of sight, all I could hear was Clint drumming his fingers on his thighs. I stared at him until he stopped.

"I'll get you some water." Clint disappeared into the kitchen for a minute, then brought out two glasses, each with a lemon wedge on the rim. He handed me my drink and sat in the armchair next to the couch, his glass resting in the circle of his hands. "I owe you a better explanation about Danielle."

"No, you don't. Really."

"I do, Sam. And I'm not going to leave tonight without giving you one. You can't walk away this time."

He was right — I literally couldn't walk away. Still, I didn't want to go there just yet. I needed to nurse this grudge for a while longer. It was a specialty of mine. So I spared him the confession.

"Your divorce didn't go through. You didn't mention it to me because you figured before things got too serious between us, it would be finalized. But then we … let our urges take over and you missed your chance to be upfront with me because you didn't have the guts to tell me the truth."

Blowing his breath out slowly, he sounded like a tire deflating. He nodded. "You're right. I was a coward. Afraid you'd write me off. Forever, maybe."

"No, I wouldn't have."

Confusion clouded his face. "What?"

"I would have waited for you." I pointed at him. "But just so we're clear, if I'd known about her, I wouldn't have done it with you that night. Wine or no wine. Anyway, my point is that, yeah, I would have listened to your side. Given you a chance. And waited. Until things with Danielle were really over."

An elbow on the armrest, he took a sip of water. "They are now."

"It doesn't matter, Clint."

Looking up at the ceiling, he slumped against the back of the chair. "What will it take for you to give me another chance, Sam?" He turned a pleading gaze on me. "Because I'm not going to give up on you that easily."

I chugged my water, suddenly realizing how parched I was. "Time, I guess. And don't ask how much. I just need to know that Danielle is out of your life for good. Maybe after she's gone back to wherever it is she came from, we can start over, slowly. Possibly. At some point."

There, I'd drawn the line. A blurry one, maybe, but a line.

"When is she leaving, by the way?"

He hesitated, swallowed. "Soon, I hope."

Somehow I had the feeling that his idea of 'soon' and mine were worlds apart.

Before I could dissect his response, he was on his feet. "I should probably take Bump out one more time for you. We'll go check out that field."

After they left, I flipped through all the TV stations. Nothing captured my attention. Probably because I kept replaying that night with Clint over and over in my head. It had been the best night of my life in over a decade. Why was I being so hard on him?

I was on my third round of channel-surfing when Clint let himself back in the house. Too bone-tired to bother getting up, I remained draped on the couch cushions like one of Ida's old afghans. Clint unclipped Bump's leash and the dog trotted over to sit beside me. He was panting heavily, like he'd just run laps at the track. Drool dripped from his tongue in long, gooey strings. Right onto Ida's clean couch.

I poked at him and told him to move, but Bump was as inert as I was.

Forcing myself upright, I planted a palm on the dog's shoulder. But before I could give him a good shove, the edges of my vision darkened.

I was aware of Clint speaking to me, but the words all blended into an unintelligible buzz.

At first I thought I must have sat up too quickly, but soon a familiar sensation started to take hold: the feeling that I was somewhere else, in some other time, in another body.

Oh, no. It was happening again. Sometimes when I touched Bump, strange things happened. The first time I'd shared one of his memories, it had been of the fire at the house of his previous owner, Bud Crawley. During that vision, I'd seen and heard snatches of Taylor coming after Crawley with a wrench. I hadn't understood it then, but it had been as real as real life: the caustic smell of smoke, the brightly flickering flames, the heat against my fur ... I'd been in Bump's mind, seen what he'd seen, heard what he'd heard, felt his fear.

Yet now, even though I didn't want to have another of his memories, I was powerless to stop it. It was like being immersed in a 3-D movie at the Omnimax, complete with surround sound and Smell-O-Vision.

A sickeningly sweet aroma wafted up my nostrils, invading my lungs and saturating my tongue. Smoke stung my eyes. It wasn't the choking smoke of a house going up in flames this time. It was a thin spire of smoke, curling upwards from a lit cigarette ... no, a joint.

Euphoria filled me. I pressed my nose to a crack above the glass of a car window. And barked. Not once, but several times.

A face, young and clean-shaven, sucked at the joint. The boy-man flicked ashes onto the ground and pushed himself away from what appeared to be an old barn.

What'd you bring the dog for?

A car door slammed. Then I heard a woman's voice beside me.

Ignore him. He's just a dumb mutt.

Feet stomped behind me, followed by a third voice, older, more authoritative, a man's.

Good. Because I'd hate to have to shoot him.

Don't you dare, the woman said. *He's a harmless pup, okay?*

"Sam, are you okay?"

I blinked until Clint's face came into focus, then nodded, even though I felt slightly nauseous. Relief rushed through me and I clamped my hands onto his face. "You didn't get shot."

"No, nobody even tried. It was quiet out there. You look a little peaked."

I let go of his face, suddenly afraid he'd take my concern as encouragement. "Just sat up too quick."

"Well, I thought you were about to keel over. I was telling you what I'd found, but your eyes had this glazed-over look. Anyway, you are not going to believe what we found." Clint dropped into the adjacent chair, a fine sheen of sweat glistening on his skin like someone had sprinkled him with glitter. I bet he tasted salty.

I leaned against the back of the couch for support. "A dead body?"

"Almost as good."

I shrugged. "The tennis ball Bump lost yesterday?"

"No."

"A pot of gold?"

"Different kind of pot. A marijuana patch."

With a satisfied grunt, Bump dropped to the ground and rolled over, legs spread eagle like he'd just finished having sex with the hottest show poodle on the block.

"Let me guess," I said. "Bump led you to it."

"Faster than if someone had laid a trail of hot dogs. I'm surprised you didn't hear him barking all the way down here. The dog has the nose of a bloodhound."

And, I was betting, a more interesting history than we had any hint of.

chapter 4

I CLICKED MY SEAT belt into place. Or tried to. It popped back out. I shoved it back in. Same thing. Yet I did it five more times, changing how much force I put into it or the angle at which I tried to jam the flat of the buckle into the clip. Then I cussed at it to see if that helped. It didn't, but I sure felt better. Like I'd accomplished something by damning it to hell. Because everyone knows seatbelts are afraid of burning for eternity.

"Here." Selma reached over and crammed the two ends together. "Now hold those there."

She reached under her seat to pull out a screwdriver, then jammed the end into the buckle clasp and wiggled it back and forth, careful not to break her inch-long, neon-pink fingernails. This time it clunked into place.

Sometimes you just have to be smarter than the seat belt.

Pink was today's color. There was a streak of it through Selma's mousy brown tresses — which may or may not have been her real hair color — and she was wearing a baby-pink tank top and tight black jeans. More the look one would expect on someone my daughter's age and not a thirty-something, but she totally rocked it. I envied her guts, though, more than her fashion sense.

I was beginning to have second thoughts about having asked my friend Selma Paradiso for a ride to the doctor. Ida was garage-saling with the gals from the Purple Hat Sisterhood, her newest social circle, since she claimed the Lion's Club was too political. And I'd loaned Dad my car to meet with the insurance agent. Archer was working.

I could've called Clint, but I didn't want to use up my favors with him since he was walking Bump every day. There was also the fact that sitting in a car with him for half an hour each way would have forced us to talk. Which might lead to other things. The longer I put that off, the better my chances of my intellect making decisions and not my hormones. Clint exuded super-pheromones, I was sure of it.

"That should hold you until we get there." Selma swung her head from me to the dashboard and back, so that her dangly rhinestone earrings twisted and sparkled. "But just so you know, it's easier to buckle than unbuckle."

Great. I'd need a switchblade to cut myself out of my seat belt. I hoped she kept one of those in the glove compartment.

With a flip of her wrist, she turned the key in the ignition switch. The fourteen year-old Camaro made a strangling noise that quickly pitched into a metallic whine. She tried again. This time it sounded like two alley cats mating. "Well, shoot."

Between that, the seat belt, the sheet of plastic in place of a rear window, and the driver-side mirror being held on with duct tape, I wasn't feeling too confident about our transportation. "How long did you say Dan had your car in his shop?"

"Oh ..." — she shoved the shifter left, then right, then back to the left — "two, three months, maybe. Why?"

Crap, this was a manual. And she had on four-inch heels. "No reason."

Selma gave the key another twist. This time it sounded worse, if that was possible. Like someone had opened the gates of hell and unleashed a thousand demons.

43

"Did you say he fixed the transmission?" I asked.

"Transfusion, honey. That and the Catalina convertor ... I think. And the calibrator. Oh, and the environmental intake cabin filter."

The air filter? Even I knew how to change one of those. "Wow. And he did all that for how much?"

"Forty-two hundred bucks. Cheaper than a new car."

And about ten times what she should have paid, given that it still hadn't been fixed.

It finally dawned on her to put a foot on the clutch. This time the engine boomed to life like a jet. It must have hit a hundred and thirty decibels inside the car. My bones were vibrating so hard I thought I might displace a few vertebrae.

She was cautious going down Ida's gravel driveway. "I don't want to bottom out if I hit a pothole," she said. "Last time I did that the muffler came loose and was dragging. The sparks almost set fire to the car."

This might be a good time to get out my cell phone and call all those people in my life I needed to apologize to.

But as soon as we hit the open road, it was like we'd suddenly been dumped into a cross-country road rally race. The back of my skull plastered against the headrest, I tried to lean left to get a look at the speedometer. The needle was stuck on zero.

"Your speedometer doesn't work."

She cracked her gum a few times. "Yeah, never has."

"How do you know how fast you're going?"

"By the tack-o-meter. There's some formula for figuring out your speed. I forget what it is, but if I get pulled over, I just talk my way out of a ticket."

I didn't ask how often she got pulled over. Or how she finagled her way out of a ticket. Or how many accidents she'd had. Judging by the dings and scratches on the car, quite a few. I resolved never to ride with her again. Even if it was a life-or-death emergency. Which this was not. But if I bailed now I'd hit the pavement at something close to eighty miles an hour. *Splat!*

"So how did you finally get the money to spring your car from Dan?" Not that I really wanted to know, or thought it was a good idea to distract her with questions, but to distract myself. My life was flashing before my eyes.

"Dylan paid it off for me."

"Loaned you the money, you mean?"

"No. Yeah. Well, maybe. That wasn't really clear. But we're on for Mexico again, and I've been watching what I eat, staying away from red meat and greasy foods so I can fit in my skinny clothes. Even joined the gym in Fullbright. I've lost twelve pounds — not that I had that much to lose, mind you, but I want to look my best for him. So if things go well there" — she winked — "he'll probably forget all about the money and never ask me for a dime."

There was a word for that, but I wasn't going to say it out loud. That she'd 'borrowed' money in return for a good time didn't concern me as much as the fact that she was back with Dylan Hawkins. I still had the feeling that he was involved in some sort of criminal activity, but I hadn't been able to link him to Jake Taylor yet. Then there was the fact that he'd pressured me for sex in exchange for information on how to sell stolen goods. If it hadn't been for the dead batteries in my voice recorder, the scumbag would be sitting in jail right now. But that was water under the bridge, and if I was ever going to get evidence on him, it would be that much harder now. I could, however, save Selma from him.

"Selma?" I tested the door lock on my side in anticipation of the need for a quick getaway, in case she pulled over to beat the snot out of me, although my aching foot would've made escaping a lost cause on my part. *Click, click, click.*

"Yeah?"

"Do you ever wonder if Dylan has cheated on you — or that he

45

would, if he had the opportunity?" *Click.* I needed to tell her about him and what he'd tried with me.

"Oh, honey, he would never cheat on me. What could be better than this?" Taking her hands off the steering wheel, she flourished them over her body. The car lurched toward the gravel shoulder before she hooked two fingers back over the steering wheel. Her D-cup breasts jutted out as she tugged her top lower with her other hand to reveal a lacy black bra that stretched across deep cleavage. "I mean, would *you* cheat on these? If you were a guy, that is. I'm not asking if you're a thespian. 'Cause it doesn't matter to me if you are."

Where did she get these ideas? "I'm not ..." — I couldn't bring myself to use the wrong word or correct her, so I worked my way around it — "one of those."

She patted my knee. "It's okay, really. Lots of people are, but they just haven't come to grips with it. Sometimes I think Dylan wishes I swung both ways, because he has some pretty kinky ideas, but it's just not my thing. I understand if you do, though. Not that I'm in the market, mind you. But you might want to tell that yummy veteran of yours. No fair stringing him along if you are."

Click, click. Click, click, click.

We whipped around a curve and I swear the car went airborne for a second. Selma gave me a sideways glance. "Are you nervous about going to see the doctor or something, Sam?"

"Veterinarian," I mumbled.

"What?"

"He's a veterinarian, not a veteran."

"Huh. I thought someone told me he'd been in the army."

Okay, so sometimes she did have the right word, just the wrong idea. But there was one idea of hers bugging me. "What makes you think I'm a ... that I like girls?"

"Isn't it obvious?"

"Not to me."

She giggled. "It's your clothes."

I glanced down at my outfit: old-fashioned Wranglers, a hoodie, and an old football jersey that used to belong to Kyle. Usually I slept in it, but it was one of the few things I had that was easy to get over my wrist brace. Besides, it reminded me of him. Over the jersey, I had on the hoodie I borrowed from Tara. I'd also pulled my curly red hair into a ponytail and skipped makeup. I thought being less well groomed might make me look more in pain. Or like a haggard crack whore, now that I thought about it.

"Honey, if you're going to hide it, you need to dress a little more feminine."

Point taken. I didn't always dress like this. Today was all about comfort. Besides, most of my clothes had been lost in the fire and I hadn't had the energy yet to go shopping. I held on to the armrest with a death grip for the rest of the ride, so in case the car broke apart upon re-entry into the atmosphere, they could find my hand still clinging to the door. The rest of my body would be scattered over several square miles if we crashed at this velocity.

We made touchdown at the Fullbright South Urgent Care Center not a moment too soon. Luckily, I hadn't suffered from a heart attack brought on by Selma's driving, but if I had I was pretty sure she could've gotten me to the hospital faster than an ambulance. Before I could wrestle with my seat belt, Selma jimmied the latch with the screwdriver and sprung me. I sucked it up and began hobbling to the door on my own before Selma could offer a shoulder. I was afraid if I clung too tightly to her, she'd interpret it as a come-on.

Halfway there I had to stop and let the pain ebb. I was wearing a pair of flip-flops I'd borrowed from Ida, and they were about three sizes too small, but my shoes had put pressure on the tender parts of my foot. Walking with my left foot rolled inward was doing a number on my ankle and knee. So I switched to curling my toes up so I could walk on my heel, but that only hurt my bad toe more.

47

Selma's spiked heels clacked behind me. She hoisted her shiny silver handbag higher onto her shoulder as she caught up with me. "Why don't you lean against that van there, Sam, while I go fetch a wheelchair?"

I was not going to let her drive me around in a wheelchair, either. "Nope. I'm good. Great, actually. I'll make it."

If my foot wasn't broken when we pulled in, it may well have been by the time I staggered into the waiting room and dove into a chair. Selma signed me in and brought me the patient questionnaire to fill out. All six pages of it. When she turned that in, they gave her an insurance form. Three more pages. Thirty minutes and a case of carpal tunnel later, I was on the schedule. The waiting room was full of people who looked like they'd just spent sixty days at sea on a life raft.

"Mooooommy?" the little girl across from us cried as she tugged at her mother's sleeve. "I think I'm going to be —"

She spewed a stream of spoiled milk and Cheerios onto the tiled floor. Her mother gathered her hair back from her face and led her into the bathroom. Even with the door shut, I could hear her hurling. The smell alone was making me sick. A receptionist mopped up the puddle near us and doused it with powerful-smelling disinfectant. Now the waiting area smelled like germ-free vomit.

"So" — Selma clacked her nails on the armrest between us — "how was dinner with Archer?"

Another patient, looking green around the gills, ran out the front door with a finger pressed to his mouth. Barely outside, he pivoted next to a bush and hunched over, his body convulsing as he brought up his last meal.

"Can we not talk about food right now?" I said.

The little girl puked again.

Selma's head swiveled toward the sound. "Oh, sure." Looking back at me, she squeezed my hand. "So how was your date?"

"It wasn't a date. There were three other people there."

"'Kay. How was your 'thing' with Archer?"

"Nice."

She squinted at me. It was the first I had noticed the glitter on her eyelids. More of a discotheque look than daytime casual. "'Nice' as in ..." — she slid her tongue around her lips — "*niiiice?*" Then her shoulders twitched in a lazy shrug. "Or just, you know, nice? Like you went to church for Easter Sunday and it was nice to dress up and the preacher didn't stare you down while talking about fornication?"

Of course, she'd gotten that word right.

"I'm not sure how to interpret either of those options, Selma. So I'll just say the conversation was pleasant, we ate well, and then Archer and I went and looked at my dad's house. It was all innocent. Then I stepped in a hole, and he carried me to the house and left just before Clint brought the dog back from a walk. And before you ask, nothing happened with Clint. We talked a little, agreed not to do anything right now, then he took the dog out to potty one more time" — I lowered my voice to a whisper — "and discovered a patch of marijuana in the field next door. Probably worth a hundred grand on the street."

Her face took on a look of concentration. She glanced around, like she was making sure no one was eavesdropping on us. "Let me get this straight. He carried you how? Over his shoulder, like he was hauling a feed sack to the barn? Or cradled like a baby, looking down into your eyes with lust like in one of those S.A. Mack novels?"

She'd invoked my secret pen name. Which reminded me I still owed her an autographed copy. I smacked her on the wrist.

"Ow!"

"Sorry. Were you listening to that last part?"

"About the illegal drugs?" she said in a voice so loud that the receptionist looked up from her desk.

Someone behind us coughed. Wonderful. Not only were we being bombarded by rampant flu germs, but we were being exposed to a respiratory infection, too. Probably tuberculosis. They coughed again.

I swiveled around to see who was hacking up globs of phlegm so I could offer them a tissue to cover their mouths.

Three seats down behind us, harsh gray eyes met mine. I'd seen those eyes before. But it was the massive bald head that ticked my memory.

Virgil. As in Dylan Hawkins' bodyguard.

I whipped around and slumped down so far I almost slid out of my chair.

Twisting sideways, Selma grabbed at my arm to stop me from hitting the floor. Just as quick, her head snapped up and she let go of me. "Virg! What are you doing here?"

"Samantha McNamee?" the nurse called from the doorway. "You may come on back now."

I shot up from my seat, yanked Selma to her feet, and slung an arm around her to drag her from the room.

AFTER I'D BEEN WEIGHED, measured, and corralled into a holding pen, Nurse Ratched — that wasn't the name on her nametag, but it suited her — wrapped a cuff around my arm and pumped it so full of air I thought she was using it as a tourniquet. Her hair was pulled up into a tight bun, stretching the skin on her face taut. She let the air out of the cuff slowly. Just when I started to regain sensation in that arm, she inflated it again.

"Hmmm, that can't be right." After the second time, she shook her head and wrote the numbers down. "Are you on any medication, currently, Ms. McNamee?"

"No." Technically, I wasn't anymore. Two days ago, I'd run out of the oxycodone they'd prescribed for me at the hospital. A part of me was hoping I could get some more, because when I was on it, I didn't care that Clint had lied to me. I didn't really care about anything then. But another part of me remembered how I'd used wine to dull the pain of losing Kyle in that car wreck a decade ago. No, I needed to learn to deal with pain, physical or otherwise. Biting my lip to keep from cussing at the nurse, I rubbed my arm to restore the blood flow, then wiggled my fingers. She'd compressed a nerve, too.

"Not even birth control?" Selma asked bluntly.

I narrowed my eyes at Selma to shush her, but the message flew right over her head.

"Because you and Clint shouldn't —"

"I'm not on any medication, but thanks for being concerned." I looked at the nurse then, the paper sheet I was sitting on crinkling as I turned in her direction. "I suppose that's a standard question?"

"Actually, it's all in the paperwork you filled out, but your blood pressure's through the roof."

The reason for that was sitting in the lobby, but that story was too long and way too involved to get into with someone I didn't hope to ever see again.

"I'm just frazzled," I told her. "It's normally fine."

"Of course it is."

My phone buzzed with a text. It was Clint, asking if he could take Bump for an early walk. I started to shoot off a reply, but Nurse Ratched was glaring at me.

"Sorry," I mumbled. I turned my phone on mute, figuring I'd just tell Clint later that this evening would be better. Somehow I'd be unavailable when he came by.

The nurse jabbed a thermometer under my tongue and pressed two fingers to the vein on my wrist as she checked her watch. Her eyebrows twitched. "Pulse is rapid, too." After the thermometer beeped, she jotted down more numbers. "The doctor will be in to see you shortly."

Which in this town meant sometime before the next harvest. And that was fine, because I intended to hide out in this room until Virgil

51

the Hulk was long gone.

While Selma and I waited, she pumped me for more information about the herbal drugs sprouting up next door, but I didn't have much to tell her.

Legs crossed, Selma swung her foot. "You're going to have to let Sheriff Driscoll know about it."

"I suppose you're right. Ida's worried about the people who planted it, though. She's afraid of them cutting through her property to get to it as long as it's there, so she wants it gone. But she's also afraid of what might go down if we do call it in."

"If?" She stopped swinging her leg and looked me dead in the eye. "Honey, there is no 'if'. You have to do your civic duty and report it. In fact, we'll stop by at the station on our way back to Ida's."

"What? No. I figured Ida could go in."

"Has Ida seen it?"

"No, but I haven't either. Maybe Clint —"

"We're stopping."

" — could go in? He's the one who —"

"We're stopping."

"But I —"

"Oh, quit being such a chicken. I will drag you in by your hair if I have to. Besides" — she reached inside her purse to jingle the car keys — "I'm driving."

My blood pressure shot up ten more points.

Fifteen minutes slogged by. I lay flat on the examining table, sat up, and lay down again. It was getting hard to stay awake. The only thing that kept me alert was the paranoia that every surface I touched and every lungful of air I inhaled were saturated with microscopic soldiers prepared to invade and wage war once they established ground somewhere in my body.

Meanwhile, Selma kept picking up pamphlets from the counter and flicking through them, pulling out the drawers, and scoping out the cabinets. So much for not taking any germs home with us.

Sitting up, I extended my left foot. The swelling was down, but it still hurt like the bejeebers if I put any weight on it. I calculated my chances of getting painkillers out of this venture, thinking they might have been better if I hadn't iced it like Archer had told me to.

Selma pulled a jar of cotton balls out of one of the cupboards, opened it up, and inhaled so deeply I thought she was going to suck one up her nose.

"What are you doing?"

She screwed the lid back on. "I always wondered what they kept in all these cabinets. Kinda hoping I might find some of those samples the drug companies are always handing out."

Never mind the fact that said samples could have been for diabetes or erectile dysfunction, both of which I was sure she didn't have a problem with.

"Say, uh, that guy out in the waiting room, Virgil — do you know him?"

"You could say that." She fanned a stack of tongue depressors, then put them back. "He's my brother."

"He is?" This wasn't good. That explained how she'd hooked up with Dylan. Or maybe she'd known Dylan first and had gotten Virgil the gig with him.

"I get that all the time. He looks like Mama. I look like Daddy."

That was an interesting picture. Their mom had to be an ugly —

"Stepbrother, actually," she elaborated. "Say, if you don't mind, I'm going to go out there and check on him. I didn't get a chance to ask what he was in for before you yanked me back here. Virgil hasn't been sick a day in his life. I'm kinda worried about the big oat."

Oaf, oaf.

"Sure." I faked a smile as she flipped a wave and backed out the door.

Crap, crap, crap. What if he told her I'd been with Dylan in the back room at the lodge? I was only trying to milk Dylan for information, but Virgil wouldn't have known that. If he told her, I might be looking for another ride home. Which actually wasn't a bad thing.

Twenty-six more minutes crept by. And yes, I was counting every single one. It figured that the one time I forgot to bring my e-reader with me to the doctor's office, I'd have to wait an eternity. But then, I'd been silly enough to think that 'urgent care' meant they'd get to you in less time than it took to die from gangrene.

My eyes drifted shut. I concentrated on my breathing, hoping to bring my blood pressure down before the doctor came in. Gradually, I began to relax. My limbs felt light, my thoughts foggy.

My head bobbed forward. I woke with a start, then decided it was better to lie down again before I fell asleep sitting up, hit my head on the floor, and was carted out of here in a coma. Since I didn't want to put pressure on my left foot, I stretched out on my other side, facing the wall.

I'd just drifted off to la-la land when the door banged open. My eyes flew wide. Heels clicked behind me. Selma had returned.

Rubbing my eyes, I exhaled loudly. "Good gosh, Selma. Give me a heart attack, will you. Would you mind going to the desk and asking what's taking them so damn long?"

"Number one," a terse female voice said, "I am *not* Selma. And number two, an outbreak of food poisoning from some dive called …" — papers rustled — "Ginny's Whistle Stop is what's taking so long. Which is probably just a little more urgent than your stubbed toe."

I knew that voice.

And if I could've made myself invisible just then and disappeared, I would have.

Slowly, I rolled over, feeling like a hog on a spit. As I sat up, I looked down at the floor to avoid eye contact until I could think of some way out of this.

My gaze slid upward, from her pointy-toed black pumps, to her tan calves, past her midthigh hemline and around perfect curves hugged by a form-fitting red knit skirt and tailored blouse, all the way up to Farrah Fawcett blond waves.

Danielle Townsley.

Apparently, she wasn't leaving the area anytime soon.

"You know what?" I rotated my foot in a tiny circle, as knives of pain jabbed at my metatarsals. "It feels all better now. I think I'll just head on home, if that's —"

"Sit," she barked.

And like any obedient dog, I sat.

chapter 5

"WE NEED TO TALK." Danielle slipped a pen into the breast pocket of her lab coat, her cool blue eyes sweeping over me like she was sizing up a side of beef and debating which cut of meat to ask the butcher for.

"Don't worry, I'm good. I'll slip the receptionist a twenty on my way out for the co-pay."

I had no sooner put my feet on the floor, determined to make my exit this time, than she stuck a fingertip in the middle of my sternum and rammed me back against the table. Okay, more like nudged me. I was still weak from my run-in with Jake Taylor. Not to mention slightly intimidated by her assertiveness. So I planted my rump back down on the paper sheet.

"First, I need to examine your foot."

She adjusted the table so I was still sitting up, but reclined enough to relax. Relaxation, however, was the furthest thing from my mind. I was ready to shove her to the floor and bolt to freedom. After stomping her head in. And strangling her with her own platinum tresses.

But as she flexed my ankle slowly back and forth, then gently probed at my foot and toe, it occurred to me that it wasn't her I

56

should be mad at. It was Clint.

So why did seeing her upset me so much? Was I ... *jealous?* Noooo.

She wiggled my little toe and I sucked air in sharply.

"So that hurt?"

"Just a little." A lot, actually. Although compared to what I'd been through recently, it was tolerable.

"Hmm." She held my feet together, looking from one to the other. Then a longer, "Hmmmmm."

"What does that mean?"

"No obvious break. No evidence of a subungual hematoma. Some discoloration of the affected area, but no open wounds, so a tetanus shot won't be necessary. I'm going to guess it's a hairline fracture of the fifth metatarsal, proximal phalange, to be exact."

"Oookay. In layman's terms, please."

She pointed to the outside of my foot. "You have a crack in this toe bone here."

"Will an X-ray confirm that?"

"Maybe, maybe not. How's your insurance coverage?"

"Terrible."

"Then we'll skip it. Treatment would be the same either way."

"So, are you going to write me a prescription?"

"For what?"

"Something for the pain, maybe? Just a few days' worth to tide me over." The addict in me was groveling. I'd resolved not to ask for it, but it was like my brain and my mouth were disconnected.

"I don't think you'll need it. Nothing a little anti-inflammatory can't take care of."

Hard liquor it was, then.

She went on to explain that treatment was precisely what Archer had already told me: rest, ice, elevation, and ibuprofen until the swelling subsided. While her bedside manner was more Dr. House than Marcus Welby, M.D., by the time she was done I didn't hate her quite as much as I had when she'd first walked in. Until —

"If you're wondering why I haven't left here yet"

— she levied a fully automatic firearm at me —

"it's because I'm making regular visits to a colleague of mine in Fort Wayne"

— and zinged a few clips at my feet before —

"who's a specialist in *in vitro* fertilization, because"

— she raised the barrel to my gut and fired at point blank range —

"I want to conceive a child. I've gone over all my options, and my optimal range for being able to carry a child naturally is rapidly diminishing. Miscarriage, pregnancy complications, and birth defects increase considerably after a certain age, which I'm getting close to. I've already achieved all of my professional goals that required traveling to locations where the risks of infectious disease and wartime casualties were high. Naturally, I didn't want to have a child only to leave him or her an orphan. A child needs a safe environment to develop in, and I intend to give them that. Currently, I'm seeking a position at a few highly regarded research hospitals near a thriving metropolis with more educational and cultural opportunities for rearing a child." She paused. "First, however, I need a sperm donor."

I had the overwhelming impulse to plunge a hand through her abdominal wall and tie her fallopian tubes in a knot. "Meaning you want Clint to be your baby-daddy? Why didn't you just have a child when you were married to him? And most importantly — why are you telling this to me?"

"Which question would you like me to answer first?"

"I don't know! Pick one."

"Very well. I don't remember the order in which you asked, but I'll do my best to answer them all. Please refresh my memory if I omit one."

What amazed me was that she could talk about this like she was discussing whether to go with warm tones or neutrals for her living room décor. What on earth had Clint ever seen in her? Besides her Barbie doll figure, that is? And her perfect hair? And an IQ that was probably twice mine?

"Why now, you asked. As I said, the timing before now was not optimal. Clinton wanted children. I did not. Not then, at least. I wasn't sure if I ever would. But working with so many ill and undernourished children in Africa touched me. Deeply. I also saw young mothers die, leaving children behind who were too young to care for themselves. The children were devastated. Lost. Deprived of the first and most important role model in their lives. And I wondered if someone would ever care that much for me. Then I began to think that perhaps I could raise a child who could go out into the world and in some way leave it a better place: cure illnesses, fight for injustice, govern the masses, enlighten humanity."

In truth, I hated her a tiny bit less for having dreams like that. I'd had similar hopes when I'd conceived Tara. Okay, maybe not *that* lofty, but I'd have been happy with a kid who didn't land in juvie or get knocked up before she could get accepted into college. So far so good.

"Why not adopt?" I asked.

"I haven't ruled it out in the long run. But I'd like to try this avenue while I still can."

So she had a primal need to procreate? In other words, her biological clock was ticking. Anyway, hadn't she heard about sperm banks?

"Why Clint, then?" I was starting to feel possessive about him. Last night, he'd vowed to win me over. Now I was sitting here with his ex, discussing whether or not they should make babies together?

"Who else? He is as near to perfect as a physical specimen could be, don't you agree?"

Well, duh.

"Not only that," she went on, "he's kind, selfless, intelligent ... He speaks fluent French, he's artistic, and he plays the piano, the guitar, and the saxophone."

The more she had rattled off, the more I realized she knew him way better than I did. And that bothered me. Greatly.

"My only other candidate at this point is the brother of one of my former roommates. He's a practicing attorney in Fort Wayne who specializes in wrongful arrest. He's amenable to the idea of fathering a child, but he's a distant, *distant* second. Besides, who could compare to Clinton? He has — how would you describe it?" She stared off into space, tugging at the neckline of her blouse like she was having a hot flash. "Ah, yes, sexual charisma. It's like his DNA is screaming out to be replicated."

That was one way of saying he was hot.

"Furthermore, I've researched his genetic history thoroughly. The indicators for longevity are stellar. I could pore through several hundred potential donors and not find one as fitting as him. So why not? Would you choose a picture from a file, a name off a piece of paper, someone who didn't have half his talents? Or would you choose Clinton?"

She had me there. If I hadn't wanted to have Clint's offspring myself before I walked in there, I did now. Still ... "I just don't get it. And I'm not talking about Clint. I do get that. Why are you telling *me* all this?"

She tucked her pen behind her ear. "Samantha, the day I showed up at Clinton's veterinary practice, when you saw us, and I noticed your reaction ... Well, it was quite obvious to me. You two are romantically involved. While I'm not sure how seriously or for how long, I want you to know I don't retain any claim to him. When I left him to go to Africa, it was with the full understanding that we were both free to pursue others. I don't want to get between you two."

I didn't have the slightest idea how to respond to her. Should I tell her there was nothing to get between? Or pretend we were totally, head over heels in love? Which for a short while I'd thought we were.

This whole thing was just so ... bizarre. I understood why someone would pick Clint to father a child, but didn't she get that doing so would change his life just as much as hers?

"Has Clint agreed to this?"

She shook her head. "Not yet."

"But he knows? Meaning, you've asked him and he didn't give you an outright no?"

"That's correct."

The more I thought about it all, the madder I got. How could he even consider it? And since I'd seen him just last night, I had to assume he and Danielle had had this discussion recently.

I had to get out of there before I totally lost it.

"Don't you have other patients to see?" I prompted.

She nodded. "Yes, I should move on. Anyway, I just wanted you to know."

How nice of her.

Bitch.

AFTER HANDING OVER MY co-pay and straightening out the confusion over my temporary address, I found Selma in the waiting area, flipping through a maternity magazine. I scanned the room. Virgil wasn't there.

Letting out a breath, I planted myself in front of Selma. When she didn't budge, I tapped her on the forehead.

Blinking, she lowered the magazine. "Do you think I'd make a good mother?"

How was I supposed to answer that? Even if I handled it with leather gloves, it was as prickly as a porcupine. Besides, I'd rather discuss whether Selma's leopard skin leggings made her butt look big than get involved in a discussion about her mothering abilities.

"Let's go." I hooked a hand under Selma's arm and guided her outside, limping toward her Camaro as fast as I could without breaking into a run.

Impatient, I grabbed the handle, expecting her to have a remote unlock like everyone else in this century. Instead, I had to wait for her to fiddle with the key, then get inside and reach across the seat to unlock my side.

Heat wrapped itself around me and seared my lungs. "It must be two hundred degrees in here."

"Sorry, hon. I always put the windows up." She started up the engine and revved it a few times. "Wouldn't want anyone to break in, hotwire my baby, and steal her."

I didn't think that would ever be a problem. In fact, she could have left the doors wide open with the key in the ignition and it probably would have still been there when we'd gotten back.

While she rummaged through her purse for a stick of gum, I scratched around the edge of my wrist brace. I couldn't wait to get the thing off and have full use of my wrist again. Just as I looked up, Selma rolled her window down and stuck her head out.

"Talk to you later, 'kay?!" she shouted. Then, with a flap of her wrist, she waved goodbye.

I leaned in her direction, but the glare off the hood blinded me.

"Talk to whom?" I asked.

She jabbed a finger to my right as she whipped out of the parking space. "Virgil."

I saw him then, sitting behind the wheel of an older model white Pontiac. He watched us like a hawk studying its prey as we rolled past him. I slid lower in the seat, keeping my head just high enough and far enough to the left to gaze out the side-view mirror on my side.

Dang if he didn't pull out behind us and go the same way.

chapter 6

"WHY IS HE FOLLOWING us?" I hunkered down lower in the seat.

Selma cracked her gum several times, like someone had lit a string of firecrackers. "Who?"

"Your brother."

"We're headed south on Highway 5. How else is he supposed to get back to Wilton?"

I hated it when she was right.

Selma had the lead foot of an Indy race car driver. Several times, she was going so fast, I was sure we'd ditched Virgil. But eventually his Pontiac would drift back into view. I was starting to wonder if he'd told Selma about my run-in with Dylan, when she flipped her turn signal on and swung a sharp left onto a country road.

I propped myself up just far enough to see Virgil's car continue on down Highway 5.

Selma gave me a hard look. "You didn't answer me."

"About what?" I wasn't good at playing dumb, but I figured with her I had a chance.

"If I'd make a good mother."

"What brought this up?" I *really* didn't want to know, but I was trapped in close quarters with her as we hurtled through the

63

countryside at light speed, and it seemed like a safer topic than asking what she'd talked about with her stepbrother while Dr. Danielle My-Biological-Clock-Is-Ticking Townsley poured out her deepest personal desires to me.

"I don't know. Sometimes I just wonder what kind of babies Dylan and I could make."

"Must be catching," I mumbled.

"Huh?"

"Uh, nothing. Just glad you can't catch food poisoning. Anyhow, you were saying?"

"Well, my birthday's coming up next week and I'm not getting any younger, you know. I may look twenty-five, but I passed that millstone a few years ago."

Milestone, millstone. She was only off by one letter. Needless to say, proofreading was not on her list of potential careers. And a *few* years ago? Try ten or fifteen.

"So do you think I would?"

"Would what?" She wasn't going to let me slip out of this noose, was she?

Selma slammed to a stop at a crossroads, then turned right. "Just answer the damn question, would you, Sam?"

Just the thought of her and Dylan procreating sounded like a precursor to a series of Maury Povich episodes. It could be its own spin-off.

If playing dumb didn't work, there was always evasion. "Do *you* think you would?"

"I'm asking you."

Touché.

"Selma, does it really matter what I say?" And if dodging the truth didn't fly, I could try confusing her. "Look, there are some questions you don't know the answer to until you ask yourself what it is you're afraid of. You either will or you won't — either way, you're right. And

64

as my dad always told me, if life gives you lemons, make yourself a hot toddy. Unless you're in the mood for a margarita, in which case you need limes."

He'd never said any such thing, but it sounded like something he'd say.

Her face went from slightly irritated, to pensive, to satisfied. Her hot-pink nails grazed my shoulder as we made another turn and pulled into a parking spot. "Thanks, I knew you'd understand."

I didn't, but the point was she'd stopped asking me about it. For now.

At the moment, though, even an awkward conversation about Selma's parenting potential was a better option than what was before me: the Humboldt County Sheriff's Office. I gripped the armrest, steeling myself. I had to go in there. All I was doing was filing a report. They'd ask me a few questions, I wouldn't have much to say, they'd promise to send an officer out, and my duty would be done. Quick and easy.

So why was my bottom superglued to the seat?

A trickle of sweat dripped from my sternum to pool in my navel. My armpits were damp. Cotton filled my mouth.

"Sam? Honey?" Selma got out of the car and came around to my side, her heels clopping on the asphalt. She opened the door, then reached across me to jimmy me from the seat belt of death. "I'll stay with you, 'kay? We'll just tell 'em you need me to help you get around. You can even squeeze my hand under the table if you want."

And then she pulled me gently up to help me inside.

A month ago, if you had given me a lineup of friend-candidates to choose from, Selma Paradiso was not who I would have picked. She was loud and garish; I was introverted and understated. She was Jersey Shore and I was PBS. Leather miniskirts and stilettos versus comfy jeans and walking shoes with memory foam. But for all those differences, she was the most loyal and honest person I'd ever met. I only wished I could have been the same to her.

By the time we stood before the front doors, my foot was aching worse than it had when I'd woken up. I reminded myself to dunk it in ice when I got home and down a double dose of ibuprofen chased by a midmorning cocktail. Had to admit I was a bit miffed I hadn't gotten any painkillers out of my medical visit, but I could ask Ida to raid the liquor section at Garber's. Except that was another dark and scary road I wasn't sure I wanted to revisit.

As Selma reached for the door, I tugged at her arm.

"Selma?"

Her jaw worked back and forth. A small pink bubble ballooned between her shiny coral lips. She sucked it back in before it could burst all over her face and popped it with a gunshot-loud crack. "Yeah?"

"Just … thanks."

"Sure." She wrapped her fingers around the handle, then paused. "For what?"

"For everything. Driving me to the clinic. Dragging me here."

For a moment, she returned a blank stare. Like she was suffering the aftereffects of electric shock therapy. Then, without warning, she yanked me into her arms and hugged me.

"Awww, any day, honeypie. What else are besties for?" After a quick pat on the back, she released me, tugging her shirt back into place. "Don't take that wrong. I wasn't coming on to you."

"Don't worry. I didn't. And I'm not —"

"Hey there, Little Willie!" she exclaimed as she swung the door open.

The same flinty-eyed, broad-girthed deputy that had manned the security checkpoint when I'd brought Dad in for questioning about the arsons squatted on his stool next to the metal detector looking like Humpty Dumpty. I was tempted to nudge him off to see if he could upright himself.

Stifling a burp, he set his pop can on the counter and opened his arms. Selma dove into his cushiony embrace. After a round of cheek pecking and arm punching, they parted.

"How're those little rug rats of yours, Willie?"

"Bunch of delinquents, as always. Washed the cat in the toilet yesterday. We saved him before they stuck him in the dryer. By the way, any chance you could babysit tonight, so Keisha and I could have some alone time?"

So *this* was Keisha's husband, William? The one who'd replaced Oren Rickman, one of Bump's former owners, on the force.

"I'd love to, honey. But I have a big date tonight with you-know-who. Planning our trip, so I don't want him making any important decisions without me."

William crossed his arms and tucked his chin into his wattle. "When's he going to pop the question, Sel?"

She lowered her voice. "Could be sooner than you think. Tell Keisha not to worry. She'll be the first to know."

"Will do, cuz."

"Say, this here's my friend, Sam McNamee. We're just stopping in to report a patch of weed off of Hilltop Road. This'll only take a minute. Mind if we slip by? You know how claustrophobic that thing makes me." She waggled a hand at the metal detector. "Plus, it looks like that doohickey from *Stargate* — you know, the one that sucks people into other dimensions? I might have a panic attack if I have to walk through it."

He squinted accusingly at me, then jerked his thumb over his shoulder at a narrow space between the metal detector and the wall. "Go right ahead."

Selma grabbed my good hand to yank me past, but I dug my heels in, stalling.

"We can't just —"

"Sure, we —"

"I'm not —"

"You are. Now come on." Selma swung me behind her as she sidestepped the detector.

Eyes shut, breath held, I hung on. But at the last second, propelled by an overwhelming fear of what might happen if I was caught evading a security checkpoint at a law enforcement facility, I broke from her grasp and darted under the arch of the detector.

A frenzied *beep-beep-beeeeeep* pierced my ears.

"Step back on the other side, ma'am," Deputy Cheerful droned. "Empty your pockets, please."

I'd forgotten I had Tara's hoodie on. A pair of nail clippers, a mini screwdriver, and a dollar and eighty-six cents in change later, I was free to go. No wonder I'd felt like a kangaroo that had swallowed a tool belt.

The moment we were out of earshot, I said to Selma, "I thought Keisha said William worked for the police department?"

"He does. That's what the uniform's for."

"This is the sheriff's department."

"And?" She pulled a tube of lipstick from her purse and smeared it on.

"The police have jurisdiction in the town. The sheriff covers the whole county."

Her face froze in bewilderment. She blotted her lips on a tissue, then smacked them together a few times while she twirled the lipstick tube in her other hand. "Sam, honey, if that was true, why would they even need police in Wilton?"

As simple as it seemed to me, it was too complicated for Selma — and apparently for Keisha, too. I brought it down to her level. "I suppose they just couldn't agree on the uniforms."

She pointed her lipstick tube at me. "Now that makes complete sense. Khaki is so unflattering, though. For the life of me, I don't know why William would choose to wear it. Makes you look all washed out. Black and white is so much sharper, don't you think?"

I nodded. "Sure."

Filling out the report took all of ten minutes. It would have gone faster if they'd been able to locate the proper forms. The female deputy that took my statement moved about as fast as a lizard sunning itself. Apparently, crops of illegal drugs were nothing new around here. Once the paperwork was signed and filed away, I retrieved Selma from the waiting area and headed toward the front door.

"Ms. McNamee?"

Dang, I'd been *that* close to freedom. Wearing my biggest smile, I turned around and tamped down the awful memories of the last time I'd seen him, when I'd had IV tubes snaking out of me. "Sheriff Driscoll, hello."

I admired the guy immensely, even liked him, but couldn't say I wanted to visit with him on a regular basis.

He strode down the corridor, backlit by a bank of fluorescent lights. Black shoes shining, pants pleated, his badge glinting with the glow of peace and justice for all. He gripped my palm in a firm, no-nonsense handshake.

"I saw you from behind," he said. "Quite a limp you have there. Still feeling it, huh?"

Like it was five minutes ago. "The limp is new. I thought it might even me out. As for the rest of me" — I lifted my braced wrist up — "getting better, gradually. Thanks for asking."

His gaze drifted to Selma. "Good seeing you here again."

Of course they would know each other.

"And I'm not even here to bail out a relative today." Selma winked as she tugged flirtatiously on Sheriff Driscoll's collar. "Nope, this time I brought my buddy Sam here to clean up the streets."

"Oh. How's that?"

I cringed, fearing this was going to turn into a thirty-minute conversation.

Selma pressed a hand to the side of her mouth secretively. "Her boyfriend found a patch of weed in the field next door to her."

I shook my head. "He's not my —"

"We'll just call him that for now, honey, 'kay? Sheriff Driscoll doesn't need to know the details about your sex life."

"Whoa, whoa, whoa. Clint Chastain just came by to walk my dog for me," I explained. "Bump sniffed the marijuana out and dragged him to it."

Driscoll's dark brows folded. "Marijuana, you say?" He tusked and shook his head. "Loads of that lately. Taking over the county, unfortunately. The farmers generally have no idea it's there until they go out to harvest and find big swaths of their fields already cut down. Costs them tens of thousands in lost revenue, sometimes."

"I had no idea it was such a huge problem," I said. "Any chance you'll be able to trace who put it there?"

"Very little. Unless they were dumb enough to drop a wallet with ID at the planting site. No, chances are we'll never find out who did it. Best bet is to just cut it all down, dispose of it, and hope they move on over to the next county for next year's crop."

Not the ideal outcome, but I was sure Ida would be happy if they at least didn't make it a habit of growing their drugs right next door. "Thanks, anyway, sheriff. When do you think someone will be by to get rid of it?"

"Later in the week, probably. Need to call in some extra hands. Meanwhile, we'll send a cruiser down your road as often as we can and someone to talk to Dr. Chastain. If you see anything suspicious, you've still got my number, right, Ms. McNamee?"

I checked my phone to confirm that I did and was halfway turned toward the front door with a farewell on my lips when Sheriff Driscoll spoke again.

"Hey, while you're here ... Funny that you came by. We were just questioning Jake Taylor again and ... I hate to bring this up, being so

70

soon after the incident and all, but he wants to talk to you. The jail is to the rear of the building. I promise it won't take more than twenty minutes. Do you have time?"

I had time, yes. The willingness to sit across a table from Jake Taylor and look him in the eye? That would be a big fat no.

I clamped my lips shut, just in case I erupted in an episode of projectile vomiting. It had been over a month, but my emotions were strong and I hadn't yet sorted them all out. I was angry and afraid and confused all at once. So far, not dealing with it had seemed like the best option.

But not dealing with a problem doesn't make it go away. Sometimes, it only makes it worse. And I *knew* that. Still …

As I struggled with a response that didn't contain expletives or running away screaming like Little Miss Moffitt being attacked by a tarantula, Sheriff Driscoll drew me aside. His voice had a persuasive, soothing effect.

"I normally wouldn't ask this of someone who's been through what you have, especially so recently, but as it turns out, the guy actually has a conscience. Now that the drugs are out of his system, he's gained some clarity. He's said he wants to apologize for what he did. Not just in a written statement, but directly. There's also a chance that he can ferret out some of the pot farmers for us. So far he won't name any of his providers, or even his fellow users. If you could talk to him, tell him there's a chance for leniency if he comes clean, well, it might help us stop some of these drugs from ever hitting the street. Some people think we should only worry about the hard drugs: crack, cocaine, methamphetamines, heroin. But it starts with the more harmless drugs like marijuana and alcohol. I've seen it time and time again. One year I'm arresting a kid for pot or underage drinking. A few years later, I'm hauling them in for doing lines in the bathroom on their work break. Last year we did four major busts at Wilton Memorial. Eight more combined in the other county schools. Four of those twelve were for the hard stuff. Three were for prescription meds they pilfered from their grandma's medicine cabinet. The problem is that the problem is growing faster than we can deal with it."

I hesitated to answer him at all. Private, selfish Sam wanted to get the hell out of there and never come back. Idealistic, can't-say-no-to-an-officer Sam waffled —

"You have a daughter, don't you, Ms. McNamee?"

— and caved.

Maybe I could make something good come out of something bad. Confront my fears, heal my inner being. Save one kid, save a generation.

Okay, maybe not, but it was worth a shot. Complacency was not my thing. Besides, I was easily guilted.

"All right, all right. I'll talk to him. But only ten minutes. Set a timer and yank me out of there when the buzzer goes off. And if I want to bail at any moment, it's my prerogative, agreed?"

"Absolutely." He dipped his head and swept a hand toward the back of the corridor. "This way."

"Wait in the lobby for me, Selma," I told her. "I'll be back in fifteen or less."

"Take your time. I'll go catch up with Will some more." She pivoted around and clacked away.

With Sheriff Driscoll's hand on the small of my back for support, I went to meet the man who'd nearly killed me.

HIS ANKLES SHACKLED, HIS wrists handcuffed, Jake Taylor looked as helpless as a half-drowned kitten. He was sitting on the far side of a wide table, a pendant lamp shedding a glaring cone of light over him. His pale hair was slicked back, the comb lines still evident in his damp, stick-straight hair. Without his ball cap, he couldn't hide his eyes beneath the shadow of the bill — and that made him look that much shiftier to me.

His eyes flicked upward as the door behind the sheriff and me thudded shut, then back down at his handcuffs. He slid his hands from the table and into his lap, his gaze fixed there, his head bent forward so that his shoulders were stooped.

For a few moments, I pitied him. Barely into his twenties, he'd been ditched by his fiancée, resorted to self-medication, ended his career, and landed himself in jail. A life wasted when it had only just begun. But then my sympathy faded, replaced by contempt.

Shit happens, and most of us wallowed in our murky little sea of self-pity until the realization sank in that it wasn't going to get us anywhere. After Kyle had swerved to avoid a deer and plowed his car into a tree, I'd walked around in a daze for years, barely functioning. And while I may have suffered inwardly, at least I'd avoided inflicting my pain on others.

Life isn't about what happens to you; it's about dealing with the failures and disappointments and kicking your sorry self in the ass to become a functioning, decent human being. One proverbial day at a time.

Jake Taylor hadn't been tough enough to take the hurt of a failed relationship when Miley Harper had chosen another guy over him. He'd fallen into a hole of despair and then proceeded to dig himself deeper: drugs, thieving to pay for the drugs, and murder and attempted murder to cover his tracks.

Why would anyone do that? I just couldn't get my head around it.

Sheriff Driscoll pulled out a chair for me. Then, he punched a button on a video recording device rigged on a shelf in the corner and took his seat beside me. Separated from Jake by the solidity of that big table, I felt a sense of safety. Emboldened. Righteous.

Placing my braced wrist squarely before me, I pinched the edge of the table with the fingers of my right hand. "How could you even —?"

Sheriff Driscoll halted me with a gentle hand over mine. "In a minute, Ms. McNamee. It's taken Jake a few days to get up the courage to speak to you. He'd like —"

"Courage?" I shirked his hand off. A tremor rose in my voice and soon my hands were shaking. "I've never known a bigger coward. I'm the courageous one. This asshat here" — I jabbed a finger at Jake, not yet meeting his eyes — "nearly killed my father when he burned down the house I grew up in. But it was *me* he was after. Me he wanted to kill, so he could save himself. When he figured out I wasn't in the house, he came after me again." I paused for breath, but I was far from done. It was only the first rumbling before the volcano blew. "Instead of just killing me on the spot, he made a game of it. Tied me up and beat the bloody hell out of me. Then, he left me there half-alive in a tinderbox doused with gasoline while he drowned himself in alcohol."

I turned a hateful gaze on Jake. "I'm not sure what would have happened to me if Archer Malone hadn't come along."

I expected him to still be looking down, but he wasn't. He looked straight back at me. Defiant. Slighted. Something in him steelier and markedly less contrite than when I'd walked in.

"You don't know how it was for me," he muttered.

"Try me."

"All right," Sheriff Driscoll interrupted, angling his body forward at a diagonal, as if he could symbolically push us apart, "you've had your say, Ms. McNamee. I brought you here for good reason, and I insist you keep silent for now so Mr. Taylor here can say his piece."

Teeth clenched, I leaned back. Jake Taylor could say whatever he damn well wanted. I wasn't feeling particularly receptive to any groveling he might have to offer up. But it might be a tad bit amusing to see what he came up with. So I kept my mouth shut.

He said nothing. Didn't move. Didn't look away. Just stared and stared at me, the muscles in his jaw twitching, a tiny vein on his temple pulsing erratically.

"Go ahead," the sheriff prodded.

His voice a controlled monotone, Jake replied, "Can't. I forget."

"Say it. Just like you told me earlier."

Slumping to one side, Jake planted an elbow on the armrest. He tilted his head back, as if to look down his nose at me. "I'm sorry ... for what I did, Ms. McNamee. I wasn't in my right mind. I had ... *have* a substance abuse problem. It was the drugs and the drink making me do crazy shit." He looked away briefly, then at Sheriff Driscoll. "Good enough?"

"Hardly. Keep talking."

Rolling his eyes ever so slightly, Jake's shoulders lifted in a shrug. I knew the body language. It was a gesture Tara had perfected well before her teenage years. One that said 'I'm saying this because it's what you expect to hear'.

Jake picked at a thread on his jailhouse orange jumpsuit, his mouth making small movements while his brain fought to put the words in order. "I know what I did was wrong, but I didn't know it then. All I wanted was my next hit, my next swallow."

I couldn't help myself then. This was all so rehearsed. And if Sheriff Driscoll was buying any of it, he was a whole lot dumber than I ever imagined. "Let me get this straight: weeks after trying to kill two people, and failing, you suddenly see the error in your ways?"

"I told you she wouldn't get it," Jake said sharply to Sheriff Driscoll.

"Just tell her the rest."

"Fine — although I don't see what good it's going to do." He expelled a breath, his eyes darting around the room nervously as he rocked in his chair. "I can't undo what I did, but maybe I can keep somebody else out of trouble."

A long pause opened up. I waited for him to go on, but it was like he was done talking, like I was supposed to understand that what he'd just said meant something more.

"I don't follow," I said. "How?"

He shrugged again. "When I get myself all straightened out, I want to talk to kids about stuff — drugs and drinking. Tell 'em not to do it."

"There are a lot of people who do that already. What's different about you, huh? Are you going to share names? *That* might make a difference."

His lips tightened. Air whistled through his nostrils as he inhaled. He shook his head.

"It's not that easy. You think it's just about me, about getting even." A wry smile warped his thin lips. "You don't know the half of it."

"Jake …" Sheriff Driscoll's chair creaked as he shifted farther forward. "You can't protect anyone on the outside from in here. But you can shake things up and put the right people behind bars so they don't ever harm anyone again."

An understanding flickered in his pupils. Jake Taylor was no Rhodes Scholar, but he was bright enough to know when something made sense.

Jake laced his fingers together. "I'll think about it."

"You do that." Sheriff Driscoll stood and slid his chair back up to the table, before pulling mine back. We headed toward the door. "Let us know when you're willing to talk more. I'm sure the judge will take it into account when your court date rolls around."

As he opened the door, a deputy I hadn't seen before stepped inside the room, then went to stand behind Jake, who took one glance at him and stiffened. The deputy was as clean-cut as they come: shaved head, milky-white complexion, mid thirties.

"Take him back to his cell, Deputy Halloway," the sheriff directed.

Halloway smiled coolly, then hooked Jake beneath the armpit

and hauled him to his feet.

I hurried away as fast as I could, given my most recent handicap. I may not have gotten Jake Taylor to rat on his cronies, but I'd stood up to him — and that made me feel more sure of myself than I'd felt in a *long* time.

chapter 7

BY THE TIME WE pulled up to Ida's house, Selma's Camaro was belching stacks of black smoke. I'd almost lost my breakfast twice on the ride home — once when she'd stopped in the middle of an intersection because she swore the stop sign hadn't been there a week ago, and a second time when she'd passed a farm tractor on a hill and put us in the path of an oncoming garbage truck. She'd swerved back into our lane with six inches to spare.

By now, I was an expert at unsnarling the seat belt. She put the car in park and a loud bang clapped from the tailpipe. I ducked, before realizing it wasn't a gunshot.

I jumped out, thankful to have made it home alive, and bent to speak into the half-open car window. "You should have that looked at."

A scowl twisted Selma's peachy-pink lips. "No way am I giving my baby back to that snake Dan."

"Is there another mechanic you could take it to?"

"In this town?"

"Good point. Maybe in Fullbright?" Although I wasn't sure her washed-up muscle car could make it that far a second time. "I'm just worried about you getting stranded on the road somewhere."

"Honey, that's what phones are for. If it dies on me, I'll just call Dylan and have him pick me up."

Inwardly, I screamed.

"Are you still going to Mexico with him?"

Her face lit up like a solar flare. "Yeah, I can't wait! He booked us a room in Can-can."

That would be Cancun for the verbally challenged.

I put my lame foot down and grimaced.

"Do you need any help?" she asked.

"Thanks, but I'll be fine." I waved goodbye to prod her along. As much as I loved Selma for reasons even I couldn't explain, I'd reached my dosage limit before noon that day.

Selma shifted her car into reverse, the gears clunking. A bang exploded from the tailpipe. She disappeared down the driveway, her car burping little clouds of smoke as she went.

I expected everyone to be home by now, but Ida's car was gone and the front door was closed. Fishing the spare key out of my purse, I hobbled up the porch steps. I fitted the key into the slot and turned it. It took me several tries, because I had to hold the key and twist the knob at the same time, one-handed, but eventually the tumbler clicked. Just as I went to open the door, something stopped me.

From inside the house came the sound of glass shattering. I froze, still gripping the knob. More glass shattering. A bump, and then a thud as something solid hit the floor.

Someone was ransacking the place.

Dropping my purse beside the door as I hunkered down, I took my phone from my pocket and pressed 9-1-1. Then, I crept to the picture window.

Waiting, waiting. I glanced at my phone. It wasn't connecting.

Another crash sounded, followed by several thumps. Carefully, I looked in. But only for a moment. I didn't see anyone, but I did see the havoc they'd wreaked.

What if they were right next to the front door with a loaded gun, ready to blow my head off? And why had I let Selma drive away? If I ran from the porch, I'd be even more obvious than if I just stayed where I was.

I scanned for something on the porch to use as a weapon. In a basket by the swing was an old garden spade. Too far. Besides the furniture and half a dozen throw pillows, there was nothing else. Curse Ida for being so tidy.

Inside, footsteps on the stairs. A mangled scream.

Oh, no. Please, no. Was that Tara?

I redialed. An anemic ring sounded on the other end of the line. *Pick up, pick up, pick up.*

Then, footsteps upstairs. Like someone trying to run away.

If Tara was in trouble, I'd never forgive myself.

Another ring. Faint. A pause. Had I lost the connection altogether? I held the phone out. Two bars. That should have been enough.

Gathering my courage, I peered inside the window. Ida's knickknacks were scattered over the floor, the shelves half-empty. Cushions and knitted afghans had been tossed about, like someone had been looking for something. Even the wingback chair that Clint had been sitting in last night was toppled.

Then I heard a voice so faint I struggled to determine where it was coming from.

"Hello?... Is anyone there?"

I held my breath. The voice was too old to be Tara, but it wasn't Ida, either.

"Is this a prank call?"

I looked down at my palm. Oh, yeah. I'd called 9-1-1.

Slapping the phone to my ear, I crouched down again and spewed out everything as fast as I could. "I need to report a break-in. And assault. I think someone's holding my daughter captive inside my friend's house. Please hurry. Oh God, hurry. I'm afraid she's hurt. I'm at 6534 Hilltop Road."

The dispatcher proceeded to ask more details, like my name and if I'd seen the perpetrators and whether or not they had a weapon, but any coherency I had possessed when I'd first spoken was rapidly diminishing, replaced by a dithering panic. All I could think of was Tara alone in the house, without any way to defend herself, and me cowering outside waiting for someone else to come to the rescue. Someone who was possibly miles and miles away.

Screw that.

"Just hurry up and get here," I told the dispatcher before ending the call and grabbing the spade.

If Tara's life was in danger, I wasn't going to worry about mine. I rushed for the door and shoved it wide. It swung back, the inside knob slamming against the wall to puncture the drywall. So much for stealth.

The house was deathly silent. They'd heard me.

I gripped the spade handle tight. It was too short to swing, to light to throw. But it did have a blunted point. I turned the handle backward, holding it back by my shoulder like a vampire stake, ready to plunge it into an eye socket.

I sank behind the couch, peering around it to scope out a better weapon. There, beside the unused fireplace, sat a pristine iron poker. I crawled toward it.

Halfway across the room, I heard them coming. I say 'them' because it had to be more than one.

I couldn't get there fast enough. Feet raced toward me. I dove on my belly, grabbing for the poker. But I was all force and no finesse. It flew from my grasp to clatter across the floor and slide into the hallway.

One-handed, I pushed myself up, ready to fight the invaders with my bare fists if I had to. But I was no sooner on my knees than a set of paws flattened me from behind.

Tucking my right arm beneath me, my jaw hit the floor with a soft whack. A long tongue flicked out to tickle my ear, slinging strings of dog slobber over my neck and cheek.

"Get. Off!" I rolled over, pushing Bump back with a knee.

He stood over me, his breath coming in steamy pants, his mouth pressed into a smile of delirium. I repeated the command. Finally, it registered. He stepped aside and folded into a sphinx position.

Then his ears perked. He coiled up like a spring, nails curled for traction.

My gaze drifted to follow his line of sight. In the doorway to the kitchen, Tiger Lily stood puffed up like she'd just stuck her paw in a light socket. Her ears were flattened against her head. Glowing yellow eyes bulged. She let out a garbled yowl. Her tail flicked in warning.

Bump inched forward on his belly, promises of feline dinner reflected in his pupils. The cat turned a shoulder, angling for an escape route. The moment she lifted a paw, Bump sprang at her, his intentions clear.

I hooked my hand in his collar barely in time, jerking him backward. His claws scrabbled on the wood floor. He strained against my hold as Tiger Lily scampered away.

So this was it. The staring contest had morphed into a game of cat-and-mouse, metaphorically speaking. There was peace, as long as the cats didn't move. But once Tiger Lily had decided to come down from her lofty perch, Bump's prey drive had launched into orbit.

And this … was the result.

Too angry to deal with him, I led Bump into the backyard and clipped him to the tie-out.

When I came back into the living room, I looked around. Saw chaos. Destruction. Objects that Ida had chosen with love and purpose and an amazing sense of matchy-matchy scattered across the floor. Bowls of colored glass now jagged shards. Porcelain figurines cracked and chipped. Old tin toys twisted and mangled. Antiques, collectibles, one-of-a-kinds.

I didn't have enough money to cover all of this. And that was just one room.

Tears of frustration flooded my vision. I crumpled to the floor and sobbed. Wailed shamelessly like a five-year-old. Because I was alone and I could. And I didn't know what the hell else to do.

Nothing was simple. And nothing was turning out like I planned.

"Sam, are you all right?"

Ah, shit.

Sucking a glob of snot down my throat, I lifted my head, feeling all of two inches tall. Clint stood in the doorway, surveying the wreckage.

"Hi, Clint. Yeah, I'm good. Just spiffy. You're early."

"I was going out for an early run. You didn't answer my text, so I stopped by, expecting someone would be here." He picked his way through the mess and crouched beside me. "What happened?"

"You sure you don't want a dog?"

"Ah." He rubbed my back, his touch sending little eddies of calmness through me. "So you didn't leave him in the crate I loaned you when you left?"

"I thought I did, but evidently not." Not even forty and my memory was going. "Honestly, he'd been so good since he came here that we all stopped thinking about that. We trusted him. And I guess everyone was in a hurry this morning."

"How did all this happen?"

"Chasing the cats."

"Oh."

That one word said everything. We both realized the gravity of it at the exact same moment. The canine-feline truce had been shattered.

"Either the dog finds a new home," I thought out loud, "or we do."

The truth of it whopped me with an unexpected sadness. The three of us living here with Ida had been crowded and crazy. But it also felt right. Like in a matter of time, we would all settle into a familiar rhythm of cards and board games, TV shows and daily dinners. Mundane, undemanding, and yet … happy.

Because of a dog — the same dog that had brought us all closer — we would also be forced apart. This was Ida's house, and Ida's cats had lived here long before Bump ever entered the picture. It wasn't fair for them to exist in terror or to restrict Bump's freedom unreasonably. He needed a yard to roam in, an environment without constant stimulation of his prey drive, and regular exercise. Clint could help with that last one, but that meant me seeing him on a regular basis and him shaping his life around a dog that wasn't even his. I could offer Bump to Clint for real, but I wasn't sure how Dad or Tara would feel about that.

I stole a glance at Clint. Our eyes met. The depth of that look, even as fleeting as it was, scared me. Because it implied so much. Before today, I'd had doubts about a relationship with him. After this morning, it was doubly so. Yet at times like this I just wanted to bury my face in his neck and feel the electricity of his hands on my body, making me forget whatever it was that was troubling me. We both looked away at the same time. As if the same temptation had surfaced in both of us and we simultaneously recognized the danger of it.

And Clint said exactly what he should have said at that moment. Which was nothing.

He simply helped me to my feet, situated me on the couch, then went and fetched a broom and a wastebasket. I'd love him if I didn't feel like crushing his family jewels. Which begged a point.

"You'll never guess who I saw today," I said.

He scooped up bits of a china plate and dumped them in the trash can. "No idea. Who?"

A distant wail pierced the air, fell away, then rose again, coming closer.

Clint went to the front door. "Is that a siren?"

I slumped down, hoping the cushions might swallow me. "I ... may have called 9-1-1."

He closed his eyes, an exasperated sigh escaping through his pinched nostrils. "You stay there." He shot me a stern look. "I'll handle it."

And I was glad to let him. The screen door banged behind Clint. I heard him exchange greetings with the officer, whose voice was unfamiliar to me. Not wanting to make myself known — after all, who wants to explain that they called 9-1-1 because their dog was hunting down a feline snack? — I went to work cleaning up the mess. A few things were salvageable, like the throws and the cushions, but over the years Ida had collected a lot of fragile goods, and in one romp of pursuit, Bump had wiped out a sizeable portion of them. Just the thought of seeing Ida come in the front door and taking inventory of it all made me sick.

"Hey." Clint popped his head inside. "We're going to take a look at the field, okay?"

"Sure." I waved him off and righted the wingback chair.

Fifteen minutes later, I was still finding bits of glass and porcelain in unlikely places when I heard Clint's and the deputy's voices again. It sounded like they were done. Relieved, I dumped the contents of the dustpan into the wastebasket and then peeked around the door frame, hoping they wouldn't notice me.

Deputy Halloway shook Clint's hand, got in his cruiser, and shut the door. The car started. But before he threw it into reverse, he tossed a glance my way. His cutting gaze lasered a hole straight through me.

I ducked behind the door, my heart pattering wildly. That man gave me the willies. Yet he hadn't said or done a single thing to warrant that reaction except look at me.

I really needed to stop being so paranoid. First Virgil, now Halloway.

"Hey."

I jerked in surprise, bumping the elbow of my braced arm against the coat-rack.

Clint caught it before it toppled over. He gave me that smile, the one that said, 'You are such a dork. A cute dork.'

"I ... uh, I was just about to come outside to see what was up. Everything good?"

"Yeah, I explained the situation here to him. As for the weed patch, he said it was the biggest he'd ever seen. He also said they'll be by in a couple of days to clear it, but they'll stop in here first before they do that."

"Oh, okay. Thanks."

He glanced around the room. "Sam, I was thinking ..."

He looked down, like a little boy about to ask for a pony when he knew it was impossible, even though he wanted it more than anything.

Outside, Bump barked. Probably at a squirrel. But it was like he was punctuating Clint's pause.

"I know that you probably saw Danielle at the clinic. Am I right?"

"I did." Although I didn't reveal what she'd shared with me. This was his chance to come clean. A test, of sorts.

"I should have told you she'd taken a position close by. It's only temporary, but still ... I should have told you."

Half-truths didn't score points. He was failing.

"Did she say anything to you about ..." — he squirmed — "becoming a mother?"

I played dumb. "Like me having another kid? Wow, you're really skipping ahead. We're not even officially a couple. Besides, I'm not sure I'm ready to start over. Tara's barely —"

"Not you. Her. *She* wants to have a kid."

"With you," I blurted, unable to dull the bitterness in my tone.

What I hated more than Danielle being in town and dangling her ova in front of him was the way Clint made me dizzy with desire one moment, then confused and betrayed the next. And the more I thought about it all, today especially, the more it dawned on me that I didn't need this kind of drama on top of what life had already dealt me. If he wanted to sow his oats, he could plant them in Danielle's fertile field. In a test tube or the way nature intended. "Yes, she may have mentioned it."

"I was afraid of that," he said, almost regretfully.

"And you actually considered it?" Because, masochist that I am, I had to know.

Nodding, he rubbed at the back of his neck.

Damn it. Deep, deep down inside, I was hoping he'd say no. That he had laughed in her face. That he'd asked her to leave town. To get out of his life for good. Because he was in love with *me*.

Obviously, he wasn't.

I shut the door on him, pressed my back to it. Waited to hear his footsteps receding. But he stayed where he was. So close. Painfully close.

"Sam? I have to tell you everything," he said through the closed door. "I thought about it. I did." There was a long pause, a deep breath. Then, quietly, "I told her no."

A minute elapsed while I processed what he'd said. He didn't move. Just stood there. Patiently.

I opened the door a crack. "You said no?"

"Yeah," he breathed, "I did." Then, several breaths later, "I told her she should get in touch with her lawyer-friend over in Fort Wayne, that maybe he could give her what she needed, no strings attached."

Out back, Bump started barking a chorus.

"Didn't you come by to walk the dog?"

He cracked a smile, hopeful. "I'll do that."

I started to shut the door, but stopped. "If you come back this

87

evening to take him out again, maybe we could … go out to dinner afterward and … talk?"

"Sure. I'd like that."

Oh, I bet he more than liked it.

IDA'S NOTE WAS PLACED squarely on the refrigerator door, surrounded by magnets collected from her many vacations: the Grand Canyon, Chicago, Hollywood, the Everglades. Was there any place in the Continental U.S. that woman had not been to?

Dear Sam,

Done with sales early. The ladies had to get back for their hair appointments. We left Bump with a bone and I took Walt to play miniature golf. Should be back around 3 p.m., unless we're having too much fun. Please call if you need us back sooner.

Love, Ida

Too much fun, huh? Those two had gone from *NCIS* once-a-week fellow junkies, to inseparable BFFs. I had no idea what was up with that, but their little spontaneous outing would buy me time to finish tidying up, not to mention how I was going to broach the subject of us moving out to Dad. We'd been avoiding it, given recent events, but now it was more urgent. Last thing I wanted was for one of Ida's cats to end up as Bump's dinner.

Done cleaning, I sat down on the couch with my foot immersed in glacial water. After the first thirty seconds, it became more bearable. My pocket buzzed. It was a text from Tara:

Almost forgot. Went to Shannon's early. Hope that's OK. Text if you need me.

It would have been good to know that before I called 9-1-1 to report that she was on the verge of being murdered. I resisted firing back a snarky reply and just told her thanks for letting me know and that someone would pick her up in the morning.

I was only vaguely aware of Bump yipping with glee as Clint took him off his line and out to his car. An hour later, I was in the guestroom that I shared with Tara, fully immersed in my work, as Clint returned Bump. Courtesy would have demanded that I go outside and thank him for exercising my dog, but I resisted. Tonight, after we'd both mulled things over, we could start fresh.

Long after I heard Clint's car head down the lane, I took Bump a fresh bowl of water. Lying down with his paws on either side of the bowl, he lapped until the bowl was empty, then flopped over on his side, a stupid grin bunching his cheeks all the way back to his ears.

I stroked his wolf-colored fur, releasing tufts of undercoat. From inside the house, I retrieved the slicker brush. After the fire, Clint had loaned me a mountain of dog supplies from when he'd had his Border Collie, Jazz. Getting a dog was like having a baby — you didn't realize all the paraphernalia that went along with them. When I came back out, Bump was still in the same position, his panting slowed to a steady rhythm, his eyes now barely open. I brushed and brushed and brushed him, collecting a mound of fur on the ground behind me that could have passed for a grungy Maltese.

"Life would be a whole lot less complicated without you," I said, as I pulled the slicker gently over his tail. "It would also be more boring."

Stretching, he let out a yodeling yawn.

"I love you." I plucked an insect from his mane. "Ticks and all."

His tail thumped ever so slightly.

89

When I went back inside and checked my messages, there was one from Archer.

Hey, Sam. Just checking up to see what the doctor said. Let me know. Hope you're feeling better today. If you need me for anything, call. Even if it's just to talk.

A twinge of guilt plucked at my conscience. I contemplated calling him back, but didn't know what I'd say. That Clint and I were patching things up now, after I'd told him just last night we'd gone our separate ways? If I did that, I'd sound like a schizophrenic nymphomaniac. I couldn't tell Archer that Clint's ex was still in town, petitioning for his sperm, either. Way too weird.

So I tapped out a chatty text, deleted it, wrote another, deleted that one, stared off into space for a while, and started over. In the end, I managed eight words: *Doing better. Thanks for your help last night.*

I wanted to call him, but somehow that felt like I'd be cheating on Clint emotionally, even though Archer was just a friend.

Maybe if I just kept telling myself that ...

I pressed the power button on my laptop and opened a file, shutting out the world and my upside-down life.

By the time Dad and Ida returned, I'd written two new chapters. Closer and closer to a finished novel. Somehow, the more chaos life threw at me, the deeper I retreated into my imaginary world. Good thing, considering I was already a month past my deadline. I closed my laptop and limped downstairs.

The front door barely open, Ida stared wide-eyed at her barren shelves. "Oh ..." Her eyes shifted to the empty mantel, then to the missing lamp that used to sit on the end table. "Ohhh my."

Dad wedged past her to put his jacket on the coat-rack. "Something the matter?"

"My things. Where are all my things?"

He looked the place over. "Looks like Sam's been cleaning." He gave me a thumbs-up. "Nice work, Sam. I like it this way."

Taking the note from my back pocket, I waved it before me. "Someone left the dog out and, well, he and the cats redecorated."

Ida and Dad looked at each other. Her eyes narrowed ever so slightly.

With a shrug, he sank into the recliner. "You said since he was asleep to just leave him there."

"No," Ida replied, "I said it would be safer to leave him in the crate."

"But you didn't *tell* me to put him away. Besides, putting him in that wire crate seems like sentencing him to prison. It's a cage, for crying out loud. How would you like to be locked up in a cage?"

He grabbed the remote and aimed it at the TV, a clear signal that the conversation was finished. When he found the noon news, he cranked the volume up.

"I'm going upstairs to wash up." Lips pursed, Ida marched from the room.

I sat on the couch across from my father. "Dad, this isn't going to work."

Without looking away from the TV, he said, "What's not going to work, Sam?"

"Us living here with Bump. He's fine in the house, except ..." I lifted my hands wide. "Those poor cats have been living in terror since we moved in with Bump. It's not fair to them for him to be here."

His face tightened. "You're not giving that dog away."

"I wasn't suggesting that. For now, Bump will have to go from his crate, to the line outside. We can't leave him loose in here."

"That's cruel, Sam."

"I know. Which is why we need to look into moving somewhere else. Maybe we could find a place with a fenced-in backyard? A nice neighborhood we could walk him in. Close to the dog park, maybe."

He hit the mute button and turned his gaze on me. "No."

"But Dad —"

"I said no. End of story."

"This won't work."

"For you, maybe not. You and Tara go ahead and move out, if it's what you want. Take Bump, too. Just don't go far. I want to be able to see my granddaughter — and the dog — regularly."

Baffled, I blinked at him. "Then where are you going to live?"

"Here."

"With Ida?"

"Sure."

"So you'd be ... living together?" I turned it over in my head a dozen times. Looked at it from every perspective conceivable. He adored Tara and Bump. Sometimes I think he even liked having me around. And I knew that he and Ida had been friends for years, but why would he want to live here, in her house, apart from us, unless ...?

Noooo. No. Freaking. Way.

Pointing to the stairs, I lowered my voice. "Tell me this isn't what I'm thinking."

He arched an eyebrow at me, a grin slowly spreading over his wrinkled lips. "What's that term your generation uses?" He wiggled his fingers on the armrests. "Friends with ... oh, something or other."

"Benefits," I whispered. "Friends with benefits." I fell against the back cushion of the couch like he'd just smacked me with a two-by-four.

"Something wrong with that?"

"No." I tried to erase images from my mind as fast as they were popping into it. Being a teenager and accidentally walking in on your married parents making love wasn't half as shocking as learning that your seventy-plus-year-old father and his longtime neighbor were doing the nasty in the room next door. "I just can't quite get my head around it, is all. Has she agreed to the, uh … the arrangement?"

"Agreed? It was her idea in the first place."

Upstairs, the pipes clanked as Ida ran water in the bathroom sink. Dad glanced at the ceiling, then met my eyes.

"Sam, you don't know how long it's been. For both of us."

Longer than it had been for me before Clint and I had hooked up, I was sure.

"You might want to think about getting some yourself," he added. "I saw you and Archer Malone cozied up on the porch swing. And what about that animal doctor? Not like you don't have prospects."

I got up from the couch. "Thanks, I'll keep that in mind."

"You don't, uh … you don't suppose you could make yourself scarce for a few hours this evening, could you? Tara's at her friend's and I figured —"

I held up a hand to stop him. "Got it. I'll make plans. Maybe Selma and I can catch a flick at the Fullbright Cinema Ten."

Selma had her own plans, and so did I, but he didn't have to know that.

I was halfway to the stairs, headed to the safe haven of my room, when he said, "And, Sam?"

Bracing myself, I turned around. "Yes?"

"We're happy this way. At our age, you never know how many chances you'll get. Hell, at any age. Don't waste a moment. If someone makes you happy, grab 'em and don't let go."

Good advice. Too bad it was never that simple.

chapter 8

AFTER CLINT TOOK BUMP for a walk and went home to shower, I met him at Wild Bill's Western Eatery, the same place we'd had our first date. Like any Saturday night in a small town with one good restaurant, the place was packed as tight as a piece of carry-on luggage for a weeklong ski trip.

The hostess wedged her way between a clump of hungry customers. "How many?"

"Two. Chastain." Clint edged up to her shoulder to peer at her clipboard. "How long's the wait?"

"Hmmm, let me see." She traced a finger down the long list of names. The aroma of steak searing on a hot grill wafted through the air. I sucked it in, dreaming of a side of baked potato loaded with sour cream and a sprinkling of chives.

Behind her, one of the waitresses called out, "Blankenship, party of eight. Blankenship, party of eight."

The hostess scratched one name off as the group squeezed through the double doors and filed into the dining area behind her. A moment later, a waiter barked, "Frantz, party of one. Frantz, party of one."

An elderly gentleman wearing a three-piece business suit shuffled after the waiter.

I whispered to Clint, "Is it even possible to be a 'party of one'?" He snickered.

The hostess drew a line through the name, then tucked the pen behind her ear. "That helps. I'd say ninety minutes."

My stomach grumbled. "Ninety minutes?"

The fact that we had to follow someone to their car for a parking spot and all the people sitting outside on benches waiting should have been our clue. But we were both starving, and this was the best place in town.

Clint frowned sympathetically at me. "Will you be all right, or do you want to try someplace else? Ginny's Whistle Stop has a good dinner buffet."

"Trust me, you don't want to go there. They were serving up a healthy dose of food poisoning earlier today." My stomach growled again. "Guess we'll have to wait."

Shifting onto my right leg, I scoped out a place to sit. With a bum foot, standing for more than five minutes wasn't an option, though. On the end of the corner bench by the hostess's podium, there was a space about half a butt-cheek wide. Next to it sat a middle-aged couple taking up four spots. If I asked them nicely to scoot over, I could perch on the edge.

"If it's okay," I said to Clint, "I'm going to have a seat."

I'd no sooner turned around to claim the spot, than a bosom the size of a pair of watermelons blocked me.

"Looks like everyone had the same idea tonight." Dawna Hawkins pushed her ruby red lips up into a fake smile that said, 'I will cut you, bitch.'

"Hi, Miss Dawna," I squeaked out, like I was a five-year-old addressing the elementary school principal. She was the female version of her ex, Dylan Hawkins. That chick could beat up a gang of motorcycle guys, even with her fake nails, big Texas hair, and a miniskirt two sizes too small.

She looked me up and down, her mouth tilting with an amused smirk. "Town's getting a little too crowded. All kinds of people showing up where they don't belong."

What did that mean? And why did I get the impression that she didn't *like* me? What had I ever done to her? Except befriend Selma, which was probably enough.

"Actually, we were just leaving."

I swung back around and grabbed Clint's hand.

"So you changed your mind?"

We were all the way out to the car before I answered him. "No, Dawna Hawkins did."

"Who?"

"Never mind. It's not important." For a guy who served the medical needs of every pet in this half of the county, there were a lot of people he still didn't know. "Where else is there to eat?"

"There's Stefano's Pizzeria. Nothing fancy, but —"

"Sounds heavenly." I buckled myself in and gestured for him to take off. After all, how long could it take to make pizza?

The answer, I discovered, was somewhere in excess of forty minutes. During which we waited in Clint's SUV. Because there were no tables inside. A fact which he'd failed to mention.

Stefano's was situated in the lower level of an older house on the last street on the south side of Wilton, which explained why I wasn't familiar with it, because I hardly ever went that way. South was farm country. Miles and miles of it. Lovely to look at, but not a place you wanted to get lost in. One cornfield looked exactly like the next one.

Clint had gone inside, again, to see if our pizza was done yet. I could see him through the plate glass window, one elbow propped on the counter to hold himself up, the fingers of his other hand drumming impatiently. With my foot propped up on the dashboard and my seat reclined, I fought sleep. So I dialed the radio to a techno dance station and cranked the volume until I wondered if I was breaking any sort of noise ordinance. Finally, he came out, bearing two cans of pop and no pizza. I hit the 'off' button on the radio.

Clint slid into his seat and pulled open the tabs on both Cokes. "Five more minutes. Turns out there were several slumber parties going on tonight and they had a rush just before we put in our order."

Only in Wilton.

"So exactly where are we eating this pizza? When we get it, that is. Because it's getting a little chilly outside, not to mention dark, in case you were thinking of an impromptu picnic. And as much as I love your car" — I flipped the lever on my seat to sit upright — "it's not exactly made for romantic dining."

He fought a smile as he sipped. In the half-light of dusk, I could see the faintest glint in his dark eyes. "Is this a romantic date, then?"

"Not so far." I set my can in the cup holder between us, not wanting to load up on carbonation and end up needing to burp if we happened to lock lips. So far, we'd been maintaining our distance, but I was quickly setting aside my self-control in favor of a little self-indulgent behavior. I'd let too much of life go by already. What Kyle and I shared had been more than being life partners — we'd reveled in each other's bodies. Why not experience at least that part again with someone else?

"Do you have someplace in mind?" Right now, I could have gone for the backseat of the SUV. "To eat, I mean."

"You're expecting me to say my house?" He winked.

A little thrill of excitement trembled in my bones. The last time we'd gone to his house, we'd ended up naked and sweaty. I kept telling myself we were going to take it slow, but chances were that was going to require more willpower than either of us possessed. Even him sitting there looking at me, that little boy grin on his face, melted my insides.

"Well," I began, "I was ordered to stay out of mine for an

unspecified length of time. Turns out Walt and Ida have something going on."

"Like what — a Trivial Pursuit tournament? Pinochle? Poker?"

"Strip poker, maybe."

He choked on his drink, then wiped his mouth, laughing. "Seriously? Good for them. I just hope when I'm their age that I'm getting —"

I slapped his knee.

"Sorry, sorry. I suppose it is your father we're talking about. Anyway, not my house, no."

A little bubble of disappointment popped inside me. If he'd taken me to his house, that would have been presumptuous on his part, but I wouldn't have said no. "Indoors, I hope."

"Ah, but a canoe on the lake in the moonlight sounds romantic, don't you think?"

I was weighing whether or not I believed him when Stefano waved through the big window.

"Be right back with our dinner."

A minute later we were on the road, heading further south on Route 379, the pizza box warming my lap. The street lamps faded away in the rearview mirror.

"Can you drive faster?" I said, inhaling a lungful of pizza sauce and oregano. "Or else I might die of hunger before we get wherever it is we're going. Where are we going, anyway?"

I couldn't see his smile, but I could hear it in his voice. "You'll see."

SHUTTERED WINDOWS WINKED FROM the upper story of a midcentury Craftsman bungalow. Crisp white trim outlined the frame of the sage-green house, complete with a picket fence and flower beds full of newly blooming mums. It was straight out of a Norman Rockwell painting.

"Whose place is this?" I asked.

A white sedan tore down the street like someone was headed to a fire. Its muffler rumbled noisily. Clint waited until it passed us, then hopped out and came around to my side to help me out as he balanced the pizza box on his other arm. "Melissa's."

The car that had just passed backfired as it pulled away from the intersection, its tailpipe clattering like it was about to fall off.

"This is your receptionist's house?" Porch lights glowed from the other houses lining the street. It was an older neighborhood, but a quiet one, less than a mile out of town. I clung to his arm for support as we made our way up the concrete sidewalk. The grass had been recently mowed and the hedges neatly trimmed. Having seen Clint's place and how tidy it was, I guessed he'd been taking care of this house, too. "She went to look after her sister and her new baby, right? When's she coming back?"

At the front door, he dug in his pocket. "She's not. She moved in with her sister in Nashville. A couple of days ago, she came back and packed up all her personal items." Turning to me, he pressed a key into my palm. "If you need a place to stay, it's yours."

Gazing down at the key, I ran my fingertip over the ridges on its edge. A blue ribbon was looped through a hole in the top. "I can't. It's too much."

The tip of his thumb grazed my cheek as he slid his hand to my neck and then down to my shoulder. "Sam, it's an empty house. You and Tara need a place to stay. A place all your own. Where Bump can't get himself into trouble."

I looked away. Down the street lined with sidewalks and mature shade trees. Where flower beds bordered groomed lawns and picket fences enclosed small backyards. Older houses, but much loved ones. A place where kids grew up safe and neighbors knew each other by name.

This was exactly what we needed, and yet ... "But my furniture is in Chicago and I couldn't move it right now anyway, even if this could work out. Plus, I'm not even sure I could afford the rent and insurance and then there's —"

"Open the door, Sam. Take a look inside."

I did. The door swung open without the slightest creak. Clint flicked on the overhead light in the foyer. The house was full of furniture true to its earlier days, from the L-shaped sofa and Scandinavian-style chairs, to the metal-and-vinyl dinette set in the breakfast nook, to the 1950s movie posters on the wall. Not entirely my style, but it was clean and more than enough space.

There was even a big-screen TV affixed to the wall, complete with a sound system. Suddenly, I had visions of Tara and me in our sweats and oversized jerseys, curled up on that coffee-colored couch, hugging bowls of popcorn while we alternately laughed and cried over sappy chick flicks.

Tara would *love* this place.

"I talked to Melissa this afternoon after I walked Bump." Clint placed his car keys on the coffee table as he opened the pizza box, then headed into the kitchen for paper towels. "She decided to go back to school to become a paralegal and doesn't want to make any decisions about the house until after that, so it's available for the next couple of years. Maybe longer. She got it in a divorce settlement and she'd like to hang onto it, but she doesn't need a lot for rent. She just wants someone who can take care of the house for her — keep the weeds down, mow, that sort of thing. If the place needs any repairs, she'll cover it. I'll get you a firm figure next time I talk to her, but it won't be much. Way less than what you'd pay per month for one of those cracker-box, one-bedroom apartments on the west side of town. And you could even have a dog here."

"The backyard, is it —?"

"It's fully fenced." He rummaged in the back of the refrigerator and took out two bottles of water. He pointed one of them toward the door at the end of the mudroom. "There's even a doggie door to outside. Might be a tight squeeze, but I think Bump can wiggle through."

So far all the boxes were being ticked. The place was affordable, small enough that it wouldn't be a nightmare to keep clean, big enough for the three of us, and just far enough from Ida's to make it feel like we'd really moved out on our own. Yet it was that last point that also bothered me.

"I'm not sure. It worries me leaving Dad and Ida alone in that house, so far from everything. I was shot at there, remember?"

"Sam, the sheriff will be out in a few days to clear out the marijuana. As soon as that's done, there won't be anything left for whoever shot at you to protect. Besides, you need to stop worrying about your dad and move on with your own life."

I couldn't find any holes in his argument, so I let it go for the moment. Except I couldn't shake the feeling that there was a lot of unfinished business relating to that one incident. It was only the tip of the iceberg. Somewhere in Humboldt County was a drug lord, a Daniel Webster's devil, preying on the weak and impressionable, promising a temporary high to replace persistent troubles.

It was absurd, though, to think I could solve all of the world's — or even Wilton's — drug problems. Clint was right: I needed to get my own life in order, not worry about everyone else's.

Clint told me to have a look around, so I roamed from room to room, taking it all in, leaning against door frames or walls whenever my foot started aching — which was less often than I expected. Maybe I hadn't broken a toe after all?

None of the appliances were brand new, but they all looked to be in good shape. There were two bathrooms: one downstairs, one up. Just off the kitchen was a small empty room that could serve as a guest room or an office. It had a good view of the backyard, so I could check on Bump without having to leave my keyboard. Curious, I wandered up the stairs. On the second floor were two good-sized bedrooms. They could use a fresh coat of paint, new curtains, and bedspreads, but if we had to make do for a while with what was there —

"Sam," Clint called from downstairs, "I thought you were hungry?"

Clutching the handrail, I made my way carefully down the stairs and over to the couch.

"I forgot she took the plates with her." He slid a paper towel with two pizza slices across the coffee table to me and patted the cushion beside him. "So, do you like the place?"

What was there not to like? All we had to do was hang our clothes in the closets. I'd have a place to do my work, Tara would have a room of her own, and Bump could go in and out as he pleased. I just hoped the next door neighbors didn't have cats, and if they did, they had better stay on their side of the fence.

"I think I can afford a few dishes."

"Good. I'll call her tomorrow and tell her." He turned the TV on and we settled into a comfortable silence as we devoured our meal. It was just as good as anything I'd ever had in Chicago, a city renowned for its pizzas.

When I'd snarfed up the last pepper off the cardboard lid, I touched Clint's knee. It was meant to be a prelude to a mention of gratitude, but when he looked at me, I realized that making that contact was so much more. His eyes went to my hand and stayed there as he twisted his body toward me.

"Thanks," I said, drawing my hand back and closing it into a fist, like I was capturing the feel of him on my fingertips and hanging onto it. "This is exactly what we need. I think … I think I could even be happy here."

He reached his left arm over the back of the couch behind me. "You deserve to be happy, Sam."

And then … he cupped my cheek. Leaned into me. Brushed my earlobe with the pad of his thumb, sending a shiver down my spine.

I couldn't breathe. Didn't dare.

Because all I could think of was that my dinner had just been loaded with onions and I desperately wanted to scrub my mouth out with minty-clean toothpaste and a jug of mouthwash.

Any inhibitions I may have had, however, vanished as he placed the lightest — and hungriest — of kisses on my lips. Flesh grazing flesh. As light as a butterfly, as brief as the beat of a hummingbird's wings. No more than a moment. Then he drew back, mere inches, and looked into my eyes, an unspoken question emanating from the depths of his: *May I?*

"I can't …" I closed my eyes. Gathered my thoughts. No, that sounded wrong. I started over. "We still have a lot to sort out. I don't want to rush into anything again. We need to take this slowly."

He tucked his face against mine, his light scruff tickling my cheek, his breath warming the curve of my neck. "I can do slow."

The murmured promise of his words thrummed in my soul. That could mean a lot of things, as torturous as they could be exquisite. If I got up and had him take me back to my car now, that meant I was holding him at arm's length, denying him, and that granted me a certain power. But how many times could I push him away and expect him to keep coming back? How long could *I* keep that up without giving in? Being around him was like snorting double-chocolate brownies while dieting. Sooner or later, I'd have to have a taste, and once I did —

At the back of my mind, there was Danielle. Classy, intellectual, Victoria's Secret perfect body Danielle. What she lacked in likeability, she probably made up for when prancing around in her lingerie.

But Danielle wasn't here now with Clint. I was.

"How slow?" I breathed, my fingers tracing along his jaw, over his Adam's apple, to his collarbone.

He wasted no time letting me know.

His arm slid down to nestle beneath the small of my back. I let myself go limp in his embrace as he lowered me to the cushions, his other hand reaching down to my opposite knee to lift it up and lay the length of my body next to his. Stretching, I rolled closer, burrowing myself against him, against his lean, *hard* body. Like melding myself to him was a reflex, not a conscious thought.

My hand slipped beneath his shirt, wandered over the ridges of his defined abdominals, found the dips between his ribs, the firmness of his pectorals. His breathing quickened. I felt the *thump-thump, thump-thump* of his heart beneath my palm, my own pulse echoing the rhythm.

With a twist of his arms, Clint tugged his shirt off, lay his hand over mine. Kissed me. Light, at first. Lips fluttering over mine. Then over my eyelids, beside my ear, at the base of my throat. A burning trail kindling my desire.

I could wake up like this, I thought. Right here. Next to him. Under a blanket. No clothes. Just my skin pressed to his. Day after day. For an eternity, even.

Or at least ... just this once.

Somehow, during all that distraction, he'd unzipped my hoodie, slid the sleeves from my arms. He glanced at the hem of my shirt, which had come untucked from my jeans, as if asking permission. I rested my hand there to give myself a moment to think.

"This isn't going at all like I'd planned," I said.

He leaned his head back. "What did you plan?"

"I thought we'd spend tonight talking."

"About ...?"

"You. Me. Us." Then more timidly, as if afraid to broach it, "Her."

His eyelids fluttered shut. Then he gave me a direct look. A hard one. Like I'd shunned his honesty once again. His lips tightened across his teeth. "I told you, Sam. There is no me and Danielle. I'm not hiding anything from you. I don't want her. I want *you*. I want to *be* with you."

I pressed a hand to his cheek. "I believe that's what you want right now."

"You don't think I can hold myself to it? That the second you're out of sight, I'd be tempted if she came around?"

"I don't think *she* can keep herself away from you." I dug my fingers into his tousled hair, wound them in his silky waves. "Because if I were her, I wouldn't."

"You're forgetting something." His mouth teased into a smile. He nudged the bottom of my shirt upward. Slowly. Agonizingly slowly.

"What?"

He lowered his mouth to my stomach, his tongue flicking across the smoothness of my belly, swirling in my navel. "*I* can't keep myself away from *you*."

My head rolled back, a moan vibrating deep in my throat. As his hand curved around the inside of my thigh, I sensed a growing dampness between my legs, heat rising deep inside me.

"Sam," he murmured against my skin, "if you don't want —"

Pinching my fingers to his lips, I silenced him. Then, I let my hand drift downward, hooked my thumb beneath the button of my jeans, and popped it.

"I want," I said.

And I wanted it bad.

chapter 9

I WOKE TO THE scream of sirens.

My blood went cold, an ice floe in my veins. Hoodie clutched to my bare chest, I sat up, scooted back against the couch cushions. My eyes were slow to adjust. A night-light glowed dimly behind a half-open door. I was disoriented. Didn't know what time it was. If not for Clint stretched out beside me, I might have had an even harder time remembering where I was.

I checked the time on my phone: 1:30 a.m. Late, but if I headed back now, Dad and Ida might not think it unreasonable for me to have been chatting it up with Selma this late. Then again, they were probably preoccupied with their own private business and thus less inclined to investigate mine.

Sweeping the cobwebs from my brain, I focused on the sirens, their distressing howl climbing in pitch, hurtling lower, then escalating again to strum at every nerve in my body. I was about to nudge Clint awake when he bolted upright.

"What was that?" He rubbed his hands over his face, opening and closing his eyes repeatedly. "Is there a fire somewhere?"

I shook my head. "I don't think so. Sounds more like the police. Or an ambulance. I'm not sure which."

Red and white lights pulsed around the gaps between the curtains and walls.

He flicked on the lamp on the end table, then gathered his clothes from the floor. "I'll go see what it is."

Grabbing my jeans, I shoved both feet in the pants legs and had them halfway pulled up before I realized I was putting them on backward. I wiggled out of them and flipped them around. "I'm coming with you."

He was fully dressed before I could even find my shirt. I put the hoodie on instead and zipped it up as I ran after him barefooted. I paused just long enough to grab my shoes from beneath the coffee table and tuck them to my chest.

When Clint opened the front door, the neighbors were already gathering on the sidewalk across the street, about three houses down. He must not have known I'd followed him, because he dove through the gathering crowd, not looking back. The closer I came to the house, the harder it was for me to see. Lights flashed, alternating near-total darkness with blinding brilliance. Clint was there ahead of me, then suddenly he wasn't. I kept going, forcing my way between people, determined not to lose him. Until I plowed into the backside of a short, plump woman.

She whirled around, her breaths coming in little bursts of indignation.

"I'm sorry," I mumbled, holding my braced arm up to shield my eyes from the light. "What's going on, anyway?"

Her sloping shoulders rolled in a lazy shrug. "Hell if I know." She elbowed the gentleman next to her. "Harmon, whose house is that again?"

Balancing on one foot at a time, I put my shoes on as they squabbled back and forth.

"You should know better than me, Maybelle."

"Do I look like the Yellow Pages to you? Must be a hundred

houses in this development."

An ambulance came down the street, the sirens wailing. It stopped in front of the house. Two EMTs hopped out and grabbed the stretcher from the back of the vehicle.

Harmon raised his voice. "You're the one who talks to every breathing soul on this street when they go out to fetch the morning paper, even as they're running back into the house in their bathrobes."

"That was only that one time with Cleora Winkelman, Harmon. Had to find out about her grandson's kidney transplant."

Their bickering was lost in the buzz of the crowd as I tried to peer above Harmon's head to see what was going on. All I could make out were two Wilton police cars, which had to be the whole fleet, in front of a small white one-story, tidy but outdated. One police officer was busy with crowd control, waving nosy neighbors back off the lawn and shaking his head every time someone asked a question. Behind him, the garage door was wide open. There was something going on in there, but I couldn't tell what.

A chill wrapped around me. The temperature had taken a dip since Clint and I first went in Melissa's house a few hours ago. Shivering, I bunched my shoulders up. I leaned to the right to get a better look and accidentally brushed up against Harmon, then took a step back.

"Sorry," I said again.

He turned around slowly.

I was so focused on trying to see what was going on that it took me a full minute to realize he was staring at my chest. I glanced down just as Maybelle turned to say something to Harmon.

She took one look at me, her jaw dropping. "Put a bra on, would you?"

My zipper had slid down. I grabbed the tab and yanked up. "Sorry, I ran out of the house when I heard the —"

Maybelle boxed Harmon in the ear. "Stop gawking!"

He rubbed at his ear, a snarl twitching at his mouth.

"This is nothing but a bunch of rubberneckers," Maybelle groused. "The police will sort this out. Let's go home and get some sleep, Harmon. Besides, Spanky's probably having a fit because we've been gone so long and you have a big week ahead of you. School starts Monday. That high school doesn't clean itself. Course, if parents these days would just teach their brats to pick up after themselves, you wouldn't have to work half as hard as you do." Spinning around, she wobbled off.

"Right behind you," Harmon said meekly. Then he turned to me, feet firmly planted, looking like he was in no hurry at all. "Say, I don't remember you. You live around here?"

"I'm, uh …" — I thumbed in the direction of Melissa's house — "just moving into the neighborhood." Although I was having serious second thoughts, given the night's developments.

"Nice to meet you, Miss …?" He offered his hand.

I shook it, his grip gentle and brief. "Sam McNamee."

"Harmon Purnell."

I felt sorry for him in a way. He got more than his fair share of being henpecked, I was sure. Otherwise, he seemed like an okay guy, despite his roving eye, and I honestly couldn't blame him for that because I did have my hoodie unzipped halfway to my navel.

"So you work at the high school?" I asked out of politeness.

"Sure do. I'm the custodian at Wilton Memorial. Been at the same job for seventeen years. Don't pay much, but the benefits are good." He looked over his shoulder, then inched closer. "Maybelle won't let me quit until I get my twenty-five years in, but after that I'm gonna open a dog kennel. That's my dream."

"So you must have a dog."

"Nope. Maybelle won't let me get one. Says they shed too much, and the vacuuming stirs up too much dust and sets her allergies off. I figure if I run a kennel, I can take care of other people's dogs. That or get a divorce." He seemed to ponder the last point deeply.

"Who's Spanky, then?"

"Maybelle's parrot," he growled. "An African Grey. Did you know they can live for *eighty* years? Sometimes I think she hopes I'll die first, so she can be alone with that stupid bird. He's always squealing on me. At least dogs are loyal. I got my revenge, though. I taught him to cuss. Told her his former owner must've had a foul mouth." Chuckling, he winked at me.

I hadn't even known Harmon five minutes and it was obvious his marriage was not a happy one. "Well, if I ever need a dog-sitter, I'll keep you in mind."

A young man in his twenties pushed his way through the crowd and rushed into the garage, calling out a name, but I couldn't quite make it out through his sobs. One of the Wilton policemen caught him by the elbow and pulled him back out. The man was clearly distraught. He kept shaking his head and reaching his hands toward the house, pleading to go in there, but the officer restrained him.

"Do things like this happen here much?" I asked.

"For the most part, the area's pretty quiet. Lots of blue-collar folk, like me. People mostly go to work, then come home to sleep. Nope, we're not used to this sort of excitement. Gotta suspect foul play, though, what with the police showing up. So if someone got knocked off, well, maybe that'll help keep the riffraff from taking over the neighborhood." He ducked his head, giving a quick look around to see if anyone had overheard him. "Sorry if that sounded mean-spirited. Just don't like it happening where I live."

"That's okay, I understand. I wouldn't either."

He shoved his hands in his pockets and rocked on the balls of his feet, having lost interest in the circus going on across the street, but not yet willing to scat back home after Maybelle. His head bobbed a few times. Finally, "Wellll … s'pose I ought to head home. Lots to do around the house tomorrow. You take care."

"I will, thanks. You, too."

"See you around," he said, backing away.

I waved goodbye as he disappeared into the gray silhouettes around him. I worked my way through the crowd, searching for Clint, but with the strobe lights it was hard to focus on any one face long enough to figure out if it was him. Eventually, I started looking for tall guys on the thinner side. It was easier to see closer to the house where all the action was going on, but he definitely wasn't there. I walked half a block either way twice, thinking maybe he'd found someone to talk to. Still no sign.

The chill was getting to me. And I was tired and my foot hurt. Not to mention starting to worry that my dad was camped out on the sofa at Ida's waiting for me to come through the door so he could grill me on my whereabouts. I'd left my cell phone at Melissa's somewhere. If I went back, I could call Clint and locate him that way. Rubbing at the goose bumps on my arms, I turned to go back to the house.

A hand grabbed my shoulder from behind. Gasping, I wheeled around.

Clint's smile gleamed in the darkness. "I thought I'd never find you."

Behind him, figures emerged from the garage. I popped up on my toes to get a better look, but the pain in my foot forced me back down. Clint swiveled around to face the same direction. The EMTs were pushing a stretcher with a body bag.

Not another one. Last time I'd seen one of those was on the night I'd first returned to Wilton.

"Oh no." I leaned against Clint, seeking the warmth of his body. His arms went around me, holding me up, and I rested my head against his chest. "Somebody died?"

"Looks like it. Sad, really. The neighbors said she was young. They all seemed to like her, but there was a lot of concern lately about the losers hanging out at her place."

111

"Huh. Harmon didn't seem to know whose house this was."

"Who?"

"Another neighbor. Any idea how she died?"

"Not really. Just a lot of speculation. But seeing as how the police showed up first ... Makes you wonder."

"Makes me wonder if this is where I want to bring my daughter. With the arrangement Dad has with Ida right now, I'm not really tied into staying in the area anymore. I'm free to leave."

As soon as the words were out of my mouth, I realized what I'd said. "I didn't mean —"

"Don't worry about it, Sam." I felt Clint's shoulders lift in a shrug, like he was trying to tell me it was no big deal, but there was the slightest tightness in his voice, like I'd just stomped on his toes. "I understand that your dad's situation changes things for you. Anyway, we're just getting started, right?" He gave me a half-hearted squeeze, his hold on me loosening. "As for what happened here tonight, I think it was just an isolated incident. Melissa assured me several times that this is a nice area. Besides, if she'd ever had any trouble with the neighbors, I'm sure I would've heard about it. She always gave me a full report every morning about anything going on in her life."

"Did they say who it was that died?"

"Didn't catch the last name, but I heard someone say 'Miley' and that she worked at the salon downtown."

A knife of cold sliced down my spine. "Miley Harper from Dawna's Beauty Studio?"

"Sounds right. You know her?"

"I met her once." I looked up at Clint. "She was Jake Taylor's fiancée. His ex, I mean."

"Huh."

And that was all he said before he herded me back to Melissa's house. It only took us a few minutes to gather up all our things and straighten the place up. He was quiet on the drive back to Wild Bill's to drop me off at my car, but I figured we were both pretty bushed and in need of some shut-eye.

He opened the passenger-side door for me, but hung across it, blocking me from getting out. "Next weekend there's a picnic at the Grand Beaver Lodge. Some sort of fundraiser." He looked down at the ground before raising his eyes again. "Would you like to go with me?"

My first concern was what Tara would think of me going out with Clint. I wasn't sure if it was good to let her in on this so soon, but eventually she'd figure out I was seeing someone. I couldn't keep lying to Dad about meeting Selma, either, because Clint and I had been out in public together and this town wasn't big enough to sneak around in. Still, a private dinner was one thing. Showing up arm in arm at a public gathering in Wilton practically meant we were engaged.

Besides, Dylan Hawkins belonged to the lodge, and I wasn't eager to rush back there because of what had happened — or almost happened — in the back room. But I could hardly let Clint in on that secret. How was I going to get out of this? All I could do was stall. "I didn't know you belonged to the lodge."

"I don't. But a friend keeps asking if I'll come. Most of the time I make up an excuse, but this occasion seemed important to him, so I told him I'd go." He ran his hand over the top of the door frame. "Sooo … will you? Please?"

He looked so desperate for me to say yes. So I did. "Sounds good to me."

I'd figure out how to dodge Hawkins when the time came. Until then, I'd just deal with the insomnia and anxiety. Anyway, if he was going to be there, chances were Selma would, too, which would provide me with a buffer if I needed one. Or it could become a title chapter from my memoir: *How I Destroyed the Only Friendship I Ever Had.*

Clint finally moved aside and we started toward my car. It was eerily dark and empty in the parking lot, but what was even stranger was that just a few hours ago Clint and I'd had no problem bridging the gap between us. Now we stood there like a couple of zombies, shell-shocked by what we'd seen and tottering awkwardly at the edge of a new stage in our relationship.

I wanted so much to enjoy what we had, just the two of us discovering each other, without my father or daughter or Danielle Townsley entering the picture. Not that I didn't want my dad or daughter getting to know Clint better, but for a while I only wanted it to be about me and him. Preferably on an uninhabited island in the South Pacific. With an endless supply of mint mojitos. And a beach blanket, so we weren't digging sand out of our private parts after the fact. And sunscreen, because ... well, if no one else was around, what would be the point of ever getting dressed?

As we arrived at my car, he took my hand and pressed Melissa's house key into it. "In case you need to get away. Or want to check it out again."

"Thanks, but don't you need it?"

"I have another spare at home. Think about it. But don't take too long. Melissa wants to list it soon if you decide you don't want it. What she really wants, though, is for the house to be lived in. Cared for. You don't even have to sign a six-month lease. If at any time, you decide it's not working for you, just let her know."

I nodded. "I'll think about it."

I already knew what I wanted to do, but the final decision wasn't mine.

I lingered beside my car, expecting him to give me a full-on goodbye kiss that would set my nether regions on fire. Instead, he brushed cool lips across the crown of my head. We mumbled our goodbyes and call-you-laters, then went our separate ways.

As I drove down dark and lonely country roads, not passing a single car along the way, I realized that everything hinged on this one decision.

Clint had offered me a place of my own and a way to find peace with my father. Yet I'd been dumb enough, and callous enough, to remind him that I was free to leave Wilton after we'd just made love.

Talk about a slap in the face.

I CAME HOME TO Ida's, the house cloaked in darkness. The moment I opened the car door, I was sure I heard the murmur of voices from over the hill. But it was only the bullfrogs in the nearby pond, croaking up a storm.

Stumbling as I set my aching foot down, I kicked a stone and sent it scuttling across the gravel driveway. I could hardly see. Clouds had shut out the moonlight and Dad hadn't even remembered to leave the porch light on for me, which made navigating my way from the car to the front door more precarious than it should have been. Somehow, I made it without breaking my other foot.

Finding the keyhole was yet another challenge. The metal tip of the key scratched over the knob. I thought I almost had it when I tried shoving the key in and realized I had it upside down. Just as I flipped the key over and pushed it in, a pinpoint of light streaked in my peripheral vision. For half a minute, I stared at the place halfway up the hill where I thought I'd seen it, but there was nothing there, no sound, no movement. Just darkness. And silence.

Inside, I locked the door behind me and crept up the stairs, mindful of each creak in the floorboards. I drifted past my dad's room. The door stood open wide, the room empty, Ida's large assortment of throw pillows still neatly arranged against the headboard.

Ida's door, however, was closed. I guess Dad telling me about them was just a way of preventing me from walking in on them at an awkward moment and figuring things out the hard way.

I kicked off my shoes and burrowed beneath the sheets in what

I'd worn that night. For a long while, though, I couldn't sleep. Questions were racing through my mind, needling my curious nature to find answers, the first of which was who Jake was protecting and whether he'd been afraid of someone taking Miley out if he gave out any information. Even though they'd broken up, it wasn't unreasonable to assume he still had feelings for her and didn't want anything to happen to her.

Finally, I tapped out a text to Archer: *Did you hear about Miley Harper???*

I hit 'Send' and laid my head down. Somehow, minutes later, I was sound asleep, adrift in dreams too delightful to wake up from.

chapter 10

I PULLED INTO THE Mullinses' driveway at 11 a.m. and was about to get out when Tara popped her head out the front door and held up a finger to let me know she'd be out in a minute. Or seven, since she was operating on teenager-time, which was a bit like dog years.

The moment he caught sight of her, Bump started whopping his tail against the backseat. He shoved his big muzzle onto my shoulder and made strange little chortling sounds of excitement.

"Get in the back," I reminded him. When a gentle suggestion didn't work, I had to shoo him back with a Stefano's menu.

Put out, he snorted in my ear before complying. Bump couldn't do anything without communicating his thoughts on the matter. In this case, he was ticked off in the first place that I hadn't let him ride shotgun — not that I ever did, mind you — and doubly hacked off that I hadn't let him run to the front door to escort Tara to the car. I knew the level of Bump's enthusiasm whenever he greeted us after we'd been gone more than a few hours and it wasn't worth the Mullinses sacrificing their front screen door because of it.

An hour ago, Dad and Ida had come down to the kitchen separately, barely looking at each other and exchanging only the most ordinary of morning chitchat. As if I didn't know they'd spent the night together *and* shared a shower that morning. Ida's pipes couldn't keep a secret.

I was still a little groggy from having to operate on less than four hours of sleep, but every time I thought back to being with Clint last night a surge of adrenaline filled me and I felt like I had enough energy to vacuum both floors of the house, push-mow the lawn, and make dinner for a family of twelve. At least until something else yanked me back to reality. Like the fact that Bump was drooling on my shoulder and shedding fistfuls of light gray hair onto my black upholstery. I hit the power button for the opposite rear window and Bump rushed over to it to hang his head out.

Judy Mullins stepped out onto the front porch and waved at me. We'd never spoken beyond exchanging a few words about when I'd be back to get Tara, but even in those brief exchanges I sensed a genuinely nice person. If Tara was going to be coming over here often, I ought to get to know her parents better. During the years we'd lived in Naperville, I'd barely been able to recognize my neighbors, let alone known their names or anything about them personally. It was about time I crawled out of my shell and made some connections around here. I never knew when I might need a favor.

Just as I put my hand on the door latch, my cell phone chirped at me. I checked the display to see who it was, intent on returning the call later. Archer's name flashed at me. I couldn't ignore him.

"Hello," I said to him as I waved back at Judy through my window. She went back inside.

"Morning, Sam. It's Archer. I got your message."

Something about hearing his voice put all my fears and worries at ease. Like I'd just had a kitten land in my lap. I leaned my head against the window. "Hey, Arch. Good morning."

He allowed the briefest of pauses before asking, "How did you know about Miley?"

Stalling, I scooped up the pennies from my ashtray and stacked them into a neat little pile. Before he'd even called, I realized how dumb of me it had been to leave him that message before the rest of Wilton would have heard about it. "Ida told me."

Liar, liar, pants on —

"At three in the morning?"

Well, that was a well-aimed fire hose. Of course my text had been time-stamped. Idiot.

"Yeah, you know Ida. She knows everything that goes on in Wilton. Must have a friend who lives in Miley's neighborhood or something."

"I heard it on the scanner at the firehouse. Man, I couldn't believe it. Stuff like this just doesn't happen in Wilton."

It shouldn't, but it had.

He must have bought my fib, because he didn't grill me on it anymore. And *that* made me feel guilty for lying to him. But even more than that, something about it bothered me on a different level. If Archer was my friend, what was my problem with admitting to him that Clint and I had spent the night together at Melissa's house? Was it just because I didn't consider him that good of a friend yet? Or because I didn't want anyone knowing how serious Clint and I were?

"I can't believe she's … gone," he said, a huskiness to his voice, almost like he was holding back tears. "It wasn't that long ago that Miley and I …"

I waited for a few seconds for him to finish, but when he didn't I prompted him. "You and Miley what?"

His sigh reached across the distance. "We hung out together for a while, during one of those times she and Jake broke it off. It was only a few times, and we were really just killing time together as friends, but it … Well, it went a little further than we were expecting one night."

Oh.

Ohhhh.

Now I felt super guilty for lying to him, because he'd told me something just as personal as what I'd lied to him about.

"I … I'm sorry, Archer. I didn't know you'd ever been that close to her. She seemed like such a nice person." I'd only met her the one time at Dawna's, but I'd liked her right away. "Do they know how she died yet?"

"Word on the street is an overdose of heroin."

"Say what?!" I tried to soak it all in, but it was like someone had just told me the earth really was flat. "Are we talking about the same Miley Harper who looked like she just got her braces off and was on her way to Sunday school?"

"I know. I don't believe it, either, Sam. They say there was drug paraphernalia lying around when they found her. But the Miley I knew a few years ago was smart enough to stay away from drugs. I know she'd gotten tangled up with the wrong crowd for a little while right after high school, but not for long. She *had* cleaned up her act."

"So you don't think she was using?"

"I'd like to think not, but who knows? People do change." After a pause, he said, "I wish I'd kept up with her better. If something was wrong, then, I might have known. Still, it just doesn't seem like her. There has to be some other explanation."

That little voice inside me said he was right. "Maybe she didn't die from an overdose after all."

"What do you mean?"

"Archer, what if …? This is just a hunch, but what if someone was trying to make it look like an overdose when it really wasn't?"

"You mean murder?"

"Yeah."

"I don't know, Sam. I suppose it's possible, but I can't think of anyone who'd want to kill her. This is all so bizarre. Maybe the police will come up with something. Until then, I'm not going to drive myself crazy wondering about it. No matter what, she didn't deserve to have her life end so soon."

"No one does. We should all live to be a hundred."

I counted my blessings, glad that Tara had a good head on her shoulders and equally glad my dad didn't have any worse vices than being perpetually contrary. Tara may have had her surly moments and Dad could be as irritating as a pebble in your shoe, but I never had to worry about them getting messed up in anything serious.

"Sam, I don't know how to say this other than just ask, but I'm in charge of a benefit picnic being hosted on the lodge grounds next week. It's to help raise money for children born to mothers with addiction problems and, well, I was wondering if you and Tara would like to go with me? There'll be a lot of kids her age there and I thought it might be a good way for her to meet some of them, seeing as how she's starting at a new school and all. I also figured we could spend some time together. I enjoyed dinner the other night. A lot."

Frick. Frick, frick, frick.

I slid down in my car seat, hanging onto the steering wheel to keep myself from disappearing under the floor mat. When Clint had asked me, I hadn't connected that Archer would be there, too. I'd been too fixated on Dylan Hawkins possibly showing up. How *stupid* could I be?

I waited so long to answer that Archer must've sensed my reluctance, because he gave me an out.

"If, uh, if you've got something else going on, that's okay. It's just a small-town event. I don't expect it'll be too exciting. High school band's playing and I heard the clarinets squeak a lot. Bunch of country hicks falling all over each other in the three-legged sack race. Old guys getting drunk on cheap beer. Enough cake and cookies to send you into a diabetic coma. That sort of thing."

"No, I ... I appreciate you asking. It's just that ..." Damn it. I *had* to tell him. "Clint already asked me. I said yes."

"Oh, I see."

Sometimes, it's not what people say that gets to you; it's what they *don't* say.

Two days ago, I'd practically sworn to him that Clint and I were done for good. There had been a moment with Archer when he pulled me up from the porch swing that the slightest spark had flickered between us. I'd been so startled by the feelings it aroused that it had left me stunned, unable to act. I wasn't sure what it had meant then. I still didn't.

But the fact was that Clint and I had a seriously serious thing going on. And I wasn't going to let myself get diverted from that. I was going to give my relationship with him the attention it deserved, because I wanted to know where it might lead.

"Archer, I —"

Tara tapped on the window of the passenger-side door and pointed down at the lock.

"I have to go," I said. "I'll see you at the picnic."

After exchanging goodbyes, I let Tara in. All at once, Bump was spinning, bouncing, and barking.

"Sit," Tara said flatly.

His rump hit the seat. He let out a warbly 'woof'.

"Hi, Bump. Now quiet." She tossed her backpack in the back and buckled up. "Lie down."

He folded with an exhaled groan. I peered in the rearview mirror to see him lying there with his chin resting on his paws, his eyes fixed adoringly on Tara.

"How do you do that?" I asked her.

She grinned. "Mind control."

"As long as you don't use it on me." I turned the car around and headed down the driveway. "How was your sleepover?"

"Fine, but" — squirming, she readjusted her seat belt — "I have to talk to you about something, Mom."

A squirrel scampered out onto the lane. I tapped on the brake, slowing, until it whipped around and went back up a tree. "What is it?

Did something happen with Shannon?"

"No way. Shannon's cool. So are her parents, before you ask."

"Okay. So spill." We pulled out onto the road.

"It's about Gramps and Ida."

"Go on."

"I saw them … you know … on the couch." She covered her eyes, as if to shut out the memory. "Together."

"Oh, you did, huh?" It was bad enough that Dad told me they'd been messing around, now Tara had seen them in action. "Do they know you saw them?" Because if they did, that would explain why Dad had confessed to me.

"I don't think so. But it was just gross. I mean, two old people kissing on the lips. Yuck!"

Kissing? And that had shocked her? I loved that my little girl was still so innocent.

"So are they dating? Because that's just … weird. Like what are they — ninety-something?"

"Not quite." I didn't dare ask her how old she thought I was.

"Anyway, that's why I left before you got home yesterday. I called Shannon early and asked if her parents could pick me up. Sorry I didn't check with you first, but it sort of grossed me out and I *had* to get out of there."

"I understand, believe me. Gramps told me yesterday they were seeing each other. I admit I was a little … Let's just say I was surprised. But you know, the more I thought about it, the more I figured they deserved to be happy together. It's all any of us wants, really."

She looked around like a gremlin was going to leap out of the backseat and cut out her tongue. "Are they home now?"

"They were when I left and as far as I know they didn't have any plans."

Her head rolled back to hit the headrest. "Great. Just great. If I see them Frenching, my corneas are going to burst into flames. And then I'll be blind, thank you."

Instead of turning onto Hilltop Road, I kept going straight. Sherlock picked it up right away.

"Hey, you missed our turn."

"No, I did that on purpose. Tara, how would you like for us to have our own house? Just you and me?"

"What about Bump?"

"Of course Bump. He's kind of the reason we need to find a place for the three of us. Seems that after you left yesterday, Gramps left him loose in the kitchen. At some point, he started chasing the cats and ... I came home to total havoc. It was like a tornado touched down *inside* the house. I figured if we had a place of our own, that wouldn't be an issue. What do you think?"

She chewed on it for a good minute while gazing out the window. Tara liked to analyze her options. "Where?"

"In Wilton. I already have something lined up. If you agree to it, that is."

She shrugged, trying to look nonchalant, but I could see the slightest glimmer of excitement in her face. "I'd have to see it."

TURNS OUT I DIDN'T have to twist her arm or dangle my parental autocracy over her head. Tara fell in love with Melissa's house as soon as she saw the retro chrome and vinyl kitchen chairs.

Tara draped herself upside down over a lime-green bean bag chair, her hair fanned out on the floor around her face. "Do we have to go back already?"

"We have to pack, don't we?"

"Sure, I suppose. That should take, what, five minutes? We are gypsies, after all."

"As soon as we have a free weekend, we can drive up to Chicago and empty our storage locker."

"I can't even remember what I put in there."

"Me, either."

She sat up like she'd just gotten an electric shock. "Shit!"

I arched an eyebrow at her.

"I mean shoot." She palmed her face with both hands and flopped onto her back. "I just remembered — school starts tomorrow. The bus is scheduled to pick me up at Ida's."

"I can take you until we get the bus switched."

She peeked between her fingers. "You sure?"

"Of course."

Bump barked three times. I peeked out the kitchen window. A squirrel was perched on a branch above him, chattering in protest over the unwelcome visitor. Wonderful. A new obsession. The squirrel would just have to take up residence somewhere else. As if it picked up my thoughts by ESP, the squirrel scampered across a branch, vaulted onto a limb of the neighbor's tree, and disappeared. Bump hit the privacy fence with his front paws, bouncing up and down a few times before he realized he couldn't see over it. His attention span being short, he was quickly distracted by a floating dandelion seed.

I cracked the window. "Time to go, Bump!"

He executed one of his famous ballet leaps and two seconds later burst through the doggie door. It had only taken one time of Tara tossing a Skittle through the opening for him to figure it out. After texting Clint to tell him to let Melissa know we'd be moving in today, the three of us piled into the car and headed home. 'Home' meaning Ida's house, which wasn't going to be our home for much longer.

The prospect of having a place of our own filled me with unexpected excitement. For now, I could stick close to Dad without having to share close quarters with him, and I could keep seeing Clint to find out where that would lead. I had no idea what life held in store, but for the short term, things were looking up. If I could just keep from falling into holes. Or poking my eye out. Or riding in Selma's car.

The biggest reason for staying in Wilton, though, was Tara. She was happy here. Happier than I'd ever seen her. She adored Ida, liked spending time with Dad, and had grown close to Shannon in a very short time. Her first best friend. All the years we lived in Naperville, I couldn't ever remember her staying over at a friend's house. She'd been invited to the occasional birthday party, but had always gone reluctantly, preferring to spend time with me — and while I loved that she liked being with me, I wanted her to have friends her own age. To just be a kid and not a forty-something in a fourteen-year-old's body.

When we pulled into Ida's driveway, she was pruning hedges at the side of the house. I'd barely put the trusty old Forester in park and hadn't even switched the ignition off, when Tara burst from the car and ran inside to start packing.

I pulled Bump from the backseat, his leash still attached. He'd proven unreliable on his recall whenever there were small furry animals anywhere within sight, so the leash was a necessary evil until he became better trained — which given his instincts might never happen. He pulled when he saw Ida, although he did that for everybody. I gave him a light correction like Clint had taught me and Bump instantly calmed. 'Calm' being a relative term. In Bump's case, that brought him from light speed down to Mach I.

"Where's Dad?"

Ida flipped the brim of her lemon-yellow sun hat up. A smear of dirt was streaked across her chin. By the looks of things, she'd been outside pulling weeds and trimming bushes since I left. Ida was seldom idle. According to her, God gave you twenty-four hours in the day and none of them should be wasted. "Inside in that old recliner with the TV on full blast again. Probably dead asleep by now. He was watching race cars go around in circles. I had to come outside for some peace and quiet."

"Did you sleep well last night?" I asked, more nosy than polite.

She flipped the brim of her hat back down, her eyes narrowing ever so slightly. "Well enough. And you? I noticed you got in late. Who did you say you were out with?"

I fessed up. "Okay, don't tell Dad, but I was out with Clint Chastain."

"Good for you. But why wouldn't you want me to tell Walt?"

"Because I don't want the third degree. You know him. And please don't blab to the ladies at the Lion's Den or the Purple Sombrero Club or whatever it is. It's hard enough to have any privacy in this town as it is."

She drew her chin back. "Sam, dear, I don't share private information about those closest to me; I only collect it on others."

"Good, because if I find out you told anyone, I'll spill the beans about you and Dad."

The clippers fell from her grip, the pointy end just missing impaling her feet. "You know?"

"Dad told me. I think he was rather proud of himself. Besides, Tara saw you two making out on the couch yesterday. And I would have been blind not to notice Dad wasn't in his own room when I came home last night."

She nodded. "Truce, then. I won't tell if you don't. A lot of those ladies from the Lion's Club are married to men who belong to the lodge. Very few of them are fond of Walt. I've been trying to stay on their good side, since I'm lobbying to head up a few committees this coming year." She retrieved the pruning shears and lopped off a dead branch from a golden privet bush, then tossed it in the wheelbarrow behind her. "Sam, this has to be terribly awkward for you — this thing between Walt and me, I mean."

"Ida, I'm happy for you. I really am. It's awkward, yes, but Tara and I will get used to it. Speaking of which — how long have you two, you know, been involved?"

"Does it matter, Sam?"

"No, but I'm just curious. When I came back to Wilton, I didn't sense anything was up between you. I just wondered if his reluctance to move into town had anything to do with you."

"Oh, who knows? Since you asked, we've always spent a lot of time together, but it wasn't until after the fire, when you were in the hospital, that —"

"Okay, fair enough. You don't need to share the details."

"You did ask." She donned a serious face. "You know he was worried sick about you, Sam, after the incident with Jake Taylor. He was sitting on the couch, trying in vain to hold back the tears because he'd nearly lost you, and I just held him for a while. It was a side of him I'd never seen. Walt doesn't like being vulnerable. But he is. More than anyone knows. One thing led to another. We weren't even sure how it happened." She pruned a few more branches, the shears making a rhythmic *snip-snip-snip* sound. "Look, I have no idea where this is going or how long it's going to last. But I haven't felt like a real woman in years. Not until these last couple of weeks. Being with Walt made me realize that there was more to me than giving my time away to others, and that I could enjoy being selfish for once. Meanwhile, I'm riding this bronco until it stops bucking. I feel like I'm twenty again."

I understood what she was saying. Not the feeling twenty part. But about enjoying being with a man again.

Setting her shears aside, she raked stray twigs into a little pile, then put them in the wheelbarrow. "Say, when you came home last night, did you notice anything unusual? I could've sworn I heard someone out in that field last night, but Walt convinced me I was just imagining things."

"Are you sure you didn't hear something?"

She tugged her gloves off. "Actually, I'm sure I did. But at three in the morning I wasn't about to go investigate. Anyway, I'd say that I'll be glad when it's gone, but I'm not sure that taking someone's cash crop out from under their noses is going to make matters any better."

"I've thought about that, too. But the bottom line is that we don't want those drugs out there in our schools."

"You're right about that. One thing I'm glad for is that dog. He may not look very intimidating, but at least he'd sound the alarm if someone showed up at the house."

I didn't have the heart to tell her right then that Bump would be moving out with Tara and me. Anyway, I honestly didn't think he'd make much of a guard dog anyway. Unless being licked to death was a threat.

Together, we walked toward the back kitchen door. I hooked Bump up to his line and went inside with her. The volume on the TV was still cranked up.

Ida flipped the lever up on the faucet and waited for the warm water, then began scrubbing up to her elbows. I went into the living room to turn the volume down. Just then, three cars and two extended-bed pickups pulled up. Bump didn't make a peep. Some watchdog he was.

Ida came out drying her hands on a dish towel. "Someone here?"

"Yeah," I said, "the sheriff."

chapter 11

SHERIFF DRISCOLL AND SIX deputies got out of their vehicles and started milling about in Ida's front yard, among them the lady deputy, who'd taken my report yesterday, and Deputy Halloway.

Despite all the door slamming and loud voices, Dad snored on. Ida poked him in the ribs to wake him up. As soon as he was coherent, we all went outside together.

Sheriff Driscoll explained to Ida that they'd come as soon as he was able to gather the manpower. A few minutes later they all piled back into their cars and trucks and drove over her yard and up the hill, leaving twin ribbons of crushed grass behind them.

Dad and Ida were headed back inside when I forced out, "Dad, Ida, I need to tell you something."

They both turned around.

"Tara and I are moving out."

Surprise wafted over their faces.

"When?" Dad asked.

"Today. Tara's upstairs packing her things already. We don't have much here. Most of our belongings are still in Chicago."

"You moving in with that animal doctor?"

"No, Dad. We're not. But Clint did find us a house. It belongs to his former receptionist. She said we could stay there in exchange for taking care of the place and a minimal rent. I thought it would be good for us to have our own space, where Bump can have a fenced-in yard and Mr. Jeeves and Tiger Lily can live in peace."

"Come on, Sam." He pointed from himself to Ida. "This is about us, isn't it?"

Ida curled a hand around his arm. "We could use some privacy, Walt. You said yourself how you didn't want Tara to catch us in the act. With the lot of us living under the same roof, it's bound to happen."

Turning his face away, he wedged his hands into his pockets. "I don't know. I'm not sure I like her and Tara living alone."

"It's Wilton, Indiana, Walt. Not New York City. Besides, they lived alone before they came here. I think they're perfectly capable of taking care of themselves. Anyway, they'll be close enough to drop by at any time." She looked at me. "Right, Sam?"

I was about to answer when Sheriff Driscoll's car came speeding down the hill. He was definitely in a hurry. We all walked out to meet him.

"Something the matter?" I asked as soon as he got out of his car. Deputy Halloway was with him.

"This is Deputy Don Halloway. He's our narcotics specialist."

Touching a finger to the brim of his hat, Halloway nodded in our general direction.

"Believe it or not," Sheriff Driscoll began, "someone beat us to the punch. Cut down every last plant out there between yesterday afternoon and last night."

Ida and I exchanged a glance.

"It's gone?" Dad asked.

"Sure is. I'd say about a hundred mature plants. Value on the street would be in excess of six figures. This wasn't some small-time dealer. We're talking serious pot farmers. Part of a drug cartel, maybe."

131

"But how did they haul it all away?" I said. "We would've noticed a vehicle on the property."

"Turns out they'd put in a crude access road in the other direction. We also found evidence just now that they'd been camping out there, probably guarding the crop."

That would explain the voices Ida and I had heard — and the gunshots aimed at Archer and me. Too bad I hadn't called Sheriff Driscoll when I got home last night, but I'd convinced myself I was just being paranoid.

The screen door on the house banged as Tara came outside to see what was going on. Bump bounded down the front steps ahead of her.

The sheriff nodded toward where the crop had been. "They did a pretty thorough job of covering their tracks. Meanwhile, if you see or find anything out of the ordinary ..."

"Thank you, sheriff," Ida said, touching his arm briefly.

"Just so you know, now that they've cleaned up this site, it's highly unlikely they'll be back. My guess is that they suspected we'd discovered the location and they'll move operations elsewhere now. We'll comb the area for a while longer, but I'm not hopeful. Whoever did this was very thorough. They're certainly not sloppy amateurs."

Bump loped toward Sheriff Driscoll, his tail swinging happily in greeting. A few feet away, he raised his muzzle in the air and took a couple of big whiffs. He veered toward Deputy Halloway, zeroing in on his shoes. His nose quivered as he loudly sniffed his way up Halloway's pants leg. Then, he shoved his nose at Halloway's hands and snorted a big glob of dog snot.

Scowling, Halloway pulled a tissue from his pocket and wiped his hands.

"Sorry about that, officer," Tara said as she jogged his way. "He always wants to say 'hi' to everyone. Bump, come here."

Ignoring her, Bump sat in front of Halloway and let out a series of barks, like he was striking up a conversation.

"No problem." Halloway stuffed the tissue — and his hands — in his pockets. "Probably smells my dog."

Tara clapped her hands at Bump. His hind end popped up and swung sideways. He met Tara's eyes briefly, before lowering his head and cocking one rear leg in the air. Before I could blurt Bump's name out, I heard the telltale hiss and plop of dog urine splattering on cop shoes. Halloway jumped back. Then, being the good sport he was, he laughed and shook his foot.

Muttering profuse apologies, I latched a hand on Bump's collar and led him back to the house. This was the second time this week I was questioning whether there were any actual benefits to dog ownership.

Near the back steps, I unwound the tie-out cable from the base of the clothesline pole and clipped the end to Bump's collar for the last time. After this, he'd be free to run in his own backyard.

He gazed up at me in his usual adoringly goofy way and sneezed three times, daintily.

"Bless you." I patted him on the nose and he ducked his head under my hand, then swung his rump around to sit on my feet. "Get off, you big goober."

But he wasn't moving.

"Get. Off."

He shifted his weight to my bad foot. Pain flared. I reached down to shove him off — and everything went black around me.

For a moment, I couldn't see or hear anything. But I knew I was on the ground. Or near it.

I was experiencing another of Bump's memories. I knew what it was, yet I couldn't separate me, Sam, from me, Bump. Couldn't tell the 'here' from the 'there', or the 'now' from the 'then'.

Gray shapes appeared at the edges of my vision, sharpening gradually. Moving from left to right, and back again. A pair of legs: light pants, dark shoes. Pacing back and forth. Kicking at a stone to

133

send it skipping across a dusty patch of dirt.

Squawks sounded. Feathers erupted into the air. I watched one drift down, then settle near a rooster, its feathers striated in a detailed pattern of black and white. It cocked its head at me, bright wattle flapping, beady eyes glinting. Behind it, a brood of hens scratched at the dirt, clucking randomly.

My blood raced, some primal urge in me awakening. The rooster strutted tauntingly toward me.

I lurched toward it, but the leash on which I'd been tethered went taut. Metal links rubbed across my windpipe, tightening.

Then another pair of legs appeared: slighter, ankles bare, the feet much, much smaller.

"'Bout time," said the gruff voice from the human next to me. *"You got it?"*

"You first."

In my peripheral vision, I was aware of them walking toward each other, but I was too intent on the flock of chickens to look at their faces.

A basket dropped to the ground, kicking up a cloud of dust. The chickens burst upward in a frenzy of beating wings. Adrenaline burst through my veins like a gunshot.

Everything went fuzzy, faded away ...

A soft woof sounded. Then, snuffles tickled my ear.

"Mom? What are you doing down there?"

Colors and shapes gathered in the darkness to bring the world back into view: blue sky laced with clouds, leafy tree limbs, freshly laundered sheets rustling in the breeze. I was flat on my back, looking up, warm dog slobber dripping onto my forehead.

Drip, drip. Drip, drip. Slurp.

I scrunched my eyes closed just in time, as Bump swiped his massive tongue across my eyelids, then proceeded to wash my face.

Tara rescued me, pushing Bump away with her knee as she helped me to my feet. "Why were you lying on the ground?"

"Just wanted to see things from a different perspective, I guess." I eyed Bump accusingly and muttered, "Next time give me a little warning, will you?"

"Huh?" Tara said.

"Nothing. Let's go inside and get our stuff, okay?"

AS WE LOADED THE last of our scant belongings into the Subaru later that afternoon, Dad and Ida stood on the top step, looking on sadly like they were sending their youngest child off to college clear on the other side of the country. Funny, it was the first time I'd looked at them as a couple. As in life partners. And oddly, somehow, they seemed to fit together.

Ida, of course, was always Ida — flitting from one charity activity to another, her social calendar brimming full, her wardrobe, house, and yard as eclectic as her life.

But Dad ... Dad was different. He was still an ornery old cuss. But an occasionally cheerful one. In the last couple of weeks, I'd seen him smile more than I had in decades. He'd even giggled at some of Tara's humorous chick flicks. While we'd been waiting for the deputies to report back from the field, Ida had talked about the two of them going to the new frozen yogurt place just outside of Fullbright. The Walter Schimmoller I knew up until recently would never have paid six dollars for a sample-sized cup of frozen yogurt with crushed candy bars and almond slivers when he could get a two-gallon tub of generic Neapolitan ice cream for half that price from the convenience store.

Somehow, over the past few years, Ida had changed him — chipped away at his granite exterior flake by flake. I wasn't sure, however, if he'd changed her at all. If he had, he'd been her anchor in an otherwise scattered life. Someone to come home to and just *be* with.

135

One thing was certain: he wasn't the man I'd run away from all those years ago. Whether they realized it yet or not, Ida hadn't changed him by answering to his manly needs in the bedroom. No, they'd connected long before the fire forced us to move in with her. Ida Oldingsells had been the beacon of light and energy at the end of a long, lonely tunnel for him.

Maybe, in the grand scheme of things, my mother, Ann Glasser, hadn't been the love of his life after all, and the only reason they'd gotten together was to create me. Maybe, the one he'd been looking for all along had turned out to live right next door. It just took him ten years and a burnt-down house to realize that.

Something in me softened toward him and maybe, just maybe, forgave him a little for being a crusty old goat all these years.

Tara gave her grandfather and Ida a quick hug, then raced back to the car and jumped in. Bump stuck his head out the window and barked at me.

"Yeah, yeah, I'm coming," I said.

"Can we help you move in, Sam?" Ida asked. "Does the place need cleaned, fixed up — anything?"

"Thanks, but honestly, I don't know what you could do. The place is furnished, it's in good shape, and everything we need is in the back of the wagon. Well, everything except dishes."

"I have extras!" Ida proclaimed.

Before I could protest, she was up the stairs and inside, leaving Dad and me standing there alone, halfway between the front steps and my trusty Subaru. I glanced toward the car. With a whimper, Bump rested his muzzle and a paw on the top edge of the window, his pale gray eyebrows twitching alternately. I turned back to my dad. He sniffed. There was a misty sheen in his eyes. He swiped a sleeve across his face.

"Dad, are you ... crying?"

He shook his head, looked away. "Damn allergies. Always making my eyes water and stuffing up my nose."

"Oh, sure. Tara has that problem, too." A fib, just like his. But if it made him feel less embarrassed …

Still avoiding my gaze, he muttered. "You take care of my dog, y'hear?"

"You can come and visit him anytime, you know."

His jaw quivered the tiniest bit, but he steeled himself. "It's not the same."

"I know it's not. But you want to be with Ida and you should be. It's just … Bump can't stay here. We both know that."

He shrugged. "We could put up a fence."

"And do what with the cats — kick them out on the street?"

"We could. I'm not particularly a cat person. Far as I see it, they're just furry shelf ornaments that holler at you one minute for a scratch behind the ears, then hiss at you the next. Hell, if one of them happened to stick a paw in a light socket tomorrow, I wouldn't —"

"Walter?" Ida pushed open the screen door. "Could you give me a hand? I put those dishes in a box on the top shelf of the pantry. I'm not sure how I even got them up there in the first place."

He raised a hand. "Coming." Then he approached the car, his steps slow, like he was trying his darnedest to delay the inevitability of our departure. Reaching into the front seat, he ruffled the top of Tara's head, messing up her carefully brushed ponytail. She hated that and he knew it. But she laughed anyway and told him she'd be back next weekend for a few games of cribbage.

Not to be ignored, Bump stretched his neck through the window, and Dad gave him a good long scratch. A groan of satisfaction emanated from the dog's maned throat. Dad stroked Bump's cheek lovingly. This was hard for him — Dad, not the dog. As far as Bump knew, we were just going for a ride to the park. Although Bump had grown used to the daily games of ball and the evenings spent lazing next to Dad as he watched his favorite TV shows, he would adjust.

But the move, the separation … it was different for my dad. The permanence of it showed on my dad's face. The realization was sinking in that this mutt, who'd been more trouble than joy at times, was no longer going to be an everyday fixture in his life.

He was trading the love of a dog, Bump, for the love of a woman, Ida. It was a hard choice, but the right one.

Shaking himself from his melancholy, Dad cleared his throat and walked back to me. "I suppose you want advance notice before we drop by for a visit?"

"Well … yes, that would be nice."

"Fine. We're coming Friday for dinner. That'll give you some time to settle in. Whatever you can fix is good. I'm not picky, but I can't speak for Ida. And I'll bring the crate in my truck. Russ Armentrout said he'd have me a new key for it by tomorrow."

"I thought you and Russ weren't speaking."

"Worms shouldn't cost an arm and a leg, Samantha. Next time, I'm digging up my own. But" — he glanced off into the distance, his voice sinking — "I *may* have apologized to him."

"You did what?"

"I need someplace to buy my hardware, don't I? A man can waste a lot of gas driving to Fullbright all the dang time. Besides, how else am I supposed to get new keys? No chance of finding the old ones. I was up there" — he hooked a thumb toward the top of the hill, where the ashen remains of his home sat — "while you were out and about this morning. Couldn't find the damn things, so Ida drove me into town and Russ and I got things straightened out."

"You mean Ida *made* you apologize, so you could get a new truck key and drive yourself around?"

He shrugged again. "Something like that."

Yeah, Ida was perfect for him.

"Walt, please?" Ida stuck her head out the door again. "It'll only take a moment."

"I'm coming!"

"Eventually, I suppose you will. But you said that five minutes ago."

"Thirty seconds, all right?"

She shook her head and disappeared inside.

The moment she was out of sight, Dad shuffled over to the garden shed and disappeared inside. Half a minute later, he came out with an old cardboard box. He held it out to me. "Here."

The sight of it sent a pang of bitterness through my chest. I knew he'd set it aside somewhere, but I'd avoided asking him about it because I didn't want to know. Out of sight, out of mind.

He thrust it closer, tilted it so I could see inside. The handwriting on the letters was formed with graceful loops and twists. The envelopes had yellowed with the years and had the creases of having been opened and carried around many times. The stamps were distinctively French. They were the letters my mom had written to him after she'd left us.

"While you were laid up in the hospital after Jake Taylor whaled on you, I took these out of your car so Ida and Tara wouldn't find them. At first, I figured maybe you'd already been through them, but when I looked again I could tell they hadn't been touched. Then you came home and I kept thinking you'd ask where they went, but you never did." When I still didn't take the box, he shook it. "Sam, I know you're still mad at your mother for leaving us, but I think you need to read these. They could change what you think about her. And me."

"For better ... or for worse?"

"That's up to you, I suppose." He pushed it at me again, like it was kryptonite and he couldn't bear its presence any longer. "You don't need to open them now. Just ... soon, okay? There are things in there you should know about. Promise you'll read them."

Reluctantly, I took the box.

I really, really, *really* didn't want to. Mom had left him for another man. Then, she'd died. Sure, I'd been mad at her. Mad as hell. Madder still that Dad hadn't always been the father I needed. It had taken me until a couple of months ago to understand that he'd had issues of his own to deal with.

Ultimately, it had all turned out okay. He and I no longer butted heads like two mountain goats sparring for dominance. It certainly wasn't all unicorns and rainbows, though. Most of the time it was still pretty bumpy. But, there were moments we were comfortable in each other's company. Moments in which he surprised me, when I glimpsed a softer side of him. Seeing him with Bump and Tara was the reason for much of that.

As I slid the box in the back of the car, Tara looked over her shoulder briefly at me from the front passenger seat. I smiled and she turned back around. I took out a letter, flipped it over in my hand, my thumb tracing the seam of the envelope. I wasn't sure I wanted anything to change between Dad and me. The way things were now ... they were so much better than I'd ever believed they'd be. Why screw with that?

The seam popped. Its edge sliced into the meat of my thumb and I winced, dropping the letter back into the box. Blood welled in a thin red line. I tipped my thumb sideways. At the end of the cut, a glimmering bead formed. I took a tissue from my pocket and pressed it to the cut, then shut the back hatch of the car.

As I turned around, Dad placed his hand on my shoulder. "Sam, promise me ... please?"

I nodded. Not because I wanted to know. I didn't. But because it meant something to him.

Whatever was in those letters, I only hoped our relationship would survive it.

Because lately, stability was the one thing that was sorely lacking in my life. I sure as hell didn't need any more excitement.

chapter 12

THERE WERE ADJUSTMENTS TO make after moving from the relative isolation of the country to a small-town neighborhood. So far, the only advantage I could see to our new location was that we were a mere five minutes from Garber's Groceries and less than two from the gas station convenience store, which was handy if you had a sudden craving for a candy bar or needed a six-pack of beer at 11 p.m. Every time I cursed at a noisy muffler or a child squealing in play, I reminded myself that Tara and I didn't have to share living quarters with anyone. There were no cats to tickle Bump's prey drive, no Ida to vacuum after us as crumbs exploded from our newly opened potato chip bags, no Dad in his plaid boxers and tatty old bathrobe to read the morning paper to us.

Yet hourly, I questioned whether my newfound independence was what I actually wanted.

The box of letters from Mom went unopened. I stashed it inside my bedroom closet, under some spare sheets and blankets that Ida had bought me as a housewarming present. I vowed to read them when life settled down. Eventually.

After three days of Bump alerting me to every little sound, I'd gone hoarse from yelling at him to stop. I'd even tried locking the dog door, but all he'd done was stare at it, whining until I let him out. Halfway through today, I'd lost the urge to correct him. The neighborhood, I learned too late, was full of barking dogs. No one seemed to pay any attention to them. So I joined the ranks of the oblivious, stuck my noise-cancelling headphones on, and cranked my music while I worked diligently at the computer.

I had just reunited my hero and heroine on the page, when Bump sounded off again. So much for these headphones being 'noise-cancelling'. I ripped them off, cursing myself for not having shelled out for the brand-name set.

His bark rose in volume and frequency. Dang it, I couldn't think with that commotion. I wanted to find out whether or not my characters, Felicity and Alexander, were going to stay together for good, because I honestly didn't know. I'd scrapped my outline four times this week alone.

Bump's barking had a different tone to it than usual. More I-want-to-lick-you-all-over, less I-want-to-devour-you-my-furry-tailed-rodent-nemesis. Before I could even glance at the clock to check the time, Bump burst through the doggie door behind me and raced to the front door. He skidded to a halt six feet away, the welcome mat folding up beneath him like an accordion. With all the intensity of a chess champion about to make his triumphant move, he stared at the doorknob, his tail thumping excitedly.

Tara was home. At least there was one bright spot to this day.

"Sooo?" I intercepted her at the front door. It was Friday afternoon, a full five days into attending Wilton Memorial for her. Today was her first day riding the bus and I wanted to make sure no one had bullied her and that she hadn't been totally ostracized for being the new kid. We'd been so busy getting settled in the new place — and me catching up on my work now that I finally had peace and privacy — that we hadn't really had a chance to talk yet.

Tara trudged past me, dropping her book bag by the coffee table before she tumbled headfirst onto the couch.

I plucked off the cushion covering her head to tuck a strand of hair behind her ear to make sure she heard me. "Tell me about your first few days at the new school. Well, new to *you*, old to me."

"There's nothing to tell. They've given us way too many books, a bunch of syllabuses, and they drone at us for *hours*. Blah, blah, blah, blah." She draped an arm over her eyes dramatically. "I already can't wait to graduate from high school."

"Yeah, but then you have to go to college."

She peeked at me under her arm. "What if I don't want to go to college?"

"No problem. You don't have to go."

She perked. "I don't?"

"Suds and Grub usually has openings. Their turnover rate is pretty high. I hear the manager is a slave driver. Lucky for you. You could be a professional sandwich maker."

"Neurosurgeon it is, then. I'll be in school forever."

"Lovely. My daughter the doctor. I'm all for it. Just don't expect me to pay your med school tuition." I motioned for her to follow me into the kitchen. "Help me out, will you? Gramps and Ida will be over later for dinner. I decided beef stew would be a safe bet, but I need some help chopping the vegetables. If we work together, we can get it in the pot and cooking in half the time."

The truth of it was that I was a disaster with a knife. The less I handled sharp objects, the better. Tara got to work cutting green beans, while I artfully browned the already-cubed bits of beef.

"Do you have any classes with Shannon?"

"Three, but get this — she was sick. On the first day of school. Can you believe it? How lucky can you get?"

"That doesn't sound like fun. Is she back yet?"

"Just today." She switched from green beans to cutting up onions, her slender fingers flying over the diced rings as deftly as a concert pianist playing Chopin. She must have inherited the manual dexterity from her father.

"Any idea what she was out with?"

"Recovering from a bad case of food poisoning. The Mullinses went to the breakfast buffet at Ginny's the other day."

"I heard about that. So who did you sit with at lunch, then?"

Her face reddened. Her focus on chopping intensified. "Nobody."

"Does 'nobody' have a name?"

She shrugged, trying to look nonchalant. "Maybe."

"How cute is he, anyway? Robert Pattinson cute or Zac Efron cute?"

"What's the difference?"

"One's a steamy vampire. The other's a boy next door who sings show tunes."

"You're not even close. He's in his own league. Remember when we went to Garber's for groceries that one day when we first got here and we were in the frozen foods section talking about me becoming a vegetarian and this super hot guy with swoopy bangs and a really cute smile came down our aisle?"

"No."

"Looked like Justin Bieber?"

"Ohhhh, him." While the beef sizzled in the bottom of the pot in a fine layer of oil, I opened a can of stewed tomatoes. "No, still don't. But go on. Start with his name."

"Cooper John."

"Any relation to Police Chief Foster John?"

"That's his dad, I think."

While I couldn't say I'd gotten a favorable impression of Foster John when I first met him, at least he was on the right side of the law. "Tell me more about him."

"Uhhh, well ..." She tugged her scrunchee loose, piled her hair on top of her head, and reassembled it into a high ponytail. "He plays basketball. Center."

"So he's tall? Is he a freshman, too?"

A snort ripped from the side of her mouth. "No."

"Sophomore?" I sat down next to her with a colander full of red potatoes that I'd rinsed earlier. Carefully, I pressed the big knife through a spud, keeping my fingers well out of the way.

"Senior."

Alarm bells went off in my head. Why does a good-looking senior befriend a lonely frosh unless he's sniffing out virgin jailbait?

"He asked if I'd go to the football game with him this Friday night."

Hell no.

But if I put it that way, she'd be sure to sneak around with him behind my back. Tara was a smart girl. She was also just as stubborn as me. Devious was the flipside of clever. I had to get her to figure this out on her own somehow.

Or, I could just be a parent and do the unpopular thing.

"That would constitute a date. You're not old enough to date."

"Say what?! You never said I couldn't —"

"New rule."

"Since when?"

"Since today." I slid the potato aside and started on a second one. I hacked it in half with one blow.

"Just because a boy asked me out? Exactly what would we do with ten thousand people there?"

"It's Wilton, pumpkin. There aren't ten thousand people in the whole town. Besides, the football team was 0 and 10 last year. Pretty sure the only people in the stands are the parents with kids on the team or in the band. Besides, those are the same bleachers as when I was a student there. Plenty of dark places." Not to mention the cornfield behind the concession stand, but I wasn't about to let her in on that.

"Mom, really. Do you think I'm that kind of girl? Anyway, if you have a problem with him picking me up in his Corvette, I could just —"

"Corvette? What high school student drives a Corvette?"

"It's an older one. And he fixed it up himself. Worked a summer job repairing cars to buy his own parts. He's not some spoiled brat."

Okay, so he had redeeming qualities. Still, it was a no-go from me. Tara was still my little girl, my pumpkin, and I wasn't comfortable with the age difference.

"I was going to say," Tara went on, "that I can go with Shannon and meet him there. Cooper and I were just going to sit together, watch the game, and chat. How is that any different from me talking to him at school? Are you going to forbid me from doing that, too? Maybe you could attach a GoPro camera to my headband and livestream my social interactions to your laptop."

She wasn't making this easy on me, but I had to stand firm. "You have to be sixteen to date."

I figured that would put the kibosh on this relationship. He'd be graduated and off to college, hooking up with some swinging sorority girl, before she'd be allowed to go on a one-on-one date. I contemplated adding that she had to have a chaperone until she was eighteen. Or was married, maybe. Just like in the early 1900s. They had their reasons back then.

"Sixteen?" Her face twisted into an ugly scowl. "That's cruel. Even Shannon has been on movie dates with her boyfriend."

"Shannon has a boyfriend?"

"She's had several, for your information. And you know what? She's *still* a virgin." She tried hard to hide her eye roll, but the surly sigh gave it away.

"I should hope so."

"So why do you think I'd be any different? It's not like you found

146

me reading *Fifty Shades of Grey* under the covers with my flashlight."

"Honey, I'm just trying to protect you. It's not you I'm worried about. Think about it. He's a seventeen-year-old boy, maybe eighteen. A senior. His hormones are almost at their peak. Senior boys don't get with freshman girls unless they want something."

"Meaning sex."

"Frankly, yes."

"Why don't you just fit me for a chastity belt, then?"

"Excuse me?"

"Nothing." Tara started on the parsnips, slicing them ruthlessly. I contemplated taking the knife away before she started whittling away at her fingers and bleeding into the pot just to spite me. Bump nudged her knee and she tossed him a small pile of vegetable pieces. He snarfed them down in three breaths and begged for more. How convenient. An ecologically friendly garbage disposal that didn't require electricity. I could scoop his poop later and fertilize the flowers.

Meanwhile, Tara's hands were busy — and so was her mind. She was stewing underneath. I let her. When she had a teenage daughter of her own someday, she'd understand.

After she was done grating, she picked up the cutting knife and started whacking the tops off more carrots like she was beheading royalty during the French Revolution. "Know what? I'm not stupid that way, but I was stupid to even mention it to you. Here I thought I'd be honest with you. A boy asked me out. A *boy*. That's never happened before. No guy has ever paid attention to me. At my last school, I was pretty sure I had cooties, they all stayed so far away from me. So this week I started at a new school and when a guy actually wanted to spend more time with me, I was over the moon and I thought …" — she choked up the tiniest bit, but Tara wasn't one to cry — "I thought maybe you'd be excited for me."

I wanted to be, but I always thought she'd play hard to get, then

147

pass notes with some shy boy in her class for a few weeks before inviting him over. Take things slowly, the way Kyle and I had. Not fall all over herself when the first slick-talker flattered her with attention.

Shaking her head, she scoffed. "I could have just gone to the game with Shannon and met him anyway. I should never have told you anything."

That hurt. She was my baby. All I wanted was to keep her safe. But I also didn't want to be so authoritarian that I drove a wedge between us. Somehow, I had to salvage this before she stormed off in a silent huff and never spoke to me again. The only way to do that was to allow her some freedom to make choices all on her own.

"All right, we'll compromise. I can't stop you from sitting with him and talking to him if he's there. Just ... be careful. Don't let him do anything that makes you uncomfortable just to make him like you, okay? I can drop you and Shannon off at the game —"

"Shannon's mom is taking us there."

"All right, I'll pick you up right afterward. If he isn't comfortable with me setting limits, then you're probably not going to be easy enough game for him. Got it?"

For a dreadfully long minute she didn't speak, just stared at the cutting board as she brutally sliced the carrots. Finally, she shoved the carrots aside and mumbled, "Fine. But you're not allowed to spy on me, got it? You have to trust me. At least a little."

"Does this mean you're not going to let me attach the video camera?"

"Not a chance."

"All right. Go to the game. Call me halfway through the fourth quarter. I'll be at the gate to pick you up when the clock runs out."

She gave me the death glare. "Can you *please* wait in the car?"

"I'll give you five minutes. You don't want me to come looking for you. Because I'll make sure everyone knows that Tara McNamee's crazy stalker-mom is on the hunt."

148

"You would, wouldn't you?"

A potato cube in one hand, I waggled the butcher knife I was holding in the other. "Tara, I'd go to the ends of the earth to save you."

Bump bounced over to me and sat obediently, his gaze locked pleadingly on the potato. I tossed it and he snapped it out of the air, swallowed it whole, and woofed at me. "Yeah, you, too, you big goofy mutt."

DAD AND IDA ARRIVED on time. No doubt a compromise between my dad's perpetual tardiness and Ida's usual fifteen minutes early. Dad was hugging a casserole dish to his chest. Ida elbowed him and he offered it to me.

"What's this?" I lifted the tea towel from the top to see rows of pecans coated in a crispy layer of brown sugar.

"My sweet potato casserole," Ida beamed. "I usually reserve it for Thanksgiving, but since this is your housewarming it seemed like a special enough occasion."

I hadn't realized that this dinner was an 'occasion', but I accepted her gift graciously. Besides, it was better than the vanilla ice cream with off-brand chocolate sauce I had planned for dessert.

Amazingly, dinner was uneventful. The stew had turned out surprisingly well, due to Tara's last-minute addition of several spices, and Ida's casserole disappeared like tuna chum in a shark tank at feeding time. Tara cleared the table just in time for Shannon's mom to pull up in the driveway to take them to the football game.

Dad warned Tara about the dangers of too much concession stand food and pounded her on the shoulder. As soon as Judy Mullins's car left, he moved to his usual spot in front of the TV. Meanwhile, Ida joined me in Tara's room, which I was starting to prep for a new paint job. We began by removing the macramé owls, needlepoint forest animals, and framed mushroom string art from the walls. Melissa had taken her retro decorating very seriously. After that, we taped off the trim and pulled furniture into the middle of the room. With Ida to talk to, the work went quickly and an hour passed without it seeming like work at all. She told me all about the gossipmongering in the Lions' Club and the shallow altruism of the Purple Hat Sisterhood.

"They aren't all like that, but I think quite a few of them volunteer just to make social connections for their husbands' businesses. You'd be surprised how many deals are hatched while a bunch of old ladies are picking up trash at the side of the road."

"I don't doubt it. But as long as good things get accomplished, does it really matter?"

"No, I suppose not. You have to wonder, though, if they'd be there at all without the opportunities to pad their retirement savings."

My phone chimed with a text. I taped off the last window and handed the roll to Ida, then checked the message. It was from Archer.

Sam, I think Tara is ready to come home. Don't worry. She's fine.

Obviously not, if Archer had to text me.

"Is that Tara?" Ida asked.

"Uh ..." I didn't want to say anything that Ida might relay to Dad that would send up an alarm. Who knew how he'd react? "Sounds like she's bored already. Never did like football. I'm going to pick her up early."

Ida frowned. "Oh, that's too bad. It can't even be halftime."

"What's too bad?" Dad said from the doorway. Bump's slobbery ball was clenched in his right hand.

"Where's the dog, Dad?"

"Getting a drink. Now what's too bad?"

"I have to pick Tara up now."

"Heh. I hear they were playing Oil City tonight. Last year's regional champs. Refs probably called the game on account of the mercy rule."

Ida's forehead creased. "What's that?"

Before he could get started, I exited the room and headed for the kitchen, where I'd left my keys, hoping to ditch Dad before he launched into a the-trouble-with-young-people-today tirade. But he was close on my heels, Ida right behind him.

"Says that if one team is up by fifty points at halftime, they call the game early. Wouldn't want anyone's feelings to get hurt. Kids today don't know how to lose. Everyone gets a trophy just for showing up. In my day, if a better team kicked your ass a hundred to nothing, you took it like a man. Stuff like that builds character. Prepares you for real life."

Secretly, I agreed with him. But if I even so much as nodded, he'd go on for half an hour about it.

They filed in behind me into the tiny galley kitchen. I stepped over Bump and grabbed my keys off the counter, then turned around to face them.

"But you know what kids today are better at?" Dad pointed a finger at me. He was going to tell me whether I answered him or not. "Everything."

There was a catch to this. Had to be. "Everything?"

"Yeah, everything. That kid of yours, Sam, is smarter at fourteen than I was at forty."

Clearly, an alien had taken over my father's body. With luck, he'd stay for a while.

chapter 13

THE FRANTIC PACE OF my heart hurried me. I didn't even bother checking my speed, just put the pedal to the metal and flew to the high school in record time. I kept glancing in my rearview mirror, expecting to see flashing lights, but they never appeared. I'd tried calling Archer back before I left the house, but he hadn't answered. Tara hadn't either. Which only worried me more, despite Archer's insistence that Tara was okay.

As expected, the parking lot was half-empty when I got to the high school. What I didn't expect were the three sheriff's cars parked at the end of the school closest to the athletic stadium.

I pulled into a parking spot and got out. Two sheriff's deputies were leaning against the trunk of one of their cars. One of them was the female deputy I'd seen twice now. They exchanged a few words, and the pot-bellied male deputy drifted over to another cruiser. In the back were two teenage girls, probably upperclassmen. A bit on the surly-looking side, but not the sort you'd cross the street to get away from.

Torn between hunting Tara down and figuring out what was going on, I decided to approach the deputies first. If Archer was keeping an eye on Tara, she was safe for the moment.

"Hello." I waved meekly as I met the female deputy's eyes. Run-ins with the police usually made me nervous — not that I'd ever broken the law. Not intentionally, at least. Except for speeding on the way here. And that one time I was daydreaming a plot for my first series and ran a stop sign, but it was 7 a.m. and it was just the sign at the end of our cul-de-sac in Naperville, not a major intersection, and the only person out on the streets was a jogger in a red velour sweatsuit half a block down. That woman was the one who ought to have been arrested for a fashion crime. Oh, and that time I'd lied to get out of jury duty. Come to think of it, I'd also forgotten to buy a dog license.

The deputy flashed me a smile. "Hello, ma'am. Can I help you?"

I bristled inwardly. Was there a certain age at which you went from being called 'miss' to 'ma'am'? It had such a ... *matronly* ring to it. So spinster-like.

I stuck my hand out. "Sam McNamee. I'm new in town. Well, not *new* new. I grew up here. Just moved back this summer. I went to college in Chicago and stayed for a job there. About fifteen years ago. Publishing. I used to proofread. Mostly romance, but a little of everything, really."

Shut. Up. I pinched my lower lip between my teeth to stop the words from spilling out. Why did I always over explain when I was nervous?

"Welcome back to Wilton, then. Deputy Carin Eklund. That's Carin with a 'C' and an 'I'." Her handshake was surprisingly firm for someone so petite. Barely taller than Ida, she had natural platinum blond hair that would have made Marilyn Monroe jealous, and she looked fresh out of cop school. "Not that you'd ever need to spell it. I suppose I just say that out of habit."

The male deputy opened the back door to the other cruiser and spoke to the kids in back.

"What's going on?" I asked.

"Smoking in the janitor's closet." Arms crossed, she shook her head. "And I'm not talking cigarettes, either."

"Ohhh." It made me think of the field behind Ida's house. Regret filled me. I wished I'd called Sheriff Driscoll last weekend when I thought I heard someone out there. Then again, even getting that crop before the growers took it down probably wouldn't have made a difference in this case. "Just those two girls?" Because I sure hoped Tara wasn't sitting in the back of the third cruiser.

"Just them. Some freshman ratted on them — after she propped a chair under the doorknob and fetched a teacher, who called us."

Now *that* sounded like my daughter.

"Would said rat happen to be Tara McNamee?"

"You must be her mom."

I nodded. Deputy Eklund pointed to an area just outside the chain-link fence surrounding the stadium. Two shadowy figures, one in a law enforcement uniform, hovered over two younger ones. I thanked her and started that way, then turned back. This was my chance to glean something from an officer of the law.

"You wouldn't happen to know anything about how Miley Harper died, would you? She lived in my neighborhood."

Pushing herself away from the cruiser, Deputy Eklund scrutinized me with newfound intensity. "Did you ... know her?"

"I'd only met her once. She seemed really nice."

"Don't they all?" Deputy Eklund curled her finger at me. I moved closer. "Why do you want to know?"

"I'm just ..." — I looked over my left shoulder, then my right — "concerned for my daughter. I moved us back here thinking we were getting away from the gangs and drive-by shootings that go on in Chicago every day."

We'd actually lived in middle-class Naperville, but Chicago usually conjured images of mobsters, ghettos, and traffic jams for folks around here. So much more dramatic.

"She was murdered, that much we know. Someone tried to make it look like a drug overdose, but the autopsy revealed suffocation."

So, my intuition had been right after all. "How?"

"Pillow, probably. There were signs of a struggle."

"Any leads on who could've done it?"

"Unfortunately, no. They took her boyfriend, Leroy Roberds, in for questioning and wanted to book him, but he had a bulletproof alibi. He works second shift at the broom factory. His shift manager confirmed he was working overtime."

No lie — Wilton had a broom factory: Brockman-Morton Brooms. It probably employed all of forty people. In reality, they made mops and long-handled dusters, too, but everyone knew it by its original purpose.

"Why did they take him in, then?"

"Jake Taylor swears up and down that Miley had told him more than once that Leroy threatened her. But then, this all didn't come out until —" She stopped herself midsentence. "You know, I shouldn't be discussing this with you. It's still under investigation. If anyone asks, you didn't hear it from me."

"Don't worry." I pretend-zipped my lips. "I won't tell a soul."

But I *would* talk to Jake Taylor again. I didn't need a murderer floating around my neighborhood, and I had a very strong hunch he knew more than he was letting on.

I would have loved to get more out of her, but that was plenty for now. I thanked her and went off to collect my daughter. A hundred feet away, a figure moved into the reach of an overhead light. It was Archer. He spotted me right away and came toward me.

"Next time give me a little more detail, will you?" I told him, my irritation evident. "I was imagining all sorts of terrible scenarios."

Sitting on a concrete parking block behind him, Tara glanced my way. She quickly lowered her eyes and pulled her knees to her chest. Shannon was beside her, looking like she had never been more mortified. Tom and Judy Mullins weren't going to like hearing about this, even if Shannon hadn't gotten in trouble. The deputy was asking them questions, jotting the answers down in a little notebook.

Archer grinned sheepishly. "Sorry. I was about to call you, but she was a little … hysterical. It seemed more important to take care of her."

"Thanks, Archer. I owe you. Again."

"Hey, it was nothing special. I'm a firefighter, remember. I save people all the time." His fingers brushed at a wisp of hair that had fallen across my cheek. All my worries melted away at his touch. I closed my eyes and instinctively turned my face toward his palm. But just like that, he drew his hand away. And with it went my tranquility.

I met Tara's eyes. Mascara was smudged beneath her lower lids, making her appear more like a frazzled raccoon than a blossoming young woman. She looked angry and lost and confused all at once.

I'd wanted so badly for her transition to Wilton Memorial to go well. Or at least not terribly. Not like this. Her first high school football game, her first police interrogation.

"Deputy Eklund told me Tara discovered a couple of upperclassmen smoking weed in the janitor's closet and locked them in, then went to get a teacher. Anything else I should know?"

"That's about all I know, too."

There had to be something more. I'd pry it out of Tara with a crowbar if I had to.

"What was she being hysterical about, then?"

"To be honest, it didn't make much sense." Archer scratched at the scruff on his neck. If Clint could pose as a model for *Fitness* magazine, Archer was the poster boy for *Field and Stream*. The more unshaven and ruggedly dressed he was, the better he looked. But in that guy-next-door kind of way. Like the neighbor you'd keep peeking at when he was out washing his car bare-chested. You knew you shouldn't be staring, but you couldn't help yourself. He patted at his face, then ran his hands over his hair. "Do I have tape on me or something?"

"Huh?" I blinked half a dozen times before finally realizing I *had* been staring. "Sorry, my mind wandered for a moment there. Do you come here every Friday?"

"When I'm not on shift and it's a home game. Some of the guys from the department and I volunteer as athletic trainers once a month. Tonight we had an extra helper, so I begged off early when I found out Tara and her friend needed help. At any rate, we make sure nobody has a concussion, ice knees, tape ankles ... stuff like that. I've been known to stick excess tape on my shirt."

Cheers erupted from the visitors' stands. The home crowd groaned collectively. Drumsticks slapped against drumheads and trumpets blared as the Marching Oilers struck up a celebratory song. Maroon and silver pompoms shook to the rhythm. One of their cheerleaders did a tumbling run that must have included a dozen backflips, and the Oil City crowd cheered again. The scoreboard flashed a new set of numbers: 63–7. The Wilton Memorial Fighting Mapleleafs weren't putting up much of a fight.

"Anyway," Archer continued, "the only thing I could get out of Tara was what a jerk he was. Whoever 'he' is."

I had a good idea.

The deputy talking to Shannon placed his foot on the bumper of a car and propped an elbow on his knee. He leaned forward to hear Shannon above the roar of the crowd. She was very soft-spoken to begin with. Some might have mistaken that trait for shyness, but she'd never seemed that way to me. As the deputy continued to question her, she nodded several times and gestured toward the school building.

"Deputy Eklund told me they took Miley's fiancé in for questioning," I said.

"Leroy? That's the last person I'd expect to be a suspect. He was pretty torn up about Miley. Besides, he's the son of the Humboldt

157

Brethren Evangelical Sanctuary of Worship's preacher."

"And was this Leroy living with Miley?"

"Technically, no. But let's just say he spent a lot of nights there. Leroy will probably be at the picnic Sunday. I'll ..." He faltered momentarily, probably remembering suddenly that I'd be there with Clint. "I'll talk to him then. By the way, hope you don't mind, but while we were waiting for you to get here, I asked the girls if they'd mind manning the dessert table at the charity picnic. We're always scrambling for help at the last minute."

"Sure, that's fine. I'll let Shannon's mom know." I wouldn't want to ask Clint if my teenage daughter could come along on our date, so I'd arrange to meet him there. First, I'd have to tell Tara that Clint and I were seeing each other. Why did I keep putting that off?

He shifted to the right to get a clear view of the scoreboard. "Hey, uh, I kind of abandoned a friend, so I'm going to go look for 'em. See you Sunday."

Before I could ask who his friend was or even say goodbye, the deputy was coming toward me. He was an older gentleman, late sixties if I had to guess, with that grandfatherly portliness and huggability factor that my own dad lacked. He nodded at me.

"You Shannon's mom — or Tara's?"

"Tara's."

"I'm Deputy Strewing. You're free to take them home. Unless, of course, they want to stay until the game's over."

Another explosion of cheers went up on the Oilers' side. They'd intercepted Wilton's first pass of the possession. "Probably not. So, you have everything you need from them?"

I searched through a line of people slipping past the stadium fencing — Wilton Memorial 'fans' eager to exit the parking lot before the final dismal countdown — but everywhere I looked there was no Archer. I'd simply turned around and he'd left.

"Yep, pretty cut and dried. If we had more kids like them, this school would be drug-free." He cuffed my arm hard enough to send me sideways a step. Thankfully to the side of my good foot. He smelled of Armor All and banana bread. Crumbs dotted his shirt just above his badge. "You should be proud of those kids."

"Thanks. I am." But Tara didn't look so proud of herself. Judging by the scowl on her face, she was set to scratch someone's eyes out.

Gravel crunched under my borrowed flip-flops. The swelling had gone down enough by now that by tomorrow I figured I could wear my regular shoes. Which was a good thing, because it was getting chilly at night, like now, and my toes were cold. I stopped a couple feet in front of Tara. She kept her eyes down, but Shannon gave me a weak smile and a little wave.

"Hey, Shannon," I said.

"Hi, Ms. McNamee. Are you going to take us home now?"

"Sure. You look like you're ready to go."

Shannon nodded emphatically and jumped up. "Let's go, Tara."

Just as I turned to go, I saw Archer across the parking lot. He opened the passenger-side door of his truck and a tall, leggy blonde with a vaguely familiar silhouette stepped up on the running board and inside. Archer got in on the other side and started the engine. The window on the passenger's side lowered, and just as the truck pulled into the line of cars exiting the parking lot I caught a very clear glimpse of the passenger. She pulled a few bobby pins from her hair and it tumbled down onto her shoulders in flaxen waves.

What was Danielle Townsley doing in Archer Malone's truck? She was the last person on earth I'd ever expected to see him with.

Heat fanned from my chest up to my face. Was I having a flare of jealousy — or was it a perimenopausal hot flash?

I jerked my gaze away and marched toward my car. Tara trudged through the parking lot behind us like she was being towed through deep snow. I was sure at any moment she was going to kick a tire so hard she'd totally deflate it, but somehow we made it to the car and all the way back to Shannon's house to drop her off without a meltdown.

Tara and I sat in the Mullinses' driveway for a few minutes in silence. I turned to Tara, but she had her forehead pressed against the passenger-side window, her breath fogging up the glass.

"You did the right thing, honey," I told her. "I know it doesn't seem like it, but —"

"You were right, okay?"

I knew what she meant, but I wanted her to say it out loud. "About what?"

"About ... *him*."

She spat the word 'him' out like I'd just shoved a bar of lye soap in her mouth. "Care to elaborate?"

"Not really," she grumbled.

Humble pie has a nasty taste to it. But I hated that I'd spooned it out to my daughter. Even worse, I hated that she'd had to learn that lesson at all.

I put the car in reverse and backed out, then headed down the lane. "Well, if you ever do want to talk, you always know you can tell me anything. And I promise not to say 'I told you so'."

The miles slipped by in darkness. The only sound was the *whoosh* of an occasional passing car and the sharp exhalation of Tara's breath through pinched nostrils. Like she was trying to get something off her chest, but didn't know how.

Finally, I couldn't stand it any longer. "Does what happened with those girls have anything to do with Cooper John?"

Her lips tightened. "Maybe."

"Tell me."

She slid her hands down her thighs, pressing hard against the stuff denim of her jeans. "He said I was being 'uptight' and told me I needed to check out the janitor's closet inside the building. I wasn't going to, but I figured I'd just see what he was talking about. So I made an excuse to get some popcorn and slipped out behind the concession stand. When I got to the building, the back door to the hallway where the janitor's closet is was propped open with a rock. Those two girls were there. In the closet. I could smell it: the marijuana. One of them must've heard me open the door, because she poked her head out of the closet. Then the other one came out. They were giggling. Like something about me was hilarious. They offered me a joint. Told me it was free, because they just wanted to be friends and I looked like I needed one. I asked them if they had enough for Shannon. They said 'sure' and went back inside the closet to wait while I went to get her." She slipped me a glance just as a pair of headlights coming from ahead lit her face, teenage angst revealed in the tiny furrow between her brows.

If she'd stopped there and if I hadn't known my daughter, I would've thought she had seriously considered their offer. But Tara was born forty. Even when she was an infant, she'd been an old soul who came with a staunch opinion of everything and a fierce determination to have her way.

"What happened then?" I asked.

Her cheeks bunched with a smug grin. "That was when I jammed the chair under the doorknob. They started pounding on the door, but I ran to get Shannon. She told me our homeroom teacher was in the ticket stand. He's the one who got the deputy who was directing traffic. The deputy got there just as those two girls — Dixie and LeAnne, I think — were trying to crawl out over the transom. The whole thing blew up from there. Pretty soon there were more cops and lots of kids standing around ..."

"Including Cooper?"

"Yeah, Cooper, too." She slumped lower in her seat. "He probably hates me."

"Maybe, but who cares? He sounds like a loser, anyway. Did he know what they were doing in there?"

"I don't know. Probably. Maybe he was joking when he told me to go find them. I don't know if he meant it or not." She blew a puff of air that lifted her bangs from her forehead. "I was just so nervous. I wanted him to like me. But half the time I didn't know what to say, and I laughed when I shouldn't have and didn't laugh when I should have ... I was *completely* stupid. A ditzy moron. Like I'd had a lobotomy. I mean, why was tonight any different from talking to him at school?"

"You weren't stupid. A stupid kid would have just walked away and not told anyone. An ever stupider kid would have taken the joint to impress him. And I'm happy to say I didn't raise a stupid kid. At least give *me* some credit, will you?" We pulled into our new driveway, which was all of fifty feet long and ended in a single-car garage that needed a good scraping and a fresh coat of paint. Funny how the longer we were here, the more I noticed what needed to be updated or repaired.

Bump barked like a proper guard dog from the backyard.

A smile cracked Tara's mouth. "I suppose doing neurosurgery would be rough if I was high."

"I suppose so." I leaned across the seats and kissed the top of her head, just like I used to do when she was little. "Do you know how much I love you?"

Smiling wider to show me those pearly whites that I'd sacrificed a few vacations to Maui for, she shook her head.

I opened my arms as far as I could, stretching them from the dashboard to the backseat. "Thiiiiiis much."

"I love you, too, Mom."

And she wrapped her arms around me and hugged me so tight that for a few seconds I couldn't inhale.

chapter 14

AMAZINGLY, THE PARKING LOT of the Humboldt Brethren Evangelical Sanctuary of Worship was empty, except for one car and the church bus. This Sunday afternoon, half of Humboldt County was at the Grand Beaver Lodge annual picnic. It was Wilton's version of the Country Music Awards, the Oscars, and the Presidential Inaugural Ball all rolled up in one.

A sign in front of the lodge entrance said 'Lot full'. I rolled to a stop as Russ Armentrout, the hardware store owner, ambled toward my car. He shifted his orange safety vest to straighten it and tapped on my window. It was already cracked, but I rolled it down farther. Which only encouraged Bump, who was sitting directly behind me, to shove his muzzle over my right shoulder for a better look. Steaming dog breath scalded my ear and neck. Tara had asked to bring him because she'd heard there was a dog costume contest.

"Hi, Russ. Where can I park?"

Leaning in to rest his elbows on the door, he nodded to Tara and Shannon in the backseat, before leveling me with an admonishing gaze. "There was plenty of parking an hour ago."

A car whooshed past us on the state highway, a little too close for comfort.

"Thanks, I'll remember that for next year. Now, where can I park?"

Squinting, he swung his head to the right as he scoped out the highway, then to the left. He took out a walkie-talkie and pressed the side button. It crackled so loud I thought it was going to explode. "Yeah, Hubert, any spots down that way? We've got a latecomer."

The flyer that Clint e-mailed me had said noon to 5 p.m. How was it possible to be late only an hour after it had started?

"Hold on," the voice on the other end groaned. "Let me check."

A dark blue sedan, older but well maintained, pulled up behind me. Russ took one look in the car, then jogged over to move the orange cones blocking the parking lot and waved them in.

It must've been my open-mouthed WTF look that spurred him to explain.

"That was Mr. and Mrs. Purnell. She has a heart condition."

I watched them park, then get out of their Buick. Mr. and Mrs. Purnell turned out to be Harmon and Maybelle from the neighborhood. Puffing on her cigarette, Maybelle hotfooted it over to the picnic area for the smorgasbord as Harmon ambled after her toting their cooler. Heart condition my —

"Still checking, Hubert?" Russ said.

"Yup. Hang on."

Russ crammed the walkie-talkie under his armpit and, bouncing on the balls of his feet, began to whistle a garbled rendition of "Hey, Jude". Which became tricky when he reached the chorus. Tara and Shannon shared a look. One of them giggled; the other nodded. They started to sing: *Naaa, naaa, na, na-na-na-naaaa, na-na-na-naaaa. Heeey, Jude!*

It got worse from there. Stretching his neck, Bump began to howl. Right in my ear. Russ bobbed and jerked to the lyrics. You couldn't call it dancing. It was more like an epileptic fit. A semi rumbled past, laying on the horn right as it passed us, nearly sending me into cardiac arrest. Oblivious to my near-fatal condition, Tara and Shannon raised their hands in the air, swaying in their seats. I shot them a *cease and desist* glare.

Their lousy singing faded to snorts of laughter, reminding me my daughter was still a teenager after all.

An older white sedan pulled to the exit of the parking lot Russ was guarding. He removed the cones and waved at the driver. "Have a nice day, Ms. Steinbrenner!"

It was Lorraine, one of the beauticians at Dawna's Beauty Studio. She flashed him a fake smile and pulled out, her car rumbling noisily down the road as she sped away.

I expected Russ to let me in, then, but he put the cones back.

"Can't I have her space?" I asked nicely. "Please?"

"Sorry, she was just making a delivery."

Delivery, huh? I'd remember that for next year.

One hand shading his brow, Russ surveyed the parking lot. "Will you be joining your father today?"

"Is he here?" He hadn't mentioned coming here to me. The last I knew, he'd sworn the lodge off.

Russ scowled. "He is. I've managed to avoid him myself so far."

"Gramps is here?" Tara chimed. "Oh, Shannon, remember those Beach Boys songs we were downloading? Gramps knows all the lyrics. It's amazing."

Squeals ensued, quickly followed by Shannon's mangled rendition of "I Get Around" and Tara's off-key falsetto.

"Is it a big car?" Hubert asked, his voice muffled in Russ's armpit.

Russ backed up, studied my car from bumper to bumper. "What would you call 'big', Hubert? It's certainly not one of those itty-bitty Smart Cars. Big, big like a monster truck? Or just kinda big like a Cadillac?"

"Ah, hell, Russ. Just tell me what kind of car it is."

Scuttling around to the back of the car, Russ bent over to read the make and model. "Says here: Sub-ah-roo For-rest-errr." He sounded the syllables out like he'd never seen the words before. Which I was pretty sure he hadn't. This was the land of Chevy, Ford, and the occasional GMC or Jeep.

"I have no idea what that is, Russ." That made two of them. "Must be Japanese. What's the closest American car you can think of?"

All this for a parking spot.

They went back and forth for another minute while Russ rested his bum on the hood. Finally, I honked at him. He jumped about three feet, then gyrated around.

"Just tell me where he is," I said. "If it doesn't fit, we'll hike."

He motioned across the road like he was signaling an airplane into its gate. About a hundred yards north in a grassy field was Hubert, his walkie-talkie glued to his ear as he sat on the tailgate of a black pickup, sipping a can of beer. More cars whooshed by at sixty miles an hour.

"Girls, you can hop out here," I told them. "Find Archer Malone and let him know you're here. We'll eat first. You can do dessert duty after that. Tara, hang onto the dog. Don't let him help himself to anyone's plate, okay?"

They piled out of the car, each balancing a casserole dish atop a small cooler, and tromped across the parking lot, Bump bouncing between them. Russ waved cheerfully as I pulled away. I was tempted to run him over, but figured there were too many witnesses.

I drove down the road nearly half a mile before I found a tractor lane leading into a soybean field to turn around in. But I couldn't pull back out right away. The traffic was so heavy on Route 379 that I sat idling for five minutes as I watched the fuel gauge dip quickly, like the gas tank had suddenly been punctured, until it went as low as I'd ever seen it. We'd left the house late because Bump had ingested a bottle cap. Three tablespoons of hydrogen peroxide later, he'd puked it up whole. I hadn't thought to stop for gas.

Come to think of it, I could've sworn I filled the tank not two days ago — and I hadn't been anywhere since but Tara's school once. Something had to be wrong with the gauge.

Finally, a gap opened up in the traffic flow. I gunned it. My trusty Forester roared with the gush of fossil fuel. The speedometer rose steadily, topping out at forty-five miles per hour. But no matter how hard I punched the accelerator, it just wouldn't go any faster. In fact, it almost felt like I was *de*celerating. A quick check of the speedometer confirmed it.

The car lurched. And not forward. The engine gasped, sputtered. It was like freefalling horizontally.

I'd lost all control of my speed. The parking field was still a quarter mile away. Concrete barriers crowded the shoulder as the state highway passed over a drainage swale. Panic compressed my ribs. In my rearview mirror, I glimpsed a semi bearing down on my tail end. The driver blared the horn, which was about as effective as shouting at an old lady in a wheelchair to speed up.

Think, Sam, think.

I could smash the car into the barrier. Not an option. I only had collision insurance on this old wreck. I could swerve into oncoming traffic and pray it parted like the Red Sea. No, that might set me up for vehicular manslaughter. Either might kill me. Then Tara would be an orphan. No can do.

I sure as hell couldn't speed up.

Where was a damn wormhole when I needed one?

I flicked on my hazard lights. And prayed. Or took the Lord's name in vain. I'm not sure which. Everything was moving so fast. Except my car.

The Subaru rolled past the end of the guard rail attached to the barrier. I yanked the steering wheel to the right. The front end dipped, plunging the car into the ditch. The wheels bounced hard, jerking my hands so the wheels craned left. I flopped around like a rag doll

167

tethered by a shoestring. Momentum carried my car up and back toward the highway.

Oh, shi—!

The semi's horn blasted: two short, one long. Its trailer whizzed past, eighteen giant wheels spinning madly. A line of cars on the other side blurred by. My front wheels hit deep gravel. Which turned out to be a blessing.

The car slowed. I corrected its trajectory — a diagonal aimed across the highway — to ease onto the right-hand shoulder and carefully tapped on the brake. The airbag mushroomed before me, punching me in the face and pushing against my stomach and chest.

Somehow, I managed to lift my head up enough to finally breathe. Because during that whole harrowing event, I'd forgotten to.

My car door swung open. Hubert stood in the opening, panting, his triple-XL gut quivering with exertion, a river of sweat cascading down his face and neck.

"Are you okay, ma'am?"

"Just dandy." After shifting the car into park, I ripped the key from the ignition and jabbed it into the airbag. It let out a gassy fart. "But don't call me ma'am."

CLINT TOOK MY FACE between his hands. "What in the heck happened to you?"

I paused while Harmon and Maybelle strolled past at snail factor negative two. Actually, Maybelle was marching like a woman on a mission, but she kept having to dawdle and nag Harmon along. He seemed to be on the alert for any reason to detach himself from his wife.

Maybelle flapped her hand in a 'hello' to Clint. The flab under her arm jiggled. Some women simply shouldn't go sleeveless.

"How's Spanky?" Clint asked.

"Getting his feathers back," Maybelle beamed. "Those vitamins did the trick. He's a new bird — more gorgeous than ever!"

"Good to hear, Mrs. Purnell. Good to hear."

When they were out of earshot, Clint tugged me over to the tree beneath which he'd put all his stuff. He backed me against the trunk, his arms on either side of me, trapping me. I yielded willingly as he planted a long, deep kiss on my mouth. The kind you gave someone when you hadn't seen them for months. My body wanted to respond, but in my mind sirens were going off. People were looking. Word was going to get around about our exhibitionism and pretty soon they'd all be asking when we were going to get married. We hadn't even gotten to the stage yet where I kept a toothbrush at his house.

Besides, I'd only just told Tara this morning that I was meeting Clint here today. The news had been received with a pouty, 'Oh'. Meanwhile, she kept asking when Archer was coming for dinner again. Since I'd given her a hard time about Cooper, I wasn't about to delve into her feelings regarding Clint. I wanted to give her time to get used to the idea of him being in my life. Even I needed time to get used it.

I slid from between his arms, but before I could get away, Clint encircled my waist and drew me back to him. He was persistent. And irresistible. His touch rendered me helpless. The truth was, I loved every second of it. Onlookers be damned. If they were going to talk, might as well give them something to talk about.

His tongue stroked mine, probing deep. The space between our bodies closed as he moved his hands downward to cup my ass. His hips pressed into my belly, moving in rhythm with his tongue. I had the sudden urge to drag him somewhere private and let my hormones do the talking, but this would be a bad time to disappear. I slid my hands between us, pushing back on him. "Hey, let a girl breathe, will you?"

With a suppressed groan, he released me and gave me a tame

peck on the nose. Then his fingers dug into my hair. He yanked. I yipped. He drew his hand back to reveal a piece of airbag material pinched between his fingers. "Are you going to tell me what happened?"

"I ... ran out of gas."

He flicked the scrap away and gave me a sideways look. The kind that said, 'You're not telling me everything.'

I looked around. "I think someone siphoned the gas out of my tank."

He lowered his voice conspiratorially. "Why would you say that?"

"Because two days ago I had a nearly full tank. I haven't gone anywhere since then. Just now, I ran out of gas on the highway. A Mack truck almost flattened me." I held one palm out flat and smacked it with the other one. "Just like that."

He tilted his head at me. "You sure you don't have a leak in the tank?"

"I would have smelled that, don't you think?"

"You last drove your car two days ago, right?"

"Yes."

"And have you been anywhere near it since?" The implication being that I was paranoid.

Hanging my head, I mumbled, "No." Because he was right. I hadn't so much as walked within ten feet of my car until we'd left for the picnic. It could've leaked a river and I wouldn't have known. There had to be an explanation. Yesterday, while Tara was busy painting the trim in her room for the new paint job, I'd closed the door of my new office and pounded out eight thousand words of my novel. Most of it inspired by fantasies of Clint lying naked on a certain alpaca rug. This morning I'd added twenty-five hundred more. It had taken all my self-control not to send him a booty call text. Hell, it was taking all my self-control right now not to jump his bones in public.

I crumpled onto the blanket he'd spread beneath the boughs of

170

the gnarly old oak tree. Without asking, I grabbed the plastic cup of iced tea he'd set down when I approached, and I chugged until it was empty.

Still standing, Clint gazed into the milling crowd, like he was searching for someone.

"Where are the girls, anyway?" I flipped open the lid on his picnic basket. Standard fare: potato salad, chipped ham and Swiss cheese sandwiches, light on the mayo, heavy on the iceberg lettuce, a bag of potato chips ... What, no drinks? I was dying of thirst.

Ah, brownies! I tore the Saran Wrap away and helped myself to one. I needed to medicate with chocolate. And then wash it down with beer. Why did it smell so much like beer around here? Then I saw it. Over by the lodge was a tent containing several coolers and kegs. In the front was a table with rows and rows of plastic cups and a line twenty deep of people waiting to shell out for their beverages.

So that's where the beer was. I squinted at the sign hanging over the table: WATER $1, POP AND ICED TEA $2, BEER $6. Despite the price-gouging, more people were walking away with beer than anything else. Obviously, that was how they were raising money at the lodge these days. Amazing that people would pay exponentially more just to drink alcohol socially. I preferred the cheap route of raiding the grocery store shelves and drinking in solitude. At least I used to.

Then I remembered Clint hadn't answered me. "The girls — where are they? They had two casserole dishes with them."

"Oh, sorry. They're with Walt and Ida. And don't worry about the food. I brought plenty."

"So my dad *is* here?"

"You sound surprised." He handed me a sandwich, then grabbed one for himself before sitting down next to me.

"It's just that I thought he'd sworn the lodge off." I leaned in close and winked. "Dodgy politics."

"Of course." His eyes roved over the crowd again as he bit into his sandwich and chewed. "That's why I don't belong to places like this."

That seemed like an odd thing to say, maybe even a little judgmental, but then I didn't belong to any organizations, either. I worked at home, alone, talking to imaginary people, if only because I could manipulate them to do what I wanted. No, I'd leave all the community fundraisers and social groups to people like Ida. I wondered where she was. If Dad was here, she had to be, too. There were so many people here, if I stayed off to the side, I could avoid being seen by most. My best bet was to stay on the defensive. Especially if Dylan or Virgil was lurking somewhere.

There was a lot going on today, more than I'd expected. In the area where a dozen old-growth trees provided welcome shade, families had either claimed the few available picnic tables or spread their blankets. We were on the fringe, closest to the lodge. The sun was blazing now, but a bank of mean gray clouds crouched on the western horizon. For the time being, though, everyone was having fun: young children squealed as they chased each other in a game of tag, teenage boys were playing half-court basketball, and a clutch of older women manned craft booths while their male counterparts lobbed beanbags in an intense tournament of corn-hole. A band of forty-somethings sporting scraggly beards and tie-dye Ts was playing a dreadfully long list of eighties cover songs. Badly. By the time they started on Blondie's "Heart of Glass", half-drunk picnic-goers had joined in. It sounded like a herd of cats in heat. I rifled through Clint's basket for paper napkins to stuff in my ears.

Clint waved a plate of potato salad under my nose. "My grandma's recipe. Want some?" Grinning, he nudged a spoonful against my lips.

I tasted it. Savory delight flooded my taste buds. I ate another bite. And another. When I'd cleaned my plate I held it out for more. "You're a liar, you know."

"Me?"

"Unless your grandmother is supplying Garber's deli section, this is not her recipe."

He heaped a few more spoonfuls on my plate. "Guilty as charged. But it does taste just like something she would have made. If she'd ever made potato salad."

Five minutes later, I was stuffed to the gills and lying face up on the blanket like a bloated fish. I closed my eyes and mumbled, "Tara had Bump with her, right?"

"I think so." He stretched out next to me. I couldn't see him, but I could sense his eyes on me. "But it was hard to tell with the neon-pink tutu and tiara. Is he in the witness protection program these days?"

I laughed. "That was Shannon's idea."

Curling a hand in mine, he moved the arch of his foot slowly over the outside of my calf. I stretched seductively, arching my back as I ran my tongue over my lips.

"Mmmm, don't do that, Sam."

"Do what?" Inhaling deeply, I tugged the neckline of my shirt down an inch. "This, you mean?" I slid the tip of my tongue around parted lips in a full, agonizingly slow circle.

Clint pressed a fingertip to my mouth. "Yes, that."

I nipped at his finger playfully, then flicked my tongue over it. This was sinfully erotic. I had to tame it down, or I was going to start with *When Harry Met Sally* orgasm sounds right here.

He traced his wet finger down my chin and neck, stopping in the little hollow of my collarbone. "Sam ... I want to whisk you away from here this very moment."

I looked into his eyes, so full of desire. Every part of me pulsed with need for him, the urge to do all sorts of naughty things I'd never dreamed of doing with a man. "I want that, too."

His smile, full of promises only a minute ago, faded to regret. He brushed the hair from my forehead. "We can't, though."

I pushed myself up onto my elbow. "Why not?"

A loud thud sounded from near the basketball hoop, startling us both. Cheers went up as water exploded from a super-giant-sized tub and splashed onto the pavement. Hoots and applause followed.

A face appeared above the tank's edge, water streaming over drenched blond hair. Archer pushed the water from his eyes, laughing. Then he hopped back up onto the levered plank on which he'd been sitting. A sign on the outside of the tub read: Dunkin' for Dollars.

Clint sat up. "Because I'm next."

"You? In the dunk tank? Get out of here!" I slapped his arm. "What are they raising money for, anyway?"

"Something called Everly's Foundation. I normally wouldn't do anything like this, but Archer asked and it's important to him. He devotes a lot of time to it. Just this last month he was in San Francisco meeting with the CEO of some huge corporation — I forget the name — about how to raise the charity's profile from a local to a national level. They want to be involved with it. There are a lot of legal technicalities to sort through, but he really wants to make it happen."

"What's Everly's Foundation? I've never heard of it."

He gave me a guarded gaze. "You should probably ask Archer."

I would. I'd also intended to ask him what he was doing with Danielle the other night.

Standing, Clint offered his hand. "Come on. I have to put on my swimming trunks."

I poked him in the ribs. "I hope you brought your Speedos."

Picking up a backpack, he hugged me to his side as we walked past one of the craft booths, where Ida's friend Gladys Detwiler was hawking crocheted pot-holders. "Are you kidding? And have these women clawing at me? I don't think so. Besides, I'm too modest to flaunt my physique."

"Hmmm, right." I lifted the bottom of his shirt to tickle his stomach. He flinched, then tucked his shirt back in. "Better keep those abs under wraps. Or else the rumors will start that you're a Chippendales dancer on the side."

While Clint went inside to change into his swimwear, I waited for Archer as two more scrawny grease monkeys heaved a softball at the paddle flipper. Both missed by miles.

Archer gave an exaggerated frown. "Sorry, Ted, but we are *not* putting you on the roster for the softball team next year. You can man the concessions, though."

Ted strutted up to the tank. "You think just because you're the league-leading homerun hitter you can poke fun at the rest of us, eh? If I didn't like you so much, I'd reach through those cage wires and yank your tonsils out."

Archer insulted Ted's choice of NFL teams and both men laughed, then promised to go out for beers next weekend. Ted and his buddy walked off. I waved at Archer and he smiled back. I liked seeing this side of him: less hero, more guy next door. Even if he did wear flannel and sing along to country music.

A few minutes later, Clint traded places with him. While Archer had taken it all in good stride, Clint looked like he'd rather be anywhere else than suspended on a skinny board above a vat full of cold water. He draped a dry towel over his bare shoulders like a cape and hugged his arms to his chest. I looked around for Archer, but he must've gone inside to change.

The scent of beef charring filled my nose. Smoke rose from a grill about thirty yards away, where a young, clean-cut man was flipping burgers. I wandered toward it. If I hadn't been so full from Clint's sandwiches, I'd have gotten a hamburger. They smelled heavenly.

Harmon and Maybelle were waiting with paper plates for theirs. Harmon glanced my way, flashed a smile, then immediately pretended not to notice me. Maybelle must have caught him looking, though, because she swatted him smack dab in the middle of the chest so hard he coughed.

"Thanks, Leroy," Maybelle said as the young man slid a thick burger onto her bun, loaded with fixings. "Sorry to hear about your gal. What an awful, *awful* thing to happen. Hope they catch whoever snuffed her out. Scary to think there's a cold-blooded murderer walking free in this town."

Leroy gawked at her, his face riddled with shock.

Yet Maybelle blabbered on. She hadn't approached Leroy to offer condolences. She was hard at work powering the rumor mill. "Really, now, what kind of a derelict takes out a sweet little thing like Miley Harper? Makes you wonder what would make a person do something like that. I mean, was it just a psycho — or someone with a motive?"

Harmon coughed, and her gaze shot to him so fast he nearly toppled over backward. Clearly there was some highly loaded tension between these two where Miley was concerned that even her death hadn't fixed.

Shoulders drooping, Leroy stared at the burger flipper in his hand. He shifted on his feet, buffed black leather shoes peeking from beneath his navy-blue slacks. He even had on a plaid, button-up shirt and looked every bit the altar boy. "I wouldn't know, Mrs. Purnell. All I can think of is how I wish she were still here, enjoying this fine day with me." Then he slapped a hamburger patty onto her bun and another on Harmon's.

"Next!" Leroy shouted to the teenage boy right behind them.

My heart twisted, seeing young Leroy Roberds like that. He was clean-cut and polite, the last type you'd ever expect to murder his fiancée. Besides, his alibi was as clean as a whistle, and he didn't have a motive to get rid of her that I could tell. Even if it had been a crime of passion, Miley would have had to have been messing around on him. She *had* ditched Jake Taylor to get with Leroy, but who wouldn't have? Jake was a sewer rat. Leroy was a preacher's son and community volunteer. Somewhere in there, Miley had dated Archer briefly, but recently she hadn't been with him, either. Maybe if I went down to Dawna's Beauty Studio, where Miley used to work, I could pick up some clues about her.

"Hey, you."

I swung around to see Selma posed in all her glitzy glory. Today was apparently Goth day. Or Biker Chick Day. Or maybe even Vampire Appreciation Day. Over a sparkly tank top — and of course she'd be a sparkly vampire — she had on a black fishnet shirt. Her skirt was black leather, fringed at the sides, and shorter than any running shorts I owned. The footwear was ... unique: a pair of black thigh-high lace-up boots with two-inch heels — conservative for her. Even her hair was jet black. The only color on her entire person was her bright red lipstick, which drew my eyes, because I kept expecting that when she opened her mouth to speak again, she'd reveal a set of fangs.

She was leaning against the backside of the building, one arm draped over her head, the other hanging limply at her side. Except for her clothes, she looked so ... subdued. Like she'd just woken up from a nap.

"Do you have a minute?" she asked meekly. "I need to talk to you."

The tone alone was enough to worry me. And since when did Selma ever ask permission to speak?

"Sure. About what?"

Drawing her arm down and turning her back to the wall, she twisted a piece of fringe around her finger. "Girl stuff, I suppose."

If she needed a tampon, my purse was all the way back in my car and I was pretty sure Tara didn't have any on her.

Tara flapped her hand at me from the dessert table. It wasn't so much a wave as it was a 'Rescue me!'

"Do you want to get some pie?" I asked her. "Tara and Shannon have quite a spread over there. I think I saw some lemon meringue.

We can walk that way, if you want."

Her gaze shifted in their direction, but stopped partway. I followed her line of sight to where a young mother was lugging a pumpkin seat as two toddlers trailed behind her. Her eyes snapped down. "Maybe later. I have to find Dylan." She pushed herself away from the wall. "See you around."

Flummoxed, I watched her go — behind the dunk tank, around the basketball court, then on past the craft tables before she disappeared into the crowd.

Hands flailing over her head, Tara jumped up and down to get my attention. I wove through the masses to her.

In front of the dessert table stood Harmon, frozen in indecision. He'd already finished his hamburger and somehow managed to detach himself from Maybelle. At the dessert table, his hand hovered over a plastic bag full of chocolate chip cookies, then reached for a paper plate full of lemon bars dusted with confectioner's sugar. He yanked his hand back and drifted to the far left of the table.

"Are those …?" He covered his mouth with a hand before placing it over his heart and pointing with the other hand to a lone plate in the corner. "Are those *dark* chocolate buckeyes?"

Shannon picked up the plate for a better look. Harmon's eyes followed intently. She showed the plate to Tara: three plump peanut butter balls coated in rich, dark chocolate.

"They are," Tara confirmed. She smiled through gritted teeth, then stomped her foot beneath the table. "Would you like them?"

His head bobbed once in a nod. "How much are they?"

"Five dollars," Shannon piped in.

Tara gave her a WTF look, before adding, "But for you, we'll take three."

He plopped down the bills and in less than fifteen seconds had stuffed all three buckeyes in his mouth.

"Were they good?" I asked.

Startled, he clutched his hands over his mouth. When he saw it was me, he ducked behind me to peek past my shoulder.

Swallowing the last of the evidence, he whispered, "Did Maybelle send you to check on me?"

"No, she didn't."

A whoosh of relief left his lungs. He stepped from behind me. "*Please* don't tell her. She thinks I shouldn't have sugar. Or chocolate. Or caffeine. Or —"

"I get it. And don't worry. Your secret is safe with me. In fact, if you happen to be out for a walk next Saturday morning and stroll by our house, I might have an extra cupcake or two."

He smiled like a five-year-old stepping onto Main Street of Disney World for the first time. "I might just take up walking, then. Starting next Saturday." He looked up and down the sidewalk, then bobbed his head a few times. "Say, have you heard anything else about that girl? You know, the one who was killed the other night?"

"Miley Harper? No, I was hoping maybe you had."

"Nope, not really. Just seems kinda mysterious, her dying that young and all. A real shame. She was a pretty gal. And nice to me. Like you. Well, I mean just the few times I spoke with her while I was out edging the lawn. Maybelle doesn't like the grass growing over the sidewalk or driveway, so I have to tidy it up every couple of weeks. Anyway, when Maybelle caught me talking to that Miss Harper gal once, she called her a crack whore. Not to her face, I mean, but to me. She said the neighborhood would be better off without the likes of her. Then she accused me of arranging to meet up with her for 'services', if you follow me."

"Oh, was she *that* kind of girl?"

"Not even close. That gal was as sugary sweet as rock candy. She went to church with Roberds every Sunday, same place as me and Maybelle. Only we don't go every week. Sometimes Maybelle has a migraine and needs me to cook and clean for her. Her headaches are so debilitating she can't do anything 'cept watch TV."

He fidgeted nervously, like his Maybelle-radar had just gone off. "Uh, yeah, I s'pose so. Look, I'd love to stay and talk some more, but I have to go get a bottle of water to gargle with before Maybelle finds me and smells the chocolate on my breath."

He disappeared into the crowd. Things were quiet over by the dunk tank. Clint sat on the board, arms crossed over his chest, gazing down at the water. No one was standing in line to dunk him. When Archer vacated the post, the bulk of the crowd had left. I did notice a small group of young women ogling Clint, though. I was about to tromp over there and stake my claim when I heard Tara's voice.

"Mooom!" Tara whined.

I turned around. A long nose peeked out from beneath the table skirt. Bump was lying under the table, jaw pressed to the ground.

Tara had her foot firmly on the leash. "Can you take him, *please?* He's eaten half a dozen cookies and a whole pie. I don't think it's good for him."

"Sure, pumpkin." I retrieved Bump's leash and led him toward the dunk tank.

But instead of going in the direction I intended, Bump yanked me the opposite way, his nose diving to the ground. I pulled back, yelling, "No, Bump, heel!"

He not only ignored me, he picked up speed. The louder I yelled, the harder he pulled. I didn't have two good hands to hold on with and people were starting to stare at me and my unruly dog, so I just shut up and hoped it looked like we were out for a playful romp.

Without warning, he took a sharp right, dragging me around a stroller with a sleeping baby, between a pair of boys flinging a Frisbee, and smack dab through a gathering of a dozen people sitting in a circle in their lawn chairs, sipping beverages.

Bump slammed to a halt before an unguarded picnic basket sitting on top of a stump. The corner of a red checkered tablecloth peeked from beneath the lid. He lifted a quivering nose, sat, and barked three times.

I looked around, ready to gush an apology, but the basket was at least fifty feet away from the nearest person. It took all my strength, but I reeled him in. His claws dug into the earth. He craned his head backward, straining toward the basket. He let out one of those ear-piercing yodels — half banshee, half Xena Warrior Princess battle cry — that only Husky-type dogs can do. I commanded him to come with me. I begged, I cajoled, I shamed him by telling him how juvenile and disobedient he was being.

In the end, I had to drag him away. And ignore the fact that a hundred or more people were watching me abuse my dog. They probably all had their smartphones out, recording it so they could post social media messages that said: 'Stop this woman!'

When we reached the edge of the crowded picnic area, I ducked between two older ladies wearing polyester skirts, pantyhose, and sensible shoes. Distracted by the fried chicken drumsticks they were waving about, Bump forgot all about the picnic basket and reverted to an oversized goofy puppy. He began walking with me, his pleading eyes skipping from face to face, his tail thwopping against my kneecaps.

Relieved, I hurried toward the building, hoping to find Archer. The hubbub of the crowd faded to a faint buzz as I squeezed between the cinder block wall and a row of parked cars. I was halfway around to the front when I heard Ted's voice, followed by Archer's laughter. I turned the corner, following the welcome sound —

And walked straight into Virgil's pro wrestler's chest.

"Looking for someone?" he said with a psychopathic grin

chapter 15

BUMP — DAMN HIS FRIENDLY nature — licked Virgil's knuckles.

Turncoat.

Head down, I muttered, "Excuse me."

Then, I stepped left, but there was a bush in the way. A very prickly bush. I'd met that bush before. Had a fight with it. And lost.

So I went right. And got as far as the end of the leash, where Bump met me on the other side of Virgil. He jumped up, paws to my chest, like we were reuniting after months apart.

A nanosecond later, I was flat on my back, gravel digging into the back of my skull, a slobbery dog tongue scraping the hair from my eyebrows.

My vision narrowed to a funnel of light. Everything sounded so *faaarrr* away. And why did it feel like someone had just bashed my skull with a baseball bat?

It was like my mind was detached from my body. I was aware of the pain, but couldn't react to it. There was also a deep voice, repeating the same thing over and over, rising in pitch at the end.

I blinked. Wiggled my fingers. Tried to remember where I was ... *Who* I was.

I heard a woman's voice, muted, like I had cotton balls stuffed in my ears. A ball rolled in front of me and I pounced on it, glee filling my chest. I scooped it up in my mouth, chomped a few times, then spat it at a pair of sandaled feet.

I'm telling you, he can sniff out anything. The woman snatched her feet away from the ball before it could touch her toes. *He finds the stash every time. No matter where I hide it. Think we could make money off of him?*

Another pair of feet wearing shiny black shoes kicked the ball away. I raced after it, caught it while it was still spinning, then returned it.

Sell him so he can find our goods? That's really bright, said the man in shiny black shoes.

So what do you think we oughta do with him? a third voice said. It sounded like another man, but younger.

Get rid of him, the older man said, *like I told you in the first place.*

I stared at the ball, willing the first man to throw it for me, but he ignored me.

Okay, okay, I'll do it, the younger man said begrudgingly.

"I said, are you okay?" Leaning over me, Virgil strong-armed Bump out of the way.

It was one time I wished I hadn't returned to my senses. Because I was up Crap Creek without a paddle. Hell, I didn't even have a canoe to keep me afloat.

Virgil pulled a cloth from his pocket. It dangled above my face menacingly. Was he going to suffocate me right here — or gag me and haul my body out of sight? Wasn't anyone watching?!

Screwing my eyes shut in denial, I gulped in a breath and tightened my abs for a big, girly scream. But then ... softness brushed over my brow. I might have been scared witless if I weren't so stunned. Was he ... was he dabbing the dog spit from my forehead with a hankie? I pried one eye open.

His hands clutching both my arms, he pulled me up gently and waited until I was steady on my feet before letting go. Lightheaded, I swayed. Meanwhile, Bump was licking my shins. I wasn't sure if he was tasting the salt on my skin or asking if I was all right, but I was too aware of Virgil's close proximity to focus on the dog long enough to shoo him away.

"Did you hit your head?" He pinched my chin between calloused fingers and tilted my head up as he leaned in close to check my pupils. Then his fingers began probing my skull, from the sides to the back. It was almost like having Mr. Clean give me a scalp massage.

I winced when he found the goose egg that was already swelling up. He pulled his hands away, checked his fingertips. No blood.

"I'm ... okay," I said, less than convincingly. But I wasn't about to let him give me a more thorough exam.

Where was Archer when I needed him?

"You should have that checked out." He indicated the front doors with his thumb. "Selma's been looking for you. She says to tell you she's inside."

Then he stepped aside.

"Thanks," I said, and kept my eyes on him as I went past. When I got to the front doors and turned back to look, he was gone. What was it with people disappearing lately?

I spotted her right away, draped over a table in the corner. Alone. Something was seriously wrong.

"Selma?" I slid onto the chair across from her. Amazingly, Bump lay down, cooling his belly on the tile floor. "Your brother said you were looking for me. What's wrong?"

"Nothing's wrong." She lifted her cup, gazed inside, and downed the last bit. I expected the telltale aroma of beer to waft my way, but then I noticed the red drops around the inside of the cup and realized she'd been drowning her sorrows in punch.

"You sure?"

Her iridescent scarlet lips turned downward in an uncharacteristic frown. "No." A sniffle leaked out of her, but she quickly shifted in her chair, her gaze darting about the room.

The main room of the lodge was an open dance hall area, the kind of place you rented for a wedding reception. Round tables surrounded by metal chairs ringed the room. In the center of the ceiling, the disco ball spun slowly, its glass tiles casting speckly squares of light around the room even with all the overhead lights on. There was no one in here except the hard drinkers at the bar — and Selma.

Instead of dance music, today they were playing country tunes. I focused on the lyrics for a moment: something about divorce, loneliness, and heartache. Normally, I'd run away from depressing music like that. I needed upbeat, energetic. But right now, Selma needed me.

I reached across the table to stroke her wrist. "Tell me."

Her eyes flicked to mine. "I just feel so … mixed up. I don't know whether to be happy, or sad, or frightened to death."

She was scaring *me*. But a woman's intuition is strong. I had an inkling where this was going. "Does this have to do with Dylan?"

She looked around, nodded. Her nails clacked on the table.

"Selma, tell me … Are you —?"

"Shhhh!" She pressed a manicured finger to her lips, but the hiss of her hushing carried.

Bump lifted his head, cocking it from side to side.

Three drunken guys at the bar twisted around, probably to see if there was a gas leak somewhere. One of them tottered on his stool. He flung a hand out to grab onto the guy next to him, which set up a domino effect. The first two guys went down in a clatter of wooden furniture and inebriated bodies. Thankfully their beer bellies had softened their falls. Their stools crashed sideways, wiping out the third stool. That man was, perhaps, less drunk than the other two, because he had the presence of mind to lean across the top of the bar to protect his drink and managed to remain upright. His elbow, however, sent the half-full bottle of Jim Beam that the bartender had just set

185

down, crashing to the floor.

That was when I noticed who the third guy was: Dylan Hawkins. His back was to us. Broad, apelike shoulders bulged against his leather motorcycle vest. The cut-off sleeves of a black T-shirt peeked from beneath it. His arms, as always, were bare, showing off a multitude of tattoos all the way down to his wrists. It was the first time I noticed that he shaved his arms as well as his head. He also worked out. Religiously.

Narrowing my eyes at Selma, I whispered, "Well, are you?"

She shrugged noncommittally, trying to act like it was no big deal. "Maybe."

"So you're late?"

Her forehead folded in confusion. "For what? I wasn't supposed to be anywhere today — except here."

"I mean, what was the date of your last period?"

"Honey, I don't know what you do all day long, but I don't do much writing, unless you count texting. And I certainly don't keep track of my punctuation. Why?"

I had to stop myself from slapping my forehead. "No, your monthly period."

"Ohhhh, oh, oh, oh. Right. My minstrel period."

Did she say minstrel, or menstrual? I swear she had an accent.

She sat back in her chair. "Yeah, that. No idea."

"You don't know?" Next to my chair, Bump stretched his legs and let out a long yawn.

"Who keeps track of it?" Selma said. "I just know I haven't had one in a while. And I've been dead tired lately."

"Have you thrown up?"

"Not since last time I had the flu, but whenever I stock the frozen food section at Garber's, it makes me queasy."

I glanced toward the bar. Dylan Hawkins hadn't noticed me yet. He was too busy explaining his tattoos to the bartender.

"Does Dylan know?"

She shook her head. "I didn't want to upset him, in case it's a false alarm. That and I really want to go to Mexico still. If I tell him, I'm afraid he'll call the trip off."

"Pregnant women fly all the time, Selma. As long as they're not too close to their due date, it's all fine. Besides, he should be happy about maybe being a dad — and if he's not, you need to dump his ass."

A pause in the music opened up. The bartender fiddled with the settings on the sound system as Dylan continued to talk at him.

"Yeah, about that ..." Selma fidgeted in her chair. It squeaked so loudly that Dylan turned around. His gaze ricocheted from her to me.

I wilted where I sat. The hangnail on my pinkie suddenly became very interesting. I needed to get out of here, find Archer.

"Sam, are you listening?" Selma scooted her chair closer and grabbed at my good wrist. "Please don't tell anyone this, but ... I'm not sure, if ... if it *is* Dylan's. If I am pregnant, that is. Which I'm still not sure I am."

"There's someone else?" I whispered, not daring to look Dylan's way.

"Was, was. It was just a fling. A one-nighter. You know, a little beer, a shoulder to cry on, a little more beer. Dylan and I were having a fight. I thought we were a done deal. Turned out he was just cranky from a long work day. But this other guy ..." The worry lines in her face softened. Her eyes took on a dreamy look. She twirled her dangly earring. "He made me feel good about myself. Special. Like he cared about me. Not that Dylan doesn't, mind you. But in a different way. Dylan makes me feel like a topnotch porn star. Like he can't get enough of me. Well, my body, that is. But this other guy, he *listened* to me. Made me feel important."

Boldly, I glanced toward the bar, but Dylan had his back turned to us again and was talking to the other two guys. "Are you sure

187

Dylan's the one you're supposed to be with?"

"If he's my baby-daddy, yeah."

"And if he's not?"

Shrugging, she spread her fingers out, pretending to inspect her manicure. "What if I'm not pregnant at all, huh?"

"Then we should find out. My place tomorrow night. I'll buy the home pregnancy test. You just show up. Okay?"

"Can't," she said firmly.

"What? Why not? You need to know, Selma. Otherwise all this fretting could be for nothing. If you're not, you can relax. And if you are ... Well, you need to start making plans."

"I'm with you on that, sugar, but I have to work the next four days straight because Jourdane's modeling chainmail at some sort of fantasy convention in Detroit — the kind with elves and hobos."

Frodo would be so disappointed to be labeled a bum.

"Evening, then? I can chase Tara off to her friend's house."

"That won't work this week, either. I have to watch Will and Keisha's kids while they go to a French class at the high school in Fullbright. They're trying to rekindle their romance, and Will wants Keisha to talk dirty to him in a foreign language." She put a hand to the side of her mouth. "Personally, I think they're just driving to the park and making whoopee in the back of their van, trying to make another baby, even though they both swear they're done having kids. That or Will's trying to keep Keisha from having a nervous breakdown by giving her some downtime. Little Willie set fire to the couch yesterday. She's convinced if she had all girls, her life would be easier. Anyway, I told her last week I heard if you have intercourse with the woman on top, then those little boy swimmers can't make it up the canal and that increases your odds of having a girl. All of a sudden they ask me if I can watch the kids. Yeah, right. I know what's going down."

I didn't have the guts to tell her Keisha had told me she'd had her tubes tied. I was sure Keisha would get around to it. Eventually.

"When, then?"

Her metal bracelets clinked as she flapped her wrist. "I'll text you. I promise. We'll do it soon, 'kay?"

"All right." If I'd been Selma, though, I would have wanted 'soon' to be yesterday. But I wasn't Selma, thankfully, and I didn't have her problems. Maybe she still needed time to come to grips with what lay in store. Bringing a life into the world and then having that little, screaming, pooping person *become* your world was a massive change — but one that brought untold joys with it, too. I wanted to be happy for her, but her situation was less than ideal. Even if Dylan was the father, I couldn't envision a rosy future for them. I had a hard time accepting her relationship with Dylan as it was now, let alone with the complications a child brought along. Whoever this other guy was, he had to be better for her than Dylan Hawkins.

"Sam?"

I looked around. Same three guys at the bar. No one on the dance floor. Front doors open and vacant.

"Behind you, Sam."

I twisted around in my chair. Cowboy boots clicking on the tile floor, Archer approached us from the back hallway, decked out in a crisp white T-shirt and ass-hugging jeans. His biceps strained against the thin material of his sleeves as he hugged a crate of bagged buns to his chest. He set the crate down on the table next to ours.

"Been looking for you for a long time." His teeth gleamed as he smiled down at me. "You been hiding from me?"

"Hey, Sel!" Dylan whistled at her from the bar. "The boys wanna see your tats."

The guys next to him chuckled. The first one elbowed the second. "She's going to show us her knockers."

The second guy whooped, but shut up when Dylan smacked him upside the head.

189

"Tattoos, you fool!" Dylan bellowed.

A blush spread from Selma's cheeks to her neck. She rolled her eyes. "He just wants to show off what his money bought. It was my three-month anniversary present. Well, three months this time around." Standing, she scooted her chair closer to mine and indicated for Archer to have a seat, then waved as she turned around and hustled to Dylan's side.

He stared at the empty chair awkwardly. "Can I get you a beer?"

I wanted to ask him about Danielle getting in his truck after the football game, but I just couldn't make myself do it without sounding like the jealous girlfriend, which was ridiculous because Clint and I were the ones dating.

"Actually," I said, "I have to drive home soon. An iced tea would be great, though." He started off, but then I remembered I needed gas. I'd have to have Clint or Ida drive me and the girls home. "Wait! Make that a beer after all."

"Coming right up."

As he made his request at the bar, Selma lifted her shirt from her lower abdomen. The two men nodded admiringly. Then Dylan tugged at the waistband of her skirt from the backside and peeked inside. She smacked his arm as she pressed herself against him. Before Archer had his drink order, Dylan and Selma were on their way out the door, Dylan's two drunken friends staggering after them.

My phone dinged with a text. It was Tara.

Is it okay if Gramps and Ida drop me off at Shannon's now? Her mom can bring me home.
What about the desserts? Aren't you on duty for another hour?
We sold out!
Sure, then. Be home by 9 PM. It's a school night.
Don't remind me.

Archer slid the beer in front of me, then gave Bump a good long scratch behind his ears. Bump groaned to let him know he'd hit the spot. I brought the beer to my nose, sniffed its golden yeastiness, and blew at the creamy froth on top. I hadn't had a beer in ... years. In fact, that glass of wine at Clint's was the first drink of anything I'd had since the night Tara was little and had a raging ear infection.

Hard as it was, I set the cup down. Had I been headed down the slippery slope of becoming an alcoholic then? Had I *been* one? If I had one drink now, what did that make me? I honestly didn't know. Maybe I was overanalyzing it all, being too hard on myself.

"Something wrong?" Archer asked. "They have light beer, ale, some of the microbrewery beers. I can get you —"

"This is perfect." I picked it up and took a deep, satisfying swallow. Amber liquid drenched my throat and poured into my waiting stomach, filling a long-dormant thirst. I drank more. And kept drinking. Until my cup was empty.

Archer brought me another. I was halfway through it when he asked, "So who's driving you home?"

"Clint, I suppose."

"Oh, of course." His voice sank the tiniest bit, like he was disappointed. "I was going to offer, but if you already have a ride ..."

I glanced his way, but he was looking out into the parking lot. His still-wet hair glistened under the harsh fluorescent lights. Every now and then, the disco ball threw a sparkle of light across his face. We started talking: about the success of the picnic, how much work he'd put into it, what his plans were for next year. I told him about running out of gas and almost getting flattened. He gave me his utter attention, clinging to every word, never once questioning my paranoia.

Fingers laced together across his abdomen, he leaned back. "That just seems odd. You keep an eye out, Sam." He jabbed an index finger on the table. "You call me if anything fishy happens. Anything at all. I don't care if your trash cans fall over in the middle of the night and you're afraid there's some crazy stalker outside your house and it turns out to be a raccoon."

I nodded, and he reached out to touch my knee reassuringly. "I mean it, call me."

My eyes were locked on his hand, his fingers lightly gripping my knee. In his touch, I felt both strength and gentleness. He was a man who could haul a limp body over his shoulder from a burning structure, rustle up a pot of Humboldt County's best chili, and sew his own buttons back on. The warmth of his palm radiated from the place where his hand lingered. His thumb stroked just above my kneecap.

"What if it really *is* the middle of the night?" I teased. "Will you come over?"

"*Any*time, Sam. You know that. I'll be there whenever you need me."

"What if you're in your birthday suit?" A picture of him showing up at the door buck naked popped into my head. I giggled. The beer was making me punchy.

He grinned, a flush of embarrassment coloring his cheeks. "Just as soon as I put my pants on."

Bump's head snapped up. His tail tapped lightly on the floor.

I hadn't noticed the shifting of feet until a throat cleared off to the side. Clint was standing about ten feet away, watching us from the shadows of the hallway to the back rooms. How long had he been there?

His clothes were soaking wet and he had a towel draped around his neck. A small puddle had already formed around his bare feet. He pointed to the back door at the end of the hallway. "I thought you two saw me come in ... but apparently not."

Awkward just got awkwarder.

"Clint, hey." Desperate to shift his attention, I raised my cup to him. There were about two sips left in it. "Want some beer?"

"Thanks, but no. Sam, I have to go. There's an emergency. A

Great Pyrenees with gastric torsion, sounds like. The owners are meeting me at the clinic. I probably have a few hours of surgery ahead. I'm sorry."

"No problem. Comes with the territory. Hope it all turns out okay."

"Me, too." He turned to Archer. "Hubert took my place. I hope you don't mind me skipping out like this."

"Not at all." He stood and shook Clint's hand. "Thanks for the help. Now go take care of business, buddy. I've got everything covered here."

Clint's glance slid toward me and the muscles in his face tightened. "I can see that." Without so much as a kiss on the cheek or a 'see you later', he left.

Shrugging, I emptied my cup. "I guess I do need a ride home after all."

chapter 16

"WHO'S EVERLY?" I SAID.

Several seconds passed while Archer kept his eyes on the road, both hands securely on the steering wheel of his truck. In the backseat, Bump panted excitedly, his breath steaming up the window. The first big drops of rain smacked the windshield, smearing the view ahead. Archer flipped the wipers on and they thunked in a monotonous rhythm. "Aren't you going to ask what Everly's Foundation is?"

"Eventually. But what I really want to know is, who is this 'Everly' person? Some rich guy looking for a tax write-off? I know a lot of charities would be floundering without help like that, but —"

"Everly was my daughter."

He said it with such simplicity and longing that my heart sank. "Oh. I'm so sorry, Archer. I didn't mean to sound flippant. Clint told me some big corporation was talking to you about taking it international, so I wondered if someone named Everly was involved. What ... what happened to your daughter?"

"Her mother was a drunk and an addict, that's what happened." His hands tightened on the steering wheel. "She put Everly in her crib and shut the bedroom door so she couldn't hear her crying. She was too busy partying with her meth head friends. Stoned, she fell asleep on the couch. Naked. Next to a guy smoking a cigarette. Couch caught fire. They got out. Didn't remember the baby until it was too late."

He took a curve a little too fast and the wheels hydroplaned for a second before making contact again. The road straightened out, and I breathed a sigh of relief.

"Everly's mother ..." I began, but stopped myself. I didn't know how to ask about her. He hadn't called her his wife, so I assumed they hadn't been married. As curious as I was about the details of their relationship, right now wasn't the time to dig that deep. "Is Everly's mother in jail?"

"No, she's not. She's dead."

"Dead?" I hadn't meant to repeat it out loud. But my brain-to-mouth filter was on the fritz. Beer — or any other alcoholic beverage — had a way of making me say or do things I normally didn't.

"Killed herself."

His voice was as flat and emotionless as a cardboard cutout. But I could see he wasn't over the events. And probably never would be.

"I'm sorry. Sorry about her, about your daughter ..." Pain, sharp and fresh, stabbed at my heart. It had been ten years since Kyle died, but I *still* felt his loss. "How long ago was this?"

"I was nineteen," he said. "She was twenty. Everly was almost two."

Wow. That meant he'd become a father before leaving high school. Obviously, he'd chosen a different path than Everly's mother. And somehow, despite all the guilt he probably carried around for not preventing his daughter's death, he'd risen above it all to make something good out of it. Now I understood why he'd become a firefighter.

"What's the foundation raise money for?" I asked.

"It's to help kids of drug- and alcohol-addicted parents."

With that, a peaceful silence settled between us. There had been enough confession for one day. Enough heartache laid raw.

I wanted to put my arms around Archer and just hold him.

We pulled into my driveway and he cut the engine. Hands still on the steering wheel, he kept his eyes forward, staring at my garage with its chipped paint and sagging gutters. When I first laid eyes on this house, I could barely see a thing wrong with it, I was so eager for my own place. But now I was starting to notice all the little things that needed fixing and I didn't have the first clue about how to go about getting them taken care of. Just like the inside of a house needed a woman's touch to make it a home, the outside and the guts of it needed a man's elbow grease. I'd always wanted to think I was a liberated woman, but the truth was I could hardly tell a Phillips screwdriver from a regular one.

"Do you want to come inside?" The moment I said it, I noticed his eyebrows lift ever so slightly. "I mean, before we get the gas can and go back to my car. Just for a while. I need to let those beers flush out of my system."

He tilted his head. "That could take more than a little while. Sure you don't need to sleep it off?"

"I'm not *that* drunk." I hiccupped. "Just a little tipsy."

"I, uh, don't think Clint would be too thrilled with me driving you home 'tipsy' and then hanging out all alone with you."

"Why can't you come inside for some lemonade and cookies, huh? We're just *friends*, Archer." I said the word 'friends' with a distinct growl.

"Friends or not, let's be honest — it would look bad."

I pivoted to face him. "Bad how?"

"Isn't that obvious?"

"Not to me."

"Clint and I are friends. Have been for years. I don't want him to think there's anything between you and me, okay?"

"Is there?"

Damn liquor talking. Why couldn't I just shut up?

"What?" Shaking his head, he got out of the truck and came around to open my door. "Come on inside. You do need to sleep it off."

After fighting with my seat belt, I slid from the truck and stumbled with the first step. He curved an arm around my waist to hold me up. It took me several tries with the key to open the door, because my vision kept blurring and I couldn't see the bloody keyhole. While I struggled with that, he let Bump into the backyard.

The rain had lightened to a fine mist, so at least I didn't get soaked while I wrestled with the lock. Finally, the knob turned and I shoved the door open with more force than needed.

In the kitchen, I tossed the keys on the counter, but they overshot it and clattered to the floor. I whirled around to face him. "You're the one who keeps telling me to call you if I need anything. Anytime, you said. For any reason. It's almost like you want a reason to rescue me."

He hunted through the fridge for a couple of cans of pop, cocked his arm back like he was going to toss me one, then thought better of it. He popped the tab and set it on the counter next to me. "I don't think you need rescuing, Sam."

"Damn straight, I don't." I chugged half the can down. Now I was a drunk on a sugar high who was going to have to pee a lake soon. The room tipped and I swayed sideways. Archer hurried forward to guide me into a chair, then sat next to me.

"And yet, I keep having to do just that." He fought a grin.

"So why don't you just say what's on your mind? The truth."

"And what would that be?"

"That you think about me. A little. Maybe even a lot." That time, it wasn't the beer talking.

He let out a breathy scoff. "Does it matter if I do? Look, I saw the two of you today."

"Kissing, you mean?"

"How could I miss it? How could anyone?"

197

He had me there. But I wasn't blind. Archer kept sending me signals, like he wanted me to respond to him. "Did you wish it was you — kissing me?"

"Where is all this coming from, Sam? I just offered you a ride home because you were out of gas and half drunk and now you're —"

"You're the one who kept bringing me beer. You also offered to come over in the middle of the night." I drummed my fingers on the table. He wasn't getting out of this without coming clean. "So, do you?"

"Do I what?"

"Think about me?"

Sighing, Archer looked out the window. Rain pattered against the glass. "I'm not going to answer that right now."

"And why not?"

His gaze shifted to me. "Because I think you already know — or else we wouldn't be having this conversation."

The earth flipped on its axis. He'd said it. Almost. It was implied, anyway. If I hadn't already been sitting down, I might have fallen over. I gripped the edge of my chair seat. Why did hearing it out loud feel so different from just thinking about it? I needed to be on solid ground, not tossed around on a roller coaster ride.

I found myself staring at my fingers, laced together on the table before me. So he did think about me. I'd sensed it all along. Known it in my gut, even though I hadn't had the slightest bit of proof. Then why was this a big surprise?

An even bigger question: where did that leave my relationship with Clint? One moment, I was on fire just thinking of him; the next, he could say a few words that would leave me feeling cold. Whenever we were alone, I couldn't get enough of him — and he certainly fulfilled my every desire. I loved *being with* Clint. I was addicted to the perfection of his body and the way mine responded to his touch.

But was that really love? Or was it simply lust?

My stomach was a tangle of snakes. A few months ago, I'd been closed off in my own little world, committed to a life of spinsterhood. Now? I was caught in confusion, like a butterfly that had only recently unfurled its wings, only to find itself ensnared in a sticky web, unable to fly free.

I knew how Archer felt now. The problem was, though, that I didn't know how I felt.

There was one way to find out.

One hand resting on the table to steady myself, I rose from my chair to stand before Archer. He watched me warily, scooting back to sit up straighter. Swinging a leg over, I straddled him. Arms stiff at his sides, he looked down at his lap. Even as I stroked a finger beneath his chin to tilt his mouth upward, he wouldn't meet my gaze. But I could hear his breathing quicken.

His eyelids fluttering shut, he tilted his head back. "What are you doing, Sam?"

In answer, I brought my mouth to his cheek, let the warmth of my skin flow into his. I let a moment pass, let it become a minute.

"I'm waiting, Archer," I murmured.

"For what?"

"For you."

A nervous cough escaped his throat. "Me?"

"Yes." I turned my face, my breath swirling with his, his lips so close to mine I could feel the heat rising off them. "For you … to make a move."

He drew in a breath, his chest expanding to brush against my breasts. A tingle, a yearning, awakened in me. Without even thinking about what I was doing, I rotated my hips, searching for the evidence of his need.

And I found it. Growing beneath me. Straining against the seam of his fly.

I wasn't thinking anymore. Wasn't analyzing what he'd said or hadn't said or wondering how the future would unfold. I just wanted to feel. Him. Completely. For as long and as intensely as I could.

His hands went around my waist, slid down as he lifted me from the chair in one swift upward movement. I wrapped my legs around his hips as he carried me from the kitchen into the living room. As we neared the couch, I loosened my arms from around his neck. He settled me onto the couch, gently lowering my upper body as I stretched my legs out.

He looked me over, his eyes swimming with a mess of emotions, reflecting mine.

Then he tugged the blanket from the back of the couch, snapped it out, and placed it over me.

"You're drunk, Sam," he said, kissing me on the top of the head like he was putting a small child to bed. "People who are drunk don't make good choices."

My stomach sank as he walked away. When he got to the front door, he turned around. "I have to go into work later, so if you need a ride to pick up your car, sorry, but I won't be able to help until tomorrow night."

The lock clunked into place as he shut the door firmly behind him.

The moment he turned over the engine of his truck, Bump came bounding through the doggie door, barking, and galloped up to the picture window. His ears perked when he saw it was Archer, and his tail swished back and forth happily, like he was hoping he'd come get him and take him for another ride. As the sound of Archer's truck faded, Bump whimpered. Then he ran to the front door and pawed at it.

"Don't scratch, Bump."

He turned his head toward me, one blue eye and one brown fixing me with a pleading gaze, the message clear.

"Sorry, buddy. He's gone."

Possibly forever.

Why was I mucking things up lately? If I wasn't jealous of Clint's ex-wife or his job, I was getting smashed in Archer's company and acting like a prostitute offering a freebie.

I pulled the blanket up to my neck as I battled tears. Even if Archer did have feelings for me, I'd made a great big fool of myself. Now what? Apologize to him for my behavior, blame it on the beer, and hope he wouldn't hate me forever? Or patch things up with Clint and just forget about Archer?

Then there was the problem of getting my car back, not to mention figuring out what had happened with that full tank of gas. I could call Ida, but then Dad would have something to say about the whole situation and I wasn't in the mood for it. Call Selma? No, I didn't want to die in a fiery auto accident. Quick way to go, but far too messy.

Ask Clint for a ride?

I contemplated how long it would take to get to my car if I started jogging there. Normally, it was a little over fifteen minutes to drive to the lodge. Wait, that was from my dad's house. I lived farther away now. So let's say twenty-two. At an average of forty-five miles per hour — given all the curves and stop signs between here and there — that meant the lodge was … fifteen or sixteen miles away? If I were to run ten-minute miles … Scratch that. I was over thirty and hadn't been on an intense exercise regime since I was in my teens and even that was just to get an A in Phys Ed … What I hated about that class was the way the locker room smelled. In one breath, I could change into my gym shorts and a T-shirt and get out the door before having to inhale again.

All right, so where was I? Did I figure it was forty-five miles to the lodge — or that it would take me twenty-two hours to jog to my car?

My head began to throb. Thinking through a word problem while still inebriated was like clearing a cobweb from my brain, one strand at a time.

I tugged my phone from the skin-tight pocket of my jeans and texted Clint. Then I laid it on my chest, too groggy by now to stretch an arm to the coffee table to set it down somewhere safe.

I had just started dreaming that I was running the marathon in the Olympics, only I was wearing a pair of Selma's spike-heeled boots on one foot and a cast on the other, when my chest started blaring out a ringtone of "Blurred Lines". Embarrassed the holy crap out of me. Lately, Tara thought it was funny to change my ring. I wasn't sure whether to ground her, or show up at her school one day wearing a hooker outfit for payback.

"Sam, I'll be there in fifteen."

Was this another word problem? And who was this?

"Huh?" I said.

"I said I'm on my way. Turned out Nero didn't have gastric torsion after all." Ah, Clint. He sounded so ... cheery. "He'd gotten into the toy box — the kids', not his. I induced vomiting. Took a while, but he eventually barfed up Woody's head. Seems he has a propensity for destroying the children's toys and eating the evidence."

I was sure he had all kinds of stories just like it. Great dinner party talk.

I searched the wall for a clock. I knew there was one in here some— Ah, there it was. 7:50. Was that a.m. or p.m.? It was an analog clock, not a digital. It was light out, barely. Had I slept through the night? Sure felt like it. But Tara would have come home by now and woken me up. She couldn't sneak past me to save her life.

So if it was still Sunday evening, I'd been asleep for close to three hours. The brain fog was clearing, but I had to pee. I rolled off the couch and headed to the half bath between the kitchen and office. Bump padded after me. Because it was some kind of dog law that you couldn't let your person go to the bathroom without supervision.

"No surgery, huh? That's good." I was trying to sound more interested than I really was. I closed the bathroom door, just in case Tara showed up, and unzipped my fly. "I'll see you soon, then. Bye."

"Wait!"

I really couldn't. I checked to make sure the toilet lid was up. Bump viewed the bowl as a great big water dish, so we'd taken to putting the lid down in between uses. Yep, it was down.

Bump whimpered a few times, then lay down on the other side of the door with a disgruntled *woompf*. He shoved his snout under the door and snorted.

"I'm kinda busy right now, Clint." The pressure on my bladder was about to make my eyeballs pop. I lifted the lid and turned around. "I'll talk to you when you get here."

"No, you need to hear this, Sam. You won't believe it. Turns out Miley Harper had been afraid for her life for a while."

I nearly peed my pants right then. I readjusted the phone to cradle it between my shoulder and ear as I slid my jeans down and lowered myself. If he insisted on talking, I could do my business without him knowing.

"Go on," I told him.

"It so happens Nero's owner is —"

Plop!

Oh … crap. Not literally. Figuratively.

I stared down into the bowl as my phone sank to the bottom with a gurgle. A moment of indecision gripped me, but was quickly overridden by desperation. I plunged my hand downward to retrieve my phone. Then, I grabbed a towel from the rack, which was luckily within arm's reach, and patted my phone dry — all while managing to relieve my bladder.

The display blipped a few times in a random pattern, then went blank.

Just … great.

I finished my business, then dumped my phone in a bowl of rice and paced the floor for fifteen minutes. Bump followed me briefly before losing interest and disappearing through the dog door. Every time I pulled my phone out to check it, it was as dead as the time before. Tara still hadn't come home, or else I could have used her phone to call Clint back, and we didn't have a landline yet. Either way, I didn't have Clint's number memorized. There was a time as a teenager when I'd had dozens of phone numbers stored away in my brain, but anymore all you had to do was punch a key or two or just say a person's name and the phone dialed itself. Pretty soon we'd all have a chip implanted in our heads that sent thought-controlled messages.

Right now, though, my thoughts were all over the place.

Bump exploded in a series of furious barks — the sort that said someone was here. I ran to the front door and looked out the little window at the top. The driveway was still empty, as was the street in front of my house. I went to the picture window and looked in both directions. The sun had just set, so it was getting hard to see, but there was nothing out there. Not even a neighbor standing on their porch or a cat crossing the street.

Bump's barking escalated. I could hear his paws slamming against the boards of the privacy fence. It had to be something out back. A squirrel, maybe, taunting him from an overhanging branch of the next-door neighbor's tree?

I headed that way, grabbing my trusty LED flashlight from the junk drawer. Before I opened the door, I peered out. Bump was racing along the fence abutting the alley, his teeth snapping along the bottom. A shadow moved along the gap at the bottom. Too big and too slow for a cat or dog passing by.

Bump pivoted, then dove at the ground to shove his nose through the gap. His hackles were standing stiff as a porcupine's quills.

Someone was out there.

chapter 17

BUMP GRUMBLED DEEP IN his belly. His head still crammed in the gap under the fence, he pushed with his hind legs and the board wobbled. In that split second when the planks gaped, I saw the distinct silhouette of a person. I flicked my flashlight on and shone it in that direction.

Suddenly, Bump yelped and pulled his head back. He sat there stunned, rubbing a paw at his nose, like he'd taken a blow to it.

A death grip on my flashlight, I flung the door open and yelled, "Whoever's out there, go away! I have a gun!"

Which was quite possibly the dumbest thing I could have ever said.

Bump slunk toward me on his belly, thinking he'd just been reprimanded again for running his mouth. Still anchored in the doorway, I stared at the place where I'd seen the person, but headlights beamed behind me, then arced across the yard, right into my eyes, momentarily blinding me before the lights were killed.

Clint was here.

Now cowering at my feet, Bump lifted his muzzle and sniffed the air. His tail thumped twice before he wedged past me, trotted through the kitchen, and went to sit at the side door there. I locked the back door before following him.

I let Clint in and, still clutching my flashlight in one hand like a baseball bat, threw my arms around his neck.

"Hey." His arms encircled my waist. He gave me a quick squeeze before pulling back to look down into my eyes. "I know you're glad to see me, but it's only been a few hours. Taking lessons from Bump?"

Next to us, Bump was bouncing up and down, his body making little curlicues in greeting. Clint ruffled the fur on top of his head, but that only seemed to wind him up tighter. Plus, he was still in a frantic state from a minute ago.

"Someone was just behind my back fence. I think they're watching me."

Clint's brows lifted and he gave me a placating nod. "What makes you say that? Could've just been a neighbor passing by."

"I don't think so. Or else they would have moved on. No, someone was just standing there, like they were watching the house."

"Maybe it was a stray dog."

"I saw them, Clint!" I slapped his chest, frustrated that he was taking this so lightly. "It was a person. There was someone out there!"

He laid a hand over mine, then brought it to his lips to brush my knuckles with a kiss. "I'm sure there was someone there. Let me take a look."

Taking my flashlight, he walked out into the backyard, made a few sweeps of the perimeter, stood on a lawn chair to look over the fence, and came back in. "No one there now."

"Of course not. They left when you pulled in."

"Did they do anything besides stand there?"

"No, but —"

"Then I don't think you have anything to worry about. Probably just some nosy neighbor. Anyway, Bump here is a good watchdog, aren't you, buddy?"

Stretching his front legs out before him, Bump yawned, then sank to the floor. Two seconds later, his eyelids were drifting shut. He flopped over on his side, pried his eyes open one last time to make sure we were still there, and let out a final grunt before dozing off.

This wasn't exactly filling me with confidence about Bump's watchdog abilities, given that he could go from hyper vigilant to comatose inside of three minutes, but already I was doubting myself. Clint had a way of getting his logic to override my paranoia. Funny, I'd always thought I had a good sense of intuition. Maybe it was my run-in with Jake Taylor that had caused me to overreact lately.

"So did you hear what I said about Nero's owners?" Clint strolled into the living room and I followed.

"Not really. I, uh, kind of dropped my phone in water. It's dead."

"Oh, bummer. I did that once — I was fishing on a yacht in the Gulf of Mexico, snagged a swordfish, and tried to take a picture with my phone when we hit a big wave. How did you manage to dunk yours?"

His story was so much more dramatic than mine.

"Let me lock up," I said. "I'll explain on the way to get my car. But first, you'll have to tell me what you learned about Miley Harper."

"NERO'S OWNERS ARE FRIENDS with Leroy Roberds?"

We were on our way to get my car, a can of gas in the rear of Clint's SUV emitting enough fumes to gag an elephant. I'd left Bump behind to guard the homestead and had used Clint's phone to call Shannon's house to tell Tara that I'd pick her up on my way home. The story of me dropping my phone in the john had taken all of thirty seconds, details omitted. It hadn't been the first time I'd done that, so thankfully I'd already learned my lesson and had all my contacts backed up.

"They are." Clint flipped the turn signal, then slowed to a stop.

He looked both ways at the last stop sign of my new neighborhood before pulling out onto the highway. "Well, more like friends with Leroy's dad, Pastor Matt. His full name is Leander Mathias Roberds, but everyone just calls him Matt."

"So, how did he and Miley get together?"

"She joined Pastor Matt's church down the road from the lodge — what's the name?"

"The Humboldt Brethren Evangelical Sanctuary of Worship?"

"Yeah, that one," Clint said. "She joined the church a couple of years after high school. Word has it she ran with the wrong crowd briefly, but wanted to clean up her act. Leroy fell in love with Miley the first time he saw her. He knew her history and wanted to get to know her better. So he suggested she set up a group for reformed addicts and have meetings in the church basement. Some of them had fallen off the wagon more than once, which is probably why Miley got a bad rap with her neighbors. But it served Leroy's purpose. They started dating right away and were engaged just a few months later."

That was all very interesting, but he hadn't told me anything I didn't already know. "What does this have to do with what you couldn't wait to tell me?"

"Because not one week before her death, Miley told Leroy that if she died before him, she wanted him to feel free to fall in love and get married to someone else."

"People say stuff like that all the time."

"Maybe someone who's been married for years, but not a young woman planning to walk down the aisle for the first time in her life in just a few months."

"Okay, it is a little ... odd. But still, it's not proof that someone was after her."

The headlights of an oncoming truck flooded Clint's face with light. Squinting against the glare, he shrugged. "I suppose not, but it seemed pretty weird to me."

"Do you know if they got the autopsy report back? I thought it was determined she died of a drug overdose." I left out that Deputy Eklund had already told me they suspected suffocation.

"I haven't heard anything definite yet. Just that drugs were found near her body. Sounds like a good question for Sheriff Driscoll, though." A weighty silence wedged between us, but only for a moment. Clint cleared his throat. "Sam, I know you wanted to have your own place, but I'm starting to think that's not wise. There could be a killer on the loose in your neighborhood."

I knew exactly where this was headed, but I did my best to avoid it.

"I don't want to move back in with Dad and Ida right now. Dad and I are getting along better than we have in years. I call him once a day to make sure he hasn't set anything on fire, and once a week we all get together for dinner. Besides, they've got their own thing going — remember?"

He let a few moments lapse, but I could see the thoughts forming behind his eyes. "I wasn't talking about you moving in with your dad. I have plenty of room at my place, even for Bump."

I gazed out the window. Why did it feel like he was pressuring me about this?

"I'm sure Bump would love seeing you every day, but what about Tara? Don't you think you and me shagging on the side would be just as awkward for her as knowing her grandfather is doing the neighbor?"

"Sam, she's fourteen. I think she's old enough to handle the thought of her mother having an adult relationship."

Is that what we had: an 'adult relationship'? Sounded like code for twenty-four-hour booty call. "So you're asking us both to move in with you, is that it? Permanently, or just as a protective measure?"

I wanted the words back the moment they sprang from my mouth. If I'd wanted to figure out where we were headed, I could have broached the subject much more diplomatically.

He lifted his foot off the accelerator. Eyes narrowed, he looked at me. "You have to ask?"

"If my daughter is part of the equation, yes, I do." What I didn't say was that I didn't want to yank her from one home to another, just in case things with Clint didn't work out.

And if that thought kept entering my mind, obviously I had doubts about us. Still, I wasn't about to say that out loud, because every relationship had its growing pains. I wanted to slow things down between us; he kept trying to speed them up.

As if he were reading my mind, Clint's eyes snapped back to the road. He grabbed the steering wheel and spun it halfway. The SUV veered to the left so fast I thought we were going to careen across the center line and into the opposite ditch. But he was just making the final turn before getting onto Highway 379. The iron cross atop the steeple of the Evangelical Sanctuary came into view and I knew we were getting close.

I watched the night scenery roll by. Moonlight painted the land in traces of faint silver, deep shadowy woods bordering broad fields ribboned in stubbled rows. "I'm sorry. It's just ... we haven't ever really talked about us. I wasn't sure if you were just looking out for Tara and me, or if you, you know ... if you see us, you and me, still together six months or a few years from now."

There, I'd bunted. Given him the chance to say what he really felt.

"Are you still concerned about Danielle? Because I haven't even seen her, or spoken to her, since the last time we talked."

That didn't exactly answer my question, but it did make me wonder why he'd asked — and if something in particular was still bothering him.

"Are you concerned that Archer gave me a ride home today?" I said, my face again turned toward the window.

"I didn't exactly like it."

Finally, I looked at him, but his eyes were steely, fixed on the road ahead. "Why? You were leaving. I had to get home somehow."

"It wasn't that he gave you a ride, Sam."

"No? Then what?"

Clint half-shrugged. "Just a sense. That maybe he'd like something more."

So I hadn't been imagining that he was miffed when he saw me inside the lodge with Archer.

"So you're trying to stake your claim?" I'd said it jokingly, but I'm sure it came off a little more snarky than I intended. Then again, maybe I did want to know if that was what he was doing.

Slowing, he pulled into the field where my loyal Subaru was sitting all alone. We bumped over the flattened hayfield until we reached my car. Clint threw his SUV into park and killed the engine.

Nostrils flaring, hands still resting on the wheel, he blinked several times. Then he turned to me, his voice soft and imploring. "Maybe I *am* trying to make a declaration. But you need to stop pushing me away whenever things get too serious, okay? Give us a chance, Sam. A real chance. That's all I ask."

"Can't we have that chance if I'm living in my own place?"

"Of course, we can. Except I don't want anything to happen to you."

I got where Clint was coming from. Still, it bothered me that he thought I couldn't fend for myself. I'd spent the last decade raising my daughter alone in a big city, where vagrants on the subway and muggings in the park were common. In some ways, I felt like he was just making the offer to keep me away from Archer. And he would have had good reason to act that way if he'd known what had gone on just a few hours ago. But he didn't.

Whatever his reason — and despite the fact that I'd just had a peeping Tom in my backyard — the timing wasn't good. Moving in together wasn't going to make a tenuous relationship suddenly magically all right.

And I had my own issues to sort out.

"I ... I don't know, Clint. It's a serious commitment."

"Marriage is a serious commitment, Sam. Getting out of it requires lawyers and paperwork and a lot of money, which isn't something I'd ever relish doing again. If living together doesn't work out, you can just pick up your stuff and go. But for now, don't you think it makes sense for us to share a place? Especially" — he drew a finger along my collarbone to send a shiver through my body — "a bed. Just think, you and me, making love every morning."

He made it sound so tantalizing, and yet ... so temporary. And even though marrying Clint wasn't something I'd thought a lot about yet, for some reason it bothered me that he may have ruled it out forever.

"I'll think about it," I told him. But only because I didn't want to tell him no right then. Even if jealousy had been part of his reason, he'd also done it out of concern and I wasn't going to rebuff him on that so quickly. "For now, Bump makes a pretty good alarm, you have to admit."

At that exact moment, I felt a tug at my gut. I'd left Bump at home, thinking that maybe if the peeping Tom came back, Bump's barks would make him think twice about loitering in the alley. But what if the person chucked a hunk of poisoned meat over the fence with the intent of silencing Bump for good?

Clint and I got out. He lugged the gas can to my car, and as he started filling the tank I said, "Clint, I have to pick Tara up from Shannon's, but would you mind following me home to make sure my car's okay and everything?"

Everything meaning Bump.

"No problem" — he flashed a perfunctory grin — "but I'm sure everything's fine."

I wouldn't be sure until I could see for myself.

I CAME HOME TO darkness — total and absolute. Why hadn't I had the good sense to leave on the outside light next to the kitchen door? Or a light inside the kitchen? I'd even left my flashlight on the counter. No, I'd been too frazzled to think straight. Now here I was standing in the driveway in pitch blackness, my heart beating franticly like a drum roll.

"Mom?"

I jumped out of my skin. Spinning around, I nearly collided with Tara, who had just come up to me. I hadn't even heard her get out of the car.

"Can we go in now?"

"No!"

"What? Why not?"

A pair of headlights swept behind her as a car pulled in behind mine. The driver killed the engine and then got out, slamming his car door. The headlights, still on, blocked my vision. I shoved Tara behind me in a surge of protectiveness.

"Don't move, pumpkin." I rifled through my keys until I found the pointiest one and gripped it tight. "I'll handle this."

"Mom, it's just Dr. Clint."

The automatic headlights dimmed, then went off, as Clint strode casually forward. "I lost you at that last stoplight. You must've been going eighty miles per hour."

"Seventy," I said, dropping the keys back in my purse, then mumbled, "*maybe* seventy-five." More like seventy-nine, actually.

It was the second time in three days that I'd broken the law speeding — and what a long day today had been. Far too eventful. And it wasn't over yet.

Bump hadn't made a sound when we pulled in. Which had me worried.

In fact, the whole neighborhood was eerily quiet. People only ever came out of their houses here to do the obligatory yardwork before scurrying back inside to their caves. In Naperville, the neighbors walked their dogs, children rode their bikes in the cul-de-sacs, and joggers were a regular occurrence. Maybe it was the fact that the houses here were closer here that made people withdraw inside. Like they wanted to get away from each other. Or put walls up between them.

On the far side of my house from the driveway was an empty lot. As soon as my brace came off, I planned to go over there and clear weeds, but for now it was just an overgrown meadow. The next door neighbor closest was a sixty-something single guy who worked third shift. I only ever knew if he was home if I happened to hear his car pull in. The garage door went up, the car went in, the garage door went down. I'd seen him once in his living room window when I came home from picking up Tara. I'd detected a scowl, then the curtains had flown shut. It was the only time I'd ever seen him. I'd contemplated sneaking the mail from his mailbox one day to pretend it had mistakenly been delivered to my house, just so I could introduce myself. But that was probably a felony and I didn't need to add it to my litany of recent misdemeanors.

Clint took his spare key out and let himself in before I could screech a warning. Tara strolled right in after him to leave me standing alone on the driveway.

I burst into the kitchen, breathless. A clatter sounded and I spun around, only to see Clint with his head halfway in the fridge. He emerged with a can of pop.

"Do you mind?" he said, holding it up. "I haven't had anything since the picnic."

"Where's Bump?" I whispered, panicking.

Shrugging, he cast a look around and lowered his own voice. "Good question."

Dad would never forgive me if I let anything happen to Bump. I tiptoed to the back door, grabbing the flashlight off the counter.

"Let me." Clint nudged past me, taking the flashlight from me. Opening the door slowly, he poked his head out, then flicked the light on and shone it over the yard. "Not here," he said, and came back in.

There was no sign of Bump, and Tara had disappeared right behind our backs. I crept to the half bath. The door was wide open. The room was empty. Same with the office. They weren't in the living room, either.

My heart was jackhammering against my ribs. The house was dark. And silent. This wasn't normal.

"Where's Tara?" I whispered to Clint.

"Tara?" he called up the stairs. No one answered. Then more loudly, "Tara?!"

The toilet flushed upstairs.

That answered where Tara was. But what about Bump?

I grabbed the butcher knife out of a kitchen drawer.

Clint snatched it away from me with an admonishing look. "Really, Sam?"

"The dog, Clint. Where's the dog?"

"Asleep, maybe? Let me handle this. You stay back."

Knife held at waist level, he crept up the stairs. I limped behind him. My foot had been doing much better, but after all of today's walking it was beginning to ache again. He reached the top step and peered around the wall.

A scream ripped from Tara's throat. Clint dropped the knife. It fell, handle down, then bounced down the steps. I yanked my foot out of the way. The knife blade grazed the end of my shoe, leaving a little nick in it next to my big toe.

Arms held wide, Clint stepped into the upstairs hallway. "Tara, Tara, it's all right. It's just me."

I rushed up after him to see Tara standing in the bathroom

215

doorway, already wearing a pair of plaid boxers and an oversized T-shirt for sleeping. She had her arms crossed over her chest to try to hide the fact that she wasn't wearing a bra.

"Why are you waving a knife at me?!" she shouted. "You scared the shit out of me. For real. I think I just crapped my pants."

"Tara," I said, "we can't find Bump."

She threw her head back, mouth open. "Is that all?" Groaning, she spun on her heel and marched into her bedroom. At her door, she pointed to her bed. "He likes to sleep there when I'm gone, okay? I guess he'd had a pretty exciting day and was out cold when we got home."

I looked. There he was, sprawled out on top of her purple comforter like a sultan waiting for his harem. The plume of his tail tapped on the bed as he gazed groggily at us.

Clint smirked. "If it will make you feel better, I'll check the other rooms before I leave."

A few minutes later, I was standing with Clint at the back door. My nerves were still frayed.

He pulled me to him, his hands sliding down my back and over my bottom to hold me firmly against him. I liked his hands there. Liked what his touch and the closeness of his body did to mine. But … I don't know what it was. Something was missing. But what? What was it that I needed from him?

Tilting my chin up with a finger, he devoured my mouth. Sucked me into the depths of his sexiness, his manly need pouring into me, demanding more.

"Sam, Sam," he murmured, a low groan vibrating in his throat. "Think about my offer. It would be … convenient. We could be together every night."

I turned my head aside. "I have to think about Tara."

"I know." He leaned sideways to look into my eyes, then his eyelids drifted shut and he planted the wettest of kisses on the curve of my neck. "Talk to her. Think about it."

"I will," I said, stepping back and opening the door for him. But I already knew my answer. I just couldn't tell him yet. Not until I could figure out how to say it.

When he left, I double-checked all the door locks and made sure the windows were all closed and latched. As I brushed my teeth, I stared into the mirror. 'It's complicated' didn't even begin to say how I felt about my love life these days. It had all been so clear and easy when Kyle and I fell in love as teenagers.

A muffled thump sounded outside the house. I poked my head out into the hallway. Bump stood in Tara's doorway, his ears perked. But was that because he heard me — or because he'd heard the sound, too?

As quietly as I could, I tiptoed down the stairs and peeked out each door. Bump padded softly behind me the whole time, looking more curious as to what I was doing than on the alert for intruders. I stood for the longest time at the kitchen window, staring out into the darkness. But I never heard the sound again, never saw anything move.

I knew I needed to stop letting my imagination get the best of me — but no matter how hard I tried lately, I couldn't shake the feeling that someone was watching.

chapter 18

I DIDN'T SLEEP WELL that night — or the night after. By the third night, I was so sleep-deprived, a tornado could've sucked up my house and dropped it in Oz and I wouldn't have woken up. Tara had managed to get herself ready for school and on the bus on time all week long. As the days slid by, that little parasite of mine called paranoia faded away. I was finally falling into a routine.

The replacement phone I got was far too advanced for me. On my old phone, I'd been able to call and text, which frankly was all I needed. But this one had more capability than my last computer. Tara showed me how to surf the web on it and download apps that somehow were supposed to save me time and provide countless conveniences, but three minutes into her technology geek fest, my eyes glazed over and my mind drifted. I heard words that were vaguely English, but their context was entirely lost on me.

"This is the best one of all," Tara beamed, shoving the screen at my face and rotating it. "If you get tired of playing *Birds of Wrath* and get hungry, you can order a pizza with just one click."

Because it had been so difficult and time-consuming to call someone and ask for one.

"How does it know what you want?"

"You tell it your preference and it saves it."

"Same for which pizza place you want it from?"

"Uh-huh. Isn't that cool?"

"Very cool. I'm not sure how I managed until now. Amazing we didn't starve to death. Does it order and deliver groceries, too?"

She closed her eyelids briefly, but I could still see her eyeballs roll.

A moment later, she was testing out ringtones. "You do know you can download songs for your ring, right?"

"Yes, but I prefer my phone to sound like, well, a phone."

This time she sighed as she rolled her eyes. I went back into my office to work while Tara played with my phone.

Whenever he didn't work too late, Clint came and took Bump for a jog. Every day, he asked if I was ready to move into his house and every day I pointed out the fact that nothing else had happened, we were fine, and besides, I couldn't uproot Tara once more in such a short time span. We'd gone from Naperville, to my dad's house, to Ida's, and were now bunking at Melissa's. I'd started to hope Melissa would sell the place to me. It might not be fancy, but it was starting to feel like home.

During another of our usual family dinner nights, while Dad was engrossed in Lisa Kudrow's genealogy show on PBS, *Who Do You Think You Are?*, Ida helped me finish painting Tara's room: a pale plum that complemented the light gray carpet beautifully. Bit by bit, the place looked less 'Melissa' and more like Sam and Tara lived here.

Bump had also gotten used to the increased stimuli, until it got to the point that the squirrel could fly from limb to limb overhead and he would barely bat an eye. The postal carrier was another matter entirely. In Bump's mind, the fact that the mail lady eventually left was proof that he'd done his job in warning her off. I finally took to crating him with a peanut butter stuffed bone during the time she usually showed up.

Tara settled in at school. Although she still didn't have many friends on account of the incident with the janitor's closet, she seemed to get along well with her teachers, and I assured her that was the most important part. She was a lot like me. Except she had Shannon, who was a lot more of a normal friend than Selma — which reminded me of something. I still needed to get together with Selma for the big 'test'. But every time I messaged her, she was either working, babysitting, or with Dylan. By all accounts, Dylan was treating her well. They went to Cancun for five days, as promised, and returned, with Selma more smitten than she'd been before. I admit — I was jealous. But who wouldn't be if their best friend had chosen a tattooed, beer-bellied, womanizing biker over them?

There came a point when I began to wonder if she was dissing me. As soon as I finished the final draft of my book, I was going to swing by Garber's Groceries and find out.

Best of all, I shed my wrist brace, and my foot, with the exception of a little morning stiffness, seemed to have fully healed. I started walking Bump through the neighborhood on my own occasionally, and often saw Harmon Purnell outside, organizing his garage, clipping his hedges, or edging his driveway. The moment I waved at him or slowed to talk, Maybelle would stick her head out the door to bark another chore at him.

Meanwhile, Dad and Ida seemed blissfully happy. They took day trips to Indianapolis together and continued to invite Tara over for board games on Wednesdays after school when Ida didn't have any committee meetings. Once a week, they came to our place for dinner. I actually started to look forward to those evenings. I was still guarded about what I said to Dad, and although he had a lot of opportunities to be cynical, he never was. It was almost like Ida had sprinkled pixie dust over him. And Ida? Well, Ida was still Ida. I wouldn't have changed a thing about her.

All was well in Wilton.

Almost.

I hadn't heard from Archer in three weeks. Although I did see him once. Never mind the fact that I'd had to drive past the firehouse twenty times at fifteen miles an hour just to catch a glimpse of him power-washing the fire engine. His back was to me. Until the car riding my bumper blasted their horn. I hit the gas then, too embarrassed to look to see if he'd noticed me. Damn tailgater.

According to the local paper, he was waist-deep in taking the steps to expand his charity. Since the response to Everly's Foundation had so rapidly grown beyond his capability to oversee it, he'd partnered with a national software corporation looking for a charity to fund. In reality, what it meant was that he was busier than ever. Too busy to have time for a crazy, messed-up friend like me — as I learned one late September morning.

I turned on the TV on the kitchen counter while waiting for my coffee to brew: pumpkin spice, whole bean, freshly ground. Anything else was like licking an ashtray. Not that I was a gourmet coffee snob or anything. Pointing my toes, I moved my foot in a circle. No pain. It was as good as new, and my wrist was fine as long as I didn't lift anything over five pounds. Clint and I were scheduled to take Bump on a jog that evening. We'd fallen into a comfortable routine, which meant we had sex — mind-blowing, intense, and occasionally kinky sex — twice a week, which was whenever I could be sure that Tara was with either my dad or Shannon. We hung out at Clint's anyway, because I was always worried that Tara would come home early and discover us desecrating the kitchen table with bare body parts.

I was in the middle of remembering the last time Clint and I had banged on Danielle's wine-stained alpaca rug when I heard Archer's wistful voice. It was only the second time I'd seen him in nearly a month. Only this time he wasn't here in Wilton. He was in New York City, bathing in the spotlight of humble heroism.

"She was my world, my life. I loved her more than anything."

The coffeemaker beeped like a hospital heart monitor. I pivoted away from it and grabbed the remote to punch up the volume.

There he was on a national morning talk show: Wilton's own Archer Malone. He smoothed the crease on his pleated trousers, looking uncomfortable in his fancy clothes, like he couldn't wait to slip back into faded jeans and a plain white T-shirt. His face, washed by the glare of studio lights, twitched. Matt Lauer uncrossed his legs and leaned forward, eyeglasses dangling from the fingertips of one hand.

Wait ... Matt Lauer! Archer was doing an interview with Matt Lauer?

"I can only imagine how hard that was," Lauer said, "losing an infant daughter in a horrific fire like that while her mother — the woman who gave birth to her — stood outside with her sexual partner, too stoned to even remember that her baby girl was inside in a mobile home being consumed by flames. You had to be devastated when you learned that."

Tucking his chin to his chest, Archer nodded. Tears glistened in his eyes. He started to speak, but the words caught in his throat. My heart ached for him. I knew how painful it was for him and that he didn't like to talk about it at all, let alone reveal his deepest torment on national TV.

Why was he doing this?

"It was, Matt. I replay the night I got that call over and over in my head. I ... I know I can't go back in time, can't change what happened." A dark furrow formed between his brows. Steepling his fingertips together, he took in two shorts breaths, forced more words out. "But I can, maybe, make a difference in someone else's life right now, someone who's struggling like Ava did."

"Do you ever blame yourself for the events that unfolded that night?"

"I used to. A lot. But then I would remind myself that I was only nineteen. I didn't know who to go to for help. Didn't think it was my place to intervene on her behalf. If there had been something like

Everly's Foundation around then, who knows?"

"Speaking of which," Lauer said, "with you this morning is the foundation's newest benefactor, Dr. Danielle Townsley. Dr. Townsley, how did you get involved in this charity?"

The camera panned to Archer's left. There, her legs crossed toward Archer and her cleavage artfully arranged, sat Danielle. She slipped her hand down over Archer's wrist. In response, he turned his hand over to clasp hers. Then she placed her other hand on top of his consolingly.

"Well, Matt," Danielle began, "I wasn't really looking to 'get involved', so to speak. It just sort of happened." She squeezed Archer's hand and they exchanged brief smiles. "Archer and I were volunteering as trainers at a local football game. I mentioned my work in Africa helping impoverished children; he told me about the foundation he'd started. One thing followed another and pretty soon I was all hands on. I couldn't help myself. I promised him I would do everything in my power to raise awareness on his behalf. I work a lot, so I don't have much spare time, but what little I do have goes to helping the mothers that Archer's charity is reaching out to."

That deceitful whore! She just wanted a reason to get her claws into him, just like she'd tried to do with Clint. Who was she going to seduce next — my dad?

Lauer touched Danielle's knee. "You're doing a good thing for others, my friends. A good thing. Mr. Malone, my condolences on your loss. I know it doesn't bring your daughter back, but maybe someone else will be saved through your efforts." He shook Archer's hand, then sat back and pointed at the camera. "Up next, what *you* can do to give your toddlers a head start on getting into college. Stay tuned."

College? I hadn't even thought that far ahead with my high school freshman, except to point out it was that or trade school.

I filled my coffee cup and took three sips, wondering why it tasted like road tar, before I realized it was black, I was that distracted. Two heaping scoops of sugar and a mound of nondairy creamer later, I was returning the caffeine levels in my blood to their proper level. I pulled a stool up to the sink and stared out the kitchen window at Bump, who was sniffing in figure eights and loops around the backyard.

Except for the surprise of seeing Archer on TV, the morning was off to a quiet start. One more pass at my manuscript and it would be off to the editor. Then I had a long list of small, but manageable tasks to tackle.

My phone rang. Or rather it played "Highway to Hell". I'd warn Tara when she got home from school not to mess with my ringtone again. I didn't recognize the number. Probably a random survey.

"Hello?"

After that, my day took the express lane straight *to* hell.

"Ms. McNamee?"

"Yes?"

"This is Principal Nina Steenkamp at Wilton Memorial," said a bland female voice. "How are you today?"

I've often wondered why people bother asking that, because they don't really want to know how you are. Usually, it was just a formality, something you said in lieu of real conversation, but I had the feeling there was a serious reason for this call. "I'm not going to like this, am I?"

"Pardon?"

"Sorry, I don't mean to sound snippy, but … why did you call? I'd imagine it's not to tell me that my daughter aced her Physical Science quiz, is it?"

"No, sorry. I wish it was."

"What, then?"

"Ms. McNamee, you need to come to the school right away. Tara has been suspended. There was a random drug search today by the sheriff's department. The dog indicated Tara's locker. We opened it and found a baggie of marijuana. Considering it was a first offense, there may not be —"

"You *can't* be serious." This was so far out in left field, it felt like I was listening in on some random conversation between strangers. She couldn't be talking about *my* daughter.

"Excuse me?" Principal Steenkamp said. "Ma'am, maybe you should just come down to the school and we can talk in person."

Ma'am? I had to bite my tongue. I *hated* that. Call me Sam, call me miss, or missus. I'll even answer to 'Hey, you' or 'Yo'. Just don't call me ma'am.

I told her I'd be there in fifteen minutes. I made it in twelve. Thank goodness the cops weren't parked on Highway 379 in their usual spot.

When I got to the school, I had to ring a buzzer beside the entry doors to even get in the building. In my day, they propped these doors open with a brick to let the breeze circulate. I half-expected metal detectors, but the Wilton school district operated on a shoestring budget. I stormed into the main office.

"Ma'am," the secretary barked, as I marched straight past her. "You'll need to sign in."

I must have looked belligerent, the way she was flagging me down with the clipboard, like she could flog me with it and knock me out cold until the police came. I ignored her anyway.

Tara was parked on a bench right next to the door to the principal's office. I could tell instantly by the look on her face that this was all a horrible mistake.

"Mom?" she croaked, tears streaking down her cheeks. "I swear I didn't —"

"Shhh. It's all right, pumpkin." I tucked her head against my stomach. "We'll figure out who did this. I know it wasn't you."

A pair of deputies walked in front of the main office. They were standing on the other side of the glass divider in the lobby. One of them was Deputy Carin Eklund. Smiling, she waved a pencil at me in greeting, as if I'd just walked in to sign my daughter out for a dentist appointment. The other one was Deputy Halloway — and he was holding onto the harness of a Belgian Malinois wearing an official vest that had 'Drug Enforcement Task Force' stitched into it. The dog had teeth like the wolf in Little Red Riding Hood. They were an intimidating pair.

Nodding, Tara sniffled loudly and hugged me tighter. The principal appeared in the doorway, and I pulled away from Tara. A blob of snot and tear stains darkened the front of my shirt. That was when I realized I was still wearing the loose tank top and sweats that I'd slept in last night. And I hadn't showered yet. Or put on deodorant. Or brushed my teeth. And my hair was piled on top of my head with a scrunchee in what must have looked like an imitation of the hairdo of Sideshow Bob, the infamous criminal sidekick of Krusty the Clown from *The Simpsons*. Thank goodness, I'd actually fallen asleep wearing a bra last night — although the purple satin spaghetti straps were probably sending the wrong message.

My look didn't exactly say 'college-educated, middle-class working mother of wrongly-accused honor roll student'. More likely it screamed 'substance-addicted, welfare-dependent, boyfriend-hopping baby-machine'.

Perfect, just what I was going for. If I wanted to convict my daughter on first impressions alone.

"Ms. McNamee?" Principal Steenkamp propped her glasses on top of her head. Her blondish-white hair was styled in a pixie cut that probably took her all of five minutes to wash and dry. Everything about her was no-nonsense, from the starched plum-colored blouse and complementary faux pearls to the tweed skirt and dark gray pumps. She indicated her office with an upturned hand. "Please."

Head down, I trudged in, feeling considerably less vigilante than when I'd arrived.

She turned out to be very nice, which was disarming, because I'd intended to come in here shouting at full lung capacity and threatening a lawsuit.

"I know this must be upsetting to you." She straightened a small stack of papers in front of her and pushed them to the side. "There's certainly nothing in Tara's records to indicate anything of this nature in her past."

"There isn't. She's an A student. A little snarky at times, maybe" — it was genetic — "but she's never so much as taken a ketchup packet she didn't need. This *has* to be a mistake."

Slender fingers dangling over the ends of the armrests, Principal Steenkamp settled back in her big leather executive chair. She had enough crow's feet to prove that she'd heard that line a hundred times.

"Yes, of course." She lowered her glasses back onto her nose and flipped through the papers. "All the parents say that."

Which was probably true. Still, I knew my kid. Possessing drugs was the last thing I'd expect of her. There had to be an explanation.

For now, though, I knew the direction this was headed in. I just didn't know how to steer this unwieldy Titanic out of the path of the iceberg.

"Unfortunately," she continued, still perusing Tara's transcripts, "we have to go on the evidence we have. Deputy Halloway's canine partner was doing a routine check along the hallway in Wing D and signaled locker #311, which belongs to your daughter, Tara McNamee. When we opened it, there was a clear plastic bag of marijuana on the top shelf, under the front cover of her geometry book. We immediately pulled her from class. Deputy Eklund questioned her and —"

"She denied it was hers, right?"

"They always do, Ms. McNamee. At least the first-time offenders. The repeats will occasionally confess, thinking they'll get a reduced punishment for being honest. She'll be expelled for ten days and not permitted to make up the work she misses in that time. That won't bode well for her grades this grading period, but with commitment, she can still keep a good overall GPA if she stays out of trouble for the rest of her stay here. As far as whether she'll be levied with criminal charges, that's up to the sheriff's department. But I'll warn you — Sheriff Driscoll takes a hard line these days. He's dedicated to cleaning up all of Humboldt County's schools and making them a safe, drug-free environment."

To her it was all cut and dried. Her job was to purge the riffraff from the building. She'd been there, done that countless times in her career and had no sympathy for those proclaiming their innocence. This was nothing new to her.

To me it was my daughter's reputation and her future on the line. I wasn't leaving without making an attempt to get it straightened out.

I pulled my shoulders back and sat up tall. Like that was going to make her forget how I was dressed. "How do we appeal this?"

Her mouth tipping in a frown, she tapped a pen on the stack of papers. "I'm not sure what you mean. There is a process for appealing suspensions, but it has to go through the school board and they don't meet until the first of next month."

That was almost three weeks away. By then, Tara would be behind. It would be a nightmare trying to rectify the situation so late. "So they can't hold an emergency meeting?"

"For something of this nature? No. Or else they'd be convening twice every week. At any rate, illegal drugs were found in Tara's —"

"Who else has access to her locker?"

"Well, I do." She tilted her head back. "The secretary, the custodian ... But that's it."

The custodian: Harmon Purnell. Since I was getting nowhere with the warden here, maybe Harmon could provide some clues. Or maybe Harmon was involved? After all, Tara had found those potheads in the janitor's closet at the football game.

On second thought, Harmon couldn't have been involved. He just wasn't the type. And I couldn't see what motive the secretary might have had. That left me with no leads.

"So what now?" I asked.

"You may take her home. Suspension begins today. The sheriff will likely visit you at home this afternoon, so I wouldn't go out of town if I were you."

Eager to leave, I stood up and turned to walk out when she sighed and added, "I'm extremely sorry, Ms. McNamee. We had such high hopes for Tara when she enrolled."

I wheeled around. "So you've already judged her guilty? You've never heard of anyone being framed for something they didn't do?" I shook my head, trying hard to contain my anger. Intellectually, I knew she was just doing her job, but the mama bear in me wanted to claw her eyes out for hurting my baby. "When I come back here with proof that she didn't do this, you'd better make a *full* apology."

I stomped from her office, jotted a few slashes on the sign-out sheet, and escorted Tara from the building. The Keystone Cops had already made themselves scarce, but I intended to speak to Deputy Eklund as soon as I cooled down. Which would likely be never.

Okay, so I'd talk to her eventually. Or I'd straighten things out with Sheriff Driscoll. First, I'd get Tara home and calmed down, because right now she was working up to a panic attack.

Halfway to the car I noticed Tara wasn't at my side anymore. I looked behind me. Right outside the front doors to the school, Tara had stopped dead. She was gulping air in tiny breaths, like a fish that had flopped up on land and was already fading. Her wide eyes were fixed on nothing, her shaking hands clutched at her chest.

Correction — she was *having* a panic attack.

I jogged to her and planted myself squarely in front of her.

"Tara? Tara, honey?" I clasped her face in my palms. "Remember how to breathe. In through your nose, out through your mouth. Relax your vocal cords."

She wasn't responding to me. No matter which way I turned her head, her eyes were not focusing on me. Her breathing was getting more rapid. Shallower. If I didn't reach her soon, she'd pass out. I really didn't need to add an ambulance run to this already crappy day.

In the school building not thirty feet from us, several students were clustered at an open window, faces pressed to the glass, watching. No doubt the discovery of drugs and Tara's subsequent removal from class had been the talk of the school all morning long. The rumors were probably more mortifying to her than the actual drug bust itself.

I patted her cheeks. "Tara?"

She made a little gurgling noise in her throat. Then came that prolonged croak, like a frog being strangled. Was she turning blue?

The heck with the lookie-loos. I slapped her. "Tara!"

She stiffened. A response. Good.

"Pull the air deep into your belly." I rubbed my hand in a light circle on her stomach. It expanded ever so slightly. "That's it. Now let it out. Slowly."

Air whooshed from her lips.

"Slower. Breathe deep. In through your nose, remember?"

She drew in a shaky breath, then let it out gradually. She sounded like a leaky tire now, which was an improvement. A few seconds later, she did it again on her own. I waved a hand in front of her face and she blinked.

When she was finally breathing normally again, I pulled her into my embrace.

"Mom? They're staring at us."

"Probably because I slapped you."

Her head on my shoulder, she sucked back snotty tears. "You did?"

"Yeah." We were both looking toward the window where all the students had been watching. The teacher must've shooed them away, because they all pulled back and returned to their seats — except for one boy, tall and good-looking.

"Hey, Tara," he called lowly. But then he jerked his head away from the window and stepped back. The teacher, an older sour-faced man with black horn-rim glasses, slammed the window shut and drew the shade down.

Tara tucked her chin against my neck. "Can we go home now?"

"Sure, pumpkin."

Back home to wait for the sheriff to question my daughter about her drug habit and decide whether or not to send her to juvenile detention. While he was at it, he could hit me with child abuse.

Maybe it was time to hire a lawyer after all?

chapter 19

"SO WHO WAS THAT in the window?" I rubbed my hair vigorously with a towel. After getting home, I'd managed to jump in the shower for five minutes while Tara was decompressing on the couch. I'd even shed my sweats for a pair of jeans and a lightweight sweater that I'd bought from the department store in Fullbright recently. Nothing fancy, but definitely more presentable than what I'd schlepped to school in that morning.

Tara pulled her fuzzy blanket around her head and sipped from her mug. Ever since she was old enough to hold her own cup and wise enough not to scald her tongue, hot chocolate had been her comfort food.

She shrugged. "There were a lot of kids in the window. Every one of them saw me lose it."

"I mean the last one. The boy who said your name."

"Oh, him." Tugging her bangs down over her eyes, she scoffed. "That was Cooper John. He was probably going to make fun of me."

Then she erupted in a fresh spate of tears. This wasn't normal for her. Anxiety attacks, yes; waterworks, no. I rubbed her back and just let her sob. At least she was breathing. Besides, for now, I really couldn't fix anything. I didn't want to call Clint to ask for the name of a lawyer, since the last one he'd chosen from these parts hadn't worked out, and honestly I was at a loss as to how to find one. Picking one out of the Yellow Pages was a gamble. Selma probably had plenty of relatives who could tell me where to find a good deal on bail bonds, but that wasn't what I needed. Not yet, anyway. I didn't dare ask Ida, because then Dad would know. Although given that Ida was always connected to the grapevine, he'd find out soon enough.

That left Archer. He was out of town, but he still might know someone. Slipping into my office for privacy, I called him, but it went straight to voicemail. I waited for the beep.

"Hey, Arch, ummm … I need some advice, sort of. Do you know any good lawyers?" I was going to say more, but I couldn't piece together how to wrap up that stunning opener before the second beep indicated that my time had run out.

No telling when he'd get back to me if he was gallivanting around the Big Apple, hobnobbing with network news celebrities. I'd wait to see how things went with Sheriff Driscoll. If he started to grill either one of us, I would plead the fifth and wait until I heard back from Archer.

Still, I couldn't shake the feeling that someone else had mentioned a lawyer to me recently. One who specialized in wrongful arrests. Who was it?

I sat down in my office chair with a *wooompf*. Now I remembered. Danielle Townsley, that was who.

Going to her for a referral would be a little like asking your mother what the best sexual position was for your wedding night. I knew what Clint's preference was. Just thinking about it made my —

My pants vibrated. I wasn't sure whether I was on the verge of being aroused or had just gotten corrected for having erotic thoughts.

After the second buzz, I realized I'd put my phone on vibrate before going into the school. I hadn't wagered on Archer responding so quickly. I answered before it buzzed again.

233

"That was quick!"

"Hello, Ms. McNamee?"

I knew that voice. It was a throwback to the silver screen of olden days, reminiscent of Cary Grant or Charlton Heston.

"Sheriff Driscoll … hi. I was expecting someone else."

"I gathered that. And I regret the circumstances for contacting you, but could you bring Tara down to the station right away?"

Shoot. They were going to book her. Take her fingerprints. Throw her in the slammer. This time tomorrow, she'd have some spiky-haired broad named Gypsy calling her 'Princess' and giving her a rubdown.

Steeling myself, I lowered my voice. "Just for questioning, right? Because this was all a big, big mistake. A setup. I'm waiting for my lawyer to get back to me, actually." Not that I had one yet, but I would. Soon. "She won't get transferred to juvenile detention, will she? Because I don't even know where that is. In Fullbright, maybe? A bit of a haul, but I'll go every day if —"

"Actually," Sheriff Driscoll interrupted, "there's someone here with information that could help her situation."

Her situation? That sounded so much less damning than 'conviction record'. Maybe there was hope, after all.

I paced back and forth in front of the window that looked out into the backyard. Next to the silver maple in the far corner, I noticed a small mound of earth.

What the —?

A clod of dirt hit the fence. I followed the source to see Bump's hind end in the air. He had widened a chipmunk hole and had his muzzle crammed down into it, as he furiously scraped away layers of dirt with his front paws.

I opened the window. "Hey, cut that out!"

His head snapped up. As soon as he saw me, his ears flattened. He went down on his belly, slinking his way to the back door.

"Pardon?"

"Not you," I said. "Sorry, I was talking to the dog. We'll be there as soon as possible."

"Very good. While I can't make any promises, it's possible that our informant could blow open an ongoing investigation."

I was less concerned about his investigation than I was about Tara's wounded pride and shattered reputation. At any rate, whoever this informant was, I just hoped he got Tara completely off the hook.

After saying goodbye to Sheriff Driscoll, I threw open the office door and grabbed the keys from the counter. At the sound of the keys clinking, Bump bounded through the doggie door. He sat at my feet, a muddy trail of paw prints behind him.

"Are you going somewhere?" Tara asked from the couch, still sitting in the exact spot she'd landed in an hour ago when we first walked in. Her eyes were so red and puffy it looked like someone had tried to gouge them out. Wads of wet tissues lay scattered around her. Her lower lip drooped pathetically. "Please don't leave me here alone."

"Put your shoes on, kiddo," I told her. "There's a snitch ready to squeal. You may not have to wear an orange jumpsuit after all."

If I hadn't seen her blow her nose, I would have thought an ocean liner was docked in the front yard and had laid on its foghorn.

"Huh?"

"Someone has information that could exonerate you. With luck, we'll have you back in school tomorrow."

"Right. About that … I've been thinking … Can I be home-schooled? I'm not really sure I want to go back there after today. Ever."

"Let's see what happens. We'll talk about it later, after we get back from the station."

Bump's ears perked at the final word. Sometimes I forgot that he was a dropout from police dog school.

Tara mopped her face dry, then picked up her jacket. Head down, she trudged toward me. When I grabbed my purse, Bump leapt into the air, then pirouetted three times before racing to the side door in the kitchen.

He woofed softly twice, which was canine speak for 'Shake your tail! We have places to go, butts to sniff.'

"Not you, buddy. This doesn't have anything to do with you. You have to stay here."

He wagged his tail harder.

"Sorry, Bump, but your job is to guard the place, okay?" I opened the door and he darted for the opening, but I grabbed his collar in time. Tara slipped by and went to sit in the car.

Bump licked my fingers — a last-ditch plea to accompany us. I leaned over and kissed him on top of the head.

My knees wobbled. The world went gray and grainy. I heard panting, hard and rapid, in my ears — my own. My heart, bursting with exhilaration, pounded inside my chest. My muscles ached with the joy of movement and spent effort.

The smell of dewy grass and rain on asphalt and wet dog fur surrounded me. I tipped my head back, felt the morning sun dance across my muzzle. A sharp bark cleaved the air and I opened my eyes to watch a slender, young German Shepherd ... no, a Malinois, sail like a gazelle over a solid board jump as high as his handler's chest. Then the dog scrambled up a pile of rubble and down the other side, slithered the length of a concrete tunnel on his belly, and bounded through a series of tire hoops.

Fingernails scratched behind my ears. *C'mon, pal. Time for us to go to work. They've put the scents out. Let's see if you can find them this time. Stay focused, all right? Ignore everything around you. Just ... smell.*

I felt a tug on my leash. As I turned to follow, the earth tipped. A blanket of white fell across my vision.

"Mom? Mom?"

I blinked until a funnel of light appeared before me. A fuzzy image, Tara was stooped over me. My back was to the cabinet nearest to the back door, my legs splayed out in front of me. Bump was sitting squarely in front of me, washing my face.

"Hey." With each blink, my vision sharpened, but I was still dizzy.

"Why are you sitting on the floor? Are you okay?"

"Sure, just giving Bump a goodbye hug." I wrapped my arms around his neck and squeezed, which only made him lick more. I pushed him away. With a snort, he dove in and licked at my eyelids, like he wasn't convinced I was completely functioning just yet.

"For five minutes?"

"Right, sorry." I pushed myself up, careful to lean against the counter for support. "I'm just going to grab a Coke. Be there in a sec."

Tara squinted at me, then finally retreated to the car. I splashed cold water on my face and chugged half a can of pop before heading out the door, hoping the sugar would kick in.

I was careful not to touch Bump on my way out this time. I never knew when those visions, or memories, were going to come through. Their effect on me seemed to be getting stronger.

Bump may have flunked out of drug dog school when he was training with Oren Rickman, but he'd loved his work.

Just like I loved him — rodent-obsessed, muddy-pawed, slobbery mutt that he was. If anything ever happened to him, there'd be a huge hole in my heart to fill.

SHERIFF DRISCOLL SAT US down in the very same room I'd had my talk with Jake Taylor in. Which didn't exactly set the right tone for me.

A huge table took up half the room, and around it were four rickety wooden chairs. The walls were blank, except for a clock that looked like it was from 1940, a mostly bare shelf, the steel door leading to the corridor, and a mirror. We all knew they could see us on the other side of the mirror.

And that pendant light. You couldn't have an interrogation without a pendant light.

Too drained from her sob fest to slip into another panic attack, Tara slumped down in her chair and plucked a fresh tissue from the box in the middle of the table. She shredded it into confetti-sized bits, piling the pieces in front of her. Four tissues later, she had a miniature version of Mount Kilimanjaro.

I took the box away and set it on the wall shelf behind us, then scooped the tissue bits into a trash can.

She started digging at a tiny nick on the table with her fingernail. "What's taking them so long? And who's this mystery person, anyway?"

"I wish I knew." I couldn't say it out loud, but this whole messed up day was just as hard on her as it was on me. At least she was allowed to fall apart. I had to keep my shit together and be the level-headed, all-knowing parent. Only I didn't know a thing and what I really wanted to do was scream about how unfair life was.

Sheriff Driscoll came in finally. But it was for less than a minute. "Bear with us. We just finished taking a statement from our informant. He'll be here soon."

Tara and I exchanged a glance.

"Who is it?" I asked.

"You'll find out shortly. Meanwhile, can I get you something to drink?"

"A shot of Jack Daniels," Tara chimed.

I gave her the death glare.

"What? It was a joke, okay? Sorry, but I'm feeling a little tense. All I did today was show up at school and I got pulled out of second period and told there were drugs in my locker. Crazy thing is that I didn't even have time to go to it this morning. My bus was late."

Sheriff Driscoll tipped his head at that new morsel. "How late?"

"I don't know — twenty minutes, maybe?"

"Excuse me. I need to make a call."

When he was gone, I said to Tara, "Why didn't you say that earlier?"

"I did. I told the principal. But she didn't believe me. Just said that they had evidence on me and they were calling you to come and get me."

A few minutes later, the sheriff returned. "I called the school. The secretary confirmed that Tara's bus had mechanical problems this morning and she signed in twenty-five minutes late. Her first period teacher confirmed she showed up less than a minute after that. Her second period class is right next door to that one. Seeing as how her locker is at the other end of the school, it's highly unlikely she would have had time to go there at all this morning."

Brightening, Tara sat up straight. "So I can go now?"

He held up a hand. "Not quite. That just tells us you didn't put anything in there this morning."

Tara plopped back down in her chair like she had just been yanked underwater by a shark.

There was a quick knock at the door, then it opened. In walked Deputy Eklund, escorting the boy from the window at school. He was tall and lanky, but athletic, and had sandy blond hair with swoopy bangs held in place by a generous dose of hair product. He flashed a sympathetic smile at Tara, distinct dimples forming in his cheeks. Tara glared back at him and his smile drooped.

"Ms. McNamee," Sheriff Driscoll began, "this is Cooper John. His father is —"

"Wilton Police Chief Foster John. Yes, I know who he is now." And I liked him about as much as I liked flat tires on rainy days. Even with the cute dimples and perfect hair.

Deputy Eklund sat next to Cooper and directly across from Tara. "Cooper came up to me after you left this morning, Tara. He has something to share." She touched Cooper's wrist. "Go ahead."

His glance darted from Tara to Sheriff Driscoll, then back to Tara. When his eyes met mine for the briefest of moments, my opinion of him shifted the tiniest bit. Dark lashes framed startlingly blue irises. There was nothing cocky behind those eyes. He looked … afraid. Although he was trying his darnedest not to show it.

Through the floor, I felt the vibration of his foot as he tapped it nervously. He checked his watch, then looked up at the clock on the wall.

"Cooper?" Deputy Eklund prompted again. "Just repeat what you told me earlier."

He puffed out a short breath. "Okay, ummm … Well, yesterday evening, I was hanging around the gym to shoot some hoops with the guys. The janitor, Mr. Purnell, told us it was time to clear the building. Rest of the guys left, but I swung by the locker room to grab my stuff. I thought the building was empty, but I heard a locker slam in Wing D and went to look, thinking maybe Brett or Andy was still around."

He stopped there, like he was having second thoughts about telling the rest.

I couldn't wait for him to summon his courage. "Who was it?"

"I … I couldn't really see. I mean, I saw two people, but couldn't make out who it was. They were right next to where Tara's locker is."

Sheriff Driscoll laced his fingers together. "Anything that would help? Tall, short, big, skinny? Kind of clothing?"

"Not really. One was shorter. Could've been a kid … or maybe a woman. The other was a bit taller, but not much. Kind of skinny, had a hat on. A man, I think."

"What kind of hat?" the sheriff asked.

"Baseball, I guess."

That was hardly helpful. Half of Wilton had a baseball hat collection. Case in point: Jake Taylor. He was still in the county jail, so we couldn't pin this on him.

"Try to remember," Sheriff Driscoll urged in a low, calming voice. "Was the hat dark or light? Did it have an emblem on it?"

Cooper shook his head. "No, I *really* couldn't see. The only light down that hallway was the exit sign behind them. When I thought one of them turned my way, I ducked around the corner. I just had this … I don't know, this sense that something was going down. They were talking, whispering, really. Then I heard Mr. Purnell coming, so I left. Didn't want him to think I was hanging around to steal or vandalize anything. Because I would never do something like that. I know, well know of kids who do, and I think it's really stupid."

"Could you hear anything they said?"

"Just the word 'sweeter', or maybe 'sweeper'. Could've been 'Swiffer', actually. I'm not sure. Sorry, I thought I'd be more helpful. I know it's not much, but I figured it was something." Cooper gave Tara an apologetic look. Chin forward, she held his gaze. She hadn't said a word yet, hadn't squirmed or sniffed or so much as rolled her eyes. "I knew you were late to school today and, well" — lowering his gaze, he shrugged — "I was going to tell you this morning how sorry I was about that night at the football game. I didn't know those girls were in there, honest. But everyone knows that's where the potheads hang out. I was just making a joke about you being so tense. I realized afterward how stupid it was, but I was too afraid to say anything to you. I figured you probably hated me for putting you in that situation, even though I didn't really mean it."

Tara scoffed ever so lightly. He seemed genuinely sorry, but she was going to make him work for her forgiveness. Sitting taller, she pursed her lips. For a moment, I thought she was going to speak. Seconds passed, each one slower than the one before. Until Cooper finally scooted his chair back and grasped the armrests, as if to stand.

"Am I done now?" He cast a pleading gaze toward Sheriff Driscoll, then glanced at Deputy Eklund. "Because I have two papers due tomorrow, plus an AP chemistry test."

"Sure, Cooper." Sheriff Driscoll shook his hand and directed him to the door. "Will you show him the way out, deputy?"

Before Cooper John left with Eklund, he looked one more time at Tara. She mouthed the word 'Thanks'. A smile lit his face.

When the door closed, I said, "So what does this mean for Tara?"

Sheriff Driscoll opened a notebook and wrote some things down. "It means she's free to go. That was enough to make me suspect that someone was trying to frame your daughter."

"Why would anyone do that?" Tara asked. Quickly followed by, "Wait ... I know. Dixie and LeAnne. They did it!"

"Mmm, I don't think so. As of this morning, they were still both at the juvenile detention facility in Fort Wayne."

"Maybe they had someone do it for them?"

"I suppose that's possible, but unlikely. They don't have communication to the outside, except for their parents, and they were all pretty upset with the situation. Lorraine Steinbrenner, in particular, was fit to be tied."

"Who's that?" I asked. Having been away from the area for so long, I no longer knew a lot of the families around here, but the first name rang a bell.

"Dixie's mom. Single mother of five. Dixie's the oldest. Lorraine's husband left her about three years ago. She struggles to make her house payments, but somehow she manages."

Now that I thought about it, the name sounded familiar. "Would that be the Lorraine who works at Dawna's Beauty Studio?"

"Yeah, I believe so." He pushed his chair away from the table to stand. Tara and I followed suit. Before he opened the door, he added, "Sadly, drugs have infiltrated even hardworking middle-class families. I've learned not to presume that only those with a heavy criminal past are suspect. So I don't rule anyone out. Every drug dealer or grower that I can make accountable eases my mind immeasurably."

We walked out into the corridor. I knew the sheriff was escorting us to the exit, but I got a wild hair and put a hand on his arm to stop him.

"Would it be possible for me to talk with Jake Taylor again? Just me and him."

Tara's eyes nearly popped out of her head. "Mom, are you crazy?"

I noticed Sheriff Driscoll resting the heel of his hand on the butt of his gun. "Are you sure? I mean, he is allowed visitors, but so far he hasn't had any. His only relative, his mother, is in a nursing home. She was in an auto accident several years ago. Not only is she wheelchair bound, but she suffered serious brain damage, so needless to say she hasn't been to see him. He used to visit her a lot, though."

As much as I detested Jake Taylor, hearing something like that spun him in a whole new light. Even the most heinous and unlikeable of people had a mother who had cared for them as babies. It made me wonder what happened to people to turn them into monsters that harmed others or broke the law.

"Yes, yes. I didn't want to see him the first time, but I still think he knows something. No offense, Sheriff Driscoll, but without an authority figure there, maybe he'd be more likely to open up and confide in someone."

He shifted on his feet.

"Mom … don't." Tara grabbed my hand. "Can't we just go home?"

"It's up to you," Sheriff Driscoll said.

I needed to connect the dots. Piece the puzzle together. Fill in the blanks. To do that, I had to talk to as many people as possible who might provide even the tiniest sliver. "I need to do this."

Tara stomped a foot in exasperation.

"Ten minutes." Then to Sheriff Driscoll. "I'm ready."

"WHO'S SWEEPER?" I ASKED.

Jake's face twitched, but he didn't look up. He had his cheek propped against a fist and was inspecting a hangnail. "How the hell should I know?" he mumbled.

Keisha's husband, William, stood behind a glass wall, looking on with boredom. He'd escorted Jake to the visitation room and had practically had to shove him through the door when he saw me. Jake and I sat on either side of a wire-grid partition. He wasn't exactly Hannibal Lecter, but just having a physical barrier of sorts between us made me a little bolder and more secure than the first time I'd spoken to him in jail.

I leaned forward, staring intently at him as if I could bore into his skull and expose his innermost secrets. "You know. Now tell me."

"What for?"

"Excuse me?"

His eyes snapped up. They were red-rimmed. I didn't think he was the sort to sit in his jail cell crying, and he certainly wasn't doped up. That left sleep deprived. "Something's keeping you awake at night. Is it your conscience?"

Laughter burst from his throat as his head rolled back. He gazed up at the ceiling, smiling. "You think you know me, huh?" Then, deadly serious, he lowered his head to meet my eyes. "I say you don't know shit."

"Clever of you. But I do know you loved Miley until the day she died. When she left you that crushed a part of your dreams. I know your mother was seriously hurt in an accident — and she's the only person who would've bothered to come see you here. You've had your share of pain. I get it. But who else hasn't?"

"You."

"Wrong. My mother abandoned my father and me when I was five for her French lover and moved out of the country. I never saw her again. My father took his bitterness out on me. My husband plastered himself against a tree and left me a widow before the age of thirty. My four-year-old daughter was in the backseat of that car. She still suffers from post-traumatic stress disorder. She remembers her father, but nothing about the accident. I still deal with the fallout of that every day."

He looked away. The weight of my confession hung in the air. I figured I had everything to gain and nothing to lose for it. If Jake Taylor learned that I had issues, too, maybe he'd stop playing the victim card and take responsibility for once in his life.

"Do you know who killed Miley?" I pressed.

"No."

His answer came too quickly. I waited, but he didn't add anything and he still wouldn't look at me. "Who does know?"

He shrugged. "Try asking Leroy Roberds."

"I already did," I lied. "He doesn't know." Actually, Maybelle was the one who'd put Leroy on the spot at the lodge picnic. It was clear to me that Miley's death had been as big a shock to him as anyone. If Jake was pointing a finger in Leroy's direction, it was because he still resented the fact that Miley had picked a church boy over him.

"Maybe Leroy was the unpredictable sort. Killed her in a jealous fit or something?"

"He was at work. You know that."

"What if he had someone do it for him? Tried to make it look like an accidental overdose?"

It was common knowledge that they'd initially speculated that was the manner of her death. Jake wasn't telling me anything of value yet.

"I don't know why you think I know who killed her. After all" — he smirked — "I've been shut up in here. Maybe you should check with the jabber-jaws she worked with. Women are always blabbing to each other about God knows what."

"Look" — I slid my chair back and stood, palms flat on the counter between us — "when you decide to share what you know, you have Sheriff Driscoll fetch me. I don't know who you're trying to protect, but one person is already dead. Whoever murdered Miley won't think twice about killing again."

I turned my back to go, but just as I took the first step Jake muttered, "Sure thing. Wouldn't want to sweep this under the rug."

Sweep?

Cooper John had said whoever was in the hallway at the high school had said a name.

I pivoted around so fast my shoes squeaked like wheels peeling out on hot pavement.

A sardonic grin twisted his mouth. He looked like Daniel Webster's devil.

A shiver ripped from the base of my spine all the way to the back of my skull.

"Who is Sweeper?" I asked again. Leroy worked at the broom factory. But he'd been cleared already. So if not Leroy, then who?

Jake scratched at the scruff on his neck. "Maybe you should check in the broom closet." He brought his fist to his mouth and cackled into it. His laughter rose to guffaws of hysteria. Like it was the funniest joke in the world.

I hurried from the room as fast as I could. Outside, I leaned against the door and rubbed at my arms, trying to get rid of the chill in my body.

"Any leads?" Sheriff Driscoll asked.

I pushed myself away from the door and we walked down the corridor toward the exit.

I shook my head. "Just a bunch of dead ends and some cryptic hint about rugs and sweeping."

"Sounds like Taylor, all right. If you ask me, the guy has a few loose screws. And yet the psychologist assures us he's not legally insane."

Tara joined us in the front lobby.

Sheriff Driscoll held the door open for us, then walked us to my car. "Sorry, it didn't help."

I got my keys out and unlocked my car doors. "Me, too. Maybe he'll come around eventually."

"If I get any other information about the marijuana field or who might have set Tara up, I'll let you know right away."

Tara had already slid into the backseat and pulled her hood over her head, like she was afraid of the paparazzi snapping photos of her after her brush with the law.

"Thanks, I'd appreciate that. And if you learn anything else about Miley Harper's case, let me know. She lives ... lived in my neighborhood. Maybe it's just coincidence, but I can't help but wonder if all these things lately are related."

"Will do."

The sheriff sent us off with a salute. While Humboldt County's finest plodded along, I was going to do a little investigating of my own to speed things up and ensure that my neighborhood and my daughter's school were safe. I knew one place in this town where a person could dig up a lot of information in a very short time.

I swung by Ida's and dropped Tara off, then left, intent on my mission. First, I had to stop at the drugstore to make an important purchase. One that just might make a difference in someone's life.

chapter 20

CHECK IN THE BROOM closet? What exactly did that mean?

I turned into the parking lot behind Garber's Groceries and pulled into a parking spot. One thing kept bugging me that I couldn't let go. If Jake had meant to point a finger at Harmon, why hadn't he just come out and said it? Things just weren't adding up.

The notion of Harmon Purnell suffocating Miley Harper was about as ludicrous as Donald Trump's comb-over. The night of Miley's murder, when I'd first run into Harmon, he didn't even seem aware that it was her house the cops were parked in front of. Plus, if he'd been out of the house for any length of time that evening, Maybelle surely would've known and said something, seeing as how untrusting she was of poor old Harmon. The old guy was a little socially awkward, but was he really a killer?

Still, why would Jake point a finger at him, of all people, if there wasn't something to it?

One thing was for sure, even though this was a small town, it was full of unpredictable characters.

Knuckles rapped lightly on my passenger-side window. My head snapped to the right.

Grinning, Russ Armentrout wiggled his fingers in a 'hello', then

248

motioned for me to roll the window down.

"How're you doing today?"

Confused. Befuddled. Worried. Concerned. Perplexed. Paranoid. Perturbed ... Did he *really* want to know?

"Fine," I forced out. "And how are you, Russ?"

"Just dandy." He tipped his head toward the grocery. "'Cept that rat, Newt Tipton, has started selling batteries and light bulbs. Since when do grocery stores dabble in household goods?"

I refrained from reminding him that all the big grocery chains sold that and more. But this was Wilton, Indiana, we were talking about. Most of the people here were still stuck in a 1970s mindset. I got out of the car and hit the remote lock, since crime seemed to be on the rise in Wilton lately. "Must be aggravating. You'd think there'd be a law against that sort of thing."

"Commerce infringement, that's what it is."

"You should contact your state senator," I told him as I started toward Garber's. "You might have something there."

"Good idea. I'll do that."

Inside the grocery store, I grabbed a cart and started filling it with everyday items: cereal, bread, boxes of mac and cheese ... At the end of Aisle 5, I lingered near the women's feminine products, slowly letting my gaze drift to the left and down. There were almost a dozen different kinds of pregnancy tests: Early, Easy Plus, Advanced ... There was even a digital one, in case peeing on a strip was too low-tech for you. They had paternity test kits, too, but those were in a special, locked glass cabinet. I couldn't imagine having to ask someone to open it for you. Maybe this was where they found people to be on the Maury Povich show?

The condoms, however, were right at eye level. Evidently, Wilton had a lot of people who still overlooked those and needed the pregnancy and then paternity tests. They had an even bigger variety of those: ribbed, thin, lubricated, snug ... Ecstasy Pack? I eased the box off the shelf and brought it close enough to read.

"Can I help you?" Newt Tipton pasted on a smile. The kind that said, 'I don't really *want* to help you, but it's my job, so I have to.' As kids, we'd ridden the school bus together. He still had the same armpit stains he did back then. The mother in me wanted to take a hankie and dab the sweat from his forehead.

I crammed the box back in place. "I'm looking for, uh, tampons. For my daughter."

"On your right here." He stepped behind me, then tapped each box as he explained it. "Light Days, Regular, Super Absor—"

I grabbed the one he was pointing to. "Thanks, that'll work. She has heavy periods. Cramps a lot."

Unfazed by my attempt to run him off through embarrassment, he blinked at me. "Oh, does she need sanitary napkins, too?"

Who calls them that anymore? "Thanks, but no. We're good on those."

"Okay. If you need anything else, I'm rearranging cleaning products in the next aisle."

I turned around to peruse the shelves behind me, then started to push my cart slowly past the adult diapers toward the cotton swabs and moisturizers. Head down, he shuffled off to Aisle 6.

When I was sure he wasn't coming back, I returned to where I'd been when he intruded. Unable to decide, I dumped three different kinds of pregnancy tests in my cart. Eager to get out of the store, I wheeled my cart down the aisle and around the end, nearly knocking Maybelle Purnell over in my haste.

Of all the luck.

She took one look at me, glanced at the contents of my cart, and fixed me with a judgmental stare. "That's an odd combination."

"Huh?" I looked and there, right next to the tampons, were the pregnancy tests. "Oh, uh, they're for a friend. Well, the tests are. The tampons are for my daughter. She's a teenager. Everything embarrasses her. Moody, too. Especially this time of month. You know how it is when girls are that age. One moment she's —"

"Hmm, are you sure the tests aren't for your daughter? Young people these days are awfully promiscuous. They're exposed to sex everywhere. Just the other day I heard a group of girls talking about that book, *Fifty Shades of* —"

"What? No! Just … no." Why was everyone in this town fixated on that book? I took a peek at her cart, hoping for some incriminating evidence like hemorrhoid cream or laxatives. Nothing but hot dog buns and mayonnaise. "You know, you really should mind your own business and worry less about others'."

She tusked at me as I squeezed past her and headed for the checkout. Selma had just finished ringing out the last customer and was putting their bags in their cart.

"Hi, Sam!" She cracked her gum three times.

"How was Mexico?" I threw my items on the belt as fast as I could, then whipped out my checkbook.

"Oh, you know, hot, sunny, lots of beans and peppers. And *everyone* had an accent. I could hardly understand a word." She paused as she picked up the first pregnancy test, holding it at arm's length with her fingertips. "Sam …?"

"They're for you," I whispered. "Come over tonight. We'll do one then. Then another, just to double-check. And if the results conflict, there's a third."

Selma was still holding the box in midair, staring at me with a dazed and lost expression.

I kept my voice low. "Unless you already know if you are … or aren't. In which case, I'll just put them back."

Without looking down, she waved the box over the scanner, before proceeding to ring up my other items. "I'll be there at eight. I still need to see your new place. Is it okay if Keisha comes, too?"

"Sure, the more the merrier."

251

"Actually, I suspect she might need to use one of the tests herself. She came in before work this morning and had a basket full of Cheez Whiz and pickled herring. Those are her go-to cravings."

"I doubt it. She told me a while back she'd had her tubes tied. Baby factory's shut down, I'm afraid." I didn't feel like keeping Selma in the dark any longer in that regard.

"What? You don't say. Well, why didn't she ever tell me? If I'd known that, I wouldn't have been babysitting for them all this time. Here I thought they were trying to promulgate."

That was Selma-speak for procreate. Correcting her would only cause more confusion.

"Maybe that's why she didn't tell you. Could be they just wanted some alone time. Anyhow, I'm on my way to Dawna's. I'll invite her myself. By the way, how's Dylan handling it?"

"Handling what?"

"Oh, Selma … You haven't told him yet?"

"There wasn't time."

"You were alone together for five solid days."

"I couldn't. He was in such a good mood. And frisky. I didn't want to turn him off talking about … you know."

"You wouldn't bring it up if he was in a bad mood, would you?"

She shrugged. "I suppose not. Tomorrow, 'kay? After we find out."

Maybelle coughed behind me.

I whipped around. How much had she heard? Might as well give her something to talk about. I turned back to Selma and said with a wink, "Maybe next week we girls can all get together and have one of those sex toy parties?"

"Sam, we've had this discussion before. I'm flattered, really I am, but I can't be that kind of" — Selma flashed the air quotes — "*girl*friend to you."

Great. Now Maybelle *really* had something to talk about. If she ever saw Harmon speaking to me again, he'd never hear the end of it. I wondered what kind of grist the Wilton rumor mill would make of this little incident by the time it got back around to me.

I paid for my stuff and stashed it in the back of my car. Next, I was going to get a manicure even if it killed me. Which, given the way things were going in this town lately, it very well could.

HUMMING, KEISHA WHISKED THE buffer across the nails of my left hand. "Girl, you need to take supplements. One with biotin. Your nails are all dry and split."

She was right. When we moved into Melissa's place, I'd started spending a lot of my spare time yanking weeds and washing paint brushes and scrubbing out the bathtub. All those things Ida had done for us that I'd taken for granted. My fingernails were a wreck.

The beauty shop looked somehow empty without Miley in it, even though there were still four people working today. Jasmine was apparently home with a migraine. Dawna was manning the first booth and front counter simultaneously, but always managed to swoop in whenever one of the better-tipping, older, blue-haired ladies showed up. We hadn't spoken since I stepped in the shop, but every once in a while I'd catch her glaring at me from the side as she was dying the hair of Ida's friend Gladys Detwiler.

Toward the back of the shop, Lorraine was emptying wastebaskets. She made a point of banging the containers sharply on the side of the big trash can as she dumped the contents. She was hacked off about something.

In the booth next to us, Tessa snipped away at Dan's hair. He was the owner of Dan's Tire Service and had once employed Jake Taylor. Dan was younger than me, and his hairline had receded so far that he'd have been better off shaving his head. Now it made sense why he

253

always wore a baseball cap. The whole cut shouldn't have taken more than two minutes, but Tessa kept going over it obsessively, combing the thin strands into place, lifting them between her tiny fingers, and scissoring a straight line, all the while with her bottom lip clenched between her teeth in concentration.

I leaned closer to Keisha. "I thought Tessa was the new girl. Why is Lorraine doing the cleaning?"

Keisha stopped humming to answer me. "Huh, yeah. Something about Tessa needing the practice. Least that's what Miss Dawna said." She hummed a few bars of a song I didn't recognize before continuing. "Personally I think it has more to do with her being miffed at Lorraine over something. But you know what's weird? The fact that Lorraine is putting up with being treated like a dishrag. Never thought I'd see the day. That's how Lorraine started out here — sweeping up after all the other girls. If she hated it then …" Her gaze flicked to Lorraine, who was muttering curse words under her breath. Then Keisha went back to humming, her cheeks bunched into a cheerful smile.

The bells on the front door tinkled and a mother ushered her twin girls in. They were wearing matching purple shirts with glittery rainbow unicorns on them and looked to be about eight years old. Both had a set of thick, unruly curls that were bordering on dreadlocks.

Lorraine scurried forth, hopeful. "Well, howdy, Jessie and Janie. Don't you look sporty in those new outfits? Did you go all the way to Fullbright to find them?"

"Welcome to Dawna's Beauty Studio." Dawna waved toward the row of chairs along the front window. "Have a seat. Tessa will be with you in a minute."

Betrayal washed over Lorraine's features. She veered toward Keisha's wastebasket. "Those are the Garfield girls," she muttered to us. "They've *always* been mine."

The moment she stepped away with the trash, Keisha said, "See what I mean?"

"What's that, Keisha?" Dawna said from across the aisle.

"Nothing, Miss Dawna. I was just telling Miss Samantha here how brittle her nails are." She grabbed my left wrist and yanked it up in the air. "See."

I winced. My wrist was pretty well healed, but every little jolt shot a splinter of pain up past my elbow to my shoulder.

Dawna squinted in my direction. "Looks like she needs a lot of work. And I mean a *lot*."

I wasn't sure how to take that. But coming from Dawna I doubted that she meant just my nails. I wasn't about to let Miss Big-Hair Clown-Face apply blue eyeshadow to my lids or get anywhere near my head with scissors, though.

At any rate, I'd been here for close to thirty minutes and hadn't learned a thing yet. Dawna the buzzard was always hovering close by, and Lorraine the piranha was in such a snit I had to keep an eye on her to make sure she didn't dart in and try to bite my head off. I didn't dare ask her what was going on. But I had to dive in soon, because Keisha was getting close to finishing my nails.

I waited until Lorraine was angrily slapping at a spider in the back corner with the broom and Dawna was busy flirting with Dan as she rang him up. Poor guy looked a little lopsided, but maybe that was the point of having a comb-over.

"What do you know about Miley Harper's death?" I asked Keisha. No sense beating around the bush. I needed answers.

Keisha's eyes bulged. She darted a look to the back of the store, then up front at the register. Her voice cracked a little. "Nothing."

"Oh, come on. Help me out, will you?"

"Everyone knows she OD'd, Sam. Besides, why're you asking me?"

"Because Jake Taylor told me to."

She slapped both hands over her mouth.

"Well, not you, exactly. But he said to talk to the folks she worked with. And as far as I can see, you're the only normal one here."

Another hasty look left and right. Then lowly, "Okay, but not here. Got it?"

"Sure thing. Come by my place between seven and eight." I jotted my address and phone number down on the back of a beauty parlor business card. "Selma's coming over after that. She might need your support for something."

She picked up the nail file, even though she'd already shaped and evened out my nails. Her eyes hardened. For a moment I thought she was going to stab my hand with it. Her upper lip twitched and she put the file in a tray full of sharp implements. "Does it have to do with that Dylan Hawkins?"

"I suppose you could say that."

"I'll be there as soon as Will gets back with the oldest two from peewee football practice and they're properly fed. Last time I let him make supper, he fed Little Willy and Jamal onion rings until they got stomachaches. Guess who stayed up with them all night while they barfed into the toilet bowl? Wasn't Will, that's for sure. Noooo." She wagged her finger in the air. "He had the night shift that week. I think he did it on purpose to get back at me for going shopping by myself earlier that day. A girl needs a little me time, you know. And a nice pair of boots every now and then. Otherwise, it's all diapers and carpooling, and screaming at the kids to quit hitting each other or coloring on the walls at the doctor's office, or trying to get them to confess who put the hamster in the silverware drawer ..." Keisha gasped. Tears welled in her eyes. The anxiety of motherhood was clearly fraying at her nerves. "That's why my mama won't baby-sit anymore. Someone — and they still won't say who — stuck the hamster in the drawer and she thought we had rats and called the exterminator. A hundred and fifty bucks for an emergency call and a dead hamster later and —"

"Keisha, honey" — I clasped her hand to stop her before she came apart at the seams — "you need to get out of the house more. And don't you dare let him guilt you into staying home tonight. You hear me? If Mama's not happy, nobody's happy."

Nodding, she wiped her eyes. "Maybe I'll just make some sandwiches and leave him with a list of instructions."

"You do that. See you at seven?"

She hesitated. "Seven thirty?"

"All right, seven thirty."

The bells on the front door tinkled as Dan left. He waved at Dawna through the window and she winked back, brushing her fingertips from her neck down to her cleavage. Dan smiled, then hurried off.

The moment he was out of sight, Dawna turned around. Just as her eyes narrowed in suspicion at Keisha and me, her cell dinged with a text. She whipped it out of her pocket, read it, then pinned Lorraine with a wilting glare — the same look my kindergarten teacher used to give just before she sent us to sit on the stool in the naughty corner back when it wasn't politically incorrect to shame kids. Sulking, Lorraine propped her broom in a corner, gathered up a couple of trash bags, and retreated to the supply room.

I glanced at Keisha, but she was pretending not to notice as she sawed away at my nails. I pulled my hand away before she could wear them down to nubs.

Fifteen minutes and a hefty tip later that left my wallet empty, I made my way out to the parking lot, head down as I carefully picked through the contents of my purse for my keys so as not to ruin my nails. The tension in the beauty parlor had been so thick, I'd hurried out of there before the last coat of nail polish had had time to set. The parking lot was behind the building, so I had to round two corners before I got there. I stopped just short of the second corner, as Lorraine's grumbles reached my ears.

"Do this. Do that. You missed some. You're not doing it right." A throaty growl rose to a barely stifled roar. "I should key her flipping car. Slash her tires. TP her house. Maybe dump some corn syrup in her hair spray. Oh, now there you go. That would be hilarious. Probably make her cry. If she thinks she can push me around like an old broom ..."

Her complaints faded back to an unintelligible mutter. Clearly, Lorraine hated working for Dawna. I'd say she should just quit, if that was the case, but we were talking about Wilton, Indiana, here. There were only so many jobs to go around. And Lorraine probably thought styling hair for little old ladies or trimming the bangs on toddlers was her calling in life. Obviously, Dawna was not an easy woman to work for. But why was she singling out Lorraine lately and riding her case?

The rough bricks of the building tugged at the threads of my shirt as I rested there. This place had more drama than a Mexican soap opera. It probably wasn't worth getting involved in. I pushed away from the wall and beelined for my car, looking down at the crumbling asphalt like I hadn't heard Lorraine's bitch fest in the first place.

My feet crunched on a pile of loose gravel and Lorraine spun around, gasping in surprise. A picnic basket with a red checkered tablecloth slipped from her hold and landed on the ground with a thud. Her eyes flew wide in horror, then she snatched the basket back to her body, her arms wrapped tightly around it like a shield.

"Oh, hi." I jingled my keys. "I didn't know you were out here." I hit the remote unlock, opened the door, and tossed my purse onto the passenger seat. "Well, see you later, I guess."

Not that I wanted to. Lorraine didn't exactly repel me, but she didn't give me warm fuzzies, either. But social protocol demanded some type of farewell, and that was the best I could do without lying outright. I mean, I *would* be in again at some point to have Keisha do my hair or nails again and Lorraine would probably be there, so I'd definitely see her — unless she got fired. Which she seemed to be trying like hell to not let happen.

Instead of saying something back, Lorraine just stood there frozen, like I'd caught her looking at porn on the Internet. Which didn't make any sense, because she was just holding a picnic basket.

Then, as if her senses had suddenly returned, she stuffed the basket into the trunk of her car, a late-model Dodge Charger with tinted windows and a spoiler, and slammed the trunk lid down tight. Didn't quite seem like the kind of car someone could afford on a hairdresser's salary, but then people had different priorities. Maybe she lived in a cardboard box and ate ramen noodles every day, just so she could cruise through Wilton in her souped-up muscle car.

"Yeah, sure." Lorraine flipped around and skedaddled through the back door to the shop, glancing over her shoulder as if to see whether or not I was following her. Or trying to jimmy the trunk open. As if I might steal some old picnic basket. If I wanted one for myself, I could just drive to the Super Wal-Mart in Fullbright and buy one, which I didn't have the time for, even if I'd wanted one.

Somehow, I was going to get Keisha to let me in on what was going on between Dawna and Lorraine. And then, as soon as Selma showed up, she was going to pee on a stick and Keisha and I would be there, holding her hand as we waited for the little plus or minus sign to show up.

No more putting it off. Selma was going to find out about the rest of her life tonight. If she was pregnant, we'd be there to give her whatever support she needed. And if she wasn't ... well, it was time to start goading her into dumping that greasy fleabag Dylan Hawkins. I wasn't about to let my best friend settle for a man just because he took her places and bought her nice things and they had terrific sex.

I pulled out onto the main drag of Wilton, my mind drifting to all the great sex Clint I had been having lately. While I couldn't deny how great we were together in bed, anytime I thought of us beyond that, not much came to mind.

Oh, fiddlesticks. Why make it more complicated than it was? What we had was good. The problem was we only had it good on one level. Well, several levels, depending on the position.

But why did I keep thinking there was something more — or that I even needed more?

I should really stop trying to self-sabotage. Things with Clint were fine.

Yeah, fine. Sandpaper was fine. Hair was fine.

Clint and I were just ... fine.

BUMP AND I STRODE through the neighborhood at a good clip. Now that my foot was feeling better, I'd discovered that brisk walks were good for loosening it up and strengthening my much-neglected muscles. It also gave me time to think. Unfortunately, I kept getting stuck on the same question: Where were Clint and I headed?

The more I thought about it, the more confused I became. So finally, I decided not to think about it at all. But I kept thinking about it anyway, and wondering why I couldn't let go of it. It was like a loop playing over and over in my head.

A prickly feeling crawled up my spine. I glanced behind us, thinking I'd heard footsteps in the distance, but there was no one out on the sidewalks, even though it was still early evening. The curtains were drawn in most of the houses, front doors closed. There were no front porches in this subdivision with little old ladies sipping iced teas, no children playing kickball in the streets.

As we turned from Cardinal Drive onto Chickadee Lane, Bump pulled on the leash, which was unusual for him to do since Clint had instilled some manners in him. I looked up and down both streets. A car pulled into a driveway ahead of us. A younger man dashed inside carrying an armload of groceries. We went on and made another turn, now halfway home.

Bump stopped, perked his ears, his head turning one direction, then another. All I heard was the faint sound of an older car with a noisy muffler. Satisfied we were in no danger, Bump continued on.

Two blocks later, I saw Harmon Purnell lugging his trash cans out to the curb. I waved. "Hi, Harmon!"

He blanched, looked behind him toward the front of his house. "Hey." He flipped a hand in greeting, then pivoted to head back to the garage.

Bump's tail wagged so hard, I thought he was going to give me an embolism from where it thwacked against my thigh.

"Harmon?" I called, remembering an offer I'd made to him earlier. "If you stop by this weekend, I should have a batch of brownies ready. I'm sure there'll be one with your name on it. I'm at 714 North —"

"Sorry, can't."

"Oh." I stopped in front of his driveway, dejected. Had I said or done something wrong? Maybe he'd gotten in trouble at work for not locking the supply closet after Dixie and LeAnne were busted for smoking pot in there and he'd made the connection between Tara and me? Or maybe he had an even bigger secret to hide.

He lingered at the door to the garage, an apologetic look weighing down his sagging jowls even further. "Maybe some other time."

A movement at the picture window caught my eye. Maybelle held the edge of the drapes back just far enough to glare at poor old Harmon. Without another word, Harmon ducked beneath the open garage door and pulled it down. It hit the concrete with a bang, followed soon by the thud of the door leading inside his house. The drape fell back into place.

It felt like someone had dropped a snake down the back of my shirt. I snapped Bump's leash and started down the street. When Clint and I had first driven through these streets, this had looked like a friendly enough neighborhood; however, it was proving to be any-thing but.

AT HOME, I LET Bump into the backyard and went into the kitchen to start on that batch of double-chocolate-chunk brownies. Since I didn't have to worry about saving any for Harmon that meant there would be extra for Tara and me. I checked the oven obsessively, dipping a knife into the brownies three times before I decided they weren't too gooey, but hadn't yet been baked to brick-like hardness. I placed the pan on the cooling rack.

The digital clock flipped over to 7:47 p.m. Keisha still hadn't shown up. No text. No 'Sorry, I'm running late' phone call. Nothing.

Shannon's dad had swung by to pick Tara up on the way home from his work, so she wasn't due back until close to ten. Bump was sacked out in the backyard under the maple tree, last I'd looked. The squirrel had wised up to his presence and made himself scarce. All alone, I'd spent the last hour dumping Ghirardelli dark chocolate chunks into brownie batter and watching it bake through the grease-splattered oven door while *Wheel of Fortune* banter played on the TV. I was pretty sure my dad was sitting in the recliner at Ida's watching the same show while shouting out the answers and calling the contestants 'idiots' for not getting the answer when the only letters up were *e* and *t*.

The timer finally dinged and I pulled the pan out. I sliced the brownies into neat little squares. Okay, not exactly little and certainly not neat. The melted chocolate chunks had left pools of goo, since I was too impatient to let them cool off. And I'd only portioned the whole eight-by-eight pan into nine pieces, whereas I usually made twelve so Tara and I wouldn't overdose on sugar. But this was confession time. The more chocolate the better. And wine. I had white zinfandel, a dark cabernet sauvignon, and a fruity local concoction, since I'd never drunk with Keisha before and didn't know what she liked. Actually, I didn't plan on having more than a few sips. I had to keep my wits about me so I could keep the facts straight. I was going to serve it in jelly jars, though, because my real wineglasses were in a box somewhere in a storage unit just outside of Chicago. The more I thought about all my old stuff, the more I realized I'd lost all attachment to it. After all, how many different kinds of drinking glasses did one person really need? It wasn't like I was going to throw a large cocktail party anytime soon. In fact, Dixie cups would work, too.

I jammed the corkscrew into the bottle of blackberry wine and tugged, expecting to hear a 'pop'. But the darn thing wouldn't budge. I gave it a few more turns and tucked the bottle under my left armpit and against my rib cage for leverage. I pulled, yanked, and pulled again, then checked the cork to see if it had eased out. Not even a millimeter. I just wanted a whiff. Maybe a tiny taste.

So I sat down on a kitchen chair and clamped the bottle between my knees. Two more twists of the cork, a good hard pull and … Nope. Wasn't budging. I had, however, managed to drive the corkscrew all the way down to the handle.

One more try. And then I'd give up on this bottle. I still had two more.

I angled the bottle down and gripped the neck. Several grunts and a blister later, it was still stuck.

Wait … if I tied the corkscrew tab to a sturdy string, anchored that to something solid, and put my whole body into it …

Three minutes later I'd fished up some clothesline that I found in the garage and lassoed it to the leg of the table. I wrapped both arms around the bottle and pitched my full weight into it — all one hundred and twenty-five pounds of me.

It worked!

Which was a bad thing. Because just as the cork popped out and the wine bottle belched air, my foot slipped on the slick linoleum.

The bottle shot from my hold like a rocket, hitting the floor with a clunk and a splash. My legs flew up in the air. And my head went backward, whacking against the floor like a hammer hitting a watermelon.

After that, the only thing I remembered was what sounded like a gunshot and the faint bellow of Bump barking from the backyard.

chapter 21

KEISHA STOOD OVER ME, fanning me with a stack of junk mail.

"You okay, honeybunch?" She batted her long black eyelashes at me, a frown of concern weighing down her mouth. Her head snapped up. "I don't think she —"

Cold water cascaded onto my forehead. The shock of it snatched my breath away. With a screech, I sat up. Once the ice cream headache eased and I could form a coherent thought, I stuttered, "W-w-what the ffff—"

Keisha slapped an arm away with the junk mail. "I was about to tell you she didn't need it. Would you pay attention?"

I sniffed. Why did it smell like blackberry jam in here? A quick survey brought me up to speed. Purple streaks marked the bottom of the kitchen cabinets and a puddle of blackberry wine spread across the flecked linoleum. Amazingly, the bottle hadn't shattered. But I'd gotten that blessed cork out. Success! Kind of. If you didn't take collateral damage into account.

There was about half a cup of wine left in the bottle. If that.

Pushing Keisha out of the way, Selma knelt next to me and clamped my face between her hands. The tips of her press-on nails dug into my skin, but she had my cheeks squeezed so tight I could

265

hardly move my jaw. "I still think we should call an ambulance," she said. "Sam, honey. Sam?" Finally, she released my face and snapped her fingers by my ears. "Can you hear me? Do you remember my name? How many fingers am I holding up?" She tucked her thumbs against her palms and held up her hands.

I waited until everything sharpened, blinked a few more times. "Eight."

"Oh, dear." She glanced at Keisha. "She's seeing double."

"You're holding up both hands," I said.

She flipped her hands around and counted, her lips moving. "Oh ... yeah, I am."

Keisha grabbed a tea towel from beside the dish-drying rack and started mopping up the mess.

"No, don't!" Selma grabbed her elbow. "You're destroying the evidence."

"Evidence? What evidence?"

"Somebody tried to knock her out with a wine bottle," Selma said.

Keisha and I snickered.

"No," I said, "I managed it all by myself." I started to get up —

"You're delusional." Selma pushed me back down. "We need to check you for a concussion. Besides, how could you possibly hit yourself in the head with a bottle so hard you'd —"

"I was pulling out the cork, slipped, and hit my head on the floor." One hand on the counter edge and with Keisha's help, I pulled myself up. The room tilted momentarily, then righted itself. I was a little lightheaded and the back of my skull throbbed, but otherwise I felt okay. As long as I didn't move. Or turn my head. Or breathe too fast. Keisha slid a stool under me and eased me onto it.

"Thanks," I said. "I tend to be accident-prone."

While Keisha mopped up my mess, Selma brought me a glass of water and some aspirin.

I glanced at the wall clock. 8:18 PM. "You're both late."

"She's pregnant, too?!" Selma stared at me in shock, then at Keisha. "How? Sam, I thought you said she'd —"

Keisha whacked me with the tail end of the tea towel. "That was personal information. Even William doesn't know. As long as he thinks he can get me pregnant, I'm more desirable to him."

"Oh, that's mean," Selma said. "But smart." Then to me, "Wait, that didn't make sense, Sam. I know I'm late, but why are you calling her late if she can't get pregnant anymore?"

"I meant you're both late getting here."

They both muttered 'Oh' simultaneously. Then Keisha frowned at Selma. "Oh, child. And here I'd been having you babysit, thinking it was the best form of birth control I could inflict on you."

"Whatever made you think I was planning this?" Selma started to look panicky. "I mean, it's not like Dylan and I were *trying* for a baby. We were taking precautions, I swear."

"Honey, I understand. Same thing happened to Will and me. Four times in a row." She wrung the towel out in the sink, then grabbed another and continued cleaning. The mother in her couldn't not clean. I was perfectly fine just staring at the mess for now, but also glad she was taking care of it.

Selma was nearing hyperventilation. When she started to wobble, Keisha led her to a chair, then handed her a plastic bag to breathe into. I kept an eye on Selma, just to make sure she didn't suffocate herself.

"So how far along are you?" Keisha asked.

"I don't know." Selma huffed into the bag a few times until her breathing slowed. "I mean, I don't even know for sure if I am ..." — her voice sank to a whispery croak — "pregnant."

Tears squeezed from her eyes. A moment later, Keisha shoved a box of tissues into her hands.

"Well, we'd best find out, then." Keisha looked at me, like she knew I had the stuff.

"It's in the bathroom," I said, "under the sink. Behind the mouthwash and toilet bowl cleaner." I'd made a point of making sure Tara didn't use the downstairs bathroom today, but just in case she did I'd hidden it behind toiletries and cleaning products I knew she wouldn't use. Last thing I wanted was for her to think *I* was pregnant.

Keisha and I stared at Selma. Selma glared at Keisha. Who then looked at me. She held a finger up. "Okay, I get why she's here" — she pointed at Selma — "and that maybe I'm here for moral support. But why did you ask me here an hour earlier? And sorry about being 'late', your highness, but I got kids, you know. And a six-foot-tall child I refer to as my husband. If I didn't have all fifty of my eyeballs on what they were doing, the whole place would explode. Or worse, nothing would happen. Ever. No home-cooked meals, no baths, no clean clothes, or laundry done, or floor swept, or —"

"You don't have to explain, Keisha. I get it. I've just got one kid and a dog ... By the way, either of you seen him?"

"Who?" they said in unison.

"Bump. I only have one dog, you know."

"I thought I heard him barking out back when I pulled in," Keisha said. Selma was crumpling into a shapeless heap on her chair, blowing her nose and throwing wadded tissues into a growing mountain.

"Anyway," I went on, "I wanted to pick your brain, Keisha, about the whole Dawna and Lorraine blow-up — and Miley's murder."

"Murder?" she whispered.

"Yeah, but it can wait. We need to take care of Selma's predicament before she checks out on us." Steadying myself with a hip against the counter, I made my way to the table, closer to Selma. "Do you need one of us to read the instructions for you? Or set a timer? I have an app on my phone that'll do that." Although I had no idea how to use it. "We'll help however we can."

"Except hold the stick," Keisha blurted. "I ain't holding no stick.

Done it plenty of times myself. If she misses —"

"I'll do it," Selma uttered flatly. She stood, took a deep breath. "And I can read the instructions myself. I'm not illegitimate, you know."

Keisha and I shared a glance as she trudged off. Then, Keisha propped a hand on her hip. "Why should we care if her parents were married? She needs to dump that baggage once and for all."

Okay, if Keisha didn't get that she'd meant 'illiterate', it wasn't worth explaining.

"So what is going on with Lorraine, anyway?" I asked. "Did Dawna start badgering her before or after Miley died?"

Looking up at the ceiling, Keisha tapped a finger against her cheek. "I suppose things got strange just a little bit before. But then ... Yeah, come to think of it, Dawna did get on her case real bad after Miley died. The day Jasmine came in and told the rest of us about Miley, I swear I saw those two look at each other and neither of them looked shook up. They said, 'Oh, that's terrible' and all that, but you know how you can tell if someone really means it or not? Well, they didn't look like they did. Not half an hour after that, I saw Dawna tip her head at Lorraine and they both ended up behind the building. They were out there for a good fifteen minutes. No idea what Dawna may have said to her, but Lorraine was pretty cowed after that. Like she was afraid to so much as sneeze."

"And you don't know what it was about — Miley, work, something else?"

"Not a clue."

A few minutes lapsed while we stared at the bathroom door.

"How had things been between them before that?" I finally asked.

"Actually, I always thought Lorraine was Dawna's favorite. Lorraine had even hinted that someday she might take that shop over — if Dawna ever decided to get out of the business." Keisha checked her watch, then leaned to her right to get a better view of the bathroom. The door was still closed and Selma hadn't made a peep. "You know, now that I think of it, Lorraine used to run a lot of errands for Dawna. In fact, she did all of them. Weird stuff, like disinfectant, bobby pins, coffee creamer. Stuff we ought to have had plenty of. And sometimes, if Lorraine went to the bank for change, it would take her over an hour." She looked at me funny, her forehead scrunched up. "The bank is only two blocks away. But she'd say how she got to talking to the teller there and just lost track of time."

"And Dawna was never miffed at her for taking so long?"

"Oh, no. She was always thanking her for doing it. She'd even let her take her car sometimes — that electric-blue Charger."

I tried to process it all. It was odd that Dawna would only let Lorraine run errands and never came down on her for taking too long, but it certainly wasn't proof of any funny business. Just favoritism, loud and bold. Especially the car —

"Wait." I slapped the table lightly. I remembered something. I'd seen Lorraine leaving the lodge picnic in her car. But what had she been driving? "The Charger is Dawna's car, not Lorraine's?"

Keisha nodded. "That's right."

"Then which car is Lorraine's?"

"The old rusty white sedan. You can always tell when she's driving it. Dang thing backfires all the time. Done that for a year. You'd think she'd get it fixed."

"Fixed?!" Selma shouted through the bathroom door. "Why're you guys talking about me like that? I don't need to get fixed. No matter what happens, I still want all my female parts."

"We're not talking about you, Selma!" Keisha shouted back. "Get over yourself." She rolled her eyes at me, then added to Selma, "How much longer you gonna be, anyway? It's not that complicated. Just start peeing, put the stick —"

The door flew open. Selma held the stick in her hand. As far from her body as she could manage. She looked at her watch. "One more minute."

She walked toward Keisha, waving the stick at her, her face turned away. "You look at it, Keisha. I can't handle the suspense."

"Sit down. Sit down." Keisha offered her chair to Selma, before taking the stick. Selma had selected the one that touted its ease of use. When the time was up, it would simply say 'Pregnant' or 'Not pregnant'.

Keisha laid it face down on the edge of the kitchen table. I pulled up a chair. Selma tapped her fingernails on the table frantically, her eyes glued to her fancy wristwatch encrusted in rhinestones. Probably a gift from Dylan. Just like that big glitzy diamond ring on her —

I smacked the table so hard Selma nearly fell off her chair. "You got engaged and didn't tell us?!"

A sheepish smile flitted across Selma's peach lips. Today's color scheme was shades of orange: a tight-fitting salmon-colored T-shirt, tangerine jeggings with a glittery white stripe down each leg, and neon-orange sneakers with three-inch heels. I'd ask where she got her outfit, but then she'd offer to take me shopping. She wiggled her fingers, the facets of the stone glinting under the overhead light. "Oh, that thing. Yeah, well … I'm not sure."

"How can you not be sure? Either you are or you aren't. Did he ask you to marry him?"

"Not exactly."

"So he didn't?"

"No."

"Then you aren't engaged?"

"I didn't say that, now did I?"

Keisha glanced at the wall clock and shook her head. "Thirty seconds."

"Okay, so what did he say?" I took her hand and tilted it to catch the light. The thing was huge. If it was real, it was the biggest diamond ring I'd ever seen outside the display case at the jewelry store.

"That he wanted to make sure everyone knew I was his." Her lip trembled. She sniffed. Not a quick, dainty sniff. A long sniff. The sniff of someone on the verge of an emotional breakdown. Tears pooled in her eyes, held back by a thick dam of mascara. "Isn't that the most romantic thing you ever heard?"

"Fifteen seconds," Keisha chimed.

"When did he give it to you?" I asked. "On your trip to Mexico?"

Selma nodded. I wasn't sure if she was about to hurl or break out in happy tears.

"Ten seconds."

"Did he mention the two of you, you know, being married, getting hitched, tying the knot, eloping, or even just shacking up?"

"Five, four, three —"

Selma gulped in a lungful of air. I gripped her hand.

"Two, one. Time!" Keisha grabbed the stick and flipped it over. "Says here, you are ... Oh, my heavens. Oh, oh, oh. I don't know what to say. You're a lucky, lucky girl, Sel."

One hand pressed above her quivering bosom, Selma breathed, "You mean I'm —"

"Not pregnant!" Keisha broke out in a wide smile, then turned to me. "So can we open both of those other wine bottles now? I just might down one all by myself. It's been a rough week."

Something deep inside Selma crumpled, like a house of cards flattened by a strong wind. She started sobbing. Not tears of relief. They were unmistakably tears of grief.

Gently, I put my arms around her. She clamped herself onto me like a baby koala clinging to its mother high up in a tree.

I let her go on for a good two minutes. Finally, Selma loosened her hold on me and Keisha slid a jelly jar of wine in front of her.

"Maybe she shouldn't —" I began to say, but Selma had already downed the wine before I could finish my sentence. "I was going to say maybe Selma should take one of those other tests. You can get false results, you know."

"Not likely," Selma blubbered. "The package said ninety-seven percent accurate."

"True," Keisha added. "Mine have never been wrong."

I took both of Selma's hands. "Humor me, then. Do one more. If that says negative, too, I'll believe it."

After a little more goading, Selma acquiesced. While she was in the bathroom preparing the test, I went to the back door to call Bump in.

I turned the knob and opened the door without him blasting into me. That was the first sign that something was wrong. I opened the door wider. "Come here, Bump."

No galloping mutt, no warbling bark.

"Bump? Time to come inside." Silence. "Bump!"

Keisha peered over my left shoulder. "Is everything okay?"

I stared into an empty yard. No tail-wagging butt in the air as he dug deep into the earth. No vigilant squirrel hunter, staring up into the branches above. No lump of snoring canine on the back stoop.

A finger jabbed me in the right shoulder. I spun around.

Selma frowned. "Negative." She waved another pee stick in front of my nose. "At least that's what I think the little dash means."

Keisha grabbed it from her. "Yep, you're right. This is the brand I used." She patted Selma on the cheek. "I'm sorry, girlfriend. I thought you'd be happy you weren't expecting."

"I would have been, at first. But then I kinda got used to it and started thinking how it would be to have a little girl and dress her up. Or a boy that Dylan could —" She finally realized we weren't hanging onto every word of her trip down Misery Lane. "What's wrong with you?"

"Her dog's gone," Keisha told her, as I stared into the yard.

"Not just gone." An eerie moan drew my attention and I looked toward the back gate. It swung on rusty hinges, back and forth, back

273

and forth, nudged by a buffeting breeze. Someone had taken bolt cutters to the padlock. "Stolen."

chapter 22

I HAD TO ADMIT, there were moments when I considered how much simpler my life would be without a crazy, wild, talkative dog in it. Not to mention quieter. But the silence was heavy, in a soul-sucking sort of way. Like someone had just turned off my hearing. It wasn't something you ever appreciated on a daily basis. Until it wasn't there anymore.

Bump was like the guts of this home. The heartbeat. He was adrenaline. He was caffeine. The pep I needed in the morning as he bounced down the stairs and raced across the kitchen linoleum to stand waiting for me while I stumbled to the back door to let him out. I'd also come to rely on him to let me know when a car passed down the back alley, or the mailman came up to the front porch to shove junk mail in the tiny little mailbox. Even as annoyed as I got at him every time he barked about those things.

I missed him panting and slobbering over his dog dish when he came back in from stalking the squirrel. I missed him tangling himself around my legs for pats on the head as I sat at my keyboard.

I even missed him following me to the bathroom and nudging open the door, just to make sure I hadn't fallen into the porcelain crater and gotten sucked away in the magical vortex.

Selma, Keisha, and I wandered through the neighborhood, calling for him until half past ten, at which point Maybelle Purnell poked her head out her front door.

"Do I need to call the sheriff on you?!" she harped. "How're we supposed to get any sleep with you maniacs out here yelling at the top of your lungs. Are you all drunk?"

I hiccupped. Maybe a little. I'd made a pit stop about an hour ago and guzzled down a couple of glasses. Which tended to affect my volume control. "Sorry, Maybelle. But someone let my dog out of my yard."

"You don't say?" She stepped out onto her front porch, tightening the belt on her ghastly plaid housecoat. A smug grin teased at her mouth. "Glad to hear it. One less irritation in this neighborhood."

With a thrust of her chin, she spun on her floppy slippers and marched back inside.

"If she'd disappear," Keisha muttered beside me, "there'd be one less Wicked Witch in Wilton."

I spied Selma trudging down the other side of the street toward us. She crossed it, shrugging as she held her hands wide.

"Sorry, no sign of your pup. I asked a few guys who were sitting in a garage, drinking beers. They said they hadn't seen any dogs or suspicious-looking people tonight."

Turning full circle, I peered into the darkness. My feet were sore, my toe was starting to throb, and my voice was getting hoarse. Still, I couldn't give up. If they'd just popped open the lock and Bump had darted out past them, then he still might be within earshot. I could only hope.

"Buuuuump!" I yelled. But it came out sounding like a dying bullfrog.

A screen door clicked open and a young woman holding a crying baby on her hip appeared on a porch across the street. "Excuse me, ma'am. I know your dog must've run away, but you woke the baby up half an hour ago. Suppose you could just continue in the morning?"

I uttered an apology, but it wasn't heartfelt. To other people, a dog was just a dog. Searching for your lost pet was like looking for the remote control. At some point, you just gave up and hoped it would turn up somewhere. I couldn't do that.

Despite me insisting that we keep looking, my friends escorted me back home.

"Maybe I could drive around and —" A hiccup jerked my chest and I staggered sideways.

Selma grabbed my arm and held on as we walked up my driveway. "Not a chance, Sam. You're not legal."

It didn't take much to put me over the limit. "Okay, you can drive and I'll yell for him."

"In case you forgot, I have issues of my own to think about. I checked my calendar before I came here, and I've missed two months of … you know. That has me kind of worried. I'm not old enough for the change of life. So I was sure I was gonna have a baby, but now, well, I'm sorta concerned that something's wrong. I'm thinking I need to see a doctor. Problem is, I'm scared to death of them."

"Why?"

"Because my momma never saw one her whole life. Then when I was fifteen, she'd been having trouble concentrating, fell a couple of times for no good reason, and was having headaches, so she went to the doctor and … he said she had a brain tumor. They operated, but they couldn't save her. Less than a month later, she died."

Keisha and I gathered her in a group hug. In my panic to find Bump, I'd forgotten all about Selma's problem. As much as I hated monthly cycles, they had a purpose. Any irregularity was something to be concerned about.

"But Selma —" I looked into her eyes, all filled with confusion and lost hope and dread — "the doctors didn't make your mother

277

sick. She already had the tumor — and probably had had it for a while. They did what they could. As for you, there are lots of reasons for skipping cycles. Many are treatable. If you don't get it checked out, whatever the cause is could get worse. Besides, what if you ignore it and it does ruin your chances of ever having a Dylan or Selma Junior?"

Pulling away from us, she crossed her arms. "I know, I know." Her face twisted in consternation. Suddenly, she wrapped me in a rib-crushing hug. "Damn you, Sam. Always making sense of things. Do you always have to be so logistical?"

"You know me," I grunted out. "Logistics are my thing."

"Look, I gotta go. Early shift tomorrow. Day after we can go to the clinic in Fullbright, okay? I don't want anyone in this town to know I have a medical problem."

The Fullbright South Urgent Care Center? No way. I couldn't. Danielle worked there. "Ummm ... I can't —"

"Do you want me to drive?"

"No! No, that's okay. I'll pick you up at nine." Then I turned to Keisha. "Can you help me look for Bump?"

"Wish I could, girlfriend. But I need to make sure Will actually put the kids to bed. School tomorrow. Keewan is crankier than hell if he doesn't get his sleep. His kindergarten teacher will have my hide if I send him in on less than six hours' worth."

She and Selma kissed cheeks, then Keisha got in her car and drove off. Selma started to go, too, but I grabbed her.

"Wait," I pleaded. "Come inside with me. Just let me make sure everything's okay. Please?"

"Sure, hon. No problem."

Thankfully, I'd left the driveway floodlight on when I'd swung by the house last time. I dug my keys out of my front jeans pocket and put my other hand on the knob. It turned before I ever put the key in. A figure appeared in the hallway by the bathroom inside, backlit by the glow of the light above the sink.

Yanking the door shut, I jumped back and grabbed Selma.

"Someone's in there," I whispered.

"Don't worry. I have pepper spray." She started to open the door.

I latched onto her elbow and dragged her back toward the garage, well out of sight of whatever scumbag had invaded my house. "What are you doing?"

"Getting the pepper spray. So I can blind him." She blinked at me like I was daft, then hitched a thumb at the door behind her. "It's in my purse."

"Which is ... inside?"

"Yeah. I left it on the counter when we ... Ohhh. Okay. Never mind." She peeked in through the garage window. "Got a baseball bat? Shovel? So I can bash his skull in? Or a hatchet? I could open up his chest from thirty feet away. I used to be the pitcher in all the backyard games as a kid."

"No, nothing like that." The only yard tools I owned were a push mower, a dull pair of clippers, and a plastic rake. I slumped against the garage wall, my heart hammering in my ears. "Maybe we should just call the sher—"

A crash sounded inside the house. Not glass shattering. More like the muffled thump of furniture being overturned.

I shoved the side door to the garage open and grabbed the first thing I found — a secondhand badminton racket. I'd bought the set off a neighbor at a garage sale last week, thinking it would be a welcome alternative to board games. I hoisted the racket above my head and charged toward the house.

The door swung open.

"Mom?"

Tara was standing in the doorway in an oversized T-shirt with a toothbrush halfway out of her mouth. She pulled the toothbrush out. "What are you doing with that?"

"This?" I swatted at nothing. "Killing June bugs. Pesky things."

"It's September. They disappeared weeks ago."

"Right. Well, some big killer insect was buzzing us. Selma and I were just saying goodnight." I waved at Selma. "See you day after tomorrow. We're going out for breakfast, right?" I winked.

"Do you have something in your eye?" Selma said.

I forgot — Selma didn't get innuendo. I wiped at my eye. "Uh, I guess. Anyway, see you."

"Sure. Later, hon."

After Selma left, I followed Tara into the kitchen.

First thing she said — "Where's Bump?" Followed by further interrogation. "Did Gramps come and get him? He's not at the vet's, is he? Oh my God, don't tell me. He ran out the front door and got hit, didn't he? I knew this was too close to the road. Probably chasing that stupid squirrel. Or Mrs. Weatherford's Siamese cat. That thing is always taunting him through the front window."

I explained Bump's disappearance as best I could, leaving out the part where I slipped and bumped my head due to my stubborn determination to pop a wine cork. Even though I tried to remain calm and convey hope, Tara was not taking it well.

She started searching through the house, convinced he had wedged himself behind the couch and fallen asleep, or was busy gnawing on a bone somewhere. But Bump had Tara radar. It was like he could sniff her scent whenever she was within a mile of the house. Every day when she got off the bus, he was already parked at the front door, tail thumping as he stared at the knob. If she came home at unscheduled times, he knew the sound of her feet hitting the concrete of the driveway.

The whole time Tara was upending the house — as if a sixty-plus-pound dog could hide in a thousand square feet without being found the first ten rounds — she babbled on and on, the pitch of her voice climbing the scale with each passing minute.

She was also starting to hyperventilate. And becoming increasingly incoherent.

"This can't be happening. Can't be. Just ..." — big shaky breath — "can't, can't, can't. How? Why would anyone ...? When did the gate ...? Stupid cat. Moronic squirrel. If I ever ... If he doesn't ..."

At that point she shuddered and collapsed into a sobbing ball.

She was too big for me to pick her up and carry to bed, so I simply folded to the floor with her and wrapped her in my arms. "We'll do our best to find him. If you get up early, you can help me make signs. While you're at school, I'll call all the vets in the area and the shelter to see if anyone has picked him up. If that doesn't help, I'll spend the day posting the signs, okay?"

Sniff, shudder, long pitiful wail. "Okay," she breathed. Then she lifted her red swollen eyes. "Can I stay home from school and help you look?"

"Sorry, I don't think searching for your lost dog is on their list of excused absences."

"I could say I'm sick."

Brushing her hair back from her wet cheeks, I shook my head. "I'll text you every hour. Sooner, if anything happens."

Somehow, I got her to bed after that, although I was sure she wouldn't get to sleep any sooner than I would. If either of us did at all.

Exhausted, yet still too worried to sleep, I picked up my new phone from the junk-collecting area on the kitchen counter and retreated to my room.

The display was flashing. I had a new text. It was Archer.

Sorry I left town without letting you know. Needed time to think about things. I have something I need to tell you.

What the blazes did that mean? Think about what? My drunken attempt to get it on with him? Maybe he wanted to be 'friends with benefits'? That or cut off our friendship completely. After all, who needed a nymphomaniac complicating their otherwise peaceful existence in rural Podunk Valley?

It took me a few minutes of conjuring all the terrible possibilities before I noticed there was a second text from him.

I'm flying back to Indy late on Friday. Can we have lunch Saturday? I've missed your company.

Missed my company? As in missed *me?* That almost sounded good. Maybe even a little more than you'd tell a friend.

Wait ... What about Clint?

But the more I thought about it, the more I realized that maybe the reason I couldn't sort out my feelings about Clint was because first I needed to understand how I felt about Archer.

chapter 23

IT WAS, QUITE POSSIBLY, the longest day of my life. Tara started off texting me every fifteen minutes. Finally, I threatened to take her phone away when she got home if one of her teachers didn't confiscate it first.

My first course of action was to call veterinary offices. No vet within a four-county radius reported anyone bringing in a dog even remotely close to fitting Bump's description. Even Clint's new receptionist said they hadn't seen a dog like him. She promised to let him know I'd called. All the shelters turned up zilch, as well.

After a lunch of plain Greek yogurt, I drove around my neighborhood and up and down Route 379, plastering up 'Lost Dog' posters with Bump's mugshot. I asked everyone I saw, the desperation in my voice mounting with each encounter.

I pulled my car up alongside a pair of elderly gentlemen out for a walk. "Have you seen a Husky mix with one blue eye around here lately?"

They both stopped, one leaning on his cane and the other cupping a hand to his ear. I could see the hearing aid as he turned that ear toward me.

"What was that?"

"I said, 'Did you see a Husky mix, bigger dog, running loose lately'?"

They looked at each other, shrugged. The old man propped up by his cane said to the other, "Did she say her husband is running around with a big, loose woman lately?"

"No, Auggie, a 'husky' woman. There's a difference."

"Uh, excuse me," I cut in, my voice raised as I enunciated each word as clearly as possible. "My *dog* is lost. I'm looking for him. He's part Husky. Like a sled dog."

"Sorry to hear that, sweetheart," the hard-of-hearing one said, shaking his head in sympathy. "Any man who would run off with your dog isn't worth keeping around. I say take him to court."

The other one nodded. "You need to go on one of those TV shows with a judge and get your dog back."

"Thanks, I'll keep that in mind." I drove off. Those two guys wouldn't know a Husky if it bit them on the kneecaps.

I interrogated a mother with four children under the age of five, the corner convenience store owner, the cable guy, the postal carrier, a pair of twenty-something chicks out jogging, and no less than half a dozen people out doing yard-work or bringing in their trash cans.

When I picked Tara up after school, I barely had the heart to tell her I hadn't turned up a single clue. I couldn't even fake a hopeful attitude, because frankly, things were looking pretty grim. While I sat blubbering in the parking lot, Tara handed me a tissue and started going over our options.

"There are lost pet groups on Facebook. If you give me your new phone, I'll post in those. Should only take a few minutes. Meanwhile, you drive around and we'll do a visual search. I'd say we should think like a dog and go where Bump would go, but he's so easily distracted that anything could have grabbed his attention." She started punching letters into my phone faster than I could have. Kids these days seemed to be born with texting thumbs. She hit 'Enter' and gave me a serious look. "You did leave your name and phone number with the shelter and vets' offices earlier, so they can call you back if they need to, right?"

I blew my nose so hard it sounded like a Canadian goose with a bad case of bronchitis. "Yes, of course. How did you get so grown-up, anyway?"

"Because I learned by watching you. Now drive. We're wasting time. And Gramps and Ida are coming at five, so we have just over two hours."

A hole opened up in my gut like someone had fired lead shot through it. I hadn't broken the news to them yet. "Ohhh, nooo. I totally forgot about that. We'll order pizza and pick it up on the way home. I'd cancel dinner, but then they'd want to know why."

"You know he's going to ask where his boy is."

"I do. Sometimes I think it's the main reason he even comes to dinner, just so he can get his Bump-fix."

"And he'll want to help look for him."

"Yeah, and last time he went looking for him he almost got lost himself."

"We should make sure Ida doesn't let him leave her sight, then."

"Good plan." Maybe I could convince her to hide his truck keys, too. I could totally see him sneaking out before dawn to do his own search. He could end up in Branson, Missouri, before he'd admit he was lost.

For nearly two hours, we scoured the back roads, calling out the window. We even kept our eyes trained on the ditches and cornfields, in case he'd gotten hit again and crawled off the road somewhere.

But there was no Bump. Anywhere.

"WHERE IS HE?" DAD PUSHED past me and headed toward the door to the backyard. He threw it open and walked outside, me right on his heels. "Hey, Bump! Come here, boy. I got you a new set of tennis balls." He rattled the can, then whistled and slapped his leg. After a few seconds of looking high and low, he started back inside. "Must be upstairs in Tara's room, right?"

"Dad, no, he's …"

He pivoted around so fast I nearly plowed into him. "He's what?" He took stock of me, his eyes tightening. "Why do you look so haggard? And why are your eyes red? Have you been drinking?"

"No, I haven't."

"That's good. I guess. Now where's Bump?"

"I … don't know."

"Don't know? What the hell does that mean?" He looked toward the gate, not fully closed, and lifted his hands from his sides. "Did you leave the gate open? How could you? And after the grief you gave me about letting him out to pee and him —"

"Someone cut the lock last night," Tara cut in, "and either took him or let him out. We've been looking since last night. You didn't see the posters on your way here?"

"Ohhh, Tara, sweetheart. No, we didn't." Ida hugged Tara to her side. "Sorry, your gramps slept on the way here, and I had a million things on my mind."

Dad jabbed a finger at me. "You're just now getting around to telling me? When all this time I could have been helping you look? Why on earth didn't you —"

"Walt" — Ida clamped a hand on his forearm, pulling his gnarly finger away from my face — "I'm sure they didn't want to disturb you last night and were probably hoping he'd show up by now. They've been busy looking for him all day, doing everything just like they should." Before he could blow another gasket, she redirected the conversation. "Have you contacted the sheriff yet? If someone broke into your yard, they should probably know about it. Who knows if whoever did it might strike again, steal someone else's beloved pet? Law enforcement could put the word out to the local TV stations, so other dog owners could be on the lookout. That could go a lot farther than just us few searching for him."

"That's a good idea, Ida." I bunched her tiny frame in my arms and kissed her cheek. "I'll do that right now."

By now, I had Sheriff Driscoll on speed dial. He picked up on the second ring. Judging by the country music in the background, I'd caught him at Wild Bill's Western Eatery.

"Who's that?" his wife said over the music. "Your mother again?"

"No, not this time, honey." Then to me, "Hold on a moment, Ms. McNamee." There was a brief pause as the music faded, followed by the thump of a door closing and the soft whoosh of nearby traffic. "Now, how can I help you?"

So I told him the story, although I realized it wasn't much to go on. He told me he'd call the station right away and get someone on it. Since Bump was something of a local hero for saving ex-postal carrier Walter Schimmoller from serial arsonist Jake Taylor, he was sure he could get it in both the Wilton and Fullbright papers, as well as on the Fort Wayne TV news.

"And next time, Ms. McNamee, don't hesitate to call me. Time is critical in cases like these."

"I know, I know. But after I called you out to Ida's house when he chased the cats around ..."

"Someone forcibly entered your property. That's reason enough to put my deputies on the alert."

While it was reassuring to know that Sheriff Driscoll was pulling out all the stops, it did nothing to change the tone over the kitchen table. My slice of pizza might as well have been made of cardboard topped with plain tomato sauce and cold pepperoni. I forced it down, knowing I had to eat. Tara didn't fare much better, stopping after two slices. She was usually good for half a medium pizza all by herself.

Usually after dinner, we'd turn on the TV and watch re-runs of old eighties sit-coms or play cards, but Dad was fixated on the local news, as if waiting for some newsbreak that would signal us about Bump's whereabouts. I retreated to the kitchen to clean up the previous few days' mess.

"Sam?"

I turned around to find Dad gripping the back of a kitchen chair.

"Did you ever read any of those letters from your mother?"

I shook my head. "I will."

"When?"

"I don't know. Right now, I'm just worried about Bump."

He reached inside his flannel shirt and pulled a letter out. "All right. Take your time. But read this one … please?"

Hands at my sides, I stayed where I was. "There's another one?"

"Yes. I was hoping you'd read the others first, so you'd get to know your mom a little better before I hit you with this doozy, but really, this is the one you oughta read." He pushed it closer. "Go ahead."

"Now?"

"Yes, now. You can't keep shoving the past aside. Ida and I … we're starting to make plans. But I'm not going to go forward with them until you know the real truth about your mother and me."

I stared at it for what seemed like an eternity: a yellowing piece of lined paper, folded and unfolded so many times the creases had nearly frayed the fibers of the paper. I pinched it between my fingers and took it over to the sink to read beneath the fluorescent light.

"And after you're done with that, have a look at this." He placed a crisp new envelope on the table. "But read your mother's letter first."

I opened it and began, the words registering slowly in my mind as I let them sink in.

Dearest Walt,

You don't deserve what I've put you through, but I want you to know this —
Samantha is the luckiest little girl in the world, because she has you. You raised
her as your own, you cared for me, loved us both. And then I broke both your
hearts by running off with Étienne. I wouldn't blame Sam at all if she hated me,
but a little girl will never understand what a grown woman might. I know you
think Étienne is just some man I met later in my life, a rich and handsome
businessman who swept me off my feet. But the truth is I've known him for a very
long time. He was my first love and kept promising he would leave his wife when
his children were old enough. After a while, though, I gave up on waiting for it to
happen. Then, you came along. You were safety and solid ground. He was empty
promises and lies.

One day, after you proposed to me, he returned and said he'd told his wife
about me and was leaving her for real. I allowed him to seduce me. But when I
woke up the next morning, everything about it felt … wrong. Like I'd betrayed
you. So I told him to go and never come back.

Then I found out I was pregnant. You still married me. Even though I'm
sure you suspected my infidelity. Yet you never forced the truth from me. And you
never held it against me. You did it because a tiny baby needed a father who would
always be there. Not a liar and a womanizer, in love with his jet-set lifestyle.

Sam was almost five when Étienne found me again. By that time, you and I
were having problems. We were very different people, Walt, trying to meld two lives
going in wildly different directions. You were stability and routine. I was the fickle
ex-model, longing for lost glamour. He was the thrill of forbidden excitement. In the
end, I couldn't resist him. But guess what? He left me for a younger woman not a
year later. Guess I got what I deserved, didn't I?

Even so, I realize now that I loved you both in different ways. Yet with either
of you, I could never be completely me. Even now, as I lie here dying, I'm not sure
who I am.

After all this time, after all I've put you through, I find it hard to believe
you're willing to take me back. Like I said, you're much too good for the likes of

me, Walter David Schimmoller. Which is why I must decline your generous offer of reconciliation. I'm staying here, in France. There is an older couple next door who take good care of me. As far as they know, I've never been anyone but Ann Glasser, the woman whose lover left her — not the cheating wife who abandoned an innocent child.

I wish with all my heart that I could let Sam know who her father is. She deserves that much. But I don't really know. Too bad there's not a way to find out, huh?

I love you both, even though I haven't been a good mother or wife. You don't have to love me back. Just know that I'm sorry, so, so sorry, for what I've done. I can't change it now, but I will always regret leaving you.

Love always,
Ann
XOXO

When I looked up, Dad was in the living room seated quietly between Tara and Ida on the couch. I could tell by the stiffness of his posture that he was waiting for me to read the contents of the second envelope and that whatever was in it was perhaps even more important.

It was addressed to him. The envelope hadn't been opened yet. The date stamp read two days ago. The return address: Double Helix Laboratories, Chicago, Illinois.

I don't remember sitting down, but when I read what was on the papers inside, I was glad I had something solid beneath me.

There were three main columns. The first said MOTHER: ANN GLASSER. The second said CHILD: SAMANTHA ANN MCNAMEE. The third said: ALLEGED FATHER: WALTER DAVID SCHIMMOLLER. On the left was a series of letters and numbers — a list of genetic markers.

At the very bottom it said this:

The alleged father does not have the matching alleles located at the loci above and therefore is excluded as the biological father of the child. There is zero probability of paternity.

I read it again, more slowly. The words didn't change. My eyes hadn't played a trick on me.

It was as though someone had suddenly delivered irrefutable evidence that the world was indeed flat. I knew it was true, but … I didn't want it to be.

Afraid that Tara might wander into the kitchen, I stuffed both letters into my purse and slid it to the back of the counter. Ever since we'd moved back to Indiana, she had latched onto him. He would never be anything but her gramps, no matter what.

But what was he to me now? A jilted husband who had raised someone else's daughter? A hero? I couldn't get my brain around either. The truth was somewhere in between. But whatever he was, aside from Tara he was the only family I had.

I don't know how long I sat there in a daze before the ringer on my phone snapped me out of it. This time Rod Stewart's raspy voice yanked me back to the 70s with "Tonight's the Night". It was Clint. I tugged my phone from my pocket and stumbled out the back door, shutting it firmly behind me.

"Sam, I've been at a veterinary symposium in Indianapolis all day. I didn't get your message from my new receptionist until about ten minutes ago. She's not very on the ball. I'm afraid I may have to fire her. Melissa was so much more responsible. Anyway, about Bump … oh, Sam. I can't believe it. What kind of a moron would do something like that? And why? You don't think it was one of your neighbors, do you? Had he been barking much since you moved in? You're home most of the time, so I wouldn't … Sam? Sam? Are you there?"

I slumped down onto the concrete of the stoop, banging my head on the doorknob so hard I was sure I'd have a lump there soon. "Yeah, I'm here."

"You sound pretty upset."

In more ways than one. But I didn't feel like filling him in on the continuing saga of my messed up childhood. "You could say that."

"I'm getting up early to run on the bike path and look for him. I thought he might end up there, if he is running loose. Do you want to come with me? I'd really like to see you. Even under the circumstances."

"Clint, I can't ..."

The silence between us lengthened until I thought maybe the call had been dropped. I was about to say something when Clint's voice began tentatively.

"Sam ... is there something else you need to tell me?"

"Tell you? No, I just wanted to let you know about Bump. Why?"

"Are you pregnant? Because you told me you were on the —"

"No! I am most certainly not pregnant. Where did you ever get that idea?" Not a second after I asked, I knew.

"Maybelle Purnell brought her parrot, Spanky, in for a beak trimming. She said she saw you buying up pregnancy tests at Garber's."

"They weren't for me! I swear."

"If not you, then who? I mean, why else would you be buying ...? Ohhh, no. Tara isn't —?"

"My God, no. Not unless she's the next Virgin Mary." Suddenly paranoid that someone might be eavesdropping, I pushed myself up and peered through the window of the door. The kitchen was empty. A light flickered in the living room and a bout of laughter sounded there. I adjusted my angle and saw *America's Funniest Home Videos* was on. That would keep Dad engrossed for a while. I stepped out into the yard, afraid that if any of them saw me they'd come out and check on me. "Trust me, Clint. It's not Tara. If I tell you, promise you'll keep it a secret."

"Of course."

"They're for Selma. I can't say any more than that, okay?"

"Oh, her. Okay, then. You don't have to tell me anything else. I can't tell you what a relief that is to hear, though. I thought that, well, it was you and ... I started to wonder what would happen between us if it was mine, and then I —"

"If it was yours?" I asked sharply. "Who else's would it be?"

But I knew damn well who he was thinking. Clint was not only worried about losing me to Archer, it had actually entered his mind that I had fooled around on him.

"Sam, I've known you less than three months. There could've been somebody before you came to Wilton."

Ohhh, how sly of him. Good cover.

"There wasn't, okay. Anyway, I don't feel like getting into this. I can't meet you tomorrow morning because Selma kind of needs me. Maybe later?"

"Sure," he said flatly. There was a lot more behind that one syllable than he was letting on, but I'd made it clear we weren't going to hash this out tonight. "Well, if anyone finds him, the microchip I gave him will alert us right away. You'll keep me posted?"

I promised to let him know if anything happened, but with each passing hour I knew the prospects for finding Bump were getting bleaker and bleaker.

Despite the inertia that had me glued to the ground, I pushed myself to my feet and went back inside. The TV volume had been turned up and Dad had pulled the recliner closer to it. Tara and Ida were involved in a game of *Uno*, although neither one seemed to care about how it went. In the alley behind the house, a car with a noisy muffler rumbled by.

Standing at the sink, I glanced through the window into the backyard, and in the fading silver light of evening, I could have sworn

I saw a wadded piece of paper sail over the top of the fence.

Someone's throwing litter in my yard now? What the —?

"So you read it?"

I whipped around. Dad was in the doorway, his shoulders bunched tight. He wandered closer.

"Yeah, I did." I avoided eye contact by rinsing off the dirty dishes that had been haphazardly piled next to the sink, then restacking them in a less precarious fashion. "How did you have a DNA test run?" I said only loud enough for him to hear. "Mom's been dead for a long time."

"A few months before she left, she cut off her braid and put it in a jewelry box. Said she wanted a pixie cut, like Twiggy, the super model. I didn't want her to cut her hair, but it actually looked good on her. Anyway, I used that. The lab told me at first that if the hair didn't have roots attached, it was no good, but then I told them I heard that the hair shaft had mitochondrial DNA, and *that*" — he held a finger up for emphasis — "could still be used to trace maternal lineage. Turns out that I was right."

His use of scientific lingo both impressed and overwhelmed me. "Where in the world did you get that idea?"

"From that TV show with Phoebe." I assumed he meant Lisa Kudrow's *Who Do You Think You Are?*, not *Friends*. Dad never could remember an actor's real name. "One time they found out this famous singer and a governor were sixteenth cousins." He lowered his voice. "She was black, he was white, by the way. That got me thinking about DNA and all that. Well, that and *NCIS*. Some guy had fallen — or was pushed, rather — into a vat of chemicals and they ID'd him by the DNA in his teeth."

"And me?"

"I collected hair from your brush while you were at Ida's."

"Oh, I see." Clever of him.

"And ...?" He glanced at the table for the envelope, then scanned the counters. "What did it say?"

"You mean you don't know?"

He shook his head. "I wanted you to find out first."

I went to him. Stood within arm's reach for an awkward length of time as he shifted on his feet. Then I pulled him gently into an embrace.

"You're my dad," I whispered in his ear.

"That's what it says?" he replied, his voice hoarse with threatening tears.

"Yeah, that's what it says."

A few sniffs, a hand dragged beneath his nose, and he finally pulled back. "Can I see?"

I put my arm around him and guided him toward the living room. "It's just a bunch of scientific mumbo jumbo, Dad. But it says without a doubt that you're my father." If the writing gig didn't pan out, I could always become an actress. That performance was worthy of an Oscar. "Now let's make a search plan for Bump, okay? Maybe we can get the lodge guys involved, or some of Ida's lady friends?"

And with that, he seemed to forget all about the paternity test results.

About an hour later, I went out into the backyard to pick up the trash someone had tossed over the fence. When I first approached, I thought it was a crumpled-up hamburger wrapper. Then I realized it was a piece of notebook paper, wrapped around a round object. I peeled it away. Beneath was an old tennis ball.

Bump's tennis ball.

My hands shook as I read the note:

We've got your dog. If you want to see him again, you'll need $4800. Tomorrow.

P.S. If you tell the cops about this, he's dead. Just like Miley Harper.

295

I turned it over several times, expecting more information. Looked around the yard and out in the alley for another note. But there was nothing.

So they were holding my dog for ransom?

Of course I wanted Bump back. But why $4800? And who was I supposed to give it to? And when?

chapter 24

DAD INSISTED I PICK him up at first light. For two hours, we drove the back roads of Humboldt County, stapling 'Lost Dog' flyers to telephone poles, the driving so slow while Dad hung out the window shouting for Bump that two school busses and a tractor passed us.

At 8:30, I dropped him back off at Ida's and made him promise that he wouldn't go looking for Bump again without Ida or Tara with him.

"What about you?" He leaned against the car door while I sat in Ida's driveway with the engine still running. "What do you have to do that's so important that you can't keep looking?"

The engine coughed a little, like it needed a tune-up, so I revved the gas pedal. It guzzled gas greedily. According to the gauge, I still had half a tank. Ever since the mysterious empty gas tank, I'd been obsessive about checking it. "If you have to know, Selma's having . . . female issues. I'm going to the doctor with her for moral support."

"Gotcha." He clammed up like I'd just started discussing incontinence products with him. He stepped back from the car. "Talk to you later, then."

As soon as I got out onto the road, I floored it. I had just enough time to get to the bank and make a withdrawal before picking Selma up. At the drive-thru window, I slipped the withdrawal slip into the plastic tube, along with my driver's license, and tried not to look like I was involved in criminal activity.

"What denomination would you like the bills in?" came the distant voice.

I'd pulled into the far drive-thru, even though the other two were empty of cars. There was a glare off the bank teller window that obscured my view, so I looked at the speaker with a smile, as if there were a tiny person hiding in there. "Um, twenties?" I didn't mean it to come out as a question, so I hastily added, "You know how it is, whenever you hand a cashier a hundred, they call the manager over to clear it. Too much hassle. We're going on vacation and I decided this year I'd pay everything in cash, so I don't overspend. I got the idea from one of those morning shows. I think it was a segment on tightening your personal finances. Not that I have money troubles, mind you, but I could probably do better. Heck, we all could, right? Anyway, walking around with all that cash kind of worries me about getting robbed, though, but I suppose if they stole your credit card they could buy even more stuff and then you'd have the headache of —"

"I'll give you twenties, ma'am. No problem."

I shut up, nodded, and thanked the voice before pulling out to head off to Selma's.

Just as I turned left onto another street, I noticed a familiar-looking car in the library parking lot. I slowed down to look. The car was empty, but it smacked me like a sledgehammer to my little toe: that was Virgil's car. I might not have thought much of it, except that the library didn't seem like the kind of place he'd frequent.

Things got suddenly stranger when, two stoplights later, I noticed that same car in my rearview mirror. I turned right onto a side street, making an impromptu detour in case he was following me. The car kept going down the main drag.

I breathed a sigh of relief, but two blocks after that, just as I made the final turn onto the road where Selma's trailer park was located, I could swear I saw the car again way in the distance on the road behind me.

I pulled in front of Selma's trailer and honked three times quickly. She came out running, the straps of her heels slung over a finger as she finished zipping up her skirt. It wasn't until she got in the car that I noticed she hadn't finished buttoning up her blouse yet.

She wiggled her feet into her pointy canary-yellow heels, then looked at me. "What are you staring at? Did I forget my lipstick?" Reaching above her head, she tilted the vanity mirror down to look herself over. "I don't see anything. What did I forget?"

"Uh, your shirt, maybe?"

She glanced down. "What about it? Is it the wrong shade, you think? Too gold, not pastel enough?" She went for the door handle. "I've got one that's more of a sunshiny yellow. If you wait —"

I shifted into reverse and started backing up before she could get out. If Virgil was tailing me again, I needed to shake him fast. "It's perfect, actually. But you might want to button it."

Her eyes swept downward. "Why?"

"Because your bra is showing, maybe?"

A light scoff escaped her. "Oh, honeybunch, that's not a bra, it's a lacy chamomile — you know, the kind with the bra built in."

Right, chamomile. A type of flowery undergarment. Not to be confused with the herbal flower known as camisole. If I hung around Selma long enough, would I start swapping out words, too? Did people in her world figure things out solely from context?

Selma drew a small glass jar out of her gigantic lemon-yellow purse. "I hope this is enough." She swirled it around, bright yellow liquid sloshing against the inside of the lid.

"Is that what I think it is?"

Tucking it back in her purse, she smiled nervously. "Yep, first morning urinal. I think. Dylan says sometimes I get up to pee in the middle of the night, but most of the time I don't even remember doing that. But I figure that's night, so it's not really morning until the sun comes up, right?"

"Sure," I agreed, although I wondered what she thought people meant when they said something like 'three in the morning'.

During the twenty-five minutes we sat in the waiting area at the Fullbright South Urgent Care Center, Selma flipped through no less than fourteen magazines. Some of them two or three times. She only stopped on the ads.

"I can't focus on the articles long enough to read." She added another to the tottering stack on the coffee table before her. The little girl sitting on the other side tore a page out of her coloring book and handed Selma three crayons. "Awww, that's sweet of you. I think I will. Thanks for sharing."

It took all her concentration to stay inside the lines, but by the time she was done she'd even managed to shade the picture and blend colors.

"Miss Pidcock? Claudette Pidcock?"

Selma jumped up. "That's me!"

I snagged the hem of her skirt. "Claudette Pidcock?"

"What? You don't have a Starbucks name?"

"Sounds more like a porn star name," I muttered as we shuffled down the corridor to the exam room.

She winked. "I may have used it a time or two to check into a motel."

After the nurse deposited Selma's urine sample with a lab tech, weighed her, and then took her blood pressure, she shut the door on us.

Selma draped her blouse and skirt over a chair, then slipped into a paper gown. "Sam, if you ever think of giving up editing those geeky textbooks and doing something more exciting —"

"Like be a porn star?"

"Don't be silly. You don't have the body for it. Unless you're thinking of getting a boob job. Are you?"

"Not a chance."

She hopped up onto the exam table, the front of her paper gown flapping wide open to reveal her D-cup melons. She laid the flaps over her chest, partially. "Anyway, if you had a made-up name, you could take up writing those risqué novels, like *Fifty* —"

"No, thanks. If anyone ever found out, not only would Tara be mortified, but then people would be asking to take selfies with me and —"

The door swung open to my worst fear: Danielle Townsley.

"Oh," Selma said, sinking back onto the table and hiking up her feet to fit them into the stirrups, "I am sooo relieved to see a familiar face." Then she launched into a detailed explanation of her frequent sexual activities, glossing over the fact that she'd missed a couple of periods. If I'd needed any ideas for sex scenes for my books, I now had enough to write a series.

Danielle barely glanced at me as she washed her hands at the sink, her eyebrows flicking upward in something between disdain and amusement.

The whole exam was over in less than five minutes, during which time Selma never stopped talking. I sat in the corner chair, skimming over a pamphlet on drug addiction in motherhood, which only made me think of Archer and wonder if he was going to call. I checked my phone for texts, since I'd put it on mute when we walked in. Nothing. My heart sank. He'd said he would call today. Had he forgotten? Not made it home? Changed his mind?

Just as I was about to put it away, it lit up with a new message. It was Clint.

Sorry, no sign of Bump. No calls at the clinic today, either. Any word

301

on your end?

I closed it without answering. Even typing in the little two-letter word 'no' might come across as a plea for help. Which would be fine, if I didn't feel so mixed up. While Clint could rock my world, it was Archer I missed talking to.

"Nurse Bailey will be back in a minute to take your blood, Miss ..." — Danielle glanced at her clipboard, one platinum eyebrow twitching — "Pidcock? Right. Anyway, as I said earlier, the test we ran on your first morning urine was also negative, but we will run a blood test as an extra measure. The good news is I didn't discern any abnormalities during the exam. Everything looks fine. I just want to check your hemoglobin levels. Given your recent diet changes and new exercise regimen, anemia is a possibility. If that's the case, some iron supplements and increased rest should return things to normal within a few weeks. A thyroid condition is another possibility, but you don't have any symptoms of that. I also want to check your hormone levels for a condition known as perimenopause. Usually, it begins to affect women a little older than your ..." — her eyes flicked to the patient information sheet again — "twenty-eight years, although it can strike earlier."

"So if I have this" — Selma groped for the word — "peri-man-pause ...?"

"Perimenopause," Danielle said with deadpan seriousness.

"Sure, that. Would I still be able to get pregnant someday? If I wanted to, that is. I'm not saying I would, but I'd just like to know if I could."

"I can't say for sure. You'd probably want to see a gynecologist who specializes in that condition." Then, as if she had no more to say about it, she clicked her pen and stuck it in her breast pocket. She put her hand on the doorknob. "You're free to get dressed now, Miss Pidcock. We'll call you with the results as soon as they're in."

The door drifted shut behind her. Selma put on her clothes in an uncharacteristically quiet manner, her breathing noticeably audible.

After a while, I couldn't stand the silence any longer. "So, maybe it's just a touch of anemia. Totally curable. No big deal, right?"

"Uh-huh. Just a little old iron pill. Fix me right up."

Nurse Ratched/Bailey came in and took three vials of blood from Selma. I expected her to be squeamish, or at least cringe, but she barely batted an eyelash as the nurse jabbed her vein and sucked the blood out with a syringe.

When we were finally outside the building, Selma drew a big breath and raised her face to the sun, eyes closed.

I wrapped my hand around hers. "Sel, were you starting to look forward to having a baby?"

She turned her eyes on me — big and brown and tinged with sorrow. "Maybe. Just a little." Deep breath in, then out. "And you know what? It didn't even have anything to do with Dylan. I realize he and I may not be together forever. Hell, I'm not even sure he's cut out to be somebody's daddy. Or that he even *is* the father. But it got me thinking ..."

Her gaze drifted away. I'd come to know Selma well enough to realize what was on her mind. And since she was my best friend, I also knew what she needed right now.

I waited until an older couple passed us and hobbled out to their '95 Cadillac, then I gave her a hug. "You'd make a fantastic mom, Selma."

She shrugged. "You really think so?"

"I know it. One thing's for sure, you'd have the best-dressed kid in Humboldt County."

Her spine straightened an inch. "Yeah, I would." Suddenly, she looked past me, her eyes pressing together in an intense squint. "Hey, that's Virgil."

There he was, parked squarely at the entrance to the clinic parking

303

lot. Like he'd been waiting for us all along.

She flapped a hand at me. "You don't mind if I beg a ride home from him, do you? I've been wanting to have beers with him for ages, but kept putting it off because I thought I might be … Anyway, maybe he can give me a lift. Hang on and I'll check."

Without giving me time to respond, she clopped off in her heels, her caution-yellow handbag swinging from the crook of her elbow. After a quick conversation through the car window with her brother, she bounced around to the other door and slid into the passenger's seat.

Two seconds later, Virgil got out and headed straight for me. It was only the fact that Selma was sitting there as a witness to my impending murder that stopped me from running. No, wait, she was busy rifling through her purse. If he pulled out a handgun with a silencer and blasted me now, I could keel over right there on the sidewalk and no one would ever know who did it. To get to my car, though, I would have had to go right past him. Or I could run for help. That way, if he shot me in the back of the head, at least I wouldn't see it coming.

I wheeled around to dash inside to safety.

"Wait!" he called.

And like a dog being commanded, I stopped and turned around. Idiot that I am.

"Uh, yeah?"

"Just wanted to tell you thanks for helping my sister out." He shoved his hands deep inside his pockets. I couldn't detect any lumps in the shape of a weapon, but then his pants weren't exactly tight-fitting. He could be hiding a spiked mace in those cargo pants, for all I knew. "She just gave me the abbreviated version of things and, well, I'm glad you were here with her."

"You're … welcome."

He looked back at his car. Selma had reclined the seat and had her eyes closed. He turned back to me. "You're probably wondering why I keep following her around."

Following *her*? What? I kept my mouth shut, curious as to where this was going and why he'd stalked me across the parking lot to tell me this.

"Dylan's ex, Dawna," he went on, "she kinda blames Selma for breaking up their marriage. She may have made a few threats."

"Ah, sooo ... Dylan put you on her tail to keep an eye on *her*?"

The corners of his eyes crinkled. He let out the lightest laugh, pulling one hand out of his pocket to rest on his quivering belly. "Oh, man. You thought I was following you?" His laughter stopped abruptly. "Why on earth would I do that?"

Did I dare bring up the incident with Dylan at the lodge? After a nanosecond of considering it, I decided not to. "No clue. It just kind of seemed that way. I'd look in my rearview mirror — and there you'd be."

He nodded. "Makes sense. Plus, there were a couple of times I thought she might be with you, but figured out she wasn't. Sorry 'bout that."

An awkward pause followed. Finally, he angled his body back toward his car. "Well, thanks again."

With a nod, he was gone, his massive shoulders diminishing with each stride. He got back in his car and pulled out of his spot, revving his engine before heading out onto the road. Selma wiggled her fingers at me as they sped away.

Wow, in one day I'd found out my dad was not my biological father, Selma wasn't pregnant but still wanted to have a baby someday, and Virgil the bouncer was actually a big ol' softie looking out for his li'l sis. Could the day get any weirder?

I checked my phone one more time. No messages — from Clint, Archer, or anyone with information about Bump. Made me wonder if my phone was even working.

I stood there on the clinic sidewalk for what must have been five minutes. Feeling very lost, ignored, upset, and just plain depressed. I wanted my dog back. If I could bury my face in his fur right now, throw him his slobbery ball, take him for a walk, then at least there would be some joy in my life.

Okay, I needed to stop being so sappy. I should go home and get busy. Help Tara finish painting her room. Take her to the mall to buy some matchy-matchy décor or new school clothes. Anything to keep my mind occupied.

Oh, who was I kidding? Tara and I were going to spend the rest of the day driving the back roads looking for Bump and tacking up posters. Maybe tomorrow I'd go to the shelter and check all the kennel runs, just to make sure they hadn't mistaken him for a German Shepherd mix and told me wrong. No, tomorrow was Sunday. They wouldn't be open. My heart sank a little bit more.

I stumbled to my car, my gaze fixed on the ground to make sure I didn't step in any potholes. But ten feet away, I stopped dead. Something was wrong. Very, very wrong.

As in broken window wrong.

The driver's side window was bashed in. Tiny shards of glass littered the asphalt. Carefully, I stepped closer. Glass crunched under my feet. On the seat, chips of glass glinted in the late-morning sun.

I did a quick scope of the parking lot. Nobody around. Except for what I figured were some employees' cars, the place was virtually empty. Whoever had done this was long gone.

My first inclination was to call Sheriff Driscoll. Then I saw it — Bump's collar, draped over the steering wheel. I reached inside and pulled it out. Twisted through the buckle clasp was a sheet of folded paper. I opened it.

Be at the old red barn on Wilkerson by the sunflower field. Noon. Not a second later.

And no cops. Or — dead dog.

Wilkerson? I didn't even remember where that was. And noon? I checked the time on my watch. That gave me exactly … twenty-two minutes?

Panic surged through my chest. I darted over to the passenger's side and yanked open the glove compartment. The envelope from the bank was still there. I didn't have time to count all the bills, but it looked like it hadn't been touched. Whoever had left the note wasn't bright enough to search the car.

Wilkerson, Wilkerson. I didn't have a map of Humboldt County. If I went home to do a computer search, I probably wouldn't have time to get to this place. Wherever it was.

Then I remembered my new phone had Internet. I turned it on, started pushing buttons, and quickly got confused. Where the hell was the map app?

"Problem?"

I spun around. Danielle Townsley was swishing her way to me, shed of her lab coat and looking ten times swankier.

"Uh, well …" My gaze skipped to my shattered window.

Her forehead puckered in concern. "Oh, dear. We haven't had this problem before. Not since I've been here, at least. Hold on." She pulled her own phone out and tapped at it. "I'll call the Fullbright Police Department for you."

"No, don't!" I blurted. Then, more calmly, "I mean, my insurance has lapsed. I was going to pick up a new policy with the local agent on Monday. If the cops come, they'll ask for my insurance info. Cruddy timing, but it's just a busted window. I can pay out of pocket."

Danielle peered in through one of the intact windows on the opposite side of the car. "They didn't damage or steal anything?"

No, but they left something. I crumpled the letter into a tight wad and stuffed it in my back pocket. "Doesn't look like it. Probably just some dumb teenager did it on a dare."

"Are you sure? You can't really drive it like that. Don't you live in Wilton?"

"Sure, but it's a warm enough day." I grabbed a discarded hoodie from the backseat and started sweeping the glass onto the car floor. "A fresh breeze won't be so bad."

She tilted her head at me skeptically. "At least let me get you a towel from inside to put on the seat. I'd hate for you to drive a glass sliver into your gluteus maximus."

"Oh, sure. That'd be nice. The towel, I mean."

In the two minutes it took her to go inside, I'd cleared the debris off the driver's seat. I took the towel from her, all neatly folded, and got in.

"Thanks." I waved, eager to be on my way. To wherever Wilkerson was. So I could get my dog. Danielle left. I shoved the key in and turned it. The engine sputtered, then made a grating sound. I tried again. It croaked an ugly, undeniable death.

No, no, noooo. This could not be happening. Not now.

I kept turning the key and pumping the gas pedal. Like I could perform CPR on my beloved ancient Subaru. "Come on, come on," I chanted in encouragement. The ignition didn't so much as click. I pounded a fist on the dash. "Start, damn you. Start! You freaking son of a —"

"Another problem?" Danielle appeared at my window. "Would you like me to call a tow truck?"

I was two breaths away from a breakdown. I only had seventeen minutes left. "It's just ..." *Breathe*, I told myself. *In, out, in, out.* Oh, God. I was starting to feel lightheaded. *Think, think, think. How do I save Bump?*

"Do you know where Wilkerson is?" I climbed out of my car and stomped the glass bits from the soles of my shoes.

"Wilkerson Road? Yes, I take it as a shortcut on my way into work some days. There's a gorgeous field of sunflowers there. Why?"

My day just got weirder. By a factor of ten thousand. Danielle Townsley was the last person on earth I wanted to ask for help. But I was about to do just that.

chapter 25

DANIELLE WAITED PATIENTLY FOR my explanation. What could I tell her? That my dog had been dognapped and I had to hurry the ransom to some old barn to get him back? She'd want to call the police and I couldn't risk that.

I shrugged. "I, uh, need to pick my dog up from a farm there. The one with a red barn." There were probably dozens of red barns in Humboldt County, but for now it was all I had to go on. "He was being boarded while I had some work done on the fence in my backyard. They close in less than fifteen minutes." I was getting better at lying. That almost sounded plausible.

"Funny. I don't remember a boarding kennel there."

"Small operation. In fact, he's probably being spoiled rotten inside their house, knowing them."

"Oh, who's the owner? And is it past Flowerdale Pike or before?"

She was being way too nosy. "I don't remember. And sorry, I don't have the exact address. My dad dropped him off for me and he's terrible about remembering house numbers. You'd think as a former mailman, he'd be good at that, but he's not. He always went by landmarks — you know, turn right at the leaning stop sign, go over the dry creek bed, take another right when you see a yellow shed with the broken-down tractor beside it …" I checked myself. I was eating up precious time. "So, do you think you could give me a ride? I normally wouldn't ask, but …" — Desperate, I glanced at my dead and battered car — "extenuating circumstances and all."

"I don't see why not. I have a blanket in the trunk I can throw in the back for the dog. Follow me."

As she marched off, I dove back into my car, grabbed the bank envelope, and stuffed it in my purse. Then I hurried to catch up with her. As we got closer, I could see where this was going to get even more interesting. She had a sports car. The two-seater kind with a tiny little storage space in back.

"Don't worry. It's bigger than it looks back there. Big enough to …" A suggestive smirk tilted Danielle's mouth. "Well, never mind."

I wedged myself into the passenger seat and soon we were cruising down Route 5 toward Wilton.

She shifted smoothly and the engine purred in response. "How's Clint?"

"Fine, I guess. I haven't seen him since … since … It's been a while."

"Oh, I thought you two were dating. Aren't you anymore?"

"To be honest, I'm not sure."

"It didn't have anything to do with what I shared with you before, did it? We really are over."

So he kept telling me. "It's kind of complicated."

"Ah, I can understand complicated. That whole baby business was more convoluted than I first thought. It wasn't just about me having a baby. I hadn't thought through how it would affect him. It was a good thing I backed out when I did."

Wait … what? I twisted in my seat to face her more squarely. "*You* backed out?"

She nodded as if it were a known fact. "I did. He was ready to be a father. Always had been. But he wanted me to stay here, in this area,

311

until the child was grown." She scoffed. "How preposterous is that? Right now I'm entertaining three offers: two from prestigious research hospitals and one —" Her voice faded away as she glanced my way. A look of sympathy flitted across her face and she returned her eyes to the road ahead. "You didn't know, I see. What did he tell you?"

"That he turned *you* down. After he thought about it."

"Hmph. He would."

"What do you mean?"

"Look, you don't have to believe me —"

At this moment, I didn't know who to believe.

" — given my history with Clinton and the fact that I just showed up in his life again shortly after he'd become a part of yours, but after I made my request for his sperm donation, I told him not to answer me right then. To think about it for a few days and then I'd reach out to him. But Clinton tends to spin things as he remembers them. It's a large part of what broke us up, although he'll tell you another story. And I really do think he does remember things differently — as if his brain filters out certain parts of a conversation. Selective recall, I guess you'd call it. But I have a condition called highly superior autobiographical memory. I remember almost everything that ever happened to me. It's a blessing and a curse. Anyway, the delay gave me time to reconsider. He'd also mentioned not wanting to leave the area because of you and, well, I came to realize that wasn't going to work for me. Indiana is merely another stopping point for me, just like Somerset, Kentucky, was. I don't know where I'll settle down eventually, or if I ever will. But thinking about what Clinton wanted me to sacrifice ... I knew I would be better off with an anonymous donor. Or maybe even adopting. So when those few days were up, I told him I'd retracted my offer."

"How did he take it?"

"Not well." She flicked her turn signal on and slowed. "Not well at all. He more or less begged me to make it happen. He ... suggested, in no uncertain terms, that we could start working on it right away. *Au naturel*, if you will. To save the time and expense of *in vitro*. Purely for procreative purposes."

Of course. Because he wouldn't have enjoyed screwing a living Barbie doll at all.

I bit the inside of my cheek. Her story was so farfetched, I —

"Ask him," she said softly. "Judge his reaction for yourself. After he propositioned me, he told me he'd made a sperm deposit at the fertility clinic in Fort Wayne. Not an anonymous deposit for a public sperm bank, but for my benefit solely. I told him I wouldn't be needing it, that I'd decided that asking him to father my child was more complex than I'd first thought. Believe me, I'm not here to steal Clinton back. I may not have entered into another serious relationship yet, but I *have* moved on emotionally. If you ask me, what he wanted was to be a father and I finally presented him with that opportunity. But it wasn't fair of me. Because he also wanted to be with you."

This was a lot to get my head around. I didn't know Danielle well enough to gauge whether or not I should believe her. I could see him offering a 'donation', but wanting to sleep with her after claiming he wanted to be with me? Maybe she was just making all this up so I'd drop him for good and he'd be all hers. "Still, if he really was willing to —"

"Sleep with me so he could impregnate me?"

Not only did she remember everything, she was a freaking mind reader, too.

"Yes, he really was," she went on. "And I know what you're thinking: that I'm fabricating this to force a wedge between you two so I can get him back. I understand why you'd think that, but I assure you it's not the case. I'm not looking for a relationship. With Clinton or anyone else. Not even a fling. And I never planned to stay here for more than six months. A year at the most. But since my plans have changed I may be leaving much sooner."

As much as I wanted to believe she was lying, the more she talked, the less I saw her as the evil temptress. Danielle Townsley was an ambitious perfectionist with uncanny intelligence who just happened to have a gorgeously irresistible body. Even I was developing something of a girl-crush on her. But one thing I couldn't see her as was a manipulator. Maybe Clint was the player. Maybe he wasn't what I thought at all.

"Sam, there's something else you should know. I left him because I found him with another woman."

My heart blasted through my bowels just as she turned one more road and a field of sunflowers appeared in the distance like discs of gold tilted up to catch the noon sun.

"What was her name?" I wasn't even sure why I asked, other than I didn't know what to say at that point. All kinds of questions started racing through my mind. Was it a hooker, a colleague, a one-night-stand? If we had stayed together, would the same thing have happened to me?

"I have no idea. It didn't matter. I opened the bedroom door, saw them, and left. I stayed a few days with a friend and when I came back, it was to pack my things to leave for Africa."

"What did he say?"

"What would you expect? He asked me to stay. Tried to convince me we could work things out."

"I mean what did he say about her — the other woman?"

"Nothing about her specifically. Again, it didn't matter. There was no justification. He said he was sorry, in the same way a dog hangs its head after it has gotten into the trash and you scold it. He was sorry he got caught, that's what I think."

We rounded a curve on Wilkerson, nothing but cornfields surrounding us. Letting her foot off the accelerator, she ducked her head to peer beneath the visor. "Is that it?"

A shabby red barn appeared above the corn tassels. Beyond that was row after row of sunflowers. The shingles of the barn were half missing and a flock of crows roosted in the rafters. Thistles and cockleburs grew alongside the stone foundation. Gaps in the siding let in shafts of light. On one side of the barn was a faded advertisement from decades ago: See Red Ro__ C__. There was no barn door, just a cavernous opening. Inside, an old rusted tractor crowded the center of the barn, the front tire completely flat, the steering wheel missing.

"Must be it," I said, both hopeful and full of dread.

Danielle turned into the driveway, a strip of weeds growing along the center of it. At the end of the drive, an equally shabby house stood. It looked like it hadn't seen a paintbrush since 1955. Two of the screens were hanging half off their windows. An upper window was completely busted out and the tail end of the faded pillowcase hanging from the inside flapped loosely.

A cat and her three kittens skittered across our path and inside the barn. Danielle stopped to let them pass and looked at me skeptically. "Your father left your dog *here*?"

"Uh, yeah. I'll talk to him about that later." According to the clock on her dashboard, I had four minutes left. A quick check of my phone confirmed it.

She put the car in park and turned off the engine, then started to open her door.

"No, no," I told her. "You stay right here. This shouldn't take more than a few minutes."

"Are you sure?"

"Positive."

I tucked my purse under my arm and hurried off, the stack of bills a bulky lump that I hoped she wouldn't notice. The steps to the porch creaked beneath my feet. A dented beer can was on its side beside an old lawn chair there. Years of sun and weather had stripped the boards clean of paint. A few planks looked rotted, so I chose my steps carefully. At the front door, I pretended to knock lightly twice. After

315

about three seconds, I pretended to knock again, then peeked inside the front window. But a pair of musty old drapes was drawn across it, so there was nothing to see.

A tiny lump of doubt mushroomed into a mountain of worry. If Bump was here after all, why hadn't he barked when he heard Danielle's car? Bump may have flunked out of police dog school because he was too friendly for his own good, but he was a passable watchdog. He never failed to alert me about the appearance of the postal carrier or an invading squirrel.

Down the steps and across the overgrown lawn I traipsed, a fake smile plastered on my face. A hasty glance at Danielle's car did nothing to ease my nerves. She was looking down at something in her lap, probably rooting around in her purse for a tube of Sexy Red #5 to reapply to those kissable lips.

Crap. What had I been thinking when I asked her to bring me here? As much as I wished she weren't around, I certainly didn't want her involved in this. Plus, even though the note hadn't said anything about coming alone, that was probably presumed. Could be that having someone else with me would totally muck up my chances of getting Bump back. Or maybe they had figured I'd have Selma with me, since she'd been in the car with me earlier? What if they weren't going to return Bump at all when I gave them the money? For all I knew, he could already be dead and this could have been a ploy to kidnap Selma or me.

How stupid had I been to come here in the first place? Sheriff Driscoll could have called out the SWAT team and surrounded the property.

With every step, my heart hammered louder in my ears. The entrance to the barn yawned ominously, a haze of dust drifting on sunbeams to shine on the decrepit old tractor, like an ode to some bygone era. To the right of the barn, chickens scratched at the dirt as they cocked their heads to peer between weed stems and grass blades in search of bugs and seeds. In their midst strutted a rooster, his red comb wobbling as he jerked his head side to side, sizing me up.

I stopped where the door should have been to let my eyes adjust. Old tools — shovels, a hoe, a pick, and three axes — hung from nails along the side walls.

A flash of gray zipped across the floor, stirring up more dust. A claw swiped at my pants leg and my attacker let out a long hiss that morphed into a warning growl. Startled, I jumped back. But it was only the mother cat defending her territory, her back arched high to make her look bigger than her scrawny eight pounds. I stomped my foot and she scampered back to the shadowy corner she'd come from.

As I looked up above that corner, I saw a series of rusty chains hanging down from the rafters, each about six feet apart. On each of them was a hook. The dirt beneath was stained dark.

I went closer, looking for clues. My first thought was that the stains were engine oil, but there was no hint of that in the air. No, the air had the faintest scent of iron in it. I sniffed, inhaled deep, trying to sort out the odors assaulting my olfactory senses. Mostly, it smelled like dirt. But mixed in was also the scent of hay and manure and rust. And ...

Blood.

The contents of my stomach curdled. I covered my mouth with my hand, stifling the urge to vomit. My breaths came in shallow pants. I tried to reason with myself. This was a farm. Maybe they had slaughtered an animal to eat. Or maybe they had stolen other people's dogs and lured them here with ransom notes to —

A scratch sounded somewhere behind me, followed by the tiniest groan.

I wheeled around. Peered into the murky darkness. I could discern nothing but haphazard piles of farm tools, discarded tractor tires, and stacks of junk metal.

The shadows shifted. I thought I heard breathing — and I was

317

sure it wasn't mine. Then footsteps. I looked harder. Was someone there?

As silently as I could, I edged back toward the light of the opening. Finally, I could see the nose of Danielle's convertible.

Just as I took my first step toward safety, the quietest *woof, woof* reached my ears. A muffled woof. But an unmistakable one.

Bump's woof.

On the other side of the barn, next to a stack of straw bales, a trapdoor was propped open: a hole leading down below. And tacked to the door was a note:

He's down here. Leave the money in the picnic basket.

chapter 26

LEAVE THE MONEY IN the picnic basket??? How big an idiot did they think I was?

Bump woofed again. Louder. And also … more desperate. Like he was in pain, dying even.

All right, then. I'd check it out, and if he was down there, I'd get him and carry him out. Danielle was sitting out in the car. She had to have seen me come in here, right? And if I didn't come out in five or ten minutes, she'd certainly come looking for me.

One minute to go.

The picnic basket was easy to spot. The checkered tablecloth peeking from inside stuck out like a sore thumb. It was sitting on a cluttered workbench about twenty feet from the trapdoor. I tossed the envelope into it and it landed inside with a telltale *thump*.

Then, I forced myself toward the hole. Stopped at the edge. Listened. All I could hear was the faint squawk of chickens from outside. I looked below. Beyond a barely visible ladder, there was only darkness.

Then … paws scratched at dirt. Bump sneezed.

I sat on the edge, lowered my feet onto the first rung. My toe ached as I settled my weight onto that foot. Bits of straw fell into the

319

hole. I clutched the sides of the ladder and swung my other foot down, found the next rung, all the while looking around me into ominous blackness. Next foot down, hands gripping. Another rung. Another.

Halfway down a rung broke. I caught myself, but not before smacking my chin on one of the upper rungs. My front teeth slammed together, pinching my lip.

"Ow!"

Behind me, Bump whimpered.

"I'm coming, buddy," I called softly to him, a drop of blood on my tongue.

Finally, my good foot hit soft dirt. I eased my other foot down. One hand still on the ladder, I twisted around to look for Bump. I couldn't tell if this was a cellar or lower level with stock pens that perhaps led to an outside entrance. It smelled strongly of manure and hay. Sickeningly sweet hay.

Or marijuana.

I'd only smelled marijuana once. It was in the restroom of a ritzy Chicago mall. Some kids had been smoking weed in the stalls and gotten busted by the mall cops. The odor had lingered long afterward. It had lingered in my memory, too.

Above me, the floorboards of the barn creaked. I looked up, toward the opening I'd just come down through. A shadow passed across.

Behind me, I heard the strike of a match, followed by the sound of a board scraping across another board.

Not a second later, the trapdoor banged shut. Laughter rang out.

I spun around. Heard a whoosh at eye level. Saw the plank just as it swung across my line of view. Felt it crack against my skull, just above my left ear.

After that, I could've sworn my brains exploded.

AN EMBER GLOWED ABOVE me. A tiny dot of orange, swelling and sparkling, then fading. Lungs sucked in air and the dot expanded again.

Leroy Roberds loomed over me, a joint pinched between his thumb and middle finger. A shadow cast by the bill of his baseball cap briefly obscured his face as he stepped beneath a dim overhead bulb. He turned the bill around backward and inhaled again, held the noxious fumes inside, and tipped his head back, a stupid smile warping his thin lips. "Ah, man. Sometimes I forget how good that is."

"You shouldn't smoke so much of it," a woman's voice chided. "You're cutting into your own profits."

"Yeah, well" — Leroy flicked a stack of ashes from his joint, watching them drift to the dirt floor with unusual fascination — "privileges of the job and all."

"If your father knew —"

"Screw Pastor Matt. Thinks he's so high and mighty. He's still disappointed I didn't go to seminary school. Well, that and that I was fornicating with Miley. Aw, God, I miss her." His lip quivered and he sniffed back tears. Then he took another drag and held the joint out. "You should try it once in a while. Maybe it would loosen you up some, Loooorraine."

Lorraine Steinbrenner? And Leroy Roberds? What an odd combination.

I blinked the cobwebs from my mind. A dull thud of pain hammered at the side of my head. Wetness oozed over my temple. Sweat? Or blood? I tried to raise a hand to wipe it away, but my hands were tied behind me with baling twine.

I was propped up in a corner. Lorraine stood in front of me, her hands braced on her hips. She stooped over and lifted my eyelids one at a time.

"I think she has a concussion," she said.

Behind her, to her right, Leroy leaned sideways from the stack of old pallets he was using as a chair. Swaying, he laughed again. His plaid button-up shirt was wide open, revealing a chest bare of all but the smallest tuft of manly hair. He looked like Opie from Mayberry on laughing gas.

"Too bad she's not dead," said another voice, much deeper, more manly.

I craned my head in that direction, but my neck was so stiff from the impact of the blow I'd received that I could only turn it partway. Still, I shifted my eyes to the side.

The uniform khakis were unmistakable. The man flipped his sunglasses up, a sinister smile on his face. Deputy Don Halloway took two strides toward me to press the heel of his hand against my forehead. In his left hand was my bank envelope, bursting with bills. He folded it, stuffed it in his front pocket, and tipped my head back so I was looking straight up at him. "You really should stop snooping around."

"Want me to take care of her?" Leroy asked eagerly.

Lorraine snorted. "Like you took care of that dog?"

She pointed to Leroy's left. There, tucked behind the pallets, was an old chicken coop, bits of feathers still stuck in the twisted wires. And scrunched inside was Bump. He didn't even have enough room to stand. Sad, mismatched eyes gazed back at me. His snout was wrapped in duct tape. He tried to bark, but the sound was lost inside his closed mouth. He swiped a front paw at the tape repeatedly, to no avail, then rubbed his muzzle against the wires.

"Hey, I made five hundred off of him when I sold him to Rickman," Leroy said. "I seem to recall that someone loaned you five hundred to start up your business, didn't they?"

Lorraine pushed her fingers through her hair, fluffing it. "That only got me a small territory. Profits from Wilton Memorial are pretty slim. Kids can't afford much."

"Yeah, but" — Leroy rubbed at his upper lip, then took one last puff before the embers singed his fingertips. He flicked the joint to the ground and stomped on it — "kids have friends. And parents. Parents who need a high."

"Shut up, you two," Halloway intervened.

Even though Halloway hadn't said much, it was clear who the brains in this operation was. Still, I didn't quite get the connection between all of them. So I figured if I could get them talking …

"I came to get my dog back. You have my money. Now give me the dog and let me go."

Halloway's mouth twitched, then curved into a gloating smile. It was the first time I'd seen him without sunglasses on. He had cold, squinty eyes, devoid of emotion. Brought to mind all those serial killers you see on TV who have a disconnect between their actions and the impact they have on other human beings.

Then I remembered those rusty hooks dangling from the barn rafters. The smell of blood. And the stains in the dirt.

"Now, now. Do you really think I'd let you go after these morons" — Halloway's gaze cut to Lorraine and then Leroy — "have blabbed? What guarantee do we have that you'd keep quiet?"

He took a step closer. The man had no fear. And probably no remorse.

Of the three of them, I could see him holding the pillow over poor Miley's face as she struggled to breathe. Leroy didn't have it in him. Lorraine, maybe. But still, I didn't peg her for a killer.

Leroy grinned nervously. "We could keep an eye on her daughter. If either one squeals …" He formed his fingers into a fake gun, put it to his temple, and pulled the trigger. "Pow!" He laughed so hard he fell off the pallet.

Halloway pivoted and kicked him in the gut, just hard enough to knock the breath from him. Leroy heaved several gasping breaths before Lorraine finally helped him back up. Clutching his stomach, Leroy slumped back against the wall.

For a few minutes, Halloway paced, while Leroy bawled like a two-year-old, fists rubbing at his eyeballs. Eventually, it was clear Leroy wasn't crying from the pain.

Lorraine extracted a tissue from her front pocket and handed it to him. "You know you shouldn't touch the stuff, Leroy. See what it does to you?"

"I can't help it." He blew his nose, looked at her with eyes full of sorrow. "Ever since someone knocked Miley off ... Just trying to dull the pain. If I ever figure out who did it —"

"Get over it, kid," Halloway barked. "Probably just some junkie who was angry because she didn't have any weed to sell him."

Now I was really confused. If Halloway had killed Miley, he seemed like the kind of guy who'd take credit for it. Then again, he also seemed like the kind of guy who'd secretly eliminate people if they got in his way.

"You're cruel, Donnie," Lorraine chided. "Miley ain't been dead a month. They were going to get hitched. Kid's got a point about this one's daughter, though, don't you think? She could be valuable."

Halloway scoffed. "Hardly. She's of no use to us."

"She can get you more money."

"Better be more than forty-eight hundred. Which one of you idiots left out the extra zero, anyway?"

Leroy's head shrank into his shoulders like a turtle pulling into its shell.

"She can get us new connections," Lorraine added. "Work for you, like I do — without the added benefits, of course." She sidled up to Halloway and slid a hand between the buttons of his shirt to caress his chest. Clearly, they were more than business partners.

Waaaait a minute. I had assumed Dawna had her claws in Lorraine. Was Lorraine working for two different people — or was

Halloway somehow connected to Dawna Hawkins? And did they have anything to do with the marijuana field next to Ida's property?

I was dying to know the answers. Well, not literally 'dying'. Figuratively. The last thing I wanted to do was leave Tara an orphan. Because then my dad would be in charge of raising her, and who knew what right-wing, socially backward thoughts he might put in her malleable teenage head?

"What do you want me to do?" I blurted, wanting the words back the moment they burst from my lips.

For a moment, no one answered. Then Lorraine spoke up, "Dixie and LeAnne are in juvie hall now because of your big-mouthed daughter."

"What does that matter to you?" I asked.

"Dixie's *my* daughter. She was good at what she did — especially about flying under the radar. She'd never even had detention before your daughter got her in trouble. She'll be out in a few weeks, but the cops will be watching her now. So we need a new liaison at Memorial, someone to arrange meet-ups with our ... associates."

By 'associates' I assumed she meant dealers. "I'd have to talk to Tara about it."

I wasn't really ever going to go through with it. I just needed to buy time to get the hell out of here before alerting Driscoll to this whole covert ring.

"There's nothing to talk about." Halloway studied me. "You want to go home alive. With your lame-brained dog ..." His chest swelled with self-importance. "You're going to do what I tell you to. Understand?"

"Just like Dawna does?" I ventured. "Or does *she* tell *you* what to do?"

The slightest tic tugged at a facial muscle just below his left eye. Aha!

He slammed a fist on the top of the empty metal barrel beside him. I jerked backward. The *boom* rattled my spine so hard I was sure it had displaced a few vertebrae.

"Nobody ..." he growled, his face reddening as he snorted through pinched nostrils, "*nobody* tells me what to do."

"I bet. You're such a tough guy."

It was such a juvenile thing to say, but it felt so good getting a rise out of him.

Rage transformed his features. Curled fingers reached toward me, hovering inches from my neck.

I was sure he was going to strangle me right then. That the last thing I saw would be his wicked face. He'd probably killed Miley in a psychotic fit, then blocked it from his memory.

As hard as it was, I held my tongue, staring back at him with reckless bravery. Arrogant jerks like him pissed me off. I wanted so badly to give him a piece of my mind — tell him what a black mark he was on law enforcement, point out all the young lives he'd ruined by funneling drugs into the schools — but none of that was going to sink in. Don Halloway wasn't a man you spoke sense to. He had his own warped view of the world.

Besides, I also had to make sure I survived this and kept Tara from harm. I couldn't do that if I kept challenging his machismo. One more snarky comment from me and next time he might follow through on his threats.

Somewhere in the barnyard, chickens flapped and clucked, like they'd been disturbed. Where the hell was Danielle? Surely, I'd been gone more than ten minutes. Had she not noticed that I hadn't returned yet — or had Halloway taken care of her?

A faint ringtone sounded, gradually rising in volume, but muffled by layers of clothing and flesh. An obnoxious ringtone.

Lorraine looked at Leroy questioningly. He shrugged.

Halloway began to search, shoving aside boxes and empty jugs to send them into disarray. "What the hell is that?"

"Someone's phone," Leroy said.

"I know that, idiot! Is it one of yours?"

"No, not mine," Leroy proclaimed.

"Not mine, either," Lorraine quickly added.

I cringed. It was my ass ringing: "I Like Big Butts".

If I got out of this alive, I was going to ground Tara until her twentieth birthday.

Halloway grabbed my shoulder and jerked me forward. His hand dipped into my pocket to extract the offending piece of technology. Gingerly, he placed it on the floor. The screen flashed with a number I didn't recognize. While it sang away, Halloway grabbed a hay rake.

What was he going to do with that?

With a flick of his wrist, he twirled the rake around and slammed the handle end into my new phone. It continued to chime, the sound tinny and mangled. Over and over, he pummeled it, until — finally, mercifully — it stopped.

Then, Halloway picked up a discarded piece of baling twine, tested its strength between his hands, and eyed my neck.

"Donnie" — Lorraine placed a hand on his back — "don't."

Halloway rammed his elbow back into her ribs to send her toppling to the floor. "*You* don't tell me what to do!"

Bump went crazy, his barks strangled by the duct tape. He banged his head against the sides of the coop and thrashed his body wildly. The coop started to rock. Feathers burst in all directions.

Slowly, Lorraine drew herself to her feet, eyes averted from Halloway, the hurt plain on her face.

"Sorry, sorry," Halloway offered, reaching toward her. She jerked her arm away, sending Bump into another frenzy.

For a moment, Leroy looked on in confusion, his reactions slowed by the drugs in his system. Just as Bump pitched his full weight against the side, Leroy threw his hands out to stop the coop from tumbling over sideways. Bump made as if to bite at him. With his

327

muzzle taped, he was no threat, but Leroy pulled his hands back instinctively.

Halloway whipped the pistol from its holster and levied it at the coop, but Leroy was in the line of fire. "Move!"

Wide-eyed, Leroy jumped aside.

Halloway took aim.

"All right," I said sharply, "I'll do whatever you want!"

His sights still focused on Bump, Halloway grinned. "Anything?"

"Yes, anything."

Slowly, he lowered his pistol. Without looking at me, he extended on open palm toward Lorraine. "Hand me the tape, Lorraine. She's said all I need to hear."

After slipping his gun back into its holster, he covered my mouth with duct tape. All the while, Bump watched with crazed desperation, his brows twitching as he looked from Halloway to me and back again, his gaze occasionally flitting to the trapdoor, as if to urge my escape.

Like I weighed no more than a sack of potatoes, Halloway scooped me up and draped me over his shoulder. He smelled like aftershave and new vinyl.

"Where're you going, Donnie, babe?" Lorraine called as he ascended the ladder.

"Miss Nosy here is going to make a withdrawal to donate to our funds." He went up a couple of rungs, then twisted around. "You two wait here for me. I'll be back. Soon."

'Soon' meaning never. I had the feeling he didn't intend to keep Lorraine, Leroy, or me around.

"Okay, babe," Lorraine replied as we continued up into the light. "Then we can celebrate later, right?"

"Right," he said blandly. "We'll do that."

"Fancy dinner?"

"Sure, I'll take you someplace *really* special." His little huff of laughter was so muted, Lorraine couldn't possibly have heard it.

At the top, he deposited me on my side beyond the trapdoor. Dust billowed around me in a golden haze. Fine bits of straw shot up my nostrils. I tried to sneeze, but couldn't open my mouth. The pressure exploded against my eardrums, leaving my hearing temporarily muffled.

Halloway climbed out, then grabbed me by the ankles to pull me free of the door. I bent my head upward, but heard the thump of the trapdoor going shut before I could see him standing over it.

"Donnie?" Lorraine called from below. "Why'd you close that up? It's stuffy down here."

"Quiet! If anyone comes looking for her, I don't want them to find you, okay?"

"Oh, okay." She sounded far from convinced.

"Hey, man," Leroy pleaded, his voice pitching to a simpering whine. "Can you leave it open a crack? Please?"

Halloway ignored them and started piling bales of straw over the door. I planted my heels on the floor and scooted back until my spine hit the wall. Leveraging my back against the rough planks, I pushed myself up. A nasty splinter pierced the fabric of my shirt and drove into the flesh just below my ribs. I winced.

Slapping a hand over his holster to draw his gun, Halloway swung his head toward me. I shrank to the floor to make a smaller target of myself. As if it would matter. He was a trained officer of the law. He probably spent weekends at the shooting range, firing at moving paper silhouettes from a hundred yards away. I wilted beneath his murderous gaze like a baby bunny trapped beneath the paws of a coyote.

His hand twitched twice before finally drifting downward. He put his gun back in its holster. Then, he snapped a piece of baling twine from a bale and descended on me. I sucked in the deepest breath I could through my nostrils and clamped my eyes shut, prepared to feel the cut of rope fibers across my throat.

Instead, his iron grip latched onto my ankles, crossing one foot over the other. He twisted the twine around them — so tight my feet went numb and cold. Then he stomped off, his breath heaving like the whoosh of a bellows.

I watched him work with obsessive purpose. In a matter of minutes, he had a dozen bales neatly arranged over the trapdoor. There was no longer any trace of it.

Through the floorboards, Lorraine's pleas rose in volume. Leroy whimpered. And Halloway — cool and collected — smiled.

"Now, now, Lorraine. I told you to wait for me. I'll be back. Eventually."

"Donnie, babe ...? What d'ya mean? Like in an hour or two?"

He walked toward me. Purposefully. A bolt of fright lanced straight through my heart. In that moment, I couldn't have acted or spoken, even if I'd been able to.

"You are coming back, right?" Lorraine shouted, her words escalating in pitch.

"Sure, sure," he muttered, just before he grabbed me by the arm and began to drag me outside. "How else could I ever get that voice out of my head — for good?"

I knew then that even if he took me to the bank and made me withdraw money for him, he had no intention of keeping me alive. I was as good as dead. Same went for Lorraine and Leroy.

Why did these things keep happening to me lately?

Sunlight blinded me in a burst of white radiance, searing my retinas. I tried to keep my eyes open, to see where he was taking me, but my reflexes kept overrunning my willpower. Rocks scraped at my hip and heels as he yanked me along. Chickens squawked and scattered. A feather landed on my forehead, then stuck to the sweat there. I focused on the itch of it, trying to take my mind away from my flesh being flayed. But my attention kept diverting to his rough handling, my mind darting to all the terrible possibilities, like the preview of some ghastly, blood-filled horror flick. Tears sprang from my eyes, both from pain and fear. He dragged me for what seemed like miles, although it couldn't have been more than a hundred yards.

I didn't want to die this way — slowly, cruelly. If Deputy Don Halloway was going to kill me, I'd rather go down in a fight.

He stopped. Dropped me to the ground so fast my cheekbone slammed into packed dirt. I heard the jangle of keys. The *pop* of a trunk opening.

The odor of car exhaust and burnt rubber overpowered me. From inside the car, a threatening growl issued, followed by a series of vicious barks. Paws slammed against glass. Teeth clicked in the air.

Through a sparkling veil of dust, I saw the police cruiser. And inside was the fiercest police dog I'd ever seen, a Belgian Malinois with its ears pinned back and rows of razor-sharp fangs. The one Halloway had had with him at Wilton Memorial. It fixed its flinty, predatory eyes on me and snarled.

I don't want to die, I don't want to die, I mumbled beneath the tape. Then I cried some more, all pride and humility gone. If I couldn't fight my way free, I'd appeal to his pity. If he even possessed any.

Halloway stripped the tape from my mouth, taking with it a layer of skin. I yelped.

That was one way to exfoliate.

His breath steamed over my face as he bent down. "You were saying something?"

"I told you," I said hoarsely, "I'll do anything. Anything you want."

And I meant it. I really, really meant it.

"Don't you get it, McNamee?" he very nonchalantly said as he reached inside the trunk as if to arrange something there. "You've already done enough."

With that, he hoisted me up. Laid me in the trunk. Gazed down at me, his face blank of expression, almost contemplative.

Fear fled from my heart. I studied his face, memorized every

331

crease, every pore on his clean-shaven jaw, the way his haircut just grazed the tops of his ears, the emptiness in his pupils.

A shadow passed behind him, briefly obscuring the halo of sunlight surrounding him. It took everything in me, but I resisted looking. Something begged me not to. It was only a cloud, I told myself. That or I was fading in and out of consciousness.

I was no longer afraid. But I was determined to have my say.

"You won't get away with this, Halloway," I told him, matter-of-fact.

He snickered. "I've been getting away with more than anyone will ever know for years."

Just as he reached up to grasp the lid, I said, "Like what?"

He lifted his jaw. "Why should I tell you?"

"Might as well brag while you can. I mean, pretty soon you won't have to worry about me blabbing to anyone. You'll make sure I'm quiet, won't you? Besides, it's not like you're going to tell anyone down at the station, are you?"

His head tilted ever so slightly. "You have a point." He readjusted his holster, took the gun out, popped open the chamber and inspected it, making sure it was fully loaded. "All right. I've been overseeing a drug ring that stretches from here to Indianapolis and across the state line into Ohio. We grow, distribute, and collect our own product. Getting rid of the middleman has been a boon to business."

"You're a smart man. Right under their noses all this time." I took it as a good sign when a smug smile danced across his mouth. The longer I could appeal to his ego, the better my chances. "What about Miley Harper? Why did you kill her? Did she threaten to expose you?"

"You're so dumb. I didn't kill her. If I had, I wouldn't have been so sloppy about it."

"Then who did? I know it wasn't Leroy. He was at work. Lorraine?"

"Good guess, but no. It definitely wasn't her. She doesn't have

332

the guts to exterminate anyone."

He was right. Lorraine didn't seem like the sort to kill in cold blood. But Halloway was. Why wouldn't he just admit it?

"Then tell me — who?"

"How should I know?" Halloway snapped the chamber of his gun closed. "Look, I'm not responsible for her death, directly or indirectly. Harper was nothing but a Goody Two-Shoes. She probably crossed one of those druggies along the way that she tried so hard to rehabilitate. I'd bet the list is pretty long."

My chances were getting slimmer by the second.

"Did Jake Taylor send someone after her?" I tossed out in desperation.

Laughing, Halloway shook his head. "I know what you're doing, McNamee." He ripped the tape from wherever he'd stuck it and slapped it across my mouth again. "Nice try, though."

Then, he kissed the muzzle of his gun and lowered it to my temple. A ring of cold metal pressed against the soft indent of my skull.

Life really does flash before your eyes. In a blink, I had visions of Tara playing cards with Dad and Ida. Selma in her colorful attire. Clint jogging with Bump. Archer standing so close I could feel the heat of his body. Kyle and all the happy years we'd had together.

I didn't think of my years wasted at a soul-crushing job. Or the deadline I'd recently missed. Or how many books I had to sell to make the New York Times bestseller list.

I thought of the things that mattered to my soul. That gave me a reason to live. The people I loved. And the dog who'd altered my world.

I closed my eyes and abandoned my fate to the universe. Dedicated my molecules to the never-ending circle of life.

Stardust — that's all any of us is. A conglomeration of atoms, whose existence originated with one epic bang.

Funny that my life would end with a bang.

A frenzied noise retrieved me from my ruminations. Halloway's dog was going berserk, racing back and forth inside the car, hitting the glass panes so hard I could feel the vehicle rock with each impact. My heart galloped like a racehorse on amphetamines.

"Quiet!" Halloway barked. But when the dog continued, he looked up for a split second. "Balthazar, if you don't stop, I'll shoot you, too."

"Not if I put a bullet through your cerebellum first," Danielle said.

Without missing a beat, Halloway jerked his arm to the right, finger poised on the trigger.

A gun blast went off, quickly followed by another. But they weren't the same gun. The back of Halloway's legs slammed against the bumper, his arms folding inward protectively as he twisted sideways. He stumbled forward, then down, disappearing from my view.

There was a scuffle. Shadows flashing across beams of sunlight. Grunts and stomps. Another crack.

A thump.

Sulfur permeated the air, overlain by the faint scent of blood.

Silence yawned for the longest of moments. Balthazar whimpered once, then grumbled deep in his throat. Growls and snarls again mounted in a crescendo of fury.

A feeble moan sounded, but it was hard to tell over Balthazar's frantic ruckus and my heavy panting whether it was Halloway or Danielle in distress.

A body scraped through dirt in starts and stops, as if crawling.

Then ... footsteps. Quick, determined, confident.

I heard a gun being kicked over the very same dirt I'd just been dragged.

"If you really were smart, Deputy Halloway," Danielle said,

"you'd stay put. The more you exert yourself, the faster the blood pumps out of your body. Unless, of course, you're trying to die. In which case, crawl all you want. Bleeding to death is such a slow way to go, though. You'll eventually feel lightheaded, then cold. Fortunately, you'll pass out long before your heart stops beating. First, though, you have to endure the pain of a gunshot. Judging by your expression, I'd say it's fairly intense."

Tears of relief pricked my eyes. I was going to be okay! Tonight, I'd hug Tara and we'd laugh about those annoying ringtones. Dad would pound me on the shoulder and tell me I didn't look too bad for someone who'd nearly had their brains blown out. Ida would stand on her tiptoes and hug me with her tiny bird-like arms, while Bump licked my shoes and thumped his Swiffer tail. And Archer would embrace me softly and, with his mouth pressed to my ear, tell me how glad he was that I hadn't been hurt.

Danielle Townsley had saved my life.

The irony of it all.

chapter 27

DANIELLE PEERED DOWN INTO the trunk.

Her brow folded in sympathy. "You can't be comfortable like that."

My feet were tucked all the way up against my butt and my neck was bent sideways, cheek crammed against the spare tire compartment in the cruiser's trunk. I hadn't even been aware of how oddly Halloway had folded me up and stuffed me inside until Danielle mentioned it. No, I'd been too damn concerned with not getting asphyxiated from exhaust fumes or having my brains splattered like cake batter at the mercy of an out-of-control blender. But my snarky reply was stifled by the duct tape on my —

"Ow!" I shouted reflexively.

Danielle looked at the square of tape pinched between her thumb and forefinger. She flicked it loose. "Sorry. Years of removing bandages have taught me it's generally easier if you don't warn the patient ahead of time. Sometimes the anticipation makes the pain worse."

I licked my lips to check for blood, but that only made them sting worse.

"You could've been a little gentler," I mumbled.

She looked away, not seeming to see a need to apologize for giving my lips and chin an impromptu wax job. "Sit tight," she commanded. "The sheriff's on his way. I'm not taking my eyes off this lunatic again."

Somehow, I managed to lever myself up with my elbow. I was far from comfortable, but at least I could see what was going on. For a moment, I felt dizzy and lightheaded, but a dull throb of pain at the side of my head quickly erased that.

Danielle's gaze was trained down the length of her arm. In her hand, she gripped a small handgun, the kind you could tuck into a pocket of your purse or the glove box of your car. Halloway was crumpled against the barn wall, blood seeping from a wound in his shoulder. She'd shot him squarely right where she needed to.

"Danielle, how did you ... learn ...?" Dust clogged my throat. A cough ripped loose.

"I learned to handle a gun out of necessity," she said, her eyes never leaving Halloway. "If it wasn't a lioness protecting her cubs, it was rebels wielding machine guns in the streets of a village while women and children hid in their huts. Don't read me wrong — I'm not an advocate of guns. But sometimes they can save a life, rather than take one. And that's what I'm about — saving lives. Even yours."

"Thank you," I croaked. I might have gotten even more sentimental, but it was hard to form words when my tongue felt like sandpaper.

"No need. There's really nothing noble about it. Just doing what I felt was right."

"But you didn't have to come looking for me."

"And let him kill you?" Danielle tilted her head. Halloway let out a gurgle of distress and she stiffened her arm at him. "Would you have sat around and let it happen if it had been me?"

"No."

"Right. So don't thank me for doing what anyone else would have done. Just don't hate me quite so much, all right?"

"I don't —"

She shot me a glance. "You do." Then she returned her focus to her captive. Seconds plodded by. The chickens had gone back to clucking. Balthazar's madness had diminished to huffs of refrained agitation. Far, far away, the hum of a tractor rolling through fields of corn sounded. Danielle shifted the gun to her other hand.

"But I understand," she added more softly. "The competition for a mate is deeply rooted in our primal DNA. Clint may not be entirely perfect as a life partner, but he is sexually desirable, you have to admit."

Although I agreed with her a hundred percent on that account, I wasn't about to launch into that conversation right now. I'd almost been abducted by a psychopath. My life had just been threatened. Discussing our carnal longings for the local hottie seemed a tad out of place, given the circumstances.

I got the gist of what she was saying, however. And, damn it, she was right. Curse her heroism. Even if she was Wonder Woman dressed up like a high-end Spice Girl, I couldn't possibly hate her — now, or ever.

I had plenty of time to think while a hot, dry September sun beat down on me, cramped in the trunk of that cruiser, waiting for the cops to show up. Plenty of time meaning about five minutes, which was all I needed. Because deep down, I'd known … Clint wasn't the one for me. Not in the long term, anyway. Maybe he'd been what I needed at this stage of my life. He'd gotten me to loosen up, to enjoy being a woman again. He'd helped me to move on from Kyle, to let go — and that was a huge step in my personal evolution.

Beyond the field of sunflowers, their golden crowns lifted heavenward, a siren wailed. Soon, the siren was joined by another, and another, until it became a chorus, their warring songs eerily out of place in the bucolic setting of an old barnyard in remotest Humboldt

County. Danielle kept her weapon pointed at Halloway, but by then he was looking close to fainting from blood loss.

Tires churned through crushed limestone. Moments later, the first cruiser skidded to a halt in the patch of dirt between the house and barn. Two more deputies' cars pulled up behind it.

Out stepped Sheriff Driscoll. Removing his mirrored shades as he walked my way, he shook his head. Two deputies, Eklund and Strewing, rushed to restrain Halloway.

"Ms. McNamee," Sheriff Driscoll said, fighting a smile as he strolled toward me, "I'd say I'm glad to see you, but ..."

"I know — not under these circumstances."

From inside the barn, the muffled pleas of Lorraine and Leroy could be heard. Hay bales landed with a soft *thump* one after another as three other deputies cleared them from the trapdoor. When that was done, two of them took aim while Deputy Eklund issued orders for Lorraine and Leroy to keep their hands in the air.

I held my hands out. "Do you have something you could cut this with? I can't feel my fingers or toes anymore."

Driscoll nodded, the silver threads at his temples catching the sunlight. "You know, I'm starting to think it would be more efficient if we just put a watch on you twenty-four/seven." He drew a switchblade from his back pocket and sawed through the twine.

The release of pressure brought an immediate tingle of blood flow back to my hands and feet. I flexed my fingers slowly, feeling the prickle of reawakening nerves. Balthazar was barking at all the commotion now, but I'd grown deaf to him. He was secured in the vehicle, able to stick his nose out, but not his entire head.

Lorraine emerged first from the hole in the barn floor, hands raised above her head. Eklund herded her off to the side, then cuffed her while she proclaimed her innocence and heaped all the blame on Halloway. A minute later, they hauled a simpering Leroy out.

An ambulance rolled to a halt by the barn. Two EMTs emerged

and went to work on Halloway as he drifted in and out of consciousness.

"On second thought," the sheriff added as he helped me out and onto solid ground, "maybe I should confine you to your house — for your own safety."

"I really don't think that's necessary, sheriff. This kind of thing can't possibly happen to me again."

He chuckled. "I'm not so sure about that. You've been in town how long — three months? — and already you've gotten yourself into situations that have led to two major busts."

"Purely coincidental, Sheriff Driscoll. It's not like I go looking for trouble."

"Maybe, but trouble sure finds you."

CLINT JUMPED OUT OF his pearl-white Lincoln Navigator and ran toward me without bothering to shut his car door. I was sitting Indian-style on the front porch, waiting for someone to bring Bump up from that musty grotto I'd barely escaped from.

By the back corner of the house, Danielle was giving Sheriff Driscoll her statement in a detailed, matter-of-fact manner. I'd just finished with mine, but I'd been so frazzled that Driscoll had cut it short, offering me the option of coming to the station tomorrow to provide more detail. I'd gratefully accepted. The whole ordeal had worn me down. Right now, I just wanted to sit on my couch wrapped up in one of Kyle's old sweatshirts, consuming my weight in Dove ice cream bars while Tara and I watched an old Gene Kelly movie.

Meanwhile, Deputy Strewing was trying to calm Balthazar before opening the cruiser door so he could slip a muzzle and leash on him and lead him away. So far, it didn't look like he was being too successful. I kept an eye on them.

"Sam, are you all right?" Clint bounded up the steps to the house in one stride and yanked me up into his arms, his hold on me tight, possessive — and a little smothering. But there was also genuine concern in his voice. "Danielle texted me. I left in the middle of an appointment to get here. I was worried something bad had happened."

His fingers grazed the lump at the side of my head, but I didn't flinch. There was a small cut there that the paramedics had cleaned up. They'd checked me for a concussion, but had found no indication of one. "I'm fine," I said, although not too convincingly, even to me. "Really."

He held on a good minute longer, his fingers stroking my back like he could erase everything that had happened. If I hadn't been so mad at him, it might have felt good. Yet every swipe of his hand was one more reminder of how he'd lied to me. Twice. First about being married. Then about having a baby with Danielle. He could be a good guy. He really could. But trust is something you build, each piece interlocking. Take away one brick — and the whole wall can come crashing down.

Lightly but firmly gripping my shoulders, Clint thrust me back just far enough to gaze down at me. So I wouldn't have to meet his eyes, I kept my head turned toward the unfolding scene: Lorraine was already sitting in the back of one of the sheriff's cars. She kicked repeatedly at the seat in front of her, threatening a lawsuit for wrongful arrest. Meanwhile, Leroy was crumpled in the backseat of the other cruiser, weeping softly.

"My daddy's gonna kill me." His shoulders jerked as a piteous sob tore through him. Then, he lifted his chin and started reciting the Lord's Prayer in broken bits.

Halloway had already been carted off via ambulance. A quick assessment by the paramedics assured Sheriff Driscoll he'd be fine, since the blood had been easily stanched. His blood pressure had merely dropped, but was already stabilizing. The bullet had missed an artery by less than an inch.

Drawing a finger down my cheek, Clint bent forward to kiss me. I pulled back reflexively.

"Sam ... what is it? Did Halloway hurt you?"

I shook my head. "No. You did." I looked at him then. Puzzlement cleaved the space between his dark brows. "Again."

"I ... what? How?"

I told him what Danielle had shared with me. And waited. For him to defend himself. Explain his way out of it. Claim she'd misconstrued the whole situation, warped the truth, made stuff up, was a crazy stalker-bitch. But he merely absorbed my accusations with bland indifference.

For several minutes he stared off into the field of sunflowers, his gaze distant. Finally, "You probably hate me."

"Why does everyone keep saying that?" I muttered.

"What?"

"Forget it. Look, the thing is — I just don't get you. And I'm not about to waste any more energy trying to figure you out. So we're done, okay? Finished, over, wrapped up, annulled, discontinued." I almost added 'put to bed', but the implications were too familiar.

"Don't say that, Sam."

"Accept it."

The clack of metal bars sounded from the barn as the deputies broke open the old coop. There was a brief yip of pain, followed by eager barking. They'd set Bump free.

"I can't," Clint said. "What I feel for you is so strong ... It makes me crazy. I'd do anything to keep you."

"I'm not yours to keep." I turned on my heel and brushed past him, headed toward the barn.

Persistent, he grabbed my arm. "Don't walk away. Listen to me. I've wanted a child long before we got together, Sam. Think about what Tara means to you. If Danielle hadn't been so tied up in her work all those years —"

I yanked my arm away, took two steps, then wheeled around and jabbed him in the sternum with my forefinger. "Leave. Me. Alone! Or I'll get a restraining order on you. Got it?"

I saw Danielle, then, coming from around the back of the house. At first I thought she was coming to talk to me, but her gaze was fixed on Clint. I was sure she'd give him hell for twisting the truth and misleading me. I'd happily let her deal with him.

Closer by, Deputy Eklund slammed the rear door of her cruiser. "Is everything okay, Ms. McNamee?"

Backing off, Clint held his hands wide. "Got it. Got it."

"Yeah, everything's fine," I told her.

Bump yipped again, a high-pitched bark that morphed into a yodel. So many times, I'd found his incessant barking to be an annoyance, but right now it was as melodic as birdsong on the first warm day of spring.

Before my foot had hit the bottom step of the porch stairs, Bump burst from the barn door opening to rush at me in great, galloping strides across the yard. The last deputy to crawl out scrambled after him, but Bump had too much of a head start. I hurried toward him, past Danielle, my heart bursting with relief.

Bump was halfway across the barnyard when Deputy Strewing cracked open the back door to the cruiser as he reached for Balthazar's leash, the straps of the muzzle looped over his wrist for easy access. Balthazar retreated to the far side of the backseat, ignoring Strewing's commands to come. Strewing opened the door wider to get inside and reach across the seat. He realized his mistake a second too late.

"Nooo—!"

Balthazar plowed him over like a monster truck flattening a cardboard cutout. Strewing flew backward, arms flailing, feet in the air, to land on his back. His head smacked so hard against the rocks of the driveway, I heard the crack of his skull from where I stood, watching mutely as the Malinois sped in my direction.

I'm not sure whether it was the look of abject terror on my face or that he'd heard the scuffle behind him, but Bump twirled around with all the skill of a martial arts master. He took two more loping strides to plant himself in Balthazar's path.

Balthazar kept coming. I wasn't sure if it was me or Danielle he was after, but I was directly between them.

A blur of gray, Bump closed the distance. Lips drawn tight against his gums, he revealed a set of Dracula fangs. His hackles bristled. He let out a snarl so wickedly menacing that he made Cujo look like an eight-week-old kitten.

"Balthazar, come!" Strewing commanded, flopping over to push himself up on an elbow.

Spittle flew as Bump snapped his teeth in the air in a final threat to stand down.

Balthazar lowered his head, ears flattened. Then, he arced around and loped back to Deputy Strewing, his tail tucked low to show Bump he conceded. Bump did not relinquish his ground until Strewing had Balthazar leashed, muzzled, and securely imprisoned in the back of his cruiser.

Clint laid a hand on my shoulder, startling me. I clamped both hands to my breast to will my heart back to beating. Soon, I felt its strong thump against the heel of my hand.

"That was close," he said.

I nodded. "It was."

"Sam, I don't mean to impose, but you look like you could use some company. Maybe I could make dinner for you and Tara? It would give us a chance to talk."

I glanced past him to where Danielle stood with her arms crossed.

He turned to look and it was as if he was noticing for the first time that she was there.

344

"Clinton," she said, "I think *we* need to talk."

He glanced at me, then nodded and walked off with her.

My eyes locked on Bump's. His cheeks bunched into a smile. His tail wagged gently behind him like a propeller as he began to trot to me. After a few more steps, he'd built up a full head of steam.

I had just enough time to shore up my balance. He hit my chest full force with his paws, but I was ready for him. I wrapped my arms around his withers and hugged him fiercely.

He let out more yips — this time of joy. His tail swished so hard, it sent us both toppling to the earth. Straddling me with his front paws, he covered me in wet, sloppy kisses. I laughed. I didn't stop him. Not even when he paused to breathe and a big string of slobber globbed onto my forehead.

Pinching his chipmunk cheeks, I kissed the moist leather of his nose. "Let's go home, okay, buddy? I've got hamburger for you. After that, you and Tara and I will go to the pet store in Fullbright and buy you all the balls and bones you want. Sound good?"

He barked a single, huge bark of approval.

Then again, this was Bump. I could've offered him the flattened, festering tail off a roadkill skunk and he would have been just as deliriously happy.

If only I could be more like him. Well, except for the roadkill. And butt-sniffing my friends. And having to potty outdoors.

How lucky I was, though, to have him in my life. Even if hitting him with my car had led to me abandoning my dream of living in the Florida Keys to remain in this one-horse town, tethered to a cranky father who wasn't really my father after all. Even if having Bump had meant getting involved with Clint, the compulsive liar. Even if I'd nearly been killed twice in the span of two months.

In spite of that all, everything had turned out all right.

Except, I still didn't know who'd killed Miley Harper. Maybe I never would.

chapter 28

I UNSCREWED THE TOP on the Coke that Sheriff Driscoll had just handed me and took a long guzzle. My throat was parched from the hour and a half I'd just spent giving my statement. Somehow, I'd recalled details that even I wasn't aware of until I connected everything together: the picnic basket, the noisy muffler on Lorraine's car, the references to 'Sweeper' ...

"So Lorraine oversaw the distribution in the schools through her daughter," I said, "and Leroy was another one of Halloway's dealers?"

"Yes, and undoubtedly there were many more. They just happened to be the two he tasked with luring you in. Roberds admitted to siphoning your gas. He says it was Lorraine, though, who lobbed the first note over your fence and broke your car window. She's pleading the fifth, for now."

I'd ask why me, but Tara's involvement in the bust of Dixie and LeAnne probably had a lot to do with it. And Bump. He'd signaled Lorraine's basket at the picnic. If I hadn't yanked him away, he'd probably have blown her cover then. I wondered what had been in the basket at the lodge picnic — money or drugs? Had Lorraine returned later to pick it up? She'd obviously gotten it back because I had seen her with it behind the beauty parlor.

346

I took another drink, waiting for the caffeine and sugar to zip through my veins. Yesterday's ordeal had exhausted me, but at least I hadn't taken the physical beating that I did when Jake Taylor kidnapped me. I really had to think about going to a self-defense class, though. These events were getting to be an unfortunate habit.

"Have you uncovered anything linking Dawna Hawkins to the drug ring?" I asked.

The sheriff drew a deep breath and leaned back in his chair. "Nothing solid yet. But I think it's only a matter of time. Leroy folded with minimal pressure, but Lorraine's being selective with information, mainly pointing the finger at Halloway. I suspect Leroy's involvement was only peripheral. He and Miley Harper were the pipeline to a small sector of users."

"But I thought Miley was trying to rehabilitate recovering addicts?"

"She was."

"Then how could she be supplying Lorraine and Halloway with new clients?"

"My guess is that Leroy was using her to bring in reformed users who were prone to relapse. She probably had no idea what he was doing."

"Do you think she confronted him about it?"

"No way to tell. Roberds is so worried about what his father's going to say, he isn't making much sense right now."

"Could he have arranged someone else to murder her?"

"Possible? Yes. Likely? No. I think that would be giving him too much credit. He's neither that sinister nor that devious. No, I just don't see it."

He was probably right on that point, but I had to think through every possibility.

"What about Lorraine?"

"We checked. She was with her kids at a movie, then took them home."

I felt sorry for Lorraine's kids. It was bad enough to be without a parent, but having your mom in the slammer for drug trafficking was a double whammy. "Who else could have done it?"

"I wish I knew." Sheriff Driscoll readjusted his tie clasp. "We'll keep digging, Samantha. Something's bound to turn up."

"I sure hope so. I know it may have been a one-time thing, but it worries me knowing a murderer could be lurking in my neighborhood."

"Understandable. I'll increase the patrols in your area." He scooted his chair back, then came and pulled mine out for me. "And as I said before, if you see or hear *anything* out of the ordinary, you have my personal phone number. Don't hesitate to call. As for Dawna Hawkins, we're going to take this slowly. Infiltrate what's left of the operation. Gather information, names. Now that we know she may be one of the big players, if we put a tail on her and bide our time, it's possible we could bring down a whole lot more than just her."

"What about Jake Taylor?" I probed. "Has he said anything else? I mean, obviously he knows more than he's letting on."

"I agree. But no, he hasn't said a word. All I can figure is that he's protecting someone."

We walked down the corridor of the station, passing closed door after closed door, the click of our heels the only sound.

In the front lobby, the receptionist cracked her gum and waved to me. It was Rhonda. We were on a first-name basis now. Pretty soon she'd be inviting me out for coffee and a slice of pie. I really needed to stop showing up at this place so much, but it wasn't like I ended up here on purpose. Stuff just seemed to happen to me.

Sheriff Driscoll pulled the door open and stood back. I cut too close and whacked my big toe on the steel edge of the door. Pain throbbed through my foot. I caught myself on the doorjamb before I could topple backward into the sheriff's chest.

He steadied me with both hands. "You all right?"

"For now, yes."

"Do me a favor and —"

"I know — stay home. Believe me, I plan to."

"Actually, I was going to say you should have some friends or family over. Someone to keep an eye on you."

"Thanks, I definitely will."

And I knew just the person to call.

"SO I'M ON THIS pill that's supposed to add more iron to my blood," Selma explained, "only I have to take it twice a day and with orange juice, not milk. Never milk. Something about the calamine interfering with the iron."

I hugged my phone between my head and shoulder as I straightened the pillows on the couch. After my talk with Sheriff Driscoll, I'd gone to Fullbright to get yet another phone. I hadn't wanted the same model, but I'd let the salesperson talk me into it, too spent to argue with him. Tara had restored my apps and settings for me, then I'd dropped her off at Shannon's and gone home. "The what interfering?"

"The calamine and the iron. Don't ask me how. I never did understand chemistry."

"Calamine? Isn't calamine lotion what you put on a poison ivy rash?"

"I don't know. Maybe. They must make it out of milk, then."

Ohhh, calcium.

"Anyway," Selma went on, "I got my period this morning. Fancy that. Never thought I'd be so happy about it. At least I'm getting back to normal. I have to go back in a few weeks and get my blood checked. Dr. Townsley says my low iron is why I've been feeling kind of tired lately. But she says I should feel good as new in a month or two. She's really nice, don't you think?"

Nice? Not quite the adjective I'd use. The woman could kick Lara Croft's ass. "She's something else, that's for sure."

"Oh! Maybe we could all get together for lunch. You know, have a girl's day out. What do you think?"

As indebted as I was to Danielle, I couldn't envision us ever being BFFs. As for her and Selma, the only thing they had in common was their cup size. "She's your doctor, Selma. No offense, but I'm sure she doesn't mix her personal and professional lives."

"Oh, you're probably right. Anyway, I hope she stays in the area. I don't feel comfortable with very many doctors, but she seems to know her stuff." She lapsed into silence, which meant she'd either been distracted by something shiny or the wheels were churning. "Hey, I was thinking ..."

This could be a revelation. "Yes?"

"For a while yesterday, after I heard what happened to you, I felt pretty bad that I didn't stick around and ride home with you, but then I figured that turned out to be a good thing. After all, if you'd been stuck with me, well ... truth is, we'd probably both be dead. You're lucky that Dr. Townsley was there and that she shot Deputy Halloway. Damn lucky."

"Yeah, I am." In some ways, it seemed like I was having a lot of bad luck lately, but as Selma pointed out I'd had more than my share of good luck, too. What I really wanted now was for life to be uneventful. Maybe even a little on the dull side.

Just to play it safe, though, I needed to do something to protect myself in the future. "Let me know if you'll go to that self-defense class I mentioned earlier. The website says it helps to have a partner to practice with between sessions."

"I'd be more likely to say 'yes' if you ever got me an autographed copy of that new S. A. Mack novel you keep promising me."

"I'll have it to you next week."

"Really? That would make me so happy! Don't suppose you could arrange a secret meeting with the author, could you? I've always wanted to meet a celebrity."

"Sorry, but she's very secretive. Even I don't know who she is in real life. Probably just some suburban housewife who doesn't want her kids' friends to know what she does for a living."

Selma snorted. "She may be brilliant, but she sounds kind of uppity to me."

I held my tongue.

"Hey, Sam ..." She sighed, like she was working the courage up to say something difficult. "Lately, I don't know what I'd do without you. I know I don't always listen, but you talk sense — and I need that. I really do. So since I'm not pregnant after all, I'm going to think long and hard about Dylan and me."

"Good, I'm glad to hear that." It was a start.

"Thanks for being the best friend a girl could ask for."

"Same to you, Sel." A little lump formed in my throat. If she didn't shut up, I was going to break down in tears.

"Anytime, Sam. Anytime. Well, talk to you later, 'kay?"

"Selma, before you hang up ..."

"What?"

"Are you ever going to tell me who the 'other man' was? The one who might have been the father?"

A pause as wide as the Amazon opened up between us. "No, Sam. Not now. Maybe never. It's not anyone you'd expect — and I don't want to say because I don't want you to think less of me for it."

I wanted to throw at her that best friends told each other *everything*, but I knew there might come a day when there was something I couldn't — or wouldn't want to — share with her. Still, my curiosity was killing me. "Is it anyone I know?"

"If I say no, you might not believe me, and if I say 'yes', you're

351

always going to wonder who it is."

That meant the answer was yes. Otherwise, she would have just said no. I'd just have to figure this out on my own.

"Okay, fair enough." I spritzed the coffee table with almond oil and began wiping it down with a paper towel. "Bye, Selma."

"Sam, wait! Are you and Tara gonna be all right there by yourselves tonight?"

I was starting to feel like I'd never get off the phone with her. "Tara's at Shannon's."

"And you? Are you staying with your dad at Ida's?"

I wasn't about to tell her who was coming over. For all I knew, nothing would come of it, anyway. "No, I'm not."

"Oh, Walt's staying there, then?"

"No."

"If not your dad, then —"

"Are you staying at Dylan's tonight?"

"I'm not saying," she muttered defensively.

"Bye, Selma." I untucked the phone from my shoulder and stared at it, trying to figure out how to turn the darn thing off. Meanwhile, she kept barraging me with questions.

"Come on, Sam. That's not fair. Why won't you tell me?"

I tapped the screen and succeeded in cranking the volume. Not quite what I was going for. Her voice sounded like she had a bullhorn pressed to my ear. Where was the button I needed?

"Is Clint bunking at your place? Archer? One of those deputies? I should know who it is, Sam. I won't even ask where they're —"

Ah, found it. I ended the call.

After giving the throw pillows one more fluff, I tossed myself in the middle of the couch. Finally, I had a moment to breathe. I was about to reach for the remote when Bump crashed through the back dog door and came galloping across the living room. He slammed his paws against the sill of the picture window. Instead of his tail wagging, his hackles went up. He let out a deep 'woof'.

I pulled my phone from my pocket and let my thumb hover over the numbers. Sheriff Driscoll was the first name on my speed dial.

Bump barked three more times, less threatening, more 'Hey, who are you?'

I crawled to the far end of the couch by the window and peered out. It was Harmon Purnell. I sighed in relief. Not that I minded him stopping by, but what was he doing here now?

I hopped off the couch and opened the front door partway. Bump tried to wedge his nose in the crack, but I pushed him back with my foot. "Hey there, Harmon. What can I do for you?"

He shifted on his worn loafers and looked over his shoulder nervously. "I was just out for a walk — thought that might be a good thing to start doing, like you suggested — and figured I'd take you up on your offer." His old face lit up in a hopeful smile. "That is, if you have any left."

No matter how hard I searched my memory, I came up empty. "You lost me. Any what?"

His mouth melted into a frown. Except for the wrinkles and pudgy jowls, his expression was that of a five-year-old boy who'd suddenly been told there weren't any candy bars at the checkout when he'd been saving his quarters all week for one. He ran a hand over his paunch to smooth the material of his Fighting Mapleleafs T-shirt. "Brownies. I came by yesterday, but you weren't here."

"I was sort of ... unavailable."

His frown drooped even more. "I heard *all* about it."

Of course he had. This was Wilton, Indiana. Twitter had nothing on the grapevine here.

"From Maybelle," he added, his upper lip twitching ever so slightly.

My knee wobbled as Bump shouldered his way through the gap between the door and the frame. I tried to grab his collar, but he was being obnoxious and managed to shove his snout at both of Harmon's pockets, pausing halfway to sniff his crotch.

"I'm so sorry, Harmon." I clamped onto Bump's collar and yanked him into a sit. Unfortunately, his nose had lingered long enough just below Harmon's fly to leave a snotty little nose print there. Hopefully, it would dry before Harmon got home to Maybelle.

"No, no. It's all right. I like dogs, remember?" He stuck his hand out for Bump to sniff. "I'd have one of my own if Maybelle weren't such a neat freak — although I don't get where feathers and bird crap all over the dining room are ..." His shoulders jerked. He pressed his eyes shut for a moment. "Sorry, I don't mean to complain about her to you. She's just not easy to live with sometimes."

"I understand."

"Actually, all the time." He stared at me expectantly. "So, do you have any?"

"Brownies, no, I —" A truck turned onto my road. I leaned out the door to get a better look. My heart took a little leap as the truck came closer. "I didn't have time to make any." The truth was that Keisha, Selma, and I had snorted them all down the night before last. I hadn't even saved any for Tara, let alone thought to set any aside for Harmon. "Next week?"

"Sure, sure." His shoulders slumped forward. I wanted to pull him into a hug and pat him on the head.

The truck slowed and then turned into my driveway.

"Who's that?" Harmon asked.

My heart was doing full-out cartwheels inside my chest now. I avoided meeting Harmon's gaze, afraid if I made eye contact with him, every emotion I was trying so hard to rein in would flash across my face like a digital billboard at Times Square.

Archer cut the engine and stepped down from his truck, hugging a grocery sack. He waved at me, then nodded at Harmon before extending his hand. "Hi, I'm Archer Malone."

"Harmon Purnell, neighbor." Harmon shook his hand, but when Archer tried to pull his away, he gripped tighter. "Your name sounds familiar." He cocked his head. "I've seen your face, too. On television."

Archer squirmed, a slight blush spreading over his cheeks. "*The Today Show*, maybe?"

"No, I don't think so." Harmon let go of Archer's hand, then tapped at his own scruffy chin in thought. "I know!" He pointed at Archer. "That reality show. The one with the single guy and about fifty good-looking broads in a mansion in Beverly Hills."

Archer handed the grocery sack to me. I set it on a chest of drawers beside the door and parted the top of the sack. The aroma of herb-roasted chicken wafted up, making my mouth water.

"No, that wasn't me," Archer said.

"Sure, it was," Harmon insisted.

"No, it —"

I shook my head at Archer and pretend-scribbled on my hand.

Brows raised, Archer laid a hand on his chest. "You got me, buddy. Would you like an autograph?"

"Sure!" Harmon said.

As I pulled Bump away to grab a piece of paper and pen from inside, I heard Harmon say, "Just so you know, I never watch the show, and Maybelle would probably have a conniption if she knew I was talking to someone infamous like you, but I figure if I ever need the money I can sell your autograph on eBay."

Archer took the paper from me and signed it. He handed the paper to Harmon. "No problem. I hope it's worth something." Clearing his throat then, he took a step toward the door. "See you around."

I let Archer in and closed the screen door, hoping Harmon would take the hint. I was trying not to be rude, but I really wanted to spend time alone with Archer. "You'll stop by next week, right, Harmon?"

Harmon bobbed his head. "Sure, next week. Or maybe we'll run into each other when you're out walking your dog again."

"I'd like that."

We waved goodbye and Harmon shuffled off, hands in his pockets.

Archer waited until Harmon was a good half a block down the sidewalk before saying, "He's a little odd, don't you think?"

"Maybe, but he's sweet. I feel kind of sorry for the old guy. His wife keeps him on a short leash. I think he just wants a friend. Anyway, he's harmless and one of the few people in this neighborhood who's even bothered to make me feel welcome. I appreciate him stopping by. It's been kind of a rough week. Yesterday, especially."

Gathering up the grocery sack, I started for the kitchen. Archer followed, Bump right on his heels.

"Sam, I saw what happened on the news. I was relieved to learn you were okay. No broken bones or bruises this time?"

"Nope, none."

"About yesterday, I know I was supposed —"

"Don't worry about it. I'm sure you had something important to take care of."

Whoa, that came out a little snarkier than I'd intended. I put the sack down on the counter. Inside, bottles clanked. I hadn't looked closely enough. Had he brought wine? Beer, maybe? I wouldn't have any. I'd tell him about my past relationship with alcohol. He'd already seen evidence of its effect on me, so he'd understand if I turned down his gift.

Archer reached past me into the sack, his arm brushing against mine. I still had my back turned to him. I couldn't turn around. He was right there, pinning me. I wanted to, though. Wanted to burrow into his protective chest, feel his arms around me, know that I was safe. He pulled out two root beers, then twisted the top off of one and handed it to me before stepping back to pull out a chair at the dinette and sit.

"*Sixty Minutes* called me for a pre-interview," he said as casually as if he were relaying a weather report. "I was on the phone with them for over an hour. By the time I got off and tried calling you, it went straight to voice mail."

"Oh." That would be because Halloway had smashed my phone. I got out the plates and silverware and set them on the table, where my Greek salad and breadsticks were already sitting. "*Sixty Minutes*, huh? Were you expecting them to call?"

"Yes, but they hadn't given me an exact time, so it took me off guard. But that wasn't the biggest thing to happen yesterday. Cirrus Software, who's been looking for a charity to support, proposed a formal plan to expand Everly's Foundation throughout North America. They want me to be the spokesperson."

"That's great!" I sat down across from him, a big fake smile plastered across my mouth. But inside, I struggled to keep the air from leaking out of my little balloon of hope. I'd fallen for Archer the firefighter. Archer my hero. The guy next door. The one who wore flannel shirts and drove around in a big truck with dually wheels and sang country songs. "So, are you going to take them up on their offer?"

His face went through so many emotions it was impossible to tell what he was thinking. "I don't know. It would require being on the road a lot, moving to San Francisco so I could be near their headquarters, lots of meetings, interviews …" He dragged a hand down over his eyes, rubbed at them. "This whole thing has snowballed so quickly, I don't know which way is up anymore. I'm starting to think it's bigger than me."

I reached across the table and took his hand. "I can't think of anyone better than you for the job. Think of all the good you could do."

Why had I said that? I mean, it was true, but by urging him to do it I was letting him go before we'd even gotten started. And yet, it was the right thing to say, so I couldn't *not* say it.

Clint had turned out to be a compulsive liar and now Archer was leaving town. So far I was batting 0 for 2. Spinsterhood it was, then. After this, I was going down to the shelter to adopt a slew of cats, so I could become the crazy old cat lady. Except Bump might eat them. Scratch that. I'd take up crocheting instead.

"Sam?" Archer turned his hand over to clutch mine. I hadn't even realized that I hadn't let go. The heat of his palm seared into mine. "I'm not going."

"Not going?" I repeated.

"No."

I slid my hand away. "But why? You could —"

"Do so much for Everly's Foundation? Yes, I know. But the fact is I already have." He laced his fingers together, stared at them for the longest time. Then he loosened them and spread his palms wide, like he was letting go of something. "In reality, it's already achieved more than I could have ever imagined. I'm not going to cut myself off from it by any means, but I also don't want to shift courses so completely. I'm negotiating with them about sitting on the board and doing occasional speaking engagements, no more than a few times a year."

I was as happy to hear that as I was confused by it. "Why wouldn't you take the position, though? If you're not in direct control, they could do things you don't agree with."

"Because it's not me. Not who I am. I'm not comfortable being in the limelight. And the truth is that they can do a lot more and get more publicity than I ever could. Besides, I love what I do here in Wilton as a firefighter. I can't imagine doing anything else."

So he was married to his job. A noble reason for staying in sleepy little Wilton, but not quite the reason I'd hoped to hear. For now, though, I'd take it. He was staying. I'd see more of him.

We ate the rest of our dinner, lapsing into comfortable conversation about how Tara was doing in school, the current state of the high school football team, and whether it was time for me to buy a new car. When our plates were cleaned, Bump lost interest in us and moseyed up the stairs to sleep in Tara's room. Meanwhile, Archer and I moved to the couch to share a batch of nachos and cheese and watch an old Fred Astaire movie that had just come on. Movies where Fred and Ginger broke out in rounds of song and dance probably weren't Archer's thing, but he was a good sport about it. Sitting there with him, laughing at the funny parts, commenting on the old cars and style of dress, the conversation flowing freely ... it just felt so *right*.

A commercial came on, and before he could get up to get another root beer, I said, "I know it was an odd request to make, but I'll feel safer knowing you're here tonight." I retrieved a pillow and set of sheets from the front closet and placed them on top of the folded blanket lying on the arm of the couch. When I'd called Archer earlier, I'd made it clear that I just needed someone to keep an eye out on both doors. He'd offered to bring the main course for dinner and to let me pick the movie — as if we were best friends who did this every weekend. Still, I felt like I was imposing on his generosity. "You sure you don't want to sleep in Tara's bed, though?"

"It's purple in there. I might go blind. Anyway, your couch is way more comfortable than the bunks at the station."

"Thanks a million, Archer."

Elbows on his knees, he tipped the nearly empty bowl of nachos toward him. "My pleasure. And I do mean that. I always look forward to spending time with you." He glanced at me, then returned his gaze to the nacho bowl. "More than you could ever imagine."

For once, I didn't question whether he meant as a friend or something more. How was it that he always knew the right words to say?

"Even after I got tipsy and threw myself at you?" I joked. "I'd think you'd be running the other way."

Unfortunately, *I* seemed to have a penchant for saying the wrong thing. I should learn to shut up more often. What if he took me up on that?

A wicked grin flitted across his lips. He popped a nacho into his mouth, then dabbed at the corners to hide it. "I'm going to be honest with you, Sam."

My little balloon of hope went dead flat. This was when he was going to tell me he was celibate, or gay, or 'not looking for a relationship'.

He pushed the bowl of chips away and scooted closer. The springs of the couch creaked beneath his shifting weight. "That night, I wished you hadn't been drunk. Because I'd been hoping for a while that you really *were* interested in me. But things between you and Clint were still too fresh. I wasn't sure where you two were at. That's why I walked away."

I hadn't been sure, either. Now, I was. "Well, we're done now. For good. And I *am* interested in you."

He smiled. A slightly embarrassed, yet delighted kind of smile. "That's what I figured when you asked me over."

I laid a hand on his knee. His gaze followed from my hand, up my arm, and all the way to my eyes. My insides went all soft and mushy. I was seventeen again, falling in love for the first time, everything new and wonderful.

He slid an arm behind me, leaned in close, his voice gentle and promising. "Sam, I've thought about you every day since I first saw you standing there in Garber's."

I'd had a messy ponytail and was probably wearing some frumpy T-shirt and tatty old jeans. I remembered how his gold-flecked hazel eyes had penetrated my soul then, even before he'd spoken a word to me.

"Lately," he added, his voice lowering to a whisper, "I've been thinking about you a lot."

"You have?"

Looking down shyly, he nodded.

I needed more. I needed specifics. "In what way?"

His shoulders twitched in the slightest shrug. He took in several breaths before he spoke. "I finally realized that my work and the foundation were just excuses to keep busy, to avoid my feelings. I don't want to get hurt again, Sam. I don't. But when I heard about what happened to you with Halloway, everything shifted. I knew I didn't want to let someone special get away." He paused and right then, Fred Astaire started to sing "The Way You Look Tonight" on TV. "Someone like you."

A million butterflies collided in my stomach — terrifying and exhilarating. I leaned toward him, slowly. Aware of what I was doing, but not entirely in control of my own body. Then I stopped myself, closing my eyes to take stock of the moment.

His lips brushed mine, soft as a dandelion seed floating on the breeze, but its impact on my heart as big as a tsunami.

My eyes snapped open and I sat back, staring at his mouth. I wanted to feel his kiss. Again. But not soft and fleeting. Deep and hungry and undeniably passionate.

More than that, though, I wanted to remember this moment. Because for once, everything ... *everything* was going exactly as it should.

about the author

N. Gemini Sasson has worked as an aquatic toxicologist, an environmental engineer, a teacher, and a cross country coach. A longtime breeder of Australian Shepherds, her articles on bobtail genetics have been translated into seven languages. Her Imagineer line of Aussies has earned ASCA's Hall of Fame Excellent distinction. She lives in rural Ohio with her husband, two nearly grown children and an ever-changing number of animals.

Long after writing about Robert the Bruce and Queen Isabella, Sasson learned she is a descendant of both historical figures.

If you enjoyed this book, please spread the word by sharing it on Facebook or leaving a review at your favorite online retailer or book lovers' site.

For more details about N. Gemini Sasson and her books, go to:
www.ngeminisasson.com

Or become a 'fan' at:
www.facebook.com/NGeminiSasson

You can also sign up to learn about new releases via e-mail at:
http://eepurl.com/vSA6z

acknowledgments

Special thanks to Jan and Tracey for reading this story in its infancy and helping to make it so much better. And to Eliza Dee for catching all the errors that I overlooked – all ten times I read my own drafts.

To the readers who asked for another Sam McNamee book – I have the best job in the world because of you.